WITHDRAWN

WITHDRAWN

Joan Tower

The Comprehensive Bio-Bibliography

Ellen K. Grolman

The Scarecrow Press, Inc.
Lanham, Maryland • Toronto • Plymouth, UK
2007

SCARECROW PRESS, INC.

Published in the United States of America
by Scarecrow Press, Inc.
A wholly owned subsidiary of
The Rowman & Littlefield Publishing Group, Inc.
4501 Forbes Boulevard, Suite 200, Lanham, Maryland 20706
www.scarecrowpress.com

Estover Road
Plymouth PL6 7PY
United Kingdom

Copyright © 2007 by Ellen K. Grolman

All rights reserved. No part of this publication may be reproduced,
stored in a retrieval system, or transmitted in any form or by any
means, electronic, mechanical, photocopying, recording, or otherwise,
without the prior permission of the publisher.

British Library Cataloguing in Publication Information Available

Library of Congress Cataloging-in-Publication Data

Schlegel, Ellen Grolman.
  Joan Tower : the comprehensive bio-bibliography / Ellen K. Grolman.
     p. cm.
  Includes bibliographical references (p.   ) and index.
  ISBN-13: 978-0-8108-5653-0 (hardcover : alk. paper)
  ISBN-10: 0-8108-5653-0 (hardcover : alk. paper)
  1. Tower, Joan, 1938—Bibliography. 2. Tower, Joan, 1938—Discography. I.
Title.

ML134.T783S35 2007
780.92—dc22
[B]   2007001928

☉™ The paper used in this publication meets the minimum requirements of
American National Standard for Information Sciences—Permanence of
Paper for Printed Library Materials, ANSI/NISO Z39.48-1992.
Manufactured in the United States of America.

Errata

The photograph of Joan Tower with her husband Jeff Litfin appears courtesy of Steve J. Sherman.

As always, to Keith and Devon.
This time, for Bari and Cory as well.

Contents

Preface

Over the course of almost five decades, Joan Tower has produced a compelling and uncompromisingly well-crafted body of work that includes compositions for orchestra, chamber ensembles, solo instruments, ballet, and symphonic band. This volume, about one of the world's most admired, celebrated, and beloved composers, explores the experiences and influences that have shaped Tower's musical voice, from her childhood and adolescence in South America, to her establishment of the Da Capo Chamber Players; from her flight from serialism, to her maturation into one of the most sought-after composers at work today.

The most esteemed soloists, chamber ensembles, and symphonic organizations commission and regularly perform Joan Tower's works, as even the most cursory survey of classical concerts over the last twenty years shows. Her compositions typically feature brilliant color palettes, a varied and striking rhythmic profile, prominent percussion, evocative titles, elements of virtuosity, and precise attention to pacing and balance. Among Tower's strongest musical influences are Beethoven, Messiaen, and Stravinsky.

The Biography, supported by published literature, correspondence with leading figures in the musical world, and extensive personal interviews with the composer, includes family history dating back to 1637. Part II covers Tower's philosophy of organicism, compositional influences, and her views on feminism and musical citizenship. In Part III, Works and Performances, compositions are categorized by genre and then listed, within that genre, alphabetically. The reader is referred throughout to relevant items in the Discography and Bibliography by "D" and "B" prefixes. A listing of early, unpublished compositions, those in progress, and compositions dedicated to Tower follows the published works.

Compositions in the Discography, Part IV, are arranged alphabetically and contain both commercial and non-commercial recordings. Part V features reflections by Tower's peers, each with a different musical perspective, about this unique composer. Appendix A is an alphabetical listing of published compositions (as of December 2006), cross-referenced with the Works and Performances section.

The annotated Bibliographic entries are affixed with sequential numbers and the letter "B," and cross-referenced with both the Works and Performances and Discography sections. A comprehensive Index follows the Appendix.

Part I: Biography

Biography

Tower Family History

According to Tower genealogist Gerry Hayes, John Tower (1609–1701), along with his friend Samuel Lincoln, boarded the *Mary Anne* in Ipswich and emigrated from Hingham, England, to Hingham, Massachusetts, reaching Boston on June 20, 1637, after a sea journey of more than two months. On February 13, 1638, less than a year after his arrival in the Massachusetts Bay Colony, John met and married Margaret Ibrook (1617–1700); they had ten children: John, Jonathan, Ibrook, Jeremiah, Elizabeth, Sarah, Hannah, Benjamin, Jemima, and Samuel.

John and Margaret's descendants fought and died in the many wars that occurred in the intervening years, including King Philip's War (1675–1676), and the American Revolutionary and Civil wars. A Daughters of the American Revolution plaque in the Tower section of the Hingham cemetery honors Malachi Tower, who fell during the Revolution. Family records show that Charlemagne Tower enlisted in the Union Army at the outbreak of the Civil War at the advanced age of 52. His son Charlemagne II was appointed first envoy extraordinary and minister plenipotentiary to Austria-Hungary (1897) by President William McKinley, and later American Ambassador to Germany by President Theodore Roosevelt.[1]

Hayes reports that "somewhere along the way," Daniel Tower, Sr., married Sarah Lincoln, descendant of John Tower's friend and fellow immigrant Samuel Lincoln and sister of Mordecai Lincoln, Jr., great-great-grandfather of Abraham Lincoln. She also notes that Joan's great-grandfather, George Warren Tower (9th generation Tower) married Abigail Adams, a direct descendant of John Adams, on March 12, 1870. A more recent descendant of patriarch John Tower (and his namesake) was the long-time Republican senator from Texas who served briefly as chairman of the armed services committee and as secretary of defense for George H. W. Bush.

The successful and prolific Tower family—all claiming descent from John Tower's arrival in the New World a mere 17 years after the landing of the *Mayflower*—celebrated in 1909 a family reunion that was announced with a booklet providing a brief history of the family along with reasons to attend the event at the Tower homestead in Hingham. Scheduled for May 29–31, 1909, its purpose was to celebrate the "Ter-Centennary of John Tower's birth."[2] The family homestead, built in the early years of the 19th century, remained in the Tower family until recently, when John Tower (13th generation) lost the house in a divorce.

Fourteen generations after John Tower arrived in the colonies, Joan Peabody Tower was born to George Warren Tower III and Anna Peabody Robinson on September 6, 1938.

Childhood through College

Joan Tower's early memories of her home at 134 Rockland Avenue in upscale Larchmont, New York, are of a big stone house on a hill, in a neighborhood filled with children of other prosperous families. Her early years typified her class: she took ballet lessons, belonged to the Campfire Girls, and studied piano. She remembers participating in numerous piano recitals and enjoying performing. A horse enthusiast as an adolescent, she also acted in school plays and played tournament tennis. In the summer, she was a camper and then a counselor at a nearby camp.

Her sister, Ellen, nine years Joan's senior, lived in the house for six years after Joan's birth; she left soon after that for boarding school. Her brother, George IV, was born in 1947, when Joan was nine years old. Because the children were born nine years apart, each had the experience of being essentially an only child.

Joan's grandfather George Warren Tower, Jr. (d. 1939) was a consulting engineer for the Securities and Exchange Commission and directed many mining companies in the United States and Mexico. His son, Joan's father George Warren Tower III, graduated *magna cum laude* from Harvard University in 1923 and followed his father into engineering. A consultant for mining companies, he worked for Thayer-Lindsey, Anaconda, and Cerro de Pasco mines. George was the son of a pianist, played the violin and sang, and ensured that Joan always had a piano at her disposal, even when the family was traveling.

Tower maintained a close relationship with her parents, even when her father, passionate about his work, was away on business for long periods of time. Joan knew few relatives on her father's side; most interactions with cousins took place at the Peabody-Endicott family home in Walpole, Massachusetts. Joan's maternal great-great-grandmother and great-grandmother each married Unitarian ministers, Ephraim Peabody and Henry Whitney Bellows, respectively. Bellows, who died in 1882, was a Harvard graduate, a civil reformer, and president of the United States Sanitary Commission under Abraham Lincoln.

Joan's mother, Anna Peabody Robinson Tower (1906–1992), attended Vassar College for a time, then graduated from Wheelock Teacher's College in Boston. Anna's sister Katherine was a recognized artist whose work hung in Boston's Museum of Fine Arts, her brother Thomas a publisher of the *Charlotte* (North Carolina) *News*. Active in the Parent-Teacher's Association of Murray Avenue Elementary School, Anna cared for the home and the children during George's frequent long absences.

For business reasons, George Tower moved the family in 1947 to La Paz, Bolivia, where he managed all the Bolivian tin mines owned by Hochschild Mines and oversaw their daily operation. The move was disruptive and difficult at first for nine-year-old Joan, especially since her sister, Ellen, didn't accompany the family, as she was enrolled in college by this time. Joan was torn from her circle of friends and the only home she'd known, and she found herself faced with a new culture, new language, and very different physical surroundings.

Located in the Andes Mountains at an altitude of 12,500 feet, the La Paz house was surrounded by gardens and came with a staff of five Indian servants. These included a cook, Mercedes; a butler, Juan; a laundress, Isabelle; a nurse/nanny, Aida; and a chauffeur, Paredes. Although their salary was paltry by North American standards, the servants viewed themselves as better situated than their peers.

Joan quickly acclimated and with a child's precocity for language was soon able to communicate in Spanish and *Aymara*, a direct descendant of the Incan language. The school she attended had a well-developed physical education program, and she remembers with fondness working on the parallel bars, the gymnastics horse, and the high jump. The students often marched in festive uniforms for parades of various kinds. Tower continued her piano studies with Denise von Stroheim, the fourth of film-maker Erich von Stroheim's four wives, and became proficient enough to perform Chopin's *Revolutionary Etude* at age eleven.[3] The family traveled frequently within the country to visit different mines, sometimes by cargo plane and sometimes by *autocaril*, a car that ran on railroad tracks. Occasionally George would take Joan into the jungle on fishing expeditions. As a protest against her father's frequent and protracted business absences, Joan ran away at age ten, accompanied by her dog, Susie, and six peanut butter sandwiches, returning before dark because she became frightened.[4]

In her daily travels with her nanny, Aida, Joan attended the frequent local celebrations of saints' days that always involved music and dancing. She recalls being given an assortment of percussion instruments to play with and participating in the music-making and dancing, absorbing the indigenous rhythms and eventually becoming a good Latin dancer. She credits these experiences with establishing her life-long affinity for the muscular, vital rhythms which characterize the majority of her compositions.

Because her parents could now afford to indulge her love of horses, they gave Joan a race horse at age 14. Naming it Aymara after the local Indian dialect, she rode the horse, fed her, and cared for her.

Coups and revolutions were monthly occurrences in Bolivia, requiring the family to take protective measures including blocking the house windows with mattresses and keeping the pantry well-stocked. George and Anna Tower were concerned enough about the political situation in 1952 to send Joan to what she called an "uptight, English church boarding school" in Santiago, Chile, for 9th and 10th grade.[5]

Santiago College was an international boarding school that prescribed green uniforms and white gloves and that used a bell to mark every change of activity during the day. By her own admission, Tower spent "most of my time trying to figure out how to break the rules."[6] One escapade involved an unauthorized leave of absence from the school in order to sunbathe at a nearby resort hotel.

She survived the strict regimens of the school and the occasional earthquake and, after two years, joined her parents in Lima, Peru, where they had relocated.

George had contracted tuberculosis and was admitted for a time to a Lima hospital before returning to the United States for treatment at New York's Saranac Sanatorium and the miracle-drug penicillin that would save his life. In the interim, Joan enrolled in secretarial school to learn typing and shorthand and in riding school to learn how to hunt and jump. She "spent a whole year doing exactly what I wanted to do because I was between schools."[7]

Admittedly boy-crazy and rarely shy, Joan also spent time in the lobby of a Lima hotel, meeting members of touring male athletic teams that came through town and bringing them home with her to family parties. In Lima she met Bob Moules, a marine stationed at the U.S. Embassy, and she left him with regret when the *Santa Maria* sailed for New York in 1954. Tower recalls vividly her first sighting of the Statue of Liberty upon her return to the States, an experience she drew on when composing *Made in America* more than fifty years later.

Joan completed the last two years of her high school education at Walnut Hill School in Natick, Massachusetts, graduating in 1956. Returning from South America a rebellious and independent young woman, fond of wearing colorful Latin clothes, she did not fit in well with the majority of Walnut Hill girls "who wore pearls and cashmere sweaters."[8]

Despite academic grades that hovered around a "C" level, Tower distinguished herself in musical and theatrical performances and on the softball and tennis teams. Her grade point average was not good enough to gain her admission to a prestigious college, and so, upon graduation from Walnut Hill, she enrolled at Wheelock College in Boston, a school that emphasized elementary teacher training for young women. Joan laughingly remembers the other students as being interested mostly in bridge and knitting.[9]

During a college interview at Radcliffe College in Boston, an observant admissions officer saved Tower from yet another school unsuitable for her (and in doing so, according to the composer, profoundly altered her life) by suggesting that Tower visit Bennington College in Vermont in 1958. Bennington was the perfect place for Tower, for it

> allowed me to flower and to get back to my real talents with a vengeance! After an exploratory side glance at physics, which fascinated me from the point of view of studying action and reaction phenomena in nature—something I have explored in music all my life—I headed straight for music and spent my three years there doing music 20 hours a day.[10]

Tower thrived in an atmosphere that not only valued, but encouraged, creativity, independence, and resourcefulness, and the college's focus on making music rather than talking or writing about it dovetailed with her natural inclinations. She writes that the college expected students to create their own vision and curriculum, and to discover where their talents lay.[11]

In one of her first classes at Bennington, Joan was asked by Professor Henry Brant to compose a piece of music, which she then heard performed by fellow students under Brant's baton. She recalls that she didn't understand the concept of composing until that memorable assignment.

> I wrote a piece for 13 instruments and it was in the style of [Maurice Ravel's] *Bolero*. I didn't know how to map a piece, so I picked the simplest map I could find and just added the instruments on one by one. Brant conducted my piece and it was the beginning of the end for me because it was so exciting to hear. I learned so much from hearing my music that I kept writing more.[12]

Although Tower found the performance of the work exhilarating, she recognized its deficiencies and was eager to modify it. "I remember hearing this piece and thinking how horrible it was. Everything was wrong with it. Too loud. Too high. Too long. Too this. Too that. I had an incredibly bad reaction to the piece, but it was . . . the beginning of a trap: I had to make it better."[13]

If Tower had not found her way to Bennington, she might never have found her way to composition. "I always wanted to be a pianist. . . . I had never met a live composer so it wasn't very real to me until I went to Bennington College. Composing then "became a new way into the music, a difficult and challenging one."[14] Under the tutelage of Professor Henry Brant, Louis Calabro, and others, Tower explored the craft in a "Bartokian-Hindemithian" style modeled after her teachers.

While at Bennington, Joan participated in the college's unique three-month winter program during which students researched, located, designed, and completed a work-oriented internship. Tower's aunt, a publisher in New York, used her connections to secure her niece an internship at *Publisher's Weekly*, for which Joan ran errands and wrote synopses of teenage romance novels. Tower praises the internship program for its emphasis on self-direction and resourcefulness.

1960s and 1970s: Finding a Life in Music

Upon graduating from Bennington in 1961 with a Bachelor's degree in Music, Tower relocated to New York City and secured a position teaching piano at the Greenwich Music House in Greenwich Village, a school founded in 1905 to provide cultural programs for newly arrived immigrants. Their stated aim was to equip students with a "thorough musical education based on the personal objectives of the student."[15]

Coming of age as a composer at a time when the twelve-tone system of composition dominated the music scene, Tower encountered contemporaries and mentors who included Mario Davidovsky, Charles Wuorinen, and Milton Babbitt, and all of whom she remembers as "very cerebral and very, very, very smart."[16] She emulated their style of composition, attended their concerts, performed their music, sought their company.

She had met Wuorinen at a Bennington College composers' summer conference several years earlier and had been impressed with his intellect and musicianship. She established a close friendship with him and actually met her first husband, jazz pianist and composer Walter Howard O'Brien ("Hod"), through Wuorinen. (The marriage lasted nine years and ended in divorce in 1975.) Joan admired Wuorinen's full immersion in music: he was at once a teacher, composer, and performer. When he started the Group for Contemporary Music series at Columbia University (where he was first a student and then a teacher), Joan participated in his concert series and then purposefully imitated him, establishing one at Greenwich House and presenting a slate of artists every Friday evening. For a time she was his teaching assistant at Columbia.

Milton Babbitt, a respected older composer, saw himself as a musical father figure to the younger generation of serial composers in New York during the 1960s and '70s, of which Joan was a member. Tower recalls him as "a caring musical citizen who attended all the concerts, wrote hundreds of recommendations, and generally looked over his flock."[17] At the time the William Shubael Conant Professor of Music at Princeton University, Babbitt wrote the following recommendation for Joan in the mid-1970s to support her application for a National Endowment for the Arts grant.

> I have had the opportunity to hear [Joan Tower's] compositions and performances over a number of years and to become aware of her impressive emergence as one of the most knowing and accomplished composers and musicians of her generation. In spite of her age, one need not speak only of her promise, but already of her considerable accomplishment, which promises achievements which appear certain.[18]

Composer Mario Davidovsky echoes Babbitt's assessment of Joan's potential in his 1974 NEA recommendation for her:

> All [of Tower's] music I have had the pleasure to know has been consistently strong structurally and most sensitive. She is a most imaginative and intelligent composer and in the last few years she has worked indefatigably as a performer of great competence through the Da Capo Chamber Players to enhance the cause of American contemporary music.[19]

In 1964, Tower graduated from Columbia University with a Master of Music degree in composition. She then began work on a doctorate in composition, a degree she would not finish until 1978. She'd enrolled in Columbia because she was already settled in New York and teaching at Greenwich Music House, because her friend and colleague Charles Wuorinen was established there, and because she knew that without advanced degrees, she would be unable to secure employment as a teacher. While at Columbia she studied composition with Jack Beeson, Otto Luening, Benjamin Boretz, Chou Wen-Chung, and Vladimir Ussachevsky. Privately, she worked with Darius Milhaud, Wallingford Riegger, Alan Sapp, and Ralph Shapey.

Tower's works from this period are fully serial and include *Percussion Quartet* (1963, rev. 1969), *Movements* for flute and piano (1968), *Prelude for Five Players* (1972), *Hexachords* (1972), *Breakfast Rhythms I* (1974), and many unpublished compositions. In a March 23, 2006, interview, she reflected that from the perspective of a composer who abandoned the serial technique long ago, those compositions represent "an older, difficult musical style that no longer really works."[20]

Tower did not find her work at Columbia entirely satisfying. She grew increasingly unhappy with the musical rewards provided her by the 12-tone system and found that the academic studies required for the degrees did not musically nourish her. She chafed against 12-tone music's restrictive over-intellectualizing, rebelled against its disdain for musical intuition, and mourned its utter lack of interest in communicating with an audience. The elitism of serial music, succinctly captured in the title of Milton Babbitt's famous essay, "Who Cares If You Listen?"[21] manifested itself in idioms that were purposely complex and which eventually alienated audiences world-wide. Tower ultimately decided that she needed to find her musical voice away from this group of composers and musicians with whom she'd aligned herself for ten years.

The Da Capo Chamber Players

Tower's series at Greenwich Music House provoked the establishment in 1969 of the Da Capo Chamber Players, first known as the Empire Chamber Players. "My personal motivation [for forming the group] at this time was to play, [but] I was also a composer and I wanted to hear my music, so I figured if I created my own venue, then I wouldn't have to send out scores, which I hate doing. . . . I don't like the rejection syndrome."[22] Thinking to form a small, mobile group with which she could form a long-term musical relationship and concertize, she sought the most talented and accomplished performers in New York and programmed them on several Greenwich concerts the first year. Documents in Tower's possession reflect the inaugural year's budget of $4,038.83 for a series of five concerts, including payment for performers; recording; piano, percussion, and music rentals; and postage.

Implicit in its name was Da Capo's effort to offer at least one work twice on the same program, so that the audience might better appreciate its complexities. The performers also attempted to resurrect 20th-century works which had had a hard time finding repeat performances.[23] The group's original membership included Tower as pianist; Allen Blustine, clarinet; Helen Harbison, 'cello; Patricia Spencer, flutist; and Joel Lester, violin. They found that they worked well together so continued giving regular performances. Joan not only founded the group, but handled fundraising, grant-writing, receptions, correspondence, promotion, piano-moving, scheduling, program duplication, marketing, and hosting duties as well.

In a grant application from 1973, Da Capo's fourth season, Tower summarizes the ensemble's raisons d'être: "(1) to continue to produce concerts featuring works of contemporary composers, (2) to commission composers to write new works for us, and (3) to record these and other works in our repertoire."[24]

In Da Capo's infancy, the group chose repertoire based on whom they thought they were expected to play: music by friends, music by famous composers, music by someone they'd heard about. After several years, they adopted a more objective method of selection that Tower had learned by being on panels:

they auditioned compositions by hearing them anonymously. The group hired a student to play tape after tape, and rated them yes, no, or maybe. "We stayed with that [system] because it was such an eye-opener to everybody. . . . That's how we picked our pieces."[25]

For their excellence in programming and performance, Tower and Da Capo Chamber Players won one of the most coveted awards for chamber musicians, the Walter W. Naumburg Chamber Music Award, in 1973. The Naumburg Foundation also arranged a 10th anniversary concert for Da Capo in 1983, in which the ensemble premiered six compositions in Alice Tully Hall in New York. Tower herself was the recipient of several National Endowment for the Arts Fellowships, MacDowell Colony and Guggenheim Fellowships in 1974 and 1975, respectively, and was selected by the Naumburg Foundation to write a concerto for Charles Neidich, winner of the Naumburg Clarinet Competition in 1987.

That Tower herself was a virtuosic performer and an ensemble player is clear in her music. Kyle Gann noted in a recent interview that "you can tell the notes originated not in blackboard gymnastics, but in the feel of playing the instruments, the give and take of chamber players cueing each other."[26] Prior to 1979, all her compositions were written for chamber groups or soloists.

Her many years with Da Capo Chamber Ensemble (1969–1984) provided her with intimate knowledge of the individual instruments' capabilities as well as their optimal combinations. She explains her transition from performer to composer: "As a pianist I learned that performing and communicating in sound was the only way I could really communicate, and then that got transferred into composing and projecting an image of sound to other people."[27] She adds, "My career in music has been largely a double kind of exploration of the two sides of music."[28] Having been a performer with Da Capo Chamber Players certainly influenced her compositional aesthetic and output, and she feels strongly that had she not been a performer, she would have been a very different composer.[29]

Over the course of her 15 years with the Da Capo Chamber Players, Tower created a solo work for each of the original instrumentalists. Although not a performer on any instrument other than piano, her pieces are written very idiomatically. Of this she says, "Composers pick up a lot of unconscious, intuitive knowledge about an instrument that they couldn't translate into technical knowledge."[30]

For violinist Joel Lester she composed *Platinum Spirals* (1976), using the evocative, image-inspired titles that would later become one of her trademarks. The work was dedicated to the memory of her father (who died in 1969) with the idea that "it would be a nice tribute to him . . . to try to tie in the idea of metal and its characteristics." *Platinum Spirals* invokes the malleability and strength of platinum, something Tower discovered by perusing her father's books on atomic structure. "The whole idea behind the piece is a stretching from the bottom of the register to the top. . . . Did you know," she asks, "that a gram of platinum can be stretched into a thread a mile long?"[31]

For clarinetist Allen Blustine, Tower composed *Breakfast Rhythms I and II for clarinet and five instruments* (1974–1975, for clarinet, flute, violin, 'cello, piano, percussion). Solo vehicles with a "supporting cast," these works were also the subject of Tower's 1978 Columbia University dissertation. In *Breakfast Rhythms II* one first begins to see the beginnings of her break with serialism.

'Cellist Helen Harbison, sister of composer John Harbison, premiered Tower's *Six Variations* for 'cello solo in 1971, and the work received a handful of additional performances in the New York area, but Tower wasn't entirely satisfied and subsequently withdrew it, writing for the instrument again (*Music for 'Cello and Orchestra*) several years later. *Hexachords* (1972) for solo flute was written for and dedicated to Patricia Spencer and has received three separate recordings to date. Written in the very midst of the twelve-tone milieu, even this early work shows signs of Tower's "defection" to compositional organicism, as evidenced by her comment that the work's five sections can be "most easily differentiated by a sense of either going somewhere or staying somewhere."[32]

As the group's membership changed, Tower continued to provide virtuosic vehicles for the performers in both solo and ensemble capacities. Tower considers André Emelianoff, for whom she wrote *Music for 'Cello and Orchestra* in 1984, the midwife of the composition. Rather than a composition for solo 'cello, Emelianoff requested a work in which the instrument interacted with a large ensemble. Tower says:

> We spent six months together meeting, working on bowings, on registers. We really created this piece together. I'm putting my child, my newborn child, into the hands of a friend, and that's very important. That was done in the 19th century all the time. Today I wish we could get back to that, since I know that a lot of performers are bored. They're playing the violin concerto for the 5,000th time. They would get so much excitement out of working with a composer.[33]

The term *midwife* above is apt, as Tower views her completed compositions as children, noting that the compositions have to be treated with patience

> and . . . disciplined thinking and hope that it comes out all right. I have some children that are kind of my "delinquent" children. They go out into the world and boy, it's difficult. Others go out and become little starlets. They get played a lot. And there are others that get . . . played now and then, and then there are some that are totally ignored! There [are] some that are actually played too much—I don't think they are strong enough to be played that much—but my opinions are quite different from what the world thinks sometimes![34]

Tower has had an ongoing love affair with the clarinet for decades. "I think of the clarinet as a powerful, flexible, virtuosic instrument that can compete with anything," she says.[35] "[It's] similar to the piano in that it has an incredible dynamic range and it can be percussive and it can be lyrical at the same time and it can be powerful and it can be soft at the same time. Not all instruments have that capability."[36]

Works which feature the clarinet include *Breakfast Rhythms I and II* (1974*), Wings* (1981), *Fantasy (. . . Those Harbor Lights)* (1983), *Clarinet Concerto* (1988), *Turning Points* (1995), and *Rain Waves* (1997).

Laura Flax, who replaced original Da Capo clarinetist Allen Blustine, was the dedicatee of *Wings,* Tower's most frequently performed solo work. Tower has said that Flax possessed "this liquid, absolutely phenomenal sound, and I wanted to write something for that."[37] Flax indicated that part of the challenge of the composition is the unusually high range,[38] and that in order to optimally perform the piece, she had to learn circular breathing, a technique that enables the wind instrumentalist to maintain a sound for long periods of time by inhaling through the nose while maintaining air flow through the instrument, using the cheeks as bellows.[39] Technically demanding and requiring extraordinary endurance (like many of Tower's solo and chamber compositions), *Wings* evokes the soaring and gliding of falcons on thermal currents. (During an address by Tower to the St. Louis [MO] Clarinet Society in September 1987, a clarinetist in the audience suggested that because of the requisite endurance, Tower should have titled the piece *Lungs* instead of *Wings.*)[40] Tower feels that solo works like *Wings* and *Platinum Spirals* and *Hexachords* require a different compositional aesthetic than ensemble works do, as "the timbral shifts [in the solo composition] are less frequent and the activity is much more pure and focused, so . . . it has to move faster." [41]

Clarinetist David Shifrin, who has performed the *Clarinet Concerto* frequently and who gave the work its West Coast premiere in 1995, says of Tower, "Each generation has composers who work with performers to extend what instruments can do, and Joan is one of those composers. Her concerto pushes the limits of the clarinet: everything's higher, faster, louder, more extreme. . . . Joan pushes the limits of orchestral technique, too."[42]

Bard College

At a poker game in the early 1970s, Joan met composer Elie Yarden, then professor of music at Bard College in Annandale-on-Hudson, New York. He persuaded her to visit the campus, intuiting that the creative environment would appeal to Tower. She liked the campus and the people she met there, and in 1972 committed to a one-day-per-week part-time position. "I needed that gradual transition in order to protect both my composing and performing time. Teaching was something I really loved to do and I didn't want to get too invested in it at a time when I wasn't sure of myself as a composer."[43]

Every few years Tower increased her presence and teaching responsibilities on campus until, upon her return from her three-year composer-in-residence position with the St. Louis Symphony in 1988, she was offered the full-time endowed Asher Edelman Professorship. Soon after that, she accepted the chairship of the Music Department at Bard, a position she held for eight years. Tower found chairing to be a complex, challenging, and ultimately overly time-consuming balancing act that she was not unhappy to relinquish; she retained, however, her professorship at Bard.

She always starts her new composition classes off with a caveat: "This is not an assignment and I never want you to *view* this as an assignment [italics mine] but I want you to write a piece you care deeply about."[44] She counsels her students to consider, initially, four questions about their composition. First: is the work coherent; second: is it (too) familiar, in other words, is the student trying to too closely emulate another composer; third: is there an element of musical risk involved; and fourth, is the student excited about the result on a fairly long-term, consistent basis.

She considers herself a self-taught composer and is of the opinion that it is essentially impossible to "teach" composition. "You can teach around it—theoretical things, harmony and counterpoint."[46] Of her own university-level training she says, "[At Columbia University] the teachers taught me more about practical notational problems, orchestrational problems, very practical things,"[47] but "everything I learned about writing music that was meaningful came from writing it and hearing it."[48]

Tower has always felt "the greatest teacher is hearing your [own] music, so I keep involving [the students] in hearing what they have written. . . . I want them to be close to what they are doing in a very passionate way."[49] Hearing what she had composed is what "hooked" Tower on composition in the late 1950s at Bennington College, and remains at the core of her teaching at Bard today.

Tower's efficacy as a teacher is evidenced by superior annual evaluations praising "the unique quality of her teaching style" and stating that "in presenting herself . . . as a questing, developing person—not an authority—she provides an encouraging and valuable model of exploration." A representative student response indicates that "[Dr. Tower] devotes the same fervent energy towards a student work [as she does to her own]."[50] Certainly for a teacher there can be no higher praise.

Tower would like to see future generations of composers and performers more involved in each other's worlds. The two groups have been separated so effectively, she says, that they have lost sight of each other's goals. Because she is both performer and composer, she can "speak the language of both parties."[51] While virtually all composers working today have been trained in a male-dominated curriculum, Tower believes that men and women approach teaching the craft a bit differently. Women, in her experience, are more intuitively inclined, less conceptual, and less systematic.[52]

1980s: International Spotlight

In 1980, Tower wrote *Sequoia*, her first orchestral work. (Two years earlier she had orchestrated *Amazon*, originally for quintet, but *Sequoia* was the first originally conceived as an orchestral composition.) "I thought it would be a disaster [since] it was my first orchestral work and there was a lot of guesswork."[53] Premiered in 1981 by the American Composers' Orchestra under Dennis Russell Davies and performed by Zubin Mehta and the New York Philharmonic the following year, the work quickly gained respect in the orchestral world.

Joseph Schwantner, at that time composer-in-residence with the St. Louis Symphony, brought the work to the attention of conductor Leonard Slatkin, who was so impressed that he programmed it with three different orchestras, acquired the recording rights, and offered Tower a composer-in-residency for 1985–1988. About Tower's music Slatkin offers, "It's tonal and it has a melodic element to it, but it's not minimal. Its long scale patterns and rhythmic complexity are of a Stravinskian nature."[54]

Tower reacted with both excitement and trepidation to Slatkin's invitation, drafting a letter to the conductor that outlined her concerns about her lack of experience writing for such large performing forces. Slatkin reminded her that she had already written one extraordinary piece for orchestra, and that with the help of the St. Louis Symphony, she would write many more.[55] Thus encouraged, Tower took a three-year leave from Bard College and accepted the residency, which was a part of the Meet the Composer/Orchestra Residencies Program, funded then by the Exxon Corporation, the Rockefeller Foundation, and the National Endowment for the Arts.

Prior to 1979, Tower had been involved almost exclusively with chamber music and chamber ensembles and was unfamiliar with the economic considerations that drive orchestras and the ways in which those considerations would impact revisions to her compositions.

Because of the economics of the symphonic world and because a new concert is presented *every* week, bringing a piece of music to life in this setting is a fast process. The time to digest and live with a new piece is in very short supply—much shorter than in chamber music. Changes can be made only on a "cosmetic" scale of dynamics, articulation, etc. This results in an enormous pressure to produce a "perfect" blueprint. Thus the notated score becomes a crucial component to the success of that performance. Corrections take up too much precious time, and the composer is put in the precarious position of making fast choices that may backfire. Should he or she wait for the orchestra to adjust the dynamics (which they have done over a longer period of time with much of the traditional repertoire) or make a change immediately that may be wrong?[56]

Tower was eager to be accepted by the musicians, but was viewed initially as an outsider; a member of management or administration, someone with authority over the conductor and performers. It took her the better part of a year to gain the players' trust and respect, something she accomplished by conducting them, playing music with them, joining them on bus tours, sharing drinks and jokes, and selecting music for them on the Discovery series she oversaw. A less public part of the residency program involved Tower sifting through the many scores submitted annually to the Symphony and making recommendations about them to Slatkin.

Tower's hand-written comments from the St. Louis Symphony's pre-recording sessions for *Sequoia* indicate that the composer knew exactly what she wanted the piece to achieve, specifying softer mallets for percussionists, providing reminders to the brass about dynamics, chiding the strings when necessary about rhythms inaccurately performed, and marking spots in the score to discuss with Maestro Slatkin ("Do you think Violin I and II up an octave would help this passage? There's something not right here").[57]

In 1982, her *Sequoia* rehearsal notes to Zubin Mehta, then conductor of the New York Philharmonic, are similar to the ones she prepared for Slatkin ("Violin II, measure 489: last chord needs tuning") and include general praise for the orchestra ("The piece improved *very* rapidly during the first rehearsal! I was amazed how fast everybody picked up on balance and rhythms the second time through a phrase"), comments of a slightly apologetic nature ("I hope I wasn't too difficult about the tempos—I think they'll settle in with the playing of longer sections"), and expressions of gratitude ("I feel so lucky and honored to have you and the New York Philharmonic do my piece—my first piece for orchestra. You took a risk with me and I appreciate that very much.")[58]

On November 10, 1982, after the New York Philharmonic's performance of the piece, Tower wrote to Mehta:

> You have made me one of the happiest "live" composers around! I can't tell you how much I appreciated your involvement in my *Sequoia*. The rehearsals and performances were so positive what with all the support I was getting from the players that I feel like a very lucky composer indeed. I hope that for you it was not just another 20th century "obligation" piece. Many, many thanks from the bottom of my heart, [signed] Joan Tower.[59]

Even in the heady aftermath of having her first orchestral work performed by one of the finest orchestras in the world, Tower is unable to avoid proselytizing: living composers should be performed and 20th-century works should not be the repertoire's "poor relations."

Tower is interested in the different lives her works lead under different batons and in different halls. "It's incredible to me how big a role the hall can play in the perception of a piece. [Each time a work is played] I can really see how that piece works, how it survives under different situations, how different orchestras handle it, how the hall makes it sound different, how the piece seems in the context of *Bolero* or *Symphonie Fantastique*, or whatever else happens to be on the program [with it]."[60]

Several years after she completed her residency with Leonard Slatkin and the St. Louis Symphony, Tower drafted a strong statement in support of the Meet the Composer program:

> I know of no other program that has had as much impact and as significant a long range consequence as the orchestral composer residency program. The presence of a living composer in the midst of the most established and visible classical organization we have in music creates an important link between the music being written today and an organization that has concentrated a large part of its efforts on playing the music of dead composers . . . . History has already proven that unless art is nourished with new works, it will die . . . . If we want to keep the classical music world a healthy and lively art, where Beethoven thrives as much as Michael Jackson does, then we have to let the new art in to help Beethoven, the same way that the new young pop/rock musicians infuse the field with new ideas and sounds to

create a lively, adventurous, *and* money-making excitement. The composer residency program is a real step in that direction.[61]

Not long after her success with *Sequoia,* Tower made the decision to leave the Da Capo Chamber Players after fifteen years with the group. "I [left] because there was a lot of work involved, and I was getting more and more commissions as a composer, so there was that kind of pressure. It took me three years to leave."[62] She adds, "Leaving was a very difficult decision because we were like a family, but the more I composed, the less time I had to practice. We even joked about it. The others would bring in monster pieces for the group to do, but I wanted a piano part written in whole notes."[63] Occasionally she will still accompany some of her own works in concert, but only the slow ones, such as *Trés Lent,* as she now has little time to practice her primary instrument.

Susan Feder's thorough liner notes accompanying the all-Tower orchestral CD of 1990 point out, "If *Sequoia* had thrust Tower into national prominence, *Silver Ladders* seem[ed] destined to do the same for her on an international scale."[64] In *Silver Ladders* (1986), the first work she produced during her St. Louis residency, Tower focused even more adroitly on the elements of contrast and balance she explored in *Sequoia. Silver Ladders* earned her a 1988 Kennedy Center Friedheim Award, the prestigious Grawemeyer Award in 1990, and numerous international performances of the work.

While appreciative of the recognition and numerous awards that she has received, Tower does not believe that her compositions are performed because of them. "Pieces get performances because they have a certain internal strength that keeps them going. Credentials [such as awards and prizes] that are attached . . . are not the real fuel."[65]

During the 1980s Tower was the subject of a 30-minute documentary produced by WGBH in Boston and National Public Television for their series *Soundings.* She was an inductee into the American Academy of Arts and Letters Institute and received several more NEA awards. Additional grants followed from the Koussevitsky, Meet the Composer, Jerome, Barlow and AT&T Foundations; the Contemporary Music Society and American Society of University Composers, and the Delaware Symphony's Alfred I. DuPont Award for Distinguished American Composers. Compositions produced during this decade remain some of the most beloved of her work, including *Petroushskates, Wings, Sequoia, Noon Dance, Snow Dreams, Fantasy . . . (Those Harbor Lights), Music for 'Cello and Orchestra, Clocks, Piano Concerto (Homage to Beethoven), Island Rhythms, Silver Ladders, Fanfare for the Uncommon Woman, Nos. 1 and 2, Clarinet Concerto, Island Prelude,* and the *Flute Concerto.*

1990–2006: "Now Completely Comfortable Speaking Her Own Language" (Violinist Elmar Oliveira about Joan Tower)

Elmar Oliveira eloquently summarizes above what the remainder of the musical world now acknowledges: Tower has found her unique, colorful, mature, and identifiable compositional voice, one that perfectly balances the elements of risk and predictability she has sought for so long.[66]

In 1990, from among 140 international entries, *Silver Ladders* won the prestigious Grawemeyer Award, the largest award available in composition. The prize netted Tower, the first female recipient, a $150,000 prize. Joan Tower had clearly been recognized as among the preeminent living composers. Several years later, she was inducted into the Academy of Arts and Sciences at Harvard University.

The most esteemed soloists, chamber ensembles, and symphonic organizations commission and regularly perform Tower's works, as even the most cursory survey of classical concerts over the last twenty years shows. In the chamber music world the Muir, Emerson, Tokyo, Vermeer, Cassatt, Degas, Cavani, Enso, Arianna, and Colorado String Quartets, the Empire Brass Quintet, the Dorian, Quintessence, and Dakota Wind Quintets, and the Vehrder and Kalich-stein-Laredo-Robinson Trios have Tower compositions in their standard repertoire.

Among soloists who present Tower's works are John Browning, Carol Wincenc, David Shifrin, Richard Woodhams, Elmar Oliveira, Paul Neubauer, Lynn Harrell, Ursula Oppens, Ani Kavafian, Chee-Yun, Cho-liang Lin, David Finckel, Wu Han, Charles Neidich, Marc André Hamlin, Evelyn Glennie, Jaime Laredo, Sharon Robinson, and Joseph Kalichstein.

The roster of orchestras programming her works reads like a *Who's Who* of the symphonic world, among them the New York Philharmonic and the St. Louis, San Francisco, Chicago, Cleveland, Philadelphia, Indianapolis, Detroit, Houston, Pittsburgh, Dallas, Cincinnati, Berlin, London, St. Paul, Louisville, Tokyo, Los Angeles, St. Luke's, American Composers', New York Chamber, and National Symphony Orchestras. Conductors Leonard Slatkin, Marin Alsop, Mariss Janssons, Yan Pascal Tortelier, Alan Gilbert, Zubin Mehta, Dennis Russell Davies, Andrew Litton, Andres Delfs, Michael Stern, JoAnn Falletta, Christof Perick, and Sergei Commissiona have all led orchestras in performances of Tower compositions.

In the decade to 2005, Tower has accepted commissions from Carnegie Hall, the Juilliard School of Music, the Pittsburgh Symphony Orchestra, Norfolk and La Jolla Music Festivals, the American Brass Quintet, Dumbarton Oaks Research Library, the Orpheus Chamber Orchestra, American Guild of Organists, Carillon Importers on behalf of Absolut Vodka, the Milwaukee Ballet, the Omaha Symphony Orchestra, the University of Wisconsin–Madison School of Music, the Dorian and Dakota Wind Quintets, the International Women's Forum, and the College Band Directors' National Association. She is in the enviable position, from a composer's standpoint, of having to turn down a significant number of requests each year due to an over-full schedule.

The occasion of her 60th birthday in 1998 prompted soloists, chamber ensembles and symphonies, conductors, and fellow composers to mount Tower celebrations across the country. Massachusetts, Michigan, Ohio, Pennsylvania, Colorado, and New York were among the locations for all-Tower concerts and celebrations. Included among the luminaries performing were Paul Neubauer,

André Emelianoff, the Verdehr Trio, Muir and Cassatt String Quartets, Columbus ProMusica, Da Capo Chamber Players, Alea III, Auros Group, and the Chamber Music Society of Lincoln Center.

About turning 60, she said, "The first thing that hit me is that time is getting shorter. So I made a list of things I want to write before I die. I've always been a composer who took risks, who tried to be adventurous with each piece. What constitutes risk-taking in music is complex. For me, it means trying to go deeper into what I think I can do, rather than trying to be something I'm not."[67]

Tower wrote prolifically during the 1990s, producing some of her most highly acclaimed and most frequently performed works including *Clarinet Concerto, Concerto for Orchestra, Fanfare for the Uncommon Woman Nos. 3, 4,* and *5, Wings (alto sax arrangement), Violin Concerto, Stepping Stones, Celebration Fanfare, Elegy, Night Fields, No Longer Very Clear, Or Like a . . . an Engine, Trés Lent, Duets for Orchestra, Turning Points, Rapids (Piano Concerto No. 2), Paganini Trills, Ascent, Holding a Daisy, Valentine Trills, Rain Waves, And . . . They're Off!, Toccanta, Wild Purple, Silver Ladders,* and *Tambor.*

Since 1999, Tower has been composer-in-residence for the New York-based Orchestra of St. Luke's. The OSL, as it is known, presented by Carnegie Hall in an annual subscription series, has commissioned one and premiered two of Tower's works. Peter Connelly conducted the premiere of *Fanfare for the Uncommon Woman, No. 2* in 1989 and Alan Gilbert the OSL-commissioned premiere of *The Last Dance* in 2000.

The American Mecca of Music, Tanglewood, has twice honored Tower as featured composer, in 2000 and 2002. In 2003, she was selected as the inaugural composer for the *Made in America* consortium program. Through the combined efforts of orchestral leaders (beginning with Robert Rosoff of the Glens Fall Symphony in upstate New York), the guidance of the American Symphony Orchestra League and Meet the Composer Foundation, and the financial backing of the Ford Motor Company Fund and the National Endowment for the Arts, the largest known orchestral commissioning consortium was realized.

Frank Oteri, editor/publisher of NewMusicBox, a monthly web magazine from the American Music Center, points out that while rock bands and jazz ensembles tour with the same set pieces year after year, orchestras, if they premiere a new work, will rarely play it more than once and that often the work is under-rehearsed and will not receive a second performance. Extended orchestral tours are so expensive and pose such logistical challenges that they are becoming a thing of the past. "Imagine," he says, "if somehow a piece of orchestral music could tour without the orchestra."[68]

Ford's *Made in America* project provided 65 smaller-budget American orchestras with the opportunity to share the costs of commissioning a composition by a major composer, perform it, and partake of the fund-raising, promotion, marketing, educational outreach, and technical resources behind the program. The grant's creators hoped to increase audiences for contemporary music and promote more such performances by American orchestras.

Between October 2005 and March 2007, *Made in America,* a fifteen-minute composition loosely based on the well-known song by the same name, was performed more than 70 times in 50 states, with Tower frequently providing pre-concert talks, putting a human face to the person behind the program notes, and occasionally conducting her own work. For a composer so deeply invested in communicating with her audience and performers, Tower and Ford *Made in America* were a perfect match.

According to John Von Rhein, the original melody is used "musically (as a unifying device), symbolically (to convey the national scope of the piece) and as a political metaphor,"[69] although Tower eschews any hidden political agenda, the composition reflecting instead the contrast between her experiences in poverty-ridden South American and in the privileged United States where she has lived for most of her life. The familiar melody undergoes various transformations throughout the piece, and Lawrence Eckerling, conductor of the Evanston Symphony Orchestra, suggests that "the use of dissonances brings an ironic undercurrent, a questioning, to the piece, that suggests things may not be as beautiful as they seem [in America]."[70] He notes that he is thrilled with the concept of the large consortium, as it both affords smaller orchestras the opportunity to participate in the creation of new works and their acceptance into the repertoire and "rescues the symphonic repertory from stagnation."[71]

The *Made in America* experience differed from Tower's past interactions with orchestras. Firstly, Tower consciously kept the technical limitations of the participating community and youth orchestras in mind while composing the work, making it accessible yet challenging for the performers. Secondly, "when you go to some of the major orchestras, they regard you as a risk—[but] not these community orchestras. I come in with a media blitz, and they treat me like a rock star. [They] are so proud to have me there, and they treat the piece with a great deal of seriousness and commitment. This surrounds the event with an excitement that's very nourishing for a composer."[72]

The first few years of the 21st century have offered Tower numerous opportunities to reflect on her success, and to allow other musicians to celebrate it. In January 2004, Carnegie Hall's *Making Music* series featured a retrospective of her work, highlighting numerous artists who regularly perform her music, including the Tokyo String Quartet, pianists Melvin Chen and Ursula Oppens, violist Paul Neubauer, oboist Richard Woodhams, and the New England Conservatory Percussion Ensemble. Most of the works were then recorded and released in August 2005 on the Naxos label. A June 2006 performance and recording session with Leonard Slatkin and the Nashville Symphony will result in yet another Naxos release, containing *Made in America, Tambor,* and *Concerto for Orchestra.*

Particularly meaningful to Tower was *Petroushskates* being identified in 2004 by Chamber Music America as one of the 101 most significant compositions for small ensembles, and New England Conservatory of Music's awarding her an honorary doctorate in May 2006. The latest in a long line of monetary awards and recognition came in the form of the 2006 Medora King Award for Musical Composition, a $25,000 prize from the University of Texas, Austin.

Tower's works since the turn of the century include *Vast Antique Cubes/Throbbing Still*, *The Last Dance*, *Big Sky*, *Fascinating Ribbons*, *Strike Zones*, *In Memory*, *DNA*, *For Daniel*, *Incandescent*, *Purple Rhapsody*, *Made in America*, *Chamber Dance*, *Copperwave*, *A Gift*, and the as-yet-untitled quintet for the Dumbarton Oaks Library.

In the past few years, Tower has turned some of her musical attention to conducting, a "natural outgrowth of composing," making her debut when she was in residence at the Scotia Festival of Music in Halifax, Nova Scotia.[73] After preparing and conducting an ambitious full-length program for the Anchorage Symphony which included *Adagio for Strings* by Samuel Barber, Janáček's *Hary Janos* Suite, Prokofiev's *Piano Concerto #3*, Bartok's *Romanian Dances*, Sibelius' *Valse Triste*, and her own *Tambor*, Tower made the decision to conduct only her own works, citing lack of formal training and experience in directing.[74]

In 1990 she established and conducted a college-community orchestra at Bard College and has conducted her *Rapids*, *In Memory*, *Flute Concerto*, *Duets*, and *Made in America* and made recent appearances as a conductor with the American Symphony, Hudson Valley Philharmonic, Scotia Festival Orchestra, Anchorage Symphony, and Kalistos Chamber Orchestra. During the 2007–08 season, Tower also wields the baton in front of the Baltimore Symphony Orchestra. When asked if her own compositions are difficult to conduct, she answers affirmatively, adding the disclaimer that she is not an experienced conductor. To conduct her pieces well, she says, the director must have a good sense of rhythm.[75]

At Home in Red Hook

Joan has shared her life for the past 32 years with Jeff Litfin, a retired businessman and writer, now a student of jazz piano. They met in New York City in the mid-1970s and finally married in 2002. (During a March 23, 2006, interview, Tower seemed a bit embarrassed that she could not recall the exact date of their anniversary.) *Island Prelude* (1989) is dedicated to Jeff; *And . . . They're Off!* (1997) may reflect his former interest in horse racing.

Joan and Jeff have numerous and deep friendships in the Red Hook, New York, community, counting among their large circle of friends faculty members at Bard College, fellow health enthusiasts at the gym, police officers, and other townspeople. Since Joan recently developed an interest in pool, 26 North Drive was remodeled to house a large billiards table. According to her husband, Joan's gotten pretty good at it.

In what other little spare time she has, Tower reads biographies of composers, having just finished one about Hildegard of Bingen and now in the midst of one about Ruth Crawford Seeger. When she travels, she prefers lighter contemporary fiction. Currently, she travels a great deal, either conducting or attending performances of the very popular *Made in America*.

In addition to her teaching and composing duties, Tower remains in great demand as speaker, panelist, coach, and judge, and appears at a handful of festivals each summer, coaching, conducting, and sometimes participating in performances of her works. During 2005 and 2006, her residencies included Vanderbilt University and the Bloch, Deer Valley, Aspen, and OKMozart festivals. Tower will be in residence at Summerfest La Jolla, Virginia Arts Center, Chamber Music Northwest, and Santa Fe Music Festival during 2007 and 2008.

At the time of this writing, Tower is approaching her 70th birthday. She vehemently denies any plans for or interest in retiring from teaching or composing and maintains a commission calendar as active as any composer in the world.

Notes

1.   Gerry Hayes, E-mail to Ellen Grolman, January 6, 2006.
2.   "Tower Genealogy," (2003), www.towergenealogy.com/pictures 4.htm. (Accessed May 6, 2006).
3.   Joan Tower, Interview by Jan Fournier. Tape Recording. Oral History American Music Project at Yale University School of Music, New Haven, CT, July 28, 1983.
4.   Tower, *Memories of Growing Up*, unpublished memoir prepared for Ellen Grolman, March 2006, 7.
5.   Tower, *Memories*, 8.
6.   Tower, Interview by Jan Fournier.
7.   Tower, Interview by Julie Niemeyer. Tape Recording. Oral History American Music Project at Yale University School of Music, New Haven, CT, April 30, 1993.
8.   Tower, Interview by Jan Fournier.
9.   Tower, *Memories*, 4.
10. Tower, *Memories*, 4.
11. Tower, Interview by Jan Fournier.
12. Richard Dyer, "Joan Tower's Bold Music Hits Boston," *Boston Globe*, May 3, 1995, E24.
13. Mark Stryker, "To Thine Own Talent Be True," *Detroit Free Press*, May 31, 2004, E1.
14. Jerry Young, "Composing Is Architecture for Tower," *Austin American-Statesman*, September 28, 1996, E1.
15. Tower, *Memories*, 8.
16. Kyle Gann, "Uptown Dropout," *The Village Voice*, no. 42 (December 1998): 132.
17. Tower, Interview by Ellen Grolman. Tape Recording. Red Hook, NY, March 22, 2006.
18. Unpublished document in possession of Joan Tower.
19. Unpublished document in possession of Joan Tower.
20. Tower, Interview by Ellen Grolman, March 23, 2006.
21. Milton Babbitt, "Who Cares If You Listen?" *Hi Fidelity* 8, no. 2 (February 1957): 38.
22. Tower, E-mail to David Gordon, August 3, 2005.
23. John Rockwell, "Da Capo Chamber Players," *New York Times*, February 6, 1974, 22.
24. Unpublished document in possession of Joan Tower.

25. Tower, E-mail to David Gordon, August 3, 2005.

26. Kyle Gann, "American Composer: Joan Tower," *Chamber Music* 18, no. 6, (2001): 42.

27. Sharon Prado, "Old Wine into New Bottles," *Contemporary Music Review*, 16, no. 1–2 (1997): 51.

28. Nancy Leckie Bonds, "An Analysis of Joan Tower's *Wings* for Solo Clarinet," D.M.A. dissertation, City University of New York, 2000: 230.

29. Mary Lou Humphrey, "An Uncommon Woman," *Stagebill Magazine*, Carnegie Hall edition (January 1990): 11.

30. Tower, Interview by Julie Niemeyer.

31. Valerie O'Brien, "Musician of the Month: Joan Tower—Her *Sequoia* Gains Establishment Status, But She Won't Rest on Her Laurels," *High Fidelity/MusicalAmerica Edition* 32, no. 6 (1982): 7.

32. "Joan Tower," musicmatch.com/album/work_Classical.cgi? (Accessed November 18, 2005).

33. Scott Cantrell, "Tower Rising in the Music World," *Times Union*, November 9, 1984, C6.

34. Tower, Interview by Julie Niemeyer.

35. Tower, Interview by Julie Niemeyer.

36. Bonds, "An Analysis of Joan Tower's *Wings*," 204.

37. Patricia Rice, "The Composer Lends a Hand to the Baton," *St. Louis Post-Dispatch*, September 14, 1984, 1.

38. Valerie O'Brien, "Musician of the Month: Joan Tower," 7.

39. "Circular Breathing," www.woodwind.org/clarinet/Study (Accessed April 26, 2006).

40. Bonds, "An Analysis of Joan Tower's *Wings*," 237.

41. Bonds, "An Analysis of Joan Tower's *Wings*," 205.

42. David Raymond, Liner notes to *Joan Tower Concertos*, d'Note Classics, DND 1016, 1997.

43. Tower, "Approaching Senior Status as a Woman and a Composer." Audiotape of Patten Foundation Lecture at Indiana University, Bloomington, IN, October 27, 1998.

44. Thomas Erdmann, "An Interview with Joan Tower," *Journal of the Conductors' Guild* 25, no. 1 (2004): 4.

45. Tower, Interview by Ellen Grolman, March 21, 2006.

46 Young, "Composing Is Architecture for Tower," E1.

47. Bonds, "An Analysis of Joan Tower's *Wings*," 195.

48. Tower, Interview by Ellen Grolman, March 22, 2006.

49. Young, "Composing Is Architecture for Tower," E1.

50. "Report on Joan Tower," Department Evaluation Committee, Bard College, Annandale-on-Hudson, NY, March 31, 1997.

51. Tower, Interview by Julie Niemeyer.

52. Lauren Rico, "Instrumental Women: Comparing Notes," broadcast on Minnesota Public Radio, February 1, 2003.

53. Rice, "The Composer Lends a Hand to the Baton," 1.

54. Margalit Fox, "A Living Composer," *Newsday*, January 2, 1994, 16.

55. Tower, Interview by Ellen Grolman, March 22, 2006.

56. Tower, "From Chamber to Orchestral Music," unpublished essay for Meet the Composer Foundation (1988): 2.

57. Tower, hand-written notes made during St. Louis Symphony pre-recording rehearsal of *Sequoia*, September 1982.

58. Joan Tower, hand-written notes made during a New York Philharmonic rehearsal of *Sequoia*, September 1982.

59. In a letter to Zubin Mehta dated November 10, 1982, Tower expresses appreciation for his interest in *Sequoia*.

60. Richard Dyer, "Joan Tower's Bold Music Hits Boston," *Boston Globe*, May 3, 1987, 103.

61. Tower, "Statement of Reasons for the Importance of the Residency Program," unpublished letter to the Meet the Composer Foundation, February 1990.

62. Tower, E-mail to David Gordon, August 3, 2005.

63. Virginia Montgomery, "Sequoia a Success Story," *Cincinnati Enquirer*, May 2, 1986.

64. Susan Feder, Liner notes to *Meet the Composer Orchestra Residency Series: Joan Tower*, Electra/Nonesuch Records 79245, 1990.

65. Tower, Interview by Jenny Raymond. Tape Recording. Oral History American Music Project at Yale University School of Music, New Haven, CT, January 4, 1998.

66. David Raymond, Liner notes to *Joan Tower Concertos*, D'note Classics 1016, 1997.

67. Ellen Pfeifer, "Classical Music," *Boston Herald*, February 2, 1999, S5.

68. Frank, J. Oteri, "Joan Tower: Made in America," September 15, 2005, www.newmusicbox.org/article.nmbx?id=4369 (Accessed April 24, 2006).

69 John Von Rhein, "Ms. Tower's Opus: How 65 Orchestras United for an American Brand," *Chicago Tribune,* February 23, 2006, 2.

70. Von Rhein, "Ms. Tower's Opus," 2.

71. Von Rhein, "Ms. Tower's Opus," 2.

72. Von Rhein, "Ms. Tower's Opus," 2.

73. Joel Jacobson, "People, Players, Composer's Reward," *The Chronicle Herald,* May 28, 1997, A6.

74. Tower, Interview by Ellen Grolman, March 21, 2006.

75. Tower, Interview by Ellen Grolman, March 21, 2006.

Part II: Tower's Musical Voice

Tower's Musical Voice

Compositional Organicism

Tower has always been in the unusual and enviable position of never having had to compose without the prospect of a performance, both because her music has always been well-received and because she has always surrounded herself with performers.

Until 1976, she relied heavily on pre-compositional maps to organize, plot, and structure her serial works. These maps helped her to navigate the infinite number of musical choices she confronted as a composer. Stylistically, one can see a movement toward change in the twelve months that separate *Breakfast Rhythms I* (1974) and *Breakfast Rhythms II* (1975), in which the strict serialism of the former gives way to a more fluid, impressionistic style dotted with tone clusters in the latter. She explores the structures of these pivotal works in her 1978 doctoral dissertation for Columbia University, "On *Breakfast Rhythms I and II*." Reflecting on the different directions in which she was being pulled when writing the works she says, "There was actually a year in between *I* and *II* where I stopped composing . . . and went through a big change of style. I had decided to branch out of [twelve-tone music], so that's why the two are quite different."[1]

One of Tower's central ideas in *Breakfast Rhythms* was to explore a pitch system in which every pitch had a unique identity and a ranked order of importance in relation to all other pitches. The more she worked with this concept, the more she found herself turning toward the tonal system and away from serial music. Tower's ten-year "compositional detour" into serial music had ultimately not been a comfortable one for her.[2] "Basically I used the serial technique because I was an insecure kind of composer [and] . . . I needed a pitch map of some kind . . . just so that I knew where my next pitches were coming from. As time wore on, I . . . started developing my own pitch structures."[3] She eventually realized that the maps were working against her inherent talents, and she left them behind, explaining, "I wanted to get away from the thick textures and pointillistic activity that characterized serialism at that time."[4]

She was also weary of the rhythmic acrobatics required of her as a pianist performing such works. Of her time with the Da Capo Chamber Players in the 1970s, she says: "It was a point of pride to be able to count very complicated music."[5] Exaggerating the serial virtuosity that was required of performers she says: "We learned how to count 15 in 3 ½ over a grace note."[6] "We rehearsed very conscientiously and professionally, and we were very good at playing the hardest pieces by everyone. At first it was a technical goal we were aiming for:

we wanted to be the best at counting that kind of complicated music. But after a while . . . I wanted to play music I felt I could project musically, not just acrobatically."[7] Hearing performances of Messiaen *Quartet for the End of Time* and George Crumb's *The Voice of the Whale* helped dislodge her from the serial trap in which she felt she was caught. She remembers thinking how "simple, direct and accessible the composers' voices were; and how gutsy."[8]

Finding, establishing, and sustaining a unique voice involved a significant element of risk, but one which provided Tower with the impetus to turn away from the serial technique she had been using. "Achieving an identity in music depends on risks. If you don't take any risks, your particular compositional talents never shine through. Creating *high-energy* music is one of my special talents; I like to see just how high I can push a work's energy level without making it chaotic or incoherent. But my lyrical nature has been emerging in snippets over the years, too."[9]

Not until 1976's *Black Topaz*, however, did Tower's natural voice begin to emerge: simpler, less dissonant, and somewhat impressionistic. After the risky decision to abandon the restrictive compositional charts, Tower was guided by a more organic, intuitive approach, one in which each idea develops from the one that precedes it and the only pre-compositional considerations are the performing forces and maybe the approximate length of the work. "I don't do sketches in advance. I do start out with a basic idea, but I'm not very 'pre-compositional' in my thinking."[10]

> Every instant of music has a past, a present, and a future. . . . For me, it's very important that the present grow out of the past, that past and present combined contain the seeds of the future. As a piece goes on it develops more and more past; it takes on more shape, and the more shape it has the more you know about where it's headed. I'm always . . . making sure that the music's present is consistent both with its past and with the future I have in mind for it.[11]

Tower admits that this intuitive process cannot be rushed: "You have to listen to the piece and let it tell you what to do."[12] And some compositions end up being harder to write than others. Of *Night Fields*, which she wrote in 1994 for the Muir String Quartet, Tower says, "It was torture to write this quartet. It was a nightmare. That's where the 'night' comes from in the title. However, *Nightmare* was too negative."[13] "You have to be aware of the context of everything; the pitch, the rhythm, the dynamics, the texture. The slowness comes in trying to hear all those levels operate simultaneously."[14]

Compositional Aesthetic

Tower doesn't think in terms of pitch systems anymore, but in terms of what she calls "simple materials": the type of scale she'll use, how she will "heat up [that] scale, and the type of action [that is] involved."[15] In order to demarcate sections or to strengthen structurally significant points within a composition, Tower often manipulates musical intensity. She effects changes in any number of musical elements: texture, density, timbre, dynamics, registration, articulation, instrumentation, dissonance, rhythm, melody, repetition, and increasingly complex chord structures, in order to increase or decrease the musical tension. In some of her solo works (as in *Hexachords*), she specifies different vibrato speeds to vary a tone's intensity.

Since her abandonment of serial technique, Tower's compositions are largely based on octatonic, chromatic, and whole tone scales, with prominent tritones. When asked if she's consciously aware of what scales she's using during the composition process and if she intentionally decides to use a particular kind of scale, Tower answers affirmatively: "It's like deciding whether to use bricks, marble, stone, wood, tile, or grass" to build a house. In her most recent octatonic pieces, she says, it's no more complicated than this: "I just use the octatonic scale, aware of which scale I'm in and what the long-range pitch relationships are, the height, depth, and heat of the harmony (more or less dissonance)—this [process] lends itself to being malleable."[16]

Tower spends a significant amount of time contemplating the long-term pitch relationships in her compositions. She recognizes the extent to which those relationships can impact a work, but continually wrestles with the constraints of her traditional theory training which privileges pitch over other musical elements. Pitch, she says, "means *nothing* without a time line, register, dynamics, etc."[17]

Margo Jones points out in her 1993 dissertation (essentially a comparison of Tower's compositions for flute pre- and post-1974) that two style constants that bridge Tower's move from serial to organic composition have been rhythmic variety and rapid meter changes.[18] Shouha identifies the common element between the two periods to be the lack of a consistent pulse, specifically citing *Island Prelude* as an examplar, but emphasizing that this is a common trait in Tower's music.[19]

Tower herself sees the lone holdover from her serial days as her use of time maps, and she finds herself gradually stepping back even from them.[20] Although her new voice is far removed from serialism, she continues to plot significant musical occurrences based on action and reaction, carefully proportioning the dramatic curve in her music. "The hardest thing is knowing what the timing, the pacing of things, is. I'm always aware of fact that if you put something in a room that's too short, you kill that room. You have to have the right length of time spent on an idea to make it hold, or it will collapse."[21] "You can write a very good tune or . . . harmonic progression . . . or interesting tapestry, but if it's not in the right place in the right time with the right length, it just dies."[22]

The placement of even a single note is crucial, she feels, since she is dealing with the delicate task of helping the work to unfold. "One triangle note placed before a set of strings holding a chord is one thing. Placing the triangle *after* the held strings-chord is another thing—it's not the same triangle note, because the context has shifted its identity."[23] As early as the mid-1970s, in her doctoral dissertation for Columbia University, Tower dealt with the concept of length and duration and timing in *Breakfast Rhythms I* and *II*, examining the compositional

process ("*how* I composed what I composed")[24] as well as the musical compo-
nents that comprise it. The durational rhythm is the element that "breathes life
into the content," she says, provides "special and general pacing," and "estab-
lishes with the content the unique rhythmic identity of that piece."[25]

She also focuses—in the dissertation and in all of her compositions—on
balance, one of the elements in Beethoven's music that she finds so satisfying
and influential. The notion of balance has many potential elemental applications:
to pitch, rhythm, and register, for example, but for Tower it also functions on a
structural level. She points out that in order to "balance something, one has to
know and understand what is being balanced—which really means identifying
the main feature (or 'itness') of any given passage," which is "dependent on its
environment for its identification."[26]

Since each musical event grows out of the previous one, beginnings of
compositions are pivotal, "because I'm carving out the world which I'm going
to inhabit."[27] She will often sculpt an opening motive to suit the intended performer's personal musical style, saying, "Perhaps the performer I'm writing for
has a lovely lyrical mode of playing, and so I will begin with a lyrical phrase."[28]
"A piece is a completely organic process, based on itself. In other words, the
starting ideas provide the fuel for the form of the piece. The whole process is
one of listening very patiently to what that piece is trying to do, rather than telling the piece what to do."[29]

Generally wary of assigning a larger architecture in the beginning stages,
believing it a potential trap, Tower most frequently makes use of a small motive
upon which to structure a composition. From a 1976 interview: "I learned long
ago that the beginning idea is very minimal, and it's what you do with the idea
that makes the piece. After all, the opening motive of Beethoven's *Fifth* [*Symphony*] is quite trivial, but look at what Beethoven does with it! The context is
everything for me; it shapes the idea and is the strength of the piece."[30]

The transformation and development of the motive, then, whether harmonic
or thematic, dictates the course of and affects all elements of the work: harmony,
melody, rhythm, tempo, and overall form.[31] As the work progresses, she gains a
better idea of its direction, describing its unfolding as the music creating itself.[32]
Tower seamlessly blends the concept of motivic development with her intuitive,
organic style.

Tower often speaks about the concept of "seams" in her compositions, as in
her interview with John Fletcher in 2002. Comparing her terminology with the
image of two pieces of fabric joined together, Fletcher asks if that is an apt description. She replies, "A seam is the end of a phrase. There's an old phrase and
a new phrase. And the seam can be very big—it can be like two movements—a
huge seam. Or it can be like a section. There is a hierarchy of seams, and . . . I
spend a lot of time making those work."[33] Tower began seriously focusing on
"seams" in *Amazon* (1977) and continued, in *Petroushskates* (1980), to explore
more deeply what she calls "seamless action."[34]

She is at all times "working on the energy line of a phrase, of an action, of a
motive . . . and . . . on continuity, or what could be described as "motivated music"; music that has a motivation rather than music that is just constructed. Mu-

sic that has impulse, a reason—an 'energy reason' for being there at that phase at that level. That's what I work at."[35] At first, she reveals, she was interested in only the energy of a musical line, "but then I became fascinated with musical motion, the energy and consequences of its actions, how lines acquire direction and shape, and musical time. Music has to be counterbalanced. It's like physics—if you throw a ball at a certain angle and speed, it will fall a certain way."[36] She recommends, in fact, that her post-1976 works may best be examined via an energy line analysis, a physics-related tool she created. In an interview with Nancy Bonds she elaborates:

[I would use an] energy line analysis [to examine my works]. There are not tools for that, and as far as I know it hasn't been explored in theory books or anything. But that would be a way of getting to my music. . . . I would start with something like a physics point of view. What direction is it going? There are three directions: one is up, one is staying, and one is down. There are three energy lines: one is up, one is staying, one is down. In other words, music can get more intense, get less intense, or it can stay the same . . . . Then I would go "okay, this is energy line one, increasing in intensity how? Well, it's getting louder, it's getting higher, the instruments are multiplying, the rhythm is getting slower. There [are] different ways of creating intensity. How is that intensity increasing? On what level?

Then I would do a space analysis on top of that because the space you're in for me is very important. Are you up here? Are you covering this grid? Are you down here? Where are you in the spatial grid? Because the energy line has a lot to do with that. How does it shift? Is it short periods, is it long periods? Then there would be a pacing line. How long does this intensity build up? And how long is this one in relationship to this one over here? What is the space here in relationship to space over here? I mean there are all kinds of maps that you could create that are not pitch maps.[37]

In the 1987 interview with Bonds, Tower deals with the inherent weaknesses of notation, telling Bonds that she continues to refine her notation because of performers' mistaken belief that notation contains "every little nuance" and the "composer's real intentions." What the performers need to do, and what the best, intuitive performers *already* do, Tower says, is "get off the page . . . listen . . . get behind the energies of . . . the line," and make sure the dynamics or articulation closely match that energy of the line—whatever the dynamics or articulation may indicate.[38] She continues to straddle the notational fence: should she make it too specific, the able but less intuitive performer will refuse to change anything in fear of going against the composer's wishes; if her notation is more open, the less able performers are apt to "kill the piece."[39]

Much has been made of Tower's self-description as a "choreographer of sound." She explains that she sees music very much like a dance in the sense "that you have an action and a reaction and it can be a physical action that's located in a particular space . . . or [it can be] low, middle or high. . . . The spatial-physical reactions are very closely related . . . between dance and music."[40]

She has had a long-term fascination with physics and the idea of forces (almost choosing to major in it in college), and her "action-reaction" approach to composition clearly reflects that interest. "What happens," she asks, "when you start with a snare roll and you crescendo over ten beats? That obviously is building up something and you've got to react to that somehow. So to me the whole issue of a good piece is about that. It's about how you create an architecture, a context . . . for how those interactions work."[41]

Titles

Pieces that date from Tower's serial period tend to have generic titles, like *Movements, Fantasia, Variations,* and *Prelude*; the majority of post-1970 compositions bear more colorful ones.

> The whole thing with titles started back in 1974. I was writing a piece for clarinet and 5 instruments and a guy [from the publisher] called and said, "We need the title right away." I said, *"Piece for Clarinet and Five Instruments."* And he said, "You can do better than that." I was looking out the window, it was a beautiful autumn day and everything was orange and red and yellow, and I was having breakfast. So I said, *"Breakfast Rhythms,"* and he said "fantastic," and hung up. When they played the piece in New York, the critic [John Rockwell from *The New York Times*] came up and said, "That's an interesting title; what does it mean?" and I said "nothing," so he put that into the review. [It was then that] I started thinking of titles that had meaning and images.[42]

Tower spends a great deal of time choosing titles for her compositions, often conferring with friends and soliciting suggestions. *Wings* (1981), for solo clarinet, began life as *Panthers* and then "the piece literally started to take off—to go up, up. And I said 'Panthers don't take off like this. . . . I've got to change it to a bird.'"[43] It then became *Falcons* and, finally, *Wings.*

The image-driven titles Tower's listeners find so provocative are normally chosen after the completion of the work, but can really appear to her at any time. She prefers that they have both broad and specific application, and some reference to action,[44] noting that "because we use words to talk about music, the choice of words for the . . . title have [*sic*] to be carefully considered."[45]

Wings is one of Tower's favorite titles "[because it is] broad enough and yet it incorporates an image of something quite specific: flying. And flying can be fast, it can be slow . . . it encompasses a lot of things."[46] One of the titles that still does not satisfy her is 1986's *Silver Ladders.* "It's not quite right," she says, "but I gave up. 'Ladders' is fine, but 'Silver' is misleading, because it makes the piece seem like it's going to be light . . . and it's not."[47] Music critic Frank Retzel argues that it actually *is* an apt title, since the musical building block of Tower's "ladder" is the octatonic scale, a word *(scala)* that means "ladder" in Latin. "The images are both concrete and abstract," he says, "and in Tower's hands, metaphoric."[48]

At times, a title will actually impact the direction a piece takes: "The image is sometimes operating while I'm writing the piece and sometimes only comes about as a result of the piece. . . . With *Amazon,* it came halfway . . . and it was a perfect image. I think that's one of the few images that really works in my pieces and that actually started to have an effect on what was coming out subsequently.[49]

Other times, the title itself will provide the impetus for the piece's popularity, as (in Tower's opinion) in the case of *Fanfare for the Uncommon Woman*.[50] She believes that the work's repeated performances (more than 500 at this point) come more from the provocative title than the music itself. Originally a tribute to Aaron Copland, identical in instrumentation to and containing musical quotes from his *Fanfare for the Common Man*, *Fanfare for the Uncommon Woman No. 1* was written for "women who take risks and are adventurous,"[51] and was immediately embraced as a "historic feminist statement in music."[52] Tamara Bernstein, who authored the liner notes to the Koch International recording of all five Tower *Fanfares*, points out that "the fact that brass sections of symphony orchestras tend to be the last stronghold against women adds a delicious irony to most performances—and a special celebratory note when some of the players, at least, are women." [53]

Tower's titles frequently come from the world of nature: *Sequoia*, *Amazon*, *Island Rhythms*, *Island Prelude*, *Rapids*, *Rain Waves*, *Wings*, *DNA*, *Snow Dreams*. Another entire series of titles reflects her father's profession in a tribute to his memory. Referred to sometimes as the "mineral series,"[54] they conjure striking images of natural elements such as gemstones, metals, and minerals. Included in this series are *Red Garnet Waltz*, *Platinum Spirals*, *Black Topaz*, *Silver Ladders*, and *Copperwave*. "Properties of metals . . . fascinate me. *Silver Ladders*, for instance, tries to symbolically capture silver's molten and gossamer qualities through the use of fluid solo lines which are juxtaposed against a kaleidoscopic panorama of rising symmetrical scales that reach, ladder-like, into space. The work's varying textures depict silver's changeable weight. *Black Topaz* metaphorically represents topaz's ability to transform into various hues."[55]

The titling of *Copperwave* (2005), written for the American Brass Quintet, was "eight months of torture! I kept delaying. . . . I wanted the image of something heavy but lustrous; weighted, in a lyrical, arch-like motion." The title is also a reference to the leaded yellow brass which composes brass instruments: 67 percent copper, 29 percent zinc, 3 percent lead, and 1 percent tin.[56]

One hallmark of a Tower title is its eclecticism. One references a popular tune from the 1930s: *Fantasy . . . (Those Harbor Lights)*; others are extracted from lines of a poem (*No Longer Very Clear*, *Or Like a . . . an Engine*, *Holding a Daisy*, *Vast Antique Cubes*, and *Throbbing Still*, all from a work by John Ashbery), while still others are more traditionally titled (*In Memory*, *Elegy*, *Chamber Dance*).

Synesthesia plays a part in the titling of two works for viola, *Purple Rhapsody* (2005) and *Wild Purple* (1998), both written for violist Paul Neubauer.

> I always thought of the viola sound as being the color purple. Its deep, resonant and luscious timbre seems to embody all kinds of hues of purple. I never thought of the viola as being particularly wild. So I decided to try and see if I could create

a piece that had wild energy in it and meet the challenge of creating a virtuosic
piece for solo viola.[57]

John Fletcher notes that although many of Tower's titles suggest general
motion (*And . . . They're Off!*, *The Last Dance*, *Turning Points*), several specifically suggest ascent. This music, including *Platinum Spirals*, *Silver Ladders*,
Stepping Stones, and *Ascent*, has elements of what Fletcher terms a "prominent
rising quality."[58]

Forms and Structures

Tower's creative titling and imagery are not evident in her concertos, whose
"genesis," she says, "springs directly from the instrument. The power of the
piece, the range of the piece, the style—everything comes directly from the instrument."[59] Tower likes concertos because they arise from a personal relationship to a performer: from their personal style, musicality, relationship to their
instrument, and unique brand of virtuosity. Typically she works closely with the
intended performer, as she did with cellist André Emelianoff in *Music for 'Cello
and Orchestra* (1984), discussing with him range, register, bowings, articulation,
fingerings, and timbres, and going so far as to call him the midwife for the
piece.[60]

Her concerti reference the elements of contrast, dialogue, and virtuosity inherent in the traditional genre, but often do so in ways which recall only blurred
outlines of the historically established form. In her violin concerto, for example,
she includes not one but two cadenzas, and unexpectedly pairs the soloist with
the concertmaster in its performance, a musical tribute to the dedicatee's (Elmar
Oliveira) deceased brother. This pairing technique also makes appearances in
Tower's clarinet and flute concertos, because the composer felt it might "break
down some of the barriers between the soloist and the orchestra . . . and . . . create collegial relationships."[61]

While traditional 19th-century cadenzas prized virtuosity over musical inte-
gration, Tower clearly eschews virtuosity for virtuosity's sake. Elmar Oliveira
comments that Tower's cadenzas contain "the kind of flashiness an audience can
relate to. Joan doesn't need avant-garde gimmicks, because now she's completely comfortable speaking her own language, one that is expressive and natural to her."[62]

The composer explains her long-time fondness for the one-movement form
by saying that she views the composition of a piece as a "one-moment experience" and that, for her, the end of a movement signals the end of that experience, a final closure that she is loathe to break up into smaller, multiple experiences.[63] The break between movements creates a musical space that is, for her,
too large; she prefers that there is always motion, a sense of moving forward.
Longer one-movement works include her concertos for flute, violin, 'cello, piano (nos. 1 and 2), percussion, orchestra, clarinet, and viola, as well as *Silver
Ladders*, *Rain Waves*, *Noon Dance*, *Made in America*, *Island Rhythms*, *Island*

Prelude, Amazon, Strike Zones, Breakfast Rhythms, Black Topaz, Petroushskates, In Memory, For Daniel, Incandescent, Duets, Copperwave, and others. The one-movement form is a multi-purpose one for Tower, since it can serve as a vehicle for a variety of instrumental combinations from string quartet, to wind quintet, to symphony. Her most recent attempt at a multi-movement work is *No Longer Very Clear: A Suite for Piano,* four pieces composed between 1994 and 2000, based on lines from the poem "No Longer Very Clear" by John Ashbery.

Until very recently, Tower has avoided setting words to music, explaining that she "has trouble with the intrusion of verbal meaning since it is shifting the agenda to the writer of those words."[64] Nevertheless, she has just accepted a commission for a short children's choir work, entitled *Can I?,* to be premiered in New York in early 2008.

Her single original work for symphonic band is *Fascinating Ribbons* (2002), a 31-ensemble commission which was the result of what dedicatee Jack Stamp of Indiana University of Pennsylvania calls persistence on his part and what Tower jokingly refers to as "composer stalking."

Tower has occasionally chosen to arrange her works for different performing forces. *Island Prelude* (1989) has been arranged for oboe and wind quartet as well as for oboe and string quartet. *Amazon* (1977) can be performed as a quintet (flute, clarinet, violin, 'cello, piano) or for full orchestra (1978). *Stepping Stones: A Ballet* began as a work for full orchestra in 1993; Daniel Forlano arranged the work for brass ensemble for Tower to conduct at the White House in September 1993. Jack Stamp, concert band director at Indiana University of Pennsylvania and conductor of the Keystone Winds, heard a recording of the brass ensemble arrangement and told Tower he thought it would be better as a work for concert band. Tower responded by inviting Stamp to re-orchestrate it, which he did in 1994. The work received its third incarnation when Tower arranged it for two pianos in 1995.

The composer sees the arrangements as one piece with different colors: "A piece of music is first and foremost a rhythm of pitches and harmonies and registers. If you play a piano version of an orchestra piece or an orchestra version of a piano piece, the difference between [them] is one of color. So you're not changing pieces, you have essentially the same piece but [with] a different coloring."[65]

In her dissertation, Tower wrote of her surprise upon hearing an orchestrated version of one of her early piano pieces, at the "sameness" of the work, shocked that the orchestral color changes did not significantly alter it. From this she surmised that the "changes in a composition had to do with pitch changes, which really meant that the *stuff* itself was much more fundamental to the piece than what one did with it. Of course, what one does with the *stuff* helps to identify what the *stuff* is in the first place."[66]

She applies the term "content-determinate" to the system described above, contrasting it to the 12-tone "order-determinate" system. She elaborates: "Pitch content seems to be the fundamental aspect of how a piece 'goes' and how a piece changes. And how significant those changes are depends on how the content changes—which in turn depends on the content itself." [67]

Rhythmic prominence has long been a hallmark of a Tower composition. She attributes her fascination with rhythm to early exposure to the complex meters of South American dance music and her personal interest in percussion as well as to the rhythmically intricate serial music she performed as a pianist for so many years. [68]

> In the 1960s I did a lot of very complicated rhythmic stuff . . . as a player and so I learned how to think rhythmically in a very intricate way. . . . [I create] musical energy on the surface of the piece through the rhythm. . . . And since I have a strong sense of rhythm, and since I can notate it, I use that as one of the things that drives my pieces. My music has a rhythmic base as a unit in the action of the piece. [69]

Although she never had any formal lessons, she became somewhat of an "accidental percussionist," performing with the Bennington College orchestra and occasionally continuing in this vein after her move to New York, when professional groups were in need of a player.

Her earliest pieces reflect her interest in percussion, among them *Percussion Quartet* (1963), *Brimset* (1965), whose title is an anagram of the word timbres, and *Breakfast Rhythms I* and *II*. As she became interested in how "a piece is moved by pitch content," she began to use more pitched-percussion instruments like vibraphone and marimba, utilizing the drums for "articulating local and large scale structures. I used to use drums as a musical gesture . . . as a sound pattern, but now I'm using it in a different way—a structural way." [70]

In her larger-scale pieces, the percussion instruments often carry that rhythmic load. She finds writing for percussion challenging; even more so when they are part of the orchestra. Tower finds herself wrestling with the role of percussion within the ensemble: "Is it an eyeliner role? Is it a punctuation role? Is it an antiphonal role? Or is it a solo role?" [71] In 1998's *Tambor*, the prominent role of the percussion in the orchestral milieu even began to influence how Tower wrote for the other instruments. She says,

> What happened while I was writing this piece was that the strong role of the percussion began to influence the behavior of the rest of the orchestra, to the point that the other instruments began to act more and more like a percussion section themselves. In other words, the main action of the work becomes more concerned with rhythm and color than with motives and melodies (though these elements do make occasional appearances here and there). [72]

Musical Influences

Tower freely admits to incorporating characteristic musical "fingerprints" of other composers into her own works and sometimes includes a musical salute in the titles of her works. *Trés Lent (Hommage à Messiaen)* (1994), *Piano Con-*

certo (Homage to Beethoven) (1985), and *Petroushskates* (1980) are three such examples, the last more than a musical nod to Igor Stravinsky's *Petrouchka*. "I think most composers would have to admit that they live, to various degrees, in the sound-worlds of other composers both old and new, and that what they consciously or unconsciously take from them enables them to discover what they themselves are interested in."[73] When asked to credit the composer who most influenced her writing, she indicates that it was more the influence of specific *pieces* she performed, rather than individual composers [italics mine].[74]

> Certain motives recur throughout a number of my compositions. One of these, a slow, straight-line upward action, can be traced back to a piece which I played for many years with . . . the Da Capo Chamber Players. In spite of my unsympathetic regard for the work of Arnold Schoenberg, whose music is so unlike my own, I remember one beautiful moment in his *Chamber Symphony Op. 9*. This slow, stately motive in rising fourths has stuck in my ears throughout the years and has appeared and reappeared in different guises in several of my works.[75]

Island Prelude, Wings, Breakfast Rhythms, and the *Clarinet Concerto* each contain the rising fourth motive Tower refers to above.

She admires the music of Olivier Messiaen, whose *Quartet for the End of Time* (1941) so influenced her own struggles with the concept of time and timing in her compositions. "What struck me was this incredible stopping of time. He would just stop everything and sit on this note, and it would just grow just magically. . . . It was always so exciting to me. It never got boring. That became another stamp in my music . . . these long gestures."[76] From Messiaen she also developed a taste for the octatonic scale.

Critics, performers, audiences, and Tower herself recognize the long shadow of Stravinsky on her music, not in the form of direct quotation, but in the music's energy, vigor, momentum, fervor, and rhythmic muscularity. Speaking with Nancy Bonds, she says, "[In Stravinsky's] *Rite of Spring* . . . near the beginning where the strings go 'ba-ba-ba-ba'. . . Oh, when I first heard that I just went bananas. . . . That is something that has been distributed throughout some of my pieces, that idea."[77]

Beethoven has long been a great love of Tower's. "Long ago, I recognized Beethoven as someone bound to enter my work at some point, because for many years I had been intimately involved in both his piano music and chamber music as a pianist. Even though my own music does not sound like Beethoven's in any obvious way, in it there is a basic idea at work which came from him, something I call the "balancing of musical energies."[78] She particularly admires the consummate sense of balance in Beethoven's works, a component of her own compositions on which she is always focused. "All the characteristics of Beethoven's phrases are balanced—and opposed—in his next phrase. He was an absolute genius at juxtaposition within a highly complex architectural design."[79] Of Tower's body of work, Patricia Rice of the *St. Louis Post-Dispatch* wrote: "The spine of her composition comes from [Beethoven]."[80]

As a Bennington College student in the late 1950s, Tower met regularly with faculty member and 'cellist George Finckel for early morning read-throughs of Beethoven 'cello and piano sonatas. David Finckel, 'cellist of the Emerson Quartet and nephew of George, recalls Joan telling the quartet about these morning sessions:

> George was a large personality and a magnetic teacher, whose enthusiasm, curiosity and courage knew no bounds. Joan, who was studying piano, was conscripted by George to read through the Beethoven 'cello and piano sonatas on a daily basis, which apparently had a profound effect on her as she still speaks of this experience with great relish and nostalgia.[81]

Tower likes to tell the story of how, when she was composing her first *Piano Concerto* (1985), she felt Beethoven enter the room and sit down next to the piano. "Everything I played seemed to have something to do with him," she says. She told him to leave, but he wouldn't, so she finally said, "'OK, if you're going to stay, you're going to have to help me.' And parts of three Beethoven sonatas came into the concerto. I welcomed him . . . instead of pushing him away."[82] As a result, the *Concerto* contains fragments of Beethoven's *Tempest, Waldstein,* and *C minor (Op. 111)* piano sonatas.

Another fundamental voice in her oeuvre is an echo of her adolescence in South America. Tower's frequent attendance at and musical participation in the Inca celebrations with her nanny led her to incorporate, often subconsciously, the Latin rhythms of samba, conga, and tango in her compositions, and to highlight their percussive natures. Tower captures and communicates the visceral excitement and abandon she experienced while listening, dancing, and playing in these festivals as a child.

Other significant sources of inspiration point to Tower's broad exposure to some of the jazz luminaries that performed in the New York clubs during the '60s and '70s. Tower pinpoints specific influences which include Berlioz, for a particular chord in the last movement of his *Symphonie Fantastique*; Philip Glass for the repetitive rhythms in *The Modern Love Waltz;* the dramatic scope of Edgar Varèse,[83] and Joseph Schwantner's method of sound attacks.[84]

The Composing Process

Tower has likened the process of composing to "creating architecture." "After laboring for a year on a composition," she says, "the blueprints get passed to an orchestra, who plays it . . . and the building goes up." Then begins the second-guessing of the structure. "You are looking at it and you say: 'Those windows are way too big for that side of the house' or 'I can't see the main window that I thought was going to be so prominent.'"[85] (She adds that the blueprint has to be far more specific if it is to go to a professional orchestra rather than a chamber music group, as the chamber group has both the luxury of more rehearsal time and the understanding that dialogue about the work is built-in to the structure of the group.)[86]

Tower composes in a spacious workspace filled with musical memorabilia, seated between a Yamaha Disklavier (which she uses almost exclusively as an acoustic instrument) and an Ensoniq electronic keyboard (for sustaining notes and use while traveling). She writes by hand in pencil, beginning with a three-or four-stave score sketch, in a manuscript which is "not the most readable."[87]

Aware that many of her students and colleagues use computer notation applications like Finale or Sibelius, Tower nevertheless insists that she needs a piano while composing, since the instrument "makes it very evident what's working and what's not working at a kind of immediate level,"[88] and also because "she has the chops and can get around [on the instrument]."[89] She has jokingly admitted to having an "instinctive resistance to being told what to do in print," so any instrument or computer program that she can't immediately interact with on an intuitive level, she eschews.[90]

Tower has never found the prospect of composing electronic music alluring, mainly because it lacked the element of connection between composer and performer, but also because of her aversion to reading manuals and directions. She says, "When I did my time in the electronic studio at Columbia University many years ago, I kept plugging the wrong plug into the wrong outlet and blowing up the speakers. I'm not mechanically minded at all."[91]

She writes each afternoon for four or five hours, putting aside all other concerns. "It is an absolutely religious habit of mine. . . . I'm very, very, very persistent, but on average complete only about three minutes of music per month. Some composers know in advance just where they're going. I don't. I have to spend *a lot* of time on where I am and where I've just been."[92] When she can devote all her time to composition, free of distractions, she can sometimes produce four minutes of music in a month, and works on only one piece at a time.

Reluctant to tinker with a piece after its completion, she makes only what she terms cosmetic changes, which might include dynamics, articulation, and orchestration. More substantive musical changes can be dangerous if not done very carefully, "because you're not inside the piece like you were when you wrote it. To come from a distance and make note or rhythm changes is dangerous."[93] An orchestral work is likely to receive fewer changes (unless a player specifically requests it); revisions for a soloist may be more involved.

Tower does not solicit opinions about a composition, share it with anyone until it's completed, nor rely on perceptions other than her own. She believes that although a completed composition will not change, one's *relationship* to it might, and that sometimes the larger world's reaction to a work will influence her own feelings about it. She cites as an example *Night Fields* (1994), a composition she struggled to write and about whose future she was not optimistic (she has used the word "disaster"). The quartet world, however, embraced the work quickly and warmly, giving it multiple performances and finally convincing Tower of its strength.

All composers must contend occasionally with negative reviews. Although reviews of her older works pose no threat to Tower, she purposely avoids reading derogatory reviews of newly launched works since she feels particularly vulnerable to a premiere. To this day, she always thinks her new pieces are terrible (until proven otherwise) and explains that is because she is so vulnerable at this point, expecting the worst is a method of protection, a way to avoid being hurt.[94] She knows, rationally, that the experience of hearing one's own music can be distorted by frustration, ego, or anxiety, so she tries to reserve final judgment until she has heard her own pieces a number of times and her perspective is clearer. She makes it a habit not to read reviews. Husband Jeff Litfin will read them—aloud if it's positive; otherwise, he says nothing. In truth, because of her strong connection to the performers, Tower is far more sensitive to players' reactions than to critics'.

Tower steadfastly believes that a strong piece will elicit repeated performances, that a work that does not have an active life after completion must have some inherent weaknesses. She examines these "weaker" pieces very closely to continue to grow as a composer. She believes in the universality of strong pieces, saying, "If a piece is good, people will like it in Utah, they will like it in New York, they will like it in Vancouver, they will like it in Lima, Peru."[95]

Reviewer Robert S. Clark describes Tower's signature style as including "phrases and note combinations that imply but stop short of tonal procedures."[96] Tower herself has difficulty ascribing a specific style to her compositional voice, a style sometimes referred to by critics as "Neo-Romantic"; she feels that the strength of music transcends any particular categorization. "There's a power in music that goes beyond style," she says. The labels of folk, classical, jazz, rock, etc., do little more than prejudice the listener. "For somebody who's musical, pieces will 'get to them'" (or not), no matter what the category.[97]

In the past, Tower has used drawings and sketches to work out both musical and personal challenges. Her scrapbooks contain a good number of these, most completed in pencil, drawings exuberant and reticent, fluid and static, many with geometric shapes. *Black Topaz* (1976) actually "derives from a drawing Tower once did of color rays emanating from a black, piano-like object. This single-movement work examines a similar projection of color from its focal point, the solo piano (black) to a six-member supporting instrumental ensemble."[98] She's created artwork for *Amazon, Wings,* and *Island Prelude*; her sketch for the last piece adorns the cover of the composition.

The State of Contemporary Music

For decades, Tower has been vocal about what she sees as the sad state of contemporary music performance in the U.S. and the rest of the world. She decries the major orchestras' reticence to program it, the superstar performers' unwillingness to perform it, the paucity of new commissions, and the lack of direct communication both between composer and audience and composer and performer. She says, "The composer today is not present . . . there is no *person* to identify with. To me, that is the main reason why new music has suffered so much."[99] Fellow composer Ned Rorem weighs in on the same subject from a different perspective: "We're the only period in history in which the past takes precedence over the present, and in which the performer is more important than what he performs. A performer makes in one evening what a composer of similar reputation makes in about a year."[100]

Outspoken about the responsibilities that the high-profile performing elite have to contemporary music, Tower praises innovators like Yo-Yo Ma for their musical curiosity and adventurousness and chides others for not connecting with today's composers and failing to regularly commission new works.[101] Tower has said that her conversations with performers often reveal that their managers are the ones veering away from new music programming.[102]

Major orchestras under-program new music for fear that the numbers of their already dwindling audiences will further decrease. Tower argues that many conductors also lack confidence in their ability to judge the quality of a piece due to their lack of familiarity with contemporary music. "The risk factor there is very large and most conductors and soloists who have big careers based on Beethoven, Brahms, and Mendelssohn are afraid their success is going to be tarnished if they pick the wrong [contemporary] piece."[103] Recording companies also bear partial responsibility, Tower feels, because as profit-making organizations, they produce what they think is most likely to sell. This results in many re-issues of established "masterpieces" and recordings with well-known artists.[104]

"In the 19th century, often the composer and the performer were the same person, which is true in the popular world today."[105] Another thing that keeps popular music like rock so creative, Tower notes, is that new music is presented all the time and consumers are passionate about it—they are familiar with it, have a great deal of input regarding its success or failure, and therefore feel empowered to have an opinion about it.[106] "The wonderful thing about new music is the reaction it provokes. Audiences could feel invested in contemporary music as well, if they had regular access to it. You don't hear people say, 'That third movement from Beethoven didn't work,'"[107] because the work has attained nearly sacred status, and its performance rarely engenders any criticism or emotion. On the other hand, an audience's experience with a newly created classical work involves them in a much more creative way. "Not being burdened with the notion of history . . . [allows] the listener to have a more individualistic response to [a composition]."[108]

Tower points out that major orchestras often precede a performance of contemporary music with a session meant to educate and prepare the audience, "but they don't bring in Beethoven or Ravel under the educational arm. They just expect you'll enjoy *that* music."[109] She is certain that audiences would quickly abandon their fear of new music if they had regular access to it. Not only does it have to be a good piece, she insists, it has to be heard. "[In pre-concert talks] I [strive to] become a person rather than an educator, [one] who is personable and approachable."[110] This accessibility is part of the reason Tower is in such high demand as composer-in-residence at music festivals throughout the world.

She jokingly refers to herself as "a composer who is above ground,"[111] and finds that one of the greatest rewards of working as a composer is the opportunity to interact with the instrumentalists performing her works.

In an ideal world, I would walk into the hall for the first rehearsal of a new piece, and a number of players would come up to me and say, 'I have a question about this passage' or 'You might want to think about writing this phrase an octave lower, because in that register it's going to be really piercing, but you can listen to it both ways. . . . It doesn't guarantee a better performance, but it's an indication of commitment to the piece.[112]

It is this connection that compels Tower to tackle the frustrations of composing, a process she's called everything from challenging to agonizing. If the music doesn't "come off the page" for the performers (whom she calls her "first audience"), should they not connect with the piece, not "pick up on the musicality, the identity, the strength of a piece,"[113] Tower blames herself. "This first linkage [with the performer] . . . has to be very strong because if a performer is playing a piece he doesn't like, he's obviously going to have some trouble projecting to the audience."[114]

Her wish for a stronger composer-audience connection has led her several times to Meet the Composer, Inc., one of whose stated aims is "to increase [composers'] visible presence as creative artists" by subsidizing the creation of new works and facilitating contact between composers and audiences.[115] Tower received grants from Meet the Composer in 1988 and again in 1990, and has acted as both board member and panelist for the organization. John Duffy, founder and president emeritus of Meet the Composer, says that despite the two-pronged challenges of sexual discrimination and antipathy toward new music, "[Joan Tower] has been fearless in reaching for more passionate musical statements and in her candor with people . . . she [has] helped do away with the baggage of the past."[116]

Former Meet the Composer associate director and current Director of Concert Music for ASCAP Fran Richards feels that Tower's importance in "recent advances for contemporary music" stems from her fierce advocacy—as a forthright spokesperson, as a panelist, and as an activist composer.[117]

Musical Citizenship and Musical Feminism

Composer Libby Larsen credits Tower for being "first-rate as both a performer and composer and as a musical citizen, which means being involved in the profession in all aspects: as an adviser, a counselor, a panel member. Whatever she does, she does holistically and with the spirit of a lioness. I've always felt a real link with her."[118]

Tower devotes countless hours to her quest for good "musical citizenship," a deeply significant aspect of her life as a composer. Since the 1960s, when a woman's presence on boards of directors was unusual, she has worked with dozens of musical organizations to evaluate new compositions and support promising composers, including the American Symphony Orchestra League, Nominating Jury for Pulitzer Prize, American Composers' Alliance, American Music Center, International Society for Contemporary Music, American Women Composers, Chamber Music America, New York Foundation for the Arts,

American Academy of Arts and Letters, National Endowment for the Arts, New York State Council on the Arts, Massachusetts Council on the Arts, Heinz Foundation, and Meet the Composer, becoming more and more vocal as she gained confidence in her ability to contribute.

She has contributed compositions for student keyboard competitions; spoken as an advocate for women composers and for contemporary music on panels; delivered scores of keynote addresses for conferences; judged composition competitions such as the National Young Composers' Competition, BMI Student Composer Awards, and National Federation of Music Clubs; coached countless chamber ensembles during summer festivals; and continued to mentor her own students at Bard. Via these channels and others, Tower challenges the classical community's slavish devotion to composers no longer living.

Tower is an untiring advocate for women composers as well as for contemporary music. She points out that since on "any program anywhere of classical composers, it's going to be 90 percent DWEMs (Dead White European Male) instead of AWAGs (American Woman Above Ground) . . . it's not just the women who are missing, it's living composers of either gender."[119] She adds that "[women are] still not part of the big discussion. We're not considered the major players—we're still put into a niche called Women Composers."[120]

Compositionally speaking, Tower believes music does not lend itself to a gendered evaluation; it is neither masculine nor feminine, only good or bad.[121] She adds that in any case, musically it's not important "because people can't tell."[122] Tower participated in a National Endowment for the Arts study during the 1970s in which a panel attempted—and failed—to determine the sex of the composer by listening to samples of their works. She adds the disclaimer, "Unless it has lyrics, I think music is genderless."[123]

Major orchestras' marketing invariably notes the gender of a composer on the program only if the composer is not male, confirming the normality and default expectations and thus the implicit *ab*normality of female composition. Tower wants to remind audiences of this inequity. "The music is the music and the fact that I'm a woman doesn't make a difference to the music . . . [but] I think some people are not aware that there are no women composers on their concerts. So for that reason, I do like to . . . remind them [that] this is a woman composer."[124] Tower indicates that to "continue to feel useful, strong, and talented as a woman composer (particularly an older one) takes a fair amount of inner perseverance and confidence as well as a keen sense of intuition and honest . . . perception about what the outside world is doing to hinder or help that."[125]

When Bruce Duffie asked Tower in a revealing 2001 interview whether she suffers discrimination as a woman composer, she responded that composers in *general* are discriminated against, and that the "woman's issue" was at the bottom of that heap.[126] She acknowledges a debt of gratitude to composers of the previous generation, such as Louise Talma and Miriam Gideon (both born in 1906), and agrees with Duffie that just as Talma and Gideon blazed trails in their time, so perhaps are she (Tower) and Ellen Taaffe Zwilich this generation's musical pioneers, especially in symphonic music.

Tower's first awareness of feminist issues came in the mid-1970s, when she asked composer Miriam Gideon (1906–96) for a Guggenheim Fellowship recommendation. When Tower received the Fellowship and expressed her appreciation to the older composer, Gideon asked Tower to write a recommendation for *her*, since she'd never received one. "[Gideon's] contemporaries were [Aaron] Copland and [Roger] Sessions, and they were getting all the attention, and she wasn't getting any. That's when I woke up and started to look at what was going on around me."[127] Discovering the feminist history behind her gave a "historical structure that I fit into, but my music still has to do the job. [Knowing the history] gave me a new confidence, not a musical confidence, but a new personal confidence."[128]

Auditing a class at Bard College in 1989 with visiting musicologist Nancy Reich had tremendous impact on Tower's awareness of the historical and contemporary roles of women in music; she describes Reich as the woman who changed her life. Reich not only provided a historical perspective for Joan, but also handed her scores to peruse and music to perform. Until this point, Tower had not been aware of nor played any music by historical women composers, but she had programmed compositions by Ursula Mamlok, Miriam Gideon, Louise Talma, Nancy Chance, Eleanor Cory, Joan La Barbara, Shulamit Ran, and other contemporary composers on her Greenwich Music house series in New York.

Tower's feminism manifests itself most effectively outside of the music itself. She sits on various boards that make musical recommendations and will often recommend women in an effort to balance inequities that still exist. If Tower herself can't accept a commission, she'll recommend another woman. If a soloist is needed for a new work, she'll suggest a woman. "It's kind of sexist, but actually I'm just trying to balance things out a little bit."[129] She also makes a habit of taking tapes of music by women composers with her when she travels and distributes them for review to orchestra managers, soloists, and conductors. "Women are still played less [frequently] than their male colleagues. Scheduling a work by one woman composer during an orchestral season is a rarity. Scheduling two . . . is a miracle."[130] She notes that there has been a significant increase in the performance of music by women since she began composing, crediting that increase to the greater numbers of women involved as presenters, administrators, managers, conductors, and performers. She finds sustenance in participating in festivals of women in music. "Projects get hatched, support networks are formed. There's less fear of being wrong or ridiculed and more freedom to pursue questions about intuition, sexuality and physicality in music."[131]

Joan Tower and other young women of her musical generation had come of age without female role models or professional mentors. The system of networking upon which young male composers depended to further their careers remained unavailable to women. Fellow composer, composition professor at University of Virginia, and former president of the American Women Composers Judith Shatin says, "In the arts, there are many situations where personal contacts make things happen. Until women are included, [any present inequities] will not change."[132]

The void has existed in higher education as well, on both sides of the desk. Composition teachers were exclusively male, female composition students were rare, and discussions of historical or contemporary women composers were absent from both undergraduate and graduate-level courses. The result, Tower states, is that women—especially women composers—have "fewer support structures and a lot less encouragement [than men]," causing them to "rely much more heavily on their inner resources to make things work for them."[133] Tower feels her strongest works provide her with the incentive, determination, and perseverance to pursue her unique compositional voice.

Tower dismisses having any protégés per se, but will admit to "helping" certain composers by offering advice or proffering an invitation to appear with her at a summer festival. Among the younger generation of composers, she recognizes Chen Yi, Jennifer Higdon, and Gabriela Frank as extremely talented.

When asked if she believes her unique voice has influenced another generation of composers, Tower laughs: "I don't like that responsibility. [In the music of] a young composer who I adore and [have] helped a lot . . . I heard this little thing in her piece and it was something that *I* do. And I said, 'Oh my God.' She doesn't realize it and I'm not going to mention it, of course, but it was this little upward scale that I do [and] she does it, too."[134]

* * *

Tower is the thinking musician's composer. This is not solely a reference to her intellect, which is formidable. She has historically striven to explore and understand her own motives, thought processes, impulses, and actions—both musical and personal. Sporadically over the years she has recorded her questions, answers, musings, and insights in journal fashion, jotting them down on manuscript paper, backs of programs, envelopes. Many take the form of Tower explaining herself to Tower, the subjects diverse as intuition in her compositions, career decisions, and relationships; in each arena, Tower's goal is self-knowledge. Like most people, she has wrestled the inner demons of doubt and insecurity; the prose is the way in which she identifies and exorcises those demons or learns to live with them

To date there are 22 theses and dissertations focusing on Tower, some with detailed analyses of specific works, some with a focus on her personal musical language, a few written as performers' or conductors' guides. Several instrumentalists who commissioned works from Tower have published documents providing both analysis and coaching, as in Carol Wincenc's thorough treatment of the *Flute Concerto* (1989), which also includes the performer's personal annotations for the flute part.[135] Tower's discography currently features a total of nearly 90 recordings of individual compositions and 11 all-Tower albums, with several more in the planning stages.

Arts critic and journalist Ted Shen noted that Tower rendered the "woman" in "woman composer" superfluous;[136] more recently, Benjamin Boretz, long-time editor of *Perspectives of New Music*, called her "a national treasure."[137] Tower's rugged persistence, sustained musical excellence, and consummate craftsmanship have earned her media superlatives and near-universal admiration and respect from the musical world. But composing is her "emotional survival,"[138] and all she wants, ultimately, is to write music that communicates. This, Tower insists, is when she feels useful.

Notes

1.   Joan Tower, Interview by Julie Niemeyer. Tape Recording. Oral History American Music Project at Yale University School of Music, New Haven, CT, April 30, 1993.
2.   Kyle Gann, "Uptown Dropout," *The Village Voice*, no. 42 (December 1998): 132.
3.   Nancy Leckie Bonds, "An Analysis of Joan Tower's *Wings* for Solo Clarinet," D.M.A. dissertation, City University of New York, 2000: 198.
4.   Barbara Jepson, "For an Uncommon Woman, *Fanfare* Comes Full Circle," *New York Times*, January 2, 1994, 30.
5.   Tower, E-mail to David Gordon, August 3, 2005.
6.   Leslie Valdes, "Women Composers Can Be in Harmony Without Making Music Together," *The Baltimore Sun*, May 30, 1981, A7.
7.   Richard Dyer, "Joan Tower's Bold Music Hits Boston," *Boston Globe*, May 3, 1987, 103.
8.   Paul Horsley, "Music: The Prime of Joan Tower," *Kansas City Star*, November 13, 2005, 1.
9.   Mary Lou Humphrey, "An Uncommon Woman," *Stagebill Magazine*, Carnegie Hall edition (January 1990): 11.
10. James Wierzbicki, "Every Instant of Music Has a Past, Present, and Future," *St. Louis Post-Dispatch*, January 4, 1987, D4.
11. Wierzbicki, "Every Instant of Music Has a Past," D4.
12. Ann Rylands, "The Violin Concertos of Ellen Taafe Zwilich and Joan Tower: Evolution of an American Style," D.M.A Dissertation, University of South Carolina, 2002: 48.
13. Edward Reichel, "Early on, Tower Preferred the Piano to Composing," *Deseret News*, July 12, 1998, E4.
14. Margalit Fox, "A Living Composer," *Newsday*, January 2, 1994, 16.
15. Tower, Interview by Julie Niemeyer.
16. Tower, Interview by Ellen Grolman. Tape Recording. Red Hook, NY, March 22, 2006.
17. Tower, Interview by Ellen Grolman, March 23, 2006.
18. Margo S. Jones, "Joan Tower's *Hexachords* for Solo Flute: An Analysis and Comparison of Its Flute Writing to Tower's *Flute Concerto*," Dissertation, University of North Texas, 1993: 4.
19. Laura Shouha, "The Musical Language of Joan Tower: An Energy Line Analysis of *Island Prelude for Oboe and Wind Quartet*," Dissertation, University of North Texas, December 2001: 11.
20. Tower, Interview by Ellen Grolman, March 22, 2006.
21. Tower, Interview by Ellen Grolman, March 23, 2006.
22. Mark Stryker, "To Thine Own Talent Be True," *Detroit Free Press*, May 31, 2004, E1.
23. Tower, Interview by Jenny Raymond. Tape Recording. Oral History American Music Project at Yale University School of Music, New Haven, CT, January 4, 1998.

24. Tower, "On *Breakfast Rhythms I* and *II*," D.M.A. Dissertation, Columbia University, 1975: 1.

25. Tower, "On *Breakfast Rhythms I* and *II*," 66.

26. Tower, "On *Breakfast Rhythms I* and *II*," 10–11.

27. Tower, Interview by Frances Harmeyer. Tape Recording. Oral History American Music Project at Yale University School of Music, New Haven, CT, January 9, 1976, 8.

28. Carol Neuls-Bates, ed., *Women in Music: An Anthology of Source Readings from the Middle Ages to the Present* (Boston, MA: Northeastern University Press; 2nd rev. edition, 1997), 355.

29. Neuls-Bates, *Women in Music*, 354.

30. Neuls-Bates, *Women in Music*, 355.

31. Rylands, "The Violin Concertos of Ellen Taafe Zwilich and Joan Tower," 75.

32. Bonds, "An Analysis of Joan Tower's *Wings*," 216.

33. John Fletcher, "Joan Tower's *Fascinating Ribbons* for Band: Genesis and Analysis," D.M.A. Dissertation, University of Oklahoma, 2002: 214.

34. Tower, Liner notes to *Joan Tower: Chamber and Solo Works*, Composers Recordings CRI 582, 1994.

35. Bonds, "An Analysis of Joan Tower's *Wings*," 199.

36. Humphrey, "An Uncommon Woman," 10.

37. Bonds, "An Analysis of Joan Tower's *Wings*," 211.

38. Bonds, "An Analysis of Joan Tower's *Wings*," 207.

39. Bonds, "An Analysis of Joan Tower's *Wings*," 207.

40. Tower, Interview by Jenny Raymond.

41. Tower, Interview by Jenny Raymond.

42. Dyer, "Joan Tower's Bold Music Hits Boston," 103.

43. Tower, Interview by Jenny Raymond.

44. Tower, Interview by Jenny Raymond.

45. Brian Wise, *Joan Tower: Composer Essay* (New York: Associated Music Publishers, 2005), 3.

46. Tower, Interview by Jenny Raymond.

47. Dyer, "Joan Tower's Bold Music Hits Boston," 103.

48. Frank Retzel, "Joan Tower: *Silver Ladders*," *Music Library Association Notes* 48, no. 2 (December 1991): 687.

49. Tower, Interview by Jan Fournier. Tape Recording. Oral History American Music Project at Yale University School of Music, New Haven, CT, July 28, 1983.

50. Tower, Interview by Ellen Grolman, March 22, 2006.

51. Tower, Interview by Ellen Grolman, March 23, 2006.

52. Tamara Bernstein, Liner notes to *Fanfares for the Uncommon Woman*, Koch International Classics, 3-7469-2, 1999.

53. Bernstein, Liner notes to *Fanfares for the Uncommon Woman*.

54. Tower, Interview by Jenny Raymond.

55. Mary Lou Humphrey and David Wright, "*Joan Tower: Composer Essay*" (1996), www.schirmer.com/Default.aspx? TabId=2419&State_2872=2&composerId_2872=1605 (Accessed January 31, 2006).

56. David Pratt, *The Juilliard Journal Online* 21, no. 8 (May 2006), www.juilliard.edu/update/journal/j_articles887.htm (Accessed May 3, 2006).

57. Tower, *Wild Purple* (New York: Associated Music Publishers, 1998).

58. John Fletcher, "Joan Tower's *Fascinating Ribbons* for Band: Genesis and Analysis," Dissertation, D.M.A. University of Oklahoma. 2002:63.

59. Tower, Interview by Julie Niemeyer.

60. Scott Cantrell, "Tower Rising in the Music World," *Times Union*, November 9, 1984, C6.
61. John Henken, "Written in a Key All Her Own," *Los Angeles Times*, October 1, 2000, 58.
62. David Raymond, Liner notes to *Joan Tower Concertos*. D'note Classics 1016, 1997.
63. Tower, Interview by Jenny Raymond.
64. Wise, *Joan Tower: Composer Essay*, 8.
65. Tower, Interview by Jan Fournier.
66. Tower, "On *Breakfast Rhythms I* and *II*," 3.
67. Tower, "On *Breakfast Rhythms I* and *II*," 4.
68. Tower, Interview by Julie Niemeyer.
69. Tower, Interview by Julie Niemeyer.
70. Tower, Interview by Frances Harmeyer.
71. Tower, Interview by Julie Niemeyer.
72. "Contemporary Youth Orchestra," www.cyorchestra.org/repertoire/?p=86 (Accessed April 23, 2006).
73. Tower, *Sequoia* program notes, www.schirmer.com/default.aspx?TabId =2420&State_2874=2&workId_2874=34028 (Accessed January 9, 2005).
74. Bonds, "An Analysis of Joan Tower's *Wings*," 195.
75. Tower, "Notes on the Program" for *Silver Ladders*, Richard Freed, program editor, The Kennedy Center, Washington, D.C.
76. Bonds, "An Analysis of Joan Tower's *Wings*," 197.
77. Bonds, "An Analysis of Joan Tower's *Wings*," 197.
78. Tower, Composer notes to *Sequoia* score (New York: Associated Music Publishers, Inc., 1981).
79. Humphrey, "An Uncommon Woman," 11
80. Patricia Rice, "The Composer Lends a Hand to the Baton," *St. Louis Post-Dispatch*, September 14, 1984, D2.
81. David Finckel, E-mail to author, March 4, 2006.
82. Stryker, "To Thine Own Talent Be True," E1.
83. Tower, Interview by Frances Harmeyer.
84. Myrna Schloss, "Out of the Twentieth Century: Three Composers, Three Musics, One Femininity," D.M.A. Dissertation, Wesleyan University, Middletown, CT, 1993: 181–183.
85. Jerry Young, "Composing Is Architecture For Tower," *Austin American-Statesman*, September 28, 1996, E1
86. Frank J. Oteri, "Joan Tower: *Made in America*" (September 15, 2005), www.newmusicbox.org/article.nmbx?id=4369 (Accessed April 24, 2006).
87. Fletcher, "Joan Tower's *Fascinating Ribbons* for Band," 224.
88. Tower, Interview by Frances Harmeyer.
89. Robert Taylor, "Joan Tower: *Fascinating Ribbons*," Northwestern University Graduate Wind Conducting Seminar, 2002: section 3,3.
90. Carol Clements, "HPR Interview: Joan Tower," *High Performance Review*, (Winter 1991–1992): 62.
91. Clements, " HPR Interview: Joan Tower," 62.
92. Wierzbicki, "Every Instant of Music Has a Past," D4.
93. Bruce Duffie (2006), "Joan Tower: The Composer in Conversation with Bruce Duffie," transcript of interview conducted in Chicago, IL, April 1987, my.voyager.net/%7Eduffie/tower.html (Accessed March 27, 2006).
94. Tower, Interview by Ellen Grolman, March 22, 2006.
95. Tower, Interview by Jan Fournier.

96. Robert S. Clark, "Music Chronicle I," *Hudson Review* 57, no. 3 (2004): 479.
97. Oteri, "Joan Tower: *Made in America.*"
98. Mary Lou Humphrey, notes in *Black Topaz* score (New York: Associated Music Publishers, Inc., 1976).
99. Valerie O'Brien, "Musician of the Month: Joan Tower—Her *Sequoia* Gains Establishment Status, But She Won't Rest On Her Laurels," *High Fidelity/MusicalAmerica Edition* 32, no. 6 (1982): 6.
100. "Overheard," *Dallas Morning News*, December 29, 2004.
101. Thomas Erdmann, "An Interview with Joan Tower," *Journal of the Conductors' Guild* 25, no. 1 (2004): 2.
102. Tower, Interview by Jan Fournier.
103. Erdmann, "An Interview with Joan Tower," 6.
104. Duffie, "Joan Tower: The Composer in Conversation."
105. Clements, "HPR Interview: Joan Tower," 62.
106. Marc Shulgold, "Moving (Ahead) with the Music on Upcoming CD; Composer, CSO Will Sound a Contemporary Theme," *Rocky Mountain News*, February 17, 1997, D6.
107. Tower, Interview by Ellen Grolman, March 22, 2006.
108. Cantrell, "Tower Rising in the Music World," C6.
109. Erdmann, "An Interview with Joan Tower," 7.
110. Erdmann, "An Interview with Joan Tower," 7.
111. Erdmann, "An Interview with Joan Tower," 8.
112. Jepson, "For an Uncommon Woman," 29.
113. Tower, Interview by Jenny Raymond.
114. Clements, "HPR Interview: Joan Tower," 62.
115. www.meetthecomposer.org (2006). Meet the Composer (Accessed February 5, 2006).
116. Jepson, "For an Uncommon Woman," 29.
117. O'Brien, "Musician of the Month: Joan Tower," 7.
118. Michael Anthony, "Tower of Power," *Star-Tribune* (Minneapolis), February 24, 2002, F2.
119. Horsley, "Music: The Prime of Joan Tower," 1.
120. Pierre Ruhe, "Ex-Atlantan a Hot Ticket in Classical Music World," *The Atlanta Journal and Constitution*, May 5, 2002.
121. Horsley, "Music: The Prime of Joan Tower," 1.
122. Erdmann, "An Interview with Joan Tower," 9.
123. Bernstein, Liner notes to *Fanfares for the Uncommon Woman.*
124. Duffie, "Joan Tower: The Composer in Conversation."
125. Tower, "A Woman Composer Approaches Senior Status," unpublished paper, 1.
126. Duffie, "Joan Tower: The Composer in Conversation."
127. Anthony, "Tower of Power," F2.
128. Johan Fleming, "Kinder, Gentler Composers They're Not," *St. Petersburg Times* (Florida), August 11, 1998, D1.
129. Jepson, "For an Uncommon Woman," 30
130. Jepson, "For an Uncommon Woman," 30
131. Jepson, "For an Uncommon Woman," 30
132. Heidi Waleson, "Women Composers Find Things Easier—Sort Of," *New York Times*, January 28, 1990, 27.
133. Tower, "A Woman Composer Approaches Senior Status," 1.
134. Tower, Interview by Jenny Raymond.

135. Carol Wincenc, "Performing Tower's *Concerto*," *Flute Talk* 19 (November 1999): 8–15.

136. Ted Shen, "Tower Leads Instrumental Journey, Orchestrates a Lesson on Rhythm," *Chicago Tribune,* February 15, 2002.

137. Benjamin Boretz, E-mail to author, April 17, 2006.

138. Neuls-Bates, *Women in Music*, 353.

Part III: Works and Performances

Works and Performances

Works for Band

W1. Celebration Fanfare (from *Stepping Stones*)
©1993 Associated Music Publishers, Inc.
Duration: 4 minutes
Dedicated to Hillary Clinton
Commissioned by the International Women's Forum
Instrumentations

> (1) Brass Ensemble, arr. Daniel Forlano from *Stepping Stones*. 4 trumpets in C, 4 horns in F, 3 trombones, tuba, timpani, 2 perc: percussion #1: glockenspiel, xylophone, 3 cymbals, snare drum, bass drum, tambourine, sleigh bells. percussion #2: 3 cymbals, snare drum, tenor drum, tambourine

> (2) Concert Band, arr. by Jack Stamp from *Celebration Fanfare*

Orchestral parts available as rental from the publisher
Premieres:

- Brass Ensemble version: September 30, 1993. Meeting of the International Women's Forum hosted by Hillary Clinton. Joan Tower, conductor. White House, Washington, D.C.
- Concert Band version: July 3, 1994. United States Military Academy Band, Lieutenant Colonel David Dietrick, conductor. Mountain Sky Festival, NY

Selected Performances:

- July 1, 1995. American Russian Youth Orchestra, Leon Botstein, conductor. Caramoor, Katonah, NY
- March 22, 2002. Community Band of Brevard, Marion Scott, conductor. Brevard Community College Fine Arts Auditorium, Cocoa Campus, Cocoa, FL

Recording:

- *Divertimento/Wind Music of American composers*. 1995. Citadel 88108. Keystone Wind Ensemble. Jack Stamp, conductor. **D9**
  See: **B205, B411, B452**

W2. Fascinating Ribbons for Symphonic Band
©2002 Associated Music Publishers, Inc.
Duration: 10 minutes
Dedicated to Jack Stamp

Commissioned by a consortium of colleges and universities via the College
Band Directors' National Association

Instrumentation:

4+pic,2+ca,3+Ebcl+bcl,ssx+asx+tsx+barsx,2+cbn4,4,4,3+btbn,2/timp,4
perc. percussion #1: xylophone, small triangle, wood block, castanets.
percussion #2: glockenspiel, timbales, low cymbal, small maraca, snare
drum, bongos, tenor tom-tom, tenor drum. percussion #3: medium
cymbal, low cymbal, temple blocks, vibraphone, medium tambourine.
percussion #4: crotales, bass drum, high cymbal, medium cymbal, low
cymbal, tam-tam, sleigh bells/pf.

Premiere:

* February 22, 2001. Keystone Winds, Jack Stamp, conductor. College
  Band Directors' National Association annual conference, University of
  North Texas, Denton, TX

Selected Performances:

* March 2, 2001. Eastern Michigan University Concert Band, Max Plank,
  conductor. Eastern Michigan University, Ypsilanti, MI
* March 29, 2006. University of Texas Symphonic Band, Jerry F. Junkin,
  conductor. Bates Recital Hall, University of Texas, Austin, TX

Recording:

* *Bandorama*. 2000. CD 1060. Indiana University Concert Band, Symphonic Band and Wind Ensemble, Timothy Mahr, conductor. **D27**

See: **B58, B173, B471, B577, B591**

Works for Stage

W3. Stepping Stones: A Ballet

©1993 Associated Music Publishers, Inc.

Duration: 25 minutes

Commissioned by Milwaukee Ballet with funding from Meet the Composer's Composer/Choreographer Project. Additional funding by the
Ford Foundation and the Pew Charitable Trusts

In memory of Daniel Forlano

Instrumentation: 2(+picc).222/4220/2perc/hp, pf(cel)/str.

Orchestral parts and recorded version for two pianos and synthetic percussion available as rental from publisher.

Premiere:

* April 1, 1993. Milwaukee Ballet and Milwaukee Ballet Orchestra,
  Kathryn Posin, choreographer; Daniel Forlano, conductor. Marcus Center for the Performing Arts, Milwaukee, WI

Selected Performances:

* February 22, 1996. BalletMet Columbus, Katherine Posin, choreogra-
  pher (synthesized piano and tape). Columbus, OH
* March 25–27, 1999. Hartford Ballet, Katherine Posin, choreographer.
  Bushnell Theatre, Hartford, CT

- March 11, 2000. Cincinnati Ballet, Katherine Posin, choreographer; Carmon DeLeone, music director. Aronoff Center, Cincinnati, OH
  See: **B99, B209, B432, B434, B508**

W4. Stepping Stones: A Ballet for Two Pianos

©1995 Associated Music Publishers, Inc. AMP 8073. First printing October 1995

Duration: ca. 25 minutes

In memory of Daniel Forlano

Instrumentation: Arranged for 2 pianos. Original 1993 scoring: 2(picc).222/4220/ 2perc/hp, pf(cel)/strings; available as rental from publisher.

I. Introductions II. Meeting III. Alone IV. Interlude V. Love and Celebration

Selected Performances:

- April 20, 1996. 20th Century Consort: Lisa Emenheiser, Edward Newman, piano. Ring Auditorium, Hirshhorn Museum and Sculpture Garden, Washington, DC
- June 24, 1997. 20th Century Consort: Lisa Emenheiser, Edward Newman, piano. Washington National Cathedral, Washington, DC
- June 9, 1998. Clarke and James Parker, piano. Glenn Gould Studio, Toronto
- December 10, 2005. 20th Century Consort: Lisa Emenheiser, Audrey Andrist, piano. Ring Auditorium, Hirshhorn Museum and Sculpture Garden, Washington, DC

Recording:

- *Black Topaz*. 1995. New World Records 80470–2. Double Edge: Edmund Niemann, Nurit Tiles, piano. **D73**
  See: **B32, B298, B319, B509**

Works for Orchestra

W5. Clarinet Concerto

©1989 Associated Music Publishers, Inc. AMP 8041.

Duration: 19 minutes

Dedicated to Charles Neidich

Commissioned by the Walter W. Naumburg Foundation.

Instrumentation: clarinet or Basset clarinet; 2(pic), 222/421+btbn, 1.2 perc: percussion #1: cymbals, large bass drum. percussion #2: cymbals, large tam-tam, triangle, 4 temple blocks, hp, pf(cel)/str

Also available: ©1990 version for clarinet and piano

Rental parts available on request from publisher.

Premiere:

- April 10, 1988. American Symphony Orchestra, Charles Neidich, clarinet; Jorge Meister, conductor. Carnegie Hall, New York, NY

Selected Performances:

- March 25, 1995. Madison Symphony Orchestra, Linda Bartley, clarinet; Elizabeth Schulze, conductor. Civic Center's Oscar Mayer Theatre, Madison, WI
- February 10, 1996. Long Beach Symphony, David Shifrin, clarinet; JoAnn Falletta, conductor. Long Beach Performing Arts Center, Long Beach, CA
- March 31, 1996. ProMusica Chamber Orchestra, Robert Spring, clarinet; Timothy Russell, conductor. Weigl Hall, Columbus, OH

Recordings:

- *Joan Tower: Music for Clarinet.* 1995. Summit Records DCD 124. Robert Spring, clarinet; Eckart Sellheim, piano, and the Ensemble 21, directed by Arthur Weisberg. **D10**
- *Joan Tower Concertos.* 1997. D'note Classics 1016. David Shifrin, clarinet; Louisville Orchestra, Max Bragado-Darman, conductor. **D11**

See: **B1, B29, B41, B63, B64, B74, B206, B347, B456**

W6. Concerto for Orchestra

©1991 Associated Music Publishers, Inc.

Duration: 30 minutes

A Meet the Composer Commission. Jointly commissioned by the Chicago Symphony Orchestra, the New York Philharmonic, and the St. Louis Symphony Orchestra

Instrumentation: 3(pic).2+ca.3(Ebcl+bcl).3(cbn)/4331/timp, 3 perc: glockenspiel cymbals (high, medium, low), temple blocks, wood blocks (4), snare drum, vibraphone, xylophone, large tam-tam, triangle, sleigh bells, crotales, tenor drum, large bass drum, castanets, mounted castanets, chimes (tubular bells) /hp,pf/strings

Composer's note:

Concerto for Orchestra *begins slowly, quietly, and simply, on a unison F-sharp that emerges from the depths of the orchestra. I had imagined a long and large landscape that had a feeling of space and distance. From the beginning I wanted to convey this sense to let the listener understand that the proportions of the piece would be spacious and that the musical materials would travel a long road.*

The energy of the piece emerges through the contrast of big alternating chords with little fast motives. These take on bigger and bigger shapes, picking up larger textures as they whirl around in fast repeated figures. There is a strong sense of direction in this piece, as in all my music, and a feeling of ascent, which comes not only from the scale motives, but from tempos, rhythms, and dynamics that cooperate to produce the different intensities.

Although it had been my intention to write a work in two parts, the content of the musical materials led me to a different form. Instead of coming to a full halt at the climactic midpoint of the composition, I felt the arrival could be answered and connected by a series of unisons (on

the note B) traversing the orchestral palette. This reaction calms things down, carries the piece forward towards its slow central section, and provides a seam that harks back toward the unison opening of the work and connects the 30-minute span of the concerto. Unity between the two halves is also provided by the slow-fast structure and by several shared motives, particularly the four-note motive that appears early in the piece and shapes the final fast section.

In every sense, Concerto for Orchestra *is my biggest work to date. It's the first piece purely for orchestra I've written since* Silver Ladders *in 1986, but it follows three solo concertos—for clarinet, flute, and violin—and reflects that experience, enabling me to take more risks between soloists and orchestra. Whereas* Silver Ladders *highlighted four solo instruments, here not only solos, but duos, trios, and other combinations of instruments form structural, timbral, and emotive elements of the piece. As in all my music, I am working here on motivating the structure, trying to be sensitive to how an idea reacts to or results from the previous ideas in the strongest and most natural way—a lesson I've learned from studying the music of Beethoven. Although technically demanding, the virtuoso sections are an integral part of the music, resulting from accumulated energy, rather than being designed purely as display elements. I thus resisted the title* Concerto for Orchestra *(with its connotations of Bartók, Lutoslawski, and Husa), and named the work only after the composing was completed, and even then reluctantly.*

Premiere:

• May 16, 1991. St. Louis Symphony, Leonard Slatkin, conductor. Powell Hall, St. Louis, MO

Selected Performances:

• January 6, 1994. New York Philharmonic, Leonard Slatkin, conductor. Lincoln Center, New York, NY
• August 2, 1996. Cabrillo Festival of Contemporary Music Orchestra, Marin Alsop, conductor. Santa Cruz Civic Auditorium, Santa Cruz, CA
• November 22, 1996. Colorado Symphony Orchestra, Marin Alsop, conductor. Boettcher Hall, Denver, CO

Recordings:

• *Fanfares for the Uncommon Woman.* 1999. Koch Int'l Classics 7469/Koch International Classics KIC 7630. Colorado Symphony Orchestra, Marin Alsop, conductor. **D14**
• In Progress: 2007. Naxos 8.559328. Nashville Symphony, Leonard Slatkin, conductor. **D88**

See: **B127, B131, B172, B175, B231, B250, B261, B266, B396, B403, B433, B459**

W7. Duets for Orchestra

Written in 1994, ©1995 Associated Music Publishers, Inc.
Duration: 19 minutes

Commissioned by and dedicated to "the wonderful Los Angeles Chamber Orchestra, Christof Perick, Music Director"

Instrumentation: 2222/2200/timp.perc: vibraphone, 3 suspended cymbals (small, medium, large), glockenspiel, temple blocks, tambourine, baby rattle, small maracas, tom-toms/str

Composer's note:

> *In three of my concertos for flute, clarinet, and violin, I explored the idea of pairing the soloist with the corresponding first chair player in featured cadenzas (an idea I got from Schumann's 'Cello Concerto). In Duets, I developed that idea within the orchestra, concentrating on pairs of 'cellos, flutes, horns, trumpets, and to a lesser degree, violins, oboes, clarinets, and percussion, creating an overall concerto grosso-like effect. Duets is divided into four sections (slow-fast-slow-fast) within one continuous movement and lasts about 19 minutes.*

Premiere:

- January 28, 1995. Los Angeles Chamber Orchestra, Christof Perick, conductor. Ambassador Auditorium, Los Angeles, CA

Selected Performances:

- May 7, 1995. American Symphony Chamber Orchestra, Leon Botstein, conductor. Olin Auditorium, Bard College, Annandale-on-Hudson, NY
- January 16 and 17, 1997. Colorado Symphony Orchestra, Marin Alsop, conductor. Boettcher Hall, Denver, CO
- April 5, 1998. ProMusica Chamber Orchestra, Timothy Russell, conductor. Weigel Hall, Ohio State University, Columbus, OH
- August 15, 1998. Cabrillo Festival of Contemporary Music Orchestra, Marin Alsop, conductor. Santa Cruz Civic Auditorium, Santa Cruz, CA
- September 4, 1998. American Symphony Chamber Orchestra, Joan Tower, conductor. Bard College, Annandale-on-Hudson, NY

Recording:

- *Fanfares for the Uncommon Woman.* 1999. Koch International Classics 7469/Koch International Classics KIC 7630. Colorado Symphony Orchestra, Marin Alsop, conductor. **D15**

See: **B30, B183, B287, B419, B424, B425, B433, B462, B535, B566**

W8. Fanfare for the Uncommon Woman (for orchestra), No. 4

©1992 Associated Music Publishers, Inc.

Duration: 5 minutes

Dedicated to JoAnn Falletta

Instrumentation: 2(pic)222/432, bass tromb,1/timp.3percussion. percussion #1: glockenspiel, wood blocks temple blocks, cymbals, maracas, small dinner bell, percussion #2 : xylophone, snare drum, tenor drum, sleigh bells, tubular bells, castanets. percussion #3: vibraphone, tambourine, cymbals, tenor drum, marimba, woodblock /str

Premiere:

- October 16, 1992. Kansas City Symphony, William McGlaughlin, conductor. Music Hall, Kansas City, MO

Selected Performances:

- May 28, 2000. Contemporary Youth Orchestra, Liza Grossman, conductor. Waetjen Auditorium, Cleveland State University, Cleveland, OH
- June 1, 2001. National Symphony Orchestra, Marin Alsop, conductor. Kennedy Center, Washington, DC

Recordings:

- *Fanfares for the Uncommon Woman.* 1999. Koch Int'l Classics 7469. Colorado Symphony Orchestra, Marin Alsop, conductor. **D22**

See: **B467**

W9. Flute Concerto

Written 1989, ©1990 Associated Music Publishers, Inc. AMP 053. First Printing: May 1992 (piano reduction)
Duration: 15 minutes
Dedicated to Carol Wincenc
Commissioned by the Fromm Foundation
Instrumentation: Flute; 1(pic).11(bcl).1/01.btbn./2perc. percussion #1: glockenspiel, temple blocks, low tom-toms, bass drum, medium cymbal. percussion #2: xylophone, vibraphone, small triangle, tenor drum, tam-tam, 3 cymbals (high, medium, low), solo flute, strings
Orchestral parts available on rental from publisher; piano reduction available.

Premiere:

- January 28, 1990. American Composer's Orchestra, Carol Wincenc, flute; Hugh Wolf, conductor. Carnegie Hall, New York, NY

Selected Performances:

- February 27, 1992. St. Louis Symphony Orchestra, Carol Wincenc, flute; Joseph Silverstein, conductor. Powell Hall, St. Louis, MO
- February 28, 1997. Charlotte Symphony Orchestra, Carol Wincenc, flute; Janna Hymes-Bianchi, conductor. North Carolina Blumenthal Performing Arts Center, Charlotte, NC
- March 24, 2001. Contemporary Youth Orchestra, Justin Berrie, flute; Liza Grossman, conductor. Waetjen Auditorium, Cleveland State University, Cleveland, OH
- April 30, 2002. Carol Wincenc, flute; Joan Tower (piano reduction). Kennedy Center Terrace Theatre, Washington, DC
- October 5, 2003. Oberlin Contemporary Music Ensemble. Lisa Blatchford, flute; Teresa McCollough (piano reduction). Finney Chapel, Oberlin College, Oberlin, OH
- August 14, 2004. Nashville Chamber Orchestra, Patricia Spencer, flute; Ransom Wilson, conductor. National Flute Association Convention, Gaylord Opryland Hotel, Nashville, TN

Recording:

- *Joan Tower Concertos.* 1997. D'note Classics 1016. Carol Wincenc, flute; Louisville Orchestra, Max Bragado-Darman, conductor. **D28**

See: **B14, B23, B77, B106, B227, B287, B392, B472, B538, B554, B580**

W10. Island Rhythms
    © 1985 Associated Music Publishers, Inc.
    Duration: 8 minutes
    Commissioned by the Florida Orchestra with a grant from Lincoln Proper-
        ties Company and dedicated to the developer of Harbour Island,
        Tampa, Michael Hogan
    Instrumentation: 2(pic).222/220+btbn.1/timp.2perc. percussion #1: glocken-
        spiel, 3 temple blocs, woodblock, medium cymbal, 3 tom-toms, me-
        dium bass drum. percussion #2: vibraphone, xylophone, triangle, high
        cymbal, low cymbal, field drum, large bass drum, 3 temple blocs, tri-
        angle, large tam-tam/strings
    Composer's note:
        *The fast outer sections, somewhat reminiscent of Caribbean drum mu-
        sic, develop and explore a repeated figure through textural, timbral,
        registral, and dynamic contrasts. The repeated tutti chord which cli-
        maxes the work was inspired by a fragment from the final movement of
        Berlioz's* Symphony Fantastique. *The central section has a slowly mov-
        ing upward direction that becomes more "luminous" as it rises. This
        was an attempt to depict a swimmer gradually rising to the water's sur-
        face from a very deep place in the ocean.*
    Premiere:
    • June 29, 1985. Florida Orchestra, Irwin Hoffman, conductor. Harbour
        Island, Tampa, FL
    Selected Performances:
    • January 22, 1987. Los Angeles Philharmonic, David Atherton, conduc-
        tor. Dorothy Chandler Pavilion, Los Angeles, CA
    • January 24 and 25, 1996. St. Louis Symphony Orchestra, Leonard Slat-
        kin, conductor. Carnegie Hall, New York, NY
    • January 25, 1997. Women's Philharmonic, Odaline de la Martinez,
        conductor. Herbst Theatre, San Francisco, CA
    Recordings:
    • *First Edition Recordings: The Louisville Symphony.* 1991. LCD006.
        Louisville Symphony, Lawrence Leighton Smith, conductor. **D37**
    • *Joan Tower.* 2004. First Edition FECD25. Louisville Orchestra, Law-
        rence Leighton Smith, conductor. **D38**
    • *The Slatkin Years.* 1995. Archmedia/SLSO. St. Louis Symphony, Leo-
        nard Slatkin, conductor. **D39**
    See: **B246, B257, B274, B302, B440, B485, B537, B553**

W11. Made in America
    ©2005 Associated Music Publishers, Inc.
    Duration: 14 minutes
    Commissioned by a consortium of 65 orchestras, the American Symphony
        Orchestra League, and Meet the Composer; funded by a grant from

Ford Motor Company Fund. Additional support from the National Endowment for the Arts, the Aaron Copland Fund for Music, JPMorgan Chase, Argosy Foundation Contemporary Music Fund, and the Amphion Foundation.
Instrumentation: 2 flute (both double piccolo), 2 oboe, 2 clarinet, 2 bassoon, 2 horn, 2 trumpets in B-flat, 1 opt picc tpt, trombone, timpani, percussion: xylophone, glockenspiel, vibraphone, large suspended cymbal, medium cymbal, low cymbal, wood block, medium maraca, egg maraca, tambourine, sleigh bells, bass drums, strings.
Composer's note:

When I was nine, my family moved to South America (La Paz, Bolivia), where we stayed for nine years. I had to learn a new language, a new culture, and how to live at 13,000 feet! It was a lively culture with many saints' days celebrated through music and dance, but the large Inca population in Bolivia was generally poor and there was little chance of moving up in class or work position. When I returned to the United States, I was proud to have free choices, upward mobility, and the chance to try to become who I wanted to be. I also enjoyed the basic luxuries of an American citizen that we so often take for granted: hot running water, blankets for the cold winters, floors that are not made of dirt, and easy modes of transportation, among many other things. So when I started composing this piece, the song "America the Beautiful" kept coming into my consciousness and eventually became the main theme for the work. The beauty of the song is undeniable and I loved working with it as a musical idea. One can never take for granted, however, the strength of a musical idea—as Beethoven (one of my strongest influences) knew so well. This theme is challenged by other more aggressive and dissonant ideas that keep interrupting, interjecting, unsettling it, but "America the Beautiful" keeps resurfacing in different guises (some small and tender, others big and magnanimous), as if to say, "I'm still here, ever changing, but holding my own." A musical struggle is heard throughout the work. Perhaps it was my unconscious reacting to the challenge of "how do we keep America beautiful?"

Premiere:
* October 2, 2005. Glens Falls Symphony Orchestra, Charles Peltz, conductor. Glens Falls High School, Glens Falls, NY
Selected Performances:
* October 15, 2005. Pine Bluff Symphony Orchestra, Charles Jones Evans, conductor. Pine Bluff Convention Center, Pine Bluff, AR
* October 22, 2005. Plymouth Philharmonic, Steven Karidoyanes, conductor. Memorial Hall, Plymouth, MA
* October 22, 2005. Vermont Symphony Orchestra, Jaime Laredo, conductor. Latchis Theatre, Burlington, VT
* October 22, 2005. Reno Chamber Orchestra, Joan Tower, conductor. Nightingale Concert Hall, Reno, NV

- October 30, 2005. Omaha Youth Symphony, Aviva Segall, conductor. Holland Performing Arts Center, Omaha, NE
- November 17, 2005. Rhode Island Philharmonic, Larry Rachleff, conductor. Veterans/Memorial Auditorium, Providence, RI
- November 19, 2005. New Philharmonia Orchestra, Ronald Knudsen, conductor. Babson College, Babson Park, MA
- February 5, 2006. Greenwich Village Orchestra, Barbara Yahr, conductor. Washington Irving High School, Manhattan, NY
- April 2, 2006. The Pro Arte Chamber Orchestra of Boston, Isaiah Jackson, conductor. Sanders Theatre, Boston, MA
- April 25, 2006. Waukesha Symphony Orchestra, Frank Almond, conductor. Shattuck Auditorium, Waukesha, WI
- April 25, 2006. Grand Junction Symphony Orchestra, Kirk Gustafson, conductor
- May 19, 2006. Mid-Coast Symphony Orchestra, Rohan Smith, conductor. Franco-American Heritage Center, Lewiston, ME
- August 18, 2006. Sunriver Music Festival Orchestra, Lawrence Leighton-Smith, conductor. Sunriver, OR
- January 27, 2007. Fairbanks Symphony, Eduard Zilberkant, conductor. Davis Concert Hall, Fairbanks, AK

Recording:
- In Progress: Naxos. Nashville Symphony, Leonard Slatkin, conductor. Recorded June 2006. **D88**

See: **B16, B17, B24, B35, B36, B48, B119, B121, B122, B123, B154, B163, B192, B197, B198, B215, B252, B279, B289, B304, B336, B353, B364, B410, B435, B436, B437, B440, B487, B536**

W12. Music for 'Cello and Orchestra
©1984 Associated Music Publishers, Inc. AMP 8006. First Printing: June 1991 (piano reduction)
Duration: 19 minutes
Dedicated to André Emelianoff and Gerard Schwarz
Commissioned by Koussevitzky Foundation
Instrumentation: 'cello; 2(pic).222/220+btbn.0/timp.2perc/hp/str
Orchestral parts available as rental from the publisher; piano reduction available.
Premiere:
- September 29, 1984. Y Chamber Symphony, André Emelianoff, 'cello; Gerard Schwarz, conductor. 92nd Street Y, New York, NY

Selected Performances:
- November 9 and 10, 1984. Albany Symphony Orchestra, André Emelianoff, 'cello; Julius Hegyi, conductor. Troy, NY Savings Bank Music Hall and Albany, NY Palace Theatre
- May 19, 1989. St. Louis Symphony Orchestra, Lynn Harrell, 'cello; Leonard Slatkin, conductor. Powell Hall, St. Louis, MO

- October 27, 1990. Berkshire Symphony Sara Sant'Ambrogio, 'cello; Ronald Feldman, conductor. Williams College, Williamstown, MA
- August 15, 1998. Cabrillo Festival Orchestra, Lee Duckles, 'cello; Marin Alsop, conductor. Cabrillo Festival of Contemporary Music, Santa Cruz Civic Auditorium, Santa Cruz, CA

Recordings:

- *Joan Tower.* 2004. First Edition FECD0025. Lynn Harrell, 'cello; St. Louis Symphony Orchestra, Leonard Slatkin, conductor. **D41**
- *Meet the Composer Orchestra Residency Series: Joan Tower.* 1990. Electra/Nonesuch Records 79245. Lynn Harrell, 'cello; St. Louis Symphony Orchestra, Leonard Slatkin, conductor. **D42**

See: **B229, B254, B343, B359, B406, B440, B489, B555**

W13. Piano Concerto No. 1 (Homage to Beethoven)
©1985 Associated Music Publishers, Inc.
Duration: 21 minutes
Commissioned by the St. Paul Chamber Orchestra and the Philharmonia Virtuosi
Instrumentation: piano; 2(pic),1,2(bcl).1/2,2,0+btbn.0/2perc/strings
Reduction for two pianos available.
Premiere:

- January 31, 1986. Hudson Valley Philharmonic Chamber Orchestra, Jacquelyn Helin, piano; Imre Pallo, conductor. Kingston Center for the Performing Arts, Kingston, NY

Selected Performances:

- February 28, 1993. Cleveland Chamber Symphony, Frederick Moyer, piano; Edwin London, conductor. Weigel Hall, Ohio State University, Columbus, OH
- June 8, 1997. Scotia Festival Orchestra, Marc André-Hamlin, piano; Joan Tower, conductor. Sir James Dunn Theatre, Halifax, Nova Scotia
- March 9, 2003. University of Wisconsin–Madison Symphony Orchestra, Caroline Moore, piano; David Becker, conductor. Mills Concert Hall, University of Wisconsin–Madison, Madison, WI

Recordings:

- *Joan Tower Concertos.* 1997. D'note Classics 1016. Ursula Oppens, piano; Louisville Orchestra, Joseph Silverstein, conductor. **D54**
- *American Piano Concertos.* 1999. Koch Schwann 313332. Paul Barnes, piano; Bohuslav Martinu Philharmonic, Kirk Trevor, conductor. **D55**

See: **B12, B37, B68, B222, B228, B330, B369, B390, B497, B562, B574**

W14. Purple Rhapsody: Concerto for Viola and Orchestra
©2005 Associated Music Publishers, Inc.
Duration: 18 minutes
Dedicated to the memory of Serge and Natalie Koussevitsky
Written for Paul Neubauer

Commissioned by the Omaha Symphony together with the Buffalo Philharmonic, Virginia Symphony, Kansas City Symphony, Pro Musica
Chamber Orchestra, the Peninsula Music Festival Orchestra, Chautauqua Symphony Orchestra. This commission was made possible by the
Serge Koussevitzky Music Foundation of the Library of Congress.
Instrumentation: 2 flute, 2 clarinet, 2 bassoon, 2 trumpets in C, 1 bass trom-
bone, timpani, percussion (glockenspiel, vibraphone, medium tam-tam,
low cymbal, high cymbal, temple blocks, piccolo wood blocks, small
maraca, medium tambourine, medium bass drum), solo viola, strings
Premiere:
*   November 4, 2005. Omaha Symphony Orchestra, Paul Neubauer, viola;
    Jo Ann Falletta, conductor. Holland Performing Arts Center, Omaha,
    NE
Selected Performances:
*   November 19 and 20, 2005. Kansas City Symphony, Paul Neubauer,
    viola; Michael Stern, conductor. Lyric Theatre, Kansas City, MO
*   February 12, 2006. ProMusica Chamber Orchestra of Columbus, Paul
    Neubauer, viola; Timothy Russell, conductor. Southern Theatre, Co-
    lumbus, OH
*   June 14, 2006. Amici Orchestra, Paul Neubauer, viola; Andres Delfs,
    conductor. OKMozart Festival, Bartelsville, OK
*   July 5, 2006. Chautauqua Symphony Orchestra, Paul Neubauer, viola;
    Uri Segal, conductor. Chautauqua, NY
*   August 10, 2006. Peninsula Music Festival Orchestra, Paul Neubauer,
    viola; Stephen Alltop, conductor. Peninsula Music Festival, Ephraim,
    WI
See: **B34, B66, B168, B185, B212, B213, B214, B216, B217, B234, B500,
B544, B567, B568, B569**

W15. Sequoia
Written between December 1979 and March 1981, ©1981
Associated Music Publishers, Inc. AMP 8020
Duration: 16 minutes
Dedicated to the concertmistress and the first horn player of American
Composers Orchestra: Jean and Paul Ingraham
Commissioned by the American Composers' Orchestra with support by a
grant from the Jerome Foundation
Instrumentation: 2(2pic).222/422+btbn.1/ 5perc: percussion #1: tom-toms
(4), small cow bell, high temple blocks (4), medium triangle, medium
bass drum. percussion #2: tom-toms (4), medium cowbell, temple
blocks (4), low cymbals (2), large bass drum, crotales [D, E, F#]. percussion #3: snare drum, tenor drum, med. cymbals (3), marimba, crotales [E-flat, F, G]. percussion #4: large cow bell, low temple blocks
(4), high cymbals (2), snare drum, tenor drum, large gong, xylophone,
glockenspiel. percussion #5: timpani (5), high cymbals, high triangle,
chimes, vibraphone. hp.pf(cel)/strings

Orchestra parts available as rental from publisher.

Composer's note:

Sequoia *opens with a very long pedal point on the note G, which expands to a four-octave G and then returns to a central G (in the trumpet part). Around this G begins a "balancing" action of harmonies that branch out on either side of the G—first above, then below—like the branching and rooting of a tree. This balancing of registers becomes more and more developed as the piece continues, and the pedal point G begins to move up and down very slowly to create a substructure of balances, a kind of counterpoint of lines. Another kind of "branching" action occurs in the contrasting of solo lines with big orchestral passages, and of soft and loud dynamics—an attempt to explore the enormous textural and dynamic range of the orchestra.*

The giant redwood tree, Sequoia, seemed to me to embody these notions in at least two senses: the incredible "balancing act" achieved in the full-grown height of the tree, and the striking contrast of very small pine needles growing upon such a large structure.

Premiere:

- May 18, 1981. American Composers' Orchestra, Dennis Russell Davies, conductor. Alice Tully Hall, New York, NY

Selected Performances:

- September 23, 1982. New York Philharmonic, Zubin Mehta, conductor. Lincoln Center for the Performing Arts, New York, NY
- October 24, 1982. New York Philharmonic, Zubin Mehta, conductor. United Nations Day. United Nations Building, New York, NY. Radio broadcast, WNET
- November 24, 1982. San Francisco Symphony, Dennis Russell Davies, conductor. Davies Symphony Hall, San Francisco, CA
- September 14 and 15, 1984. St. Louis Symphony, Leonard Slatkin, conductor. Powell Hall, St. Louis, MO
- October 4, 1984. Omaha Symphony Orchestra, Bruce Hangen, conductor. Orpheum Theatre, Omaha, NE
- October 25–27, 1984. National Symphony Orchestra, Leonard Slatkin, conductor. John F. Kennedy Center for the Performing Arts, Washington, DC
- May 2 and 3, 1986. Cincinnati Symphony Orchestra, Bernard Rubenstein, conductor. Music Hall, Cincinnati, OH
- (Choreographed version) October 11, 1989. Winnipeg Ballet; Winnipeg Ballet Orchestra. Mark Godden, choreographer. Manitoba Centennial Concert Hall, Winnipeg, Manitoba
- March 25, 26, 28, 30, 1992. Toronto Symphony, Gunther Herbig, conductor. Roy Thomson Hall, Toronto, Canada.
- (Choreographed version) July 8, 1992. Banff Festival Orchestra, Max Bell Auditorium, Banff, Canada. Note: This performance was choreographed by Marc Godden, choreographer/former principal dancer, Winnipeg Ballet

- August 5, 1995. Cabrillo Festival of Contemporary Music Orchestra, Marin Alsop, conductor. Santa Cruz Civic Auditorium, Santa Cruz, CA
- April 5, 1996. Colorado Symphony Orchestra, Peter Oundjian, conductor. Boettcher Hall, Denver, CO
- June 2, 2002. Orquesta Nacional de Cuba, Sebrina Maria Alfonso, conductor. Havana, Cuba

Recordings:

- *Meet the Composer Orchestra Residency Series: Joan Tower.* 1990. Electra/Nonesuch Records 79245. St. Louis Symphony Orchestra, Leonard Slatkin, conductor. **D63**
- *The Infernal Machine.* 1986. Nonesuch 79118. St. Louis Symphony Orchestra, Leonard Slatkin, conductor. **D64**
- *New York Philharmonic: An American Celebration Sampler, vol. 2.* 1999. New York Philharmonic, Zubin Mehta, conductor. **D65**
- *Joan Tower.* 2004. First Edition. FECD0025. St. Louis Symphony Orchestra, Leonard Slatkin, conductor. **D66**

See: **B3, B26, B43, B67, B81, B105, B107, B126, B137, B151, B162, B171, B184, B189, B208, B237, B254, B265, B268, B328, B329, B346, B368, B383, B406, B413, B426, B427, B429, B440, B482, B504, B529, B531, B546, B564, B590**

W16. Silver Ladders

Written in 1986; ©1987 Associated Music Publishers, Inc. AMP 8017. First Printing: December 1989 (full score)

Duration: 23 minutes

Dedicated "with admiration to Leonard Slatkin"

Commissioned by the St. Louis Symphony Orchestra, Leonard Slatkin, music director and conductor, and Meet the Composer, Inc., through the Meet the Composer Orchestra Residencies Program, with major funding from Exxon Corporation, the Rockefeller Foundation, and the National Endowment for the Arts

Instrumentation: 2+pic.2+ca.2+bcl.2+cbn/432+btbn.1/timp. 4 percussion: percussion #1: tam-tam (medium), cymbals (low and medium), tom-tom (low), bass drum (medium), triangle, crotales, glockenspiel, xylophone. percussion #2: large wood block, cymbals (medium), tenor drum, bass drum (large), snare drum, triangle, glockenspiel. percussion #3: tam-tam (medium), cymbals (medium), tom-tom (low, tuned), snare drum, triangle, temple blocks (high), glockenspiel, vibraphone. percussion #4: tam-tam (large), cymbals (medium to high), tenor drum, temple blocks (low to medium), triangle, wood block, chimes, marimba, hp.pf[=cel]/str

Won the 1990 Grawemeyer Award for Music Composition and a finalist prize in the 1988 Kennedy Center/Friedheim Awards

Composer's note: (in collaboration with Sandra Hyslop)

The images and feelings of this composition are reflected in the title. Its many upward-moving lines suggest nothing so much as a giant ladder, reaching to the sky and moving into space. Just as the metal silver has many contrasting qualities, so the textures of this music range from heavy to light, solid to fluid. Instrumental solos spin forth slowly like liquid metal, fluid and silvery, providing contrast to the solid orchestral ladder surrounding them. Silver Ladders *was composed in 1986 for the St. Louis Symphony during Joan Tower's tenure as composer-in-residence. It is dedicated to Leonard Slatkin with "admiration for his unswerving musical integrity and confidence in presenting the music of his own time." The four solos in this piece were written for four distinguished players of the St. Louis Symphony: George Silsies (principal clarinet), Peter Bowman (principal oboe), John Kasica (percussion), and Susan Slaughter (principal trumpet).*

Premieres:

- January 9, 1987. St. Louis Symphony, Leonard Slatkin, conductor. Powell Symphony Hall, St. Louis, MO
- (Choreographed version) April 30, 1998. San Francisco Ballet Orchestra, Emil deCou, conductor. War Memorial Opera House, San Francisco, CA. Note: this performance was choreographed by Helgi Tomasson, San Francisco Ballet

Selected Performances:

- April 9, 1987. Chicago Symphony Orchestra, Leonard Slatkin, conductor. Symphony Hall, Chicago, IL
- May 3, 1987. St. Louis Symphony, Leonard Slatkin, conductor. Symphony Hall, Boston, MA.
- April 7, 1989. Dallas Symphony Orchestra, James Rives-Jones, conductor. Fair Park Music Hall, Dallas, TX
- September 30, 1996. University of Texas Symphony, Timothy Muffit, conductor. Bates Recital Hall, University of Texas, Austin, TX
- October 22, 1998. San Francisco Ballet Orchestra, Emil deCou, conductor. War Memorial Opera House, San Francisco, CA. Note: this performance was choreographed by Helgi Tomasson, San Francisco Ballet
- March 12, 1999. San Francisco Ballet Orchestra, Emil deCou, conductor. War Memorial Opera House, San Francisco, CA. Note: this performance was choreographed by Helgi Tomasson, San Francisco Ballet

Recordings:

- *Meet the Composer Orchestra Residency Series: Joan Tower.* 1990. Electra/Nonesuch Records 79245. St. Louis Symphony Orchestra, Leonard Slatkin, conductor. **D67**
- *First Edition Music: World Premiere Collection.* 2005. Naxos FECD 0032. St. Louis Symphony Orchestra, Leonard Slatkin, conductor. **D68**
- *Joan Tower.* 2004. First Edition LCD006. St. Louis Symphony Orchestra, Leonard Slatkin, conductor. **D69**

See: **B4, B19, B52, B118, B136, B150, B224, B225, B226, B254, B271, B312, B318, B381, B406, B440, B505, B552, B563, B587, B589**

W17. Rapids (Piano Concerto No. 2)
©1996 Associated Music Publishers, Inc.
Duration: 15 minutes
Dedicated to Ursula Oppens
Commissioned by University of Wisconsin–Madison School of Music for
    their 100th Anniversary, 1995–1996.
Instrumentation: piano; 2222/2210/timp, percussion: bongos, gong, mara-
    cas, snare drum, suspended cymbals (high, medium, low), tambourine,
    temple blocks, tenor drum, wood blocks, xylophone/strings
Premiere:
* March 2, 1996. University of Wisconsin–Madison Symphony Orches-
    tra, Ursula Oppens, piano; David Becker, conductor. UW–Madison
    School of Music, Madison, WI
Selected Performances:
* April 5, 1998. ProMusica Chamber Orchestra, Ursula Oppens, piano;
    Timothy Russell, conductor. Weigel Hall, Ohio State University, Co-
    lumbus, OH
* February 25, 1999. Louisiana Philharmonic Orchestra, Ursula Oppens,
    piano; Uriel Segal, conductor. Orpheum Hall, New Orleans, LA
Recording:
* *The Centennial Commissions: Celebrating the 100th Anniversary of the
    University of Wisconsin–Madison School of Music.* 2002. Ursula Op-
    pens, piano, University of Wisconsin–Madison Symphony Orchestra,
    David E. Becker, conductor. **D60**
See: **B5, B12, B62, B65, B305, B308, B502, B534, B566, B574**

W18. Strike Zones (Percussion Concerto)
©2001 Associated Music Publishers, Inc.
Duration: 25 minutes
Written for Evelyn Glennie
Commissioned by the National Symphony Orchestra of Washington, DC,
    Leonard Slatkin, music director, through a grant from the John and
    June Hechinger Commissioning Fund for new orchestral works
Instrumentation: percussion solo; 2(2pic), 222/4330/timp, 2perc/pf(cel)/str
Premiere:
* October 4, 2001. National Symphony Orchestra, Evelyn Glennie, per-
    cussion; Leonard Slatkin, conductor. Kennedy Center, Washington, DC
Selected Performances:
* October 13, 2001. National Symphony Orchestra, Evelyn Glennie, per-
    cussion; Leonard Slatkin, conductor. Carnegie Hall, New York, NY
See: **B174, B240, B263, B311, B350, B510**

W19. Tambor
©1998 Associated Music Publishers, Inc.
Duration: 15 minutes
Commissioned by Mariss Jansons and the Pittsburgh Symphony Society

Instrumentation: 2(pic), 22(bcl).2/432+btbn.1/timp. 3 percussion: snare drum, tenor drum, bass drums (medium, large), conga drums, 5 cymbals (low to high), hi-hat, bell tree, 4 timbales (low to high), tambourines (small and large), sleigh bells, maracas, ratchet, chimes, glockenspiel, marimba, vibraphone/str

Composer's note:

What happened while I was writing this piece was that the strong role of the percussion began to influence the behavior of the rest of the orchestra, to the point that the other instruments began to act more and more like a percussion section themselves. In other words, the main action of the work becomes more concerned with rhythm and color than with motives and melodies (though these elements do make occasional appearances here and there).

Premiere:

- May 7, 1998. Pittsburgh Symphony Orchestra, Mariss Jansons, conductor. Heinz Hall, Pittsburgh, PA

Selected Performances:

- January 25, 2000. National Symphony Orchestra, Leonard Slatkin, conductor. Carnegie Hall, New York, NY
- May 7, 2000. Syracuse Youth Orchestra, Charles Peltz, conductor. Mulroy Civic Center Theater. Syracuse, NY
- November 4, 2000. Anchorage Symphony Orchestra, Joan Tower, conductor. Atwood Concert Hall, Anchorage, AK
- March 24, 2001. Contemporary Youth Orchestra, Liza Grossman, conductor. Waetjen Auditorium, Cleveland State University, Cleveland, OH
- June 22, 2002. Dallas Symphony Orchestra, Andrew Litton, conductor. Meyerson Symphony Center, Dallas, TX
- June 10, 2004. Pittsburgh Symphony Orchestra, Yan Pascal Tortelier, conductor. Heinz Hall, Pittsburgh, PA
- August 5, 2005. Utah Symphony, Edwin Outwater, conductor. Deer Valley Amphitheater, Deer Valley, UT

Recording:

- In Progress. 2007. Naxos 8.559328. Nashville Symphony, Leonard Slatkin, conductor. Recorded June 2006. **D88**

See: **B27, B95, B96, B112, B113, B114, B115, B142, B158, B379, B392, B395, B511**

W20. The Last Dance

©2000 Associated Music Publishers, Inc..

Duration: 15 minutes

Commissioned for the Orchestra of St. Luke's in celebration of its 25th anniversary with funds provided by the Mary Flagler Cary Charitable Trust

Instrumentation: 2(pic).222/220+btbn.0/timp.2perc/str

Premiere:

- February 24, 2000. Orchestra of St. Luke's, Alan Gilbert, conductor. Carnegie Hall, New York, NY
See: **B125, B512**

W21. Violin Concerto
©1992 Associated Music Publishers, Inc. AMP 8076. First Printing: December 1994
Duration: 19 minutes
Dedicated with admiration to Elmar Oliveira
Commissioned by Snowbird Institute, Snowbird, UT and Brigham Young University's Barlow Endowment for Music Composition with a grant from Meet the Composer/Reader's Digest Commissioning Program, in partnership with the NEA and the Lila Wallace-Reader's Digest Fund
Finalist for the Pulitzer Prize in 1993
Instrumentation: violin; 2222/2210/2perc/str
Piano reduction available for purchase; orchestral parts available as rental through publisher
Composer's note:
> *My concerto is really a fantasy for violin and orchestra that explores different kinds of feelings ranging from a robust Romantic tune for the orchestra to sharply etched rhythmic punctuations to a very soft passage that descends from the highest celestial regions of the violin. There are two violin duets for the soloist and the concertmaster that were written as a tribute to Elmar Oliveira's brother (also a violinist and one of Oliveira's teachers), who passed away in the fall of 1991. The last section is fast, and takes as its thematic basis a motive from Bartók's* Contrasts for Clarinet, Violin, and Piano, *an idea that has frequently appeared in other works of mine.*

Premiere:
- April 24, 1992. Utah Symphony, Elmar Oliveira, violin; Joseph Silverstein, conductor. Symphony Hall, Salt Lake City, UT
Selected Performances:
- November 19, 1993. Kansas City Symphony, Elmar Oliveira, violin; William McGlaughlin, conductor. Lyric Theatre, Kansas City, MO
- October 6, 2000. Thornton Symphony Orchestra, Michelle Kim, violin; Joan Tower, conductor. University of Southern California, Los Angeles, CA
Recording:
- *Joan Tower Concertos.* 1997. D'note Classics 1016. Elmar Oliveira, violin. Louisville Orchestra, Joseph Silverstein, conductor. **D77**
See: **B23, B49, B187, B188, B373, B520, B575, B585**

W22. Yet Another Set of Variations (on a Theme by Paganini): Paganini Trills
©1996 Associated Music Publishers
Duration: c. 2 minutes

Written as a farewell to outgoing conductor of the St. Louis Symphony Leonard Slatkin. Former composers-in-residence Joan Tower, Joseph Schwantner, William Bolcom, Claude Baker, Donale Erb each contributed to the *Yet Another Set of Variations*. Slatkin added a variation of his own.

Instrumentation: 2222/2220/2percussion: glockenspiel, low tom-tom, maraca, temple block, xylophone/strings

Available as rental from publisher

Premiere:

- May 19, 1996. St. Louis Symphony, Leonard Slatkin, conductor. Powell Hall, St. Louis, MO

Works for Chamber Ensemble

W23. Amazon I

©1977 Associated Music Publishers, Inc. AMP 8065
Duration: 13 minutes
Instrumentation: flute, clarinet, violin, 'cello, piano
Commissioned by the Contemporary Music Society
Written for and dedicated to the Da Capo Chamber Players
Composer's note:

> I grew up in South America and have long wanted to write a piece as a tribute to my experiences there. The opportunity presented itself to me when the image of a river, as a musical metaphor, became the focus of this piece. The title refers to the great Brazilian river, the Amazon, and the images and actions that a journey on such a river might provide. I was concerned with creating a kind of seamless, flowing action within which, along the way, one might sense changes of pace through the speed of the notes, sometimes resulting in a "cascade" of many notes, other times in a slowing down that almost stops the action entirely. A ripple effect can be heard in the trill sections.
>
> The other reason I chose "Amazon" as a title was the fact that I was reading many books by and about women at the time, and I liked the feminist connotation of the title. I have never actually seen the Amazon River.

Premiere:

- January 11, 1978. The Da Capo Chamber Players. Carnegie Hall, New York, NY

Selected Performances:

- October 21, 1979. 20th-Century Consort: Sara Stern, flute; Edward Johnson, clarinet; Lambert Orkis, piano; Dan Rouslin, violin; Glenn Garlick, 'cello. Ring Auditorium, Hirshhorn Museum, Washington, DC
- December 5, 1992. 20th Century Consort. Ring Auditorium, Hirshhorn Museum, Washington, DC

- February 27, 2001. Da Camera of Houston: Leone Buyse flute; Michael Webster, clarinet; Curtis Macomber, violin; Timothy Hester, piano; Norman Fischer, 'cello. Menil Collection, Houston, TX
- January 22, 2002. SOLI Chamber Ensemble: Stephanie Key, clarinet; Martha Fabrique, flute; Ertan Torgul, violin; David Mollenauer, 'cello; Carolyn True, piano. Trinity University, Ruth Taylor Concert Hall, San Antonio, TX
- March 22, 2005. The Fulcrum Point Ensemble: Mary Stolper, flute; Dileep Gangolli, clarinet; Sharon Polifrone, violin; Mark Brandfonbrener, 'cello; Andrea Swan, piano. Harris Theater for Music and Dance, Chicago, IL

Recordings:

- *Joan Tower: Platinum Spirals, Noon Dance, Wings, Amazon.* 1984. Composers' Recordings CRI SD517. Da Capo Chamber Players, Collage, Joel Smirnoff. **D1**
- *Joan Tower: Chamber and Solo Works.* 1994. Composers' Recordings CRI 582. Da Capo Chamber Players. **D2**

See: **B117, B132, B155, B195, B201, B313, B360, B407, B409, B443, B543**

W24. Amazon II for Chamber Orchestra

©1979 Associated Music Publishers, Inc.
Duration: 14 minutes
Instrumentation (arranged by the composer from the original quintet): 2(pic).222/2211/3(3 optional)percussion: percussion #1: 4 timpani, bass drum, snare drum, 3 cymbals (low, medium, high), marimba, vibraphone. percussion #2: 4 tom-toms, 3 cymbals (low, medium, high), marimba, vibraphone, hp,pf[=cel]/strings
Premiere:

- November 10, 1979. Hudson Valley Philharmonic, Imre Pallo, conductor. Kingston Center for the Performing Arts, Kingston, NY

Selected Performances:

- March 12, 1983. Houston Symphony, William Harwood, conductor. Jones Hall, Houston, TX
- May 12, 1985. Columbus Symphony Chamber Orchestra, Tania León, conductor. Ohio Theater, Columbus, OH

See: **B2, B194, B444**

W25. A Gift

Written 2006
Duration: 2 ½ minutes
Instrumentation: flute and clarinet
Commissioned by Chamber Music Northwest
Premiere:

- July 10, 2006. Chamber Music Northwest. David Shifrin, clarinet; Tara O'Connor, flute. Portland, OR

W26. And . . . They're Off!
©1997 Associated Music Publishers, Inc.
Duration: 3 minutes
Dedication: to Gwen and Desmond
Instrumentation: violin, 'cello, piano
Premiere:

- June 4, 1997. Scotia Festival of Music. Gwen Hoebig, violin; Desmond Hoebig, 'cello; David Moroz, piano. Scotia Festival, Halifax, Nova Scotia

Selected Performances:

- February 20, 1998. Desmond Hoebig, 'cello; Jeanne Kierman, piano; Kenneth Goldsmith, violin. Duncan Recital Hall, Rice University, Houston, TX
- September 10, 1999. Da Capo Chamber Players. Merkin Concert Hall, New York, NY
- August 6, 2000. Chee-Yun, violin; David Finckel, 'cello; Wu Han, piano. La Jolla Chamber Music Society's SummerFest, La Jolla, CA
- June 15, 2006. Nai-Yuan Hu, violin, Fred Sherry, 'cello; Wu Han, piano. OKMozart Festival, Bartlesville, OK

See: **B445**

W27. Big Sky
©2000 Associated Music Publishers, Inc.
Duration: 7 minutes
Instrumentation: violin, 'cello, piano
Commissioned by Silvia and Brian Devine for Summerfest La Jolla
Composer's note:

> Big Sky *has an image of a big landscape, a Montana-like sky and maybe a lone wild stallion roaming freely within that. Sometimes he is staring at the peaceful gigantic blue sky, other times running wildly and freely over the green mountains.*

Premiere:

- August 6, 2000. Chee-Yun, violin; David Finckel, 'cello; Wu Han, piano. La Jolla Chamber Music Society's SummerFest, La Jolla, CA

Selected Performances:

- June 5, 2001. Da Capo Chamber Players, Joan Tower, piano. Merkin Concert Hall, New York, NY
- August 10, 2002. Muneko Otani, violin; Caroline Stinson, 'cello; Joan Tower, piano. Maverick Concert Hall, Woodstock, NY
- January 25, 2004. The Calyx Piano Trio. James Library and Center for the Arts, Norwell, MA
- February 18, 2004. eighth blackbird. Modlin Center, University of Richmond, Richmond, VA
- April 30, 2002. Eva Gruesser, violin; André Emelianoff, 'cello; Joan Tower, piano. Kennedy Center Terrace Theatre, Washington, DC

- April 6, 2002. Orchestra of St. Luke's. Dia Center for the Performing Arts, New York, NY
- June 5, 2004. Orchestra of St. Luke's. Chelsea Museum of Art, New York, NY
- June 15, 2006. Ani Kavafian, violin; Raman Ramakrishnan, 'cello; Wu Han, piano. OKMozart Festival, Bartlesville, OK

Recording:
- *Joan Tower: Instrumental Music.* Naxos 8559215. 2005. Chee-Yun, violin; André Emelianoff, 'cello; Joan Tower, piano. **D4**

See: **B33, B77, B87, B98, B102, B103, B135, B177, B182, B193, B356, B363, B400, B402, B414, B448**

W28. Black Topaz

©1976. Associated Music Publishers, Inc.

Duration: 13 minutes

Dedicated to Robert Miller and the Group for Contemporary Music

Commissioned by the Group for Contemporary Music with a grant from the National Endowment for the Arts

Instrumentation: piano, flute, clarinet (bcl), trumpet, trombone, 2 percussion (2 marimbas, 2 vibraphones, temple blocks, and tom-toms)

Notes from score (by Mary Lou Humphrey):

> *Joan Tower's* Black Topaz *derives from a drawing she once did of color rays emanating from a black, piano-like object. This single-movement work examines a similar projection of color from its focal point, the solo piano (black), to a six-member supporting instrumental ensemble.* Black Topaz *was one of Joan Tower's first compositions to move away form an earlier quasi-serial style in favor of a more fluid, organic style. Here a large-scale musical architecture reigns, emphasizing metamorphosis of color and musical time, and an ever-increasing level of harmonic consonance.*

Premiere:
- November 15, 1976. Group for Contemporary Music, Robert Miller, piano, Charles Wuorinen, conductor. Manhattan School of Music, New York, NY

Selected Performances:
- September 22, 1986. Voices of Change, Jo Boatright, conductor. Caruth Auditorium, Southern Methodist University, Dallas, TX
- October 3, 2003. Oberlin Contemporary Music Ensemble, Timothy Weiss, conductor. Finney Chapel, Oberlin College, Oberlin, OH
- October 2, 2004. Members of the New World Symphony, David Krehbiel, conductor. Lincoln Theatre, Miami Beach, FL

Recording:
- *Black Topaz.* 1995. New World Records, CD 80470–2. Laura Flax, clarinet; Michael Powell, trombone; Patricia Spencer, flute; Jonathan Haas and Deborah Moore, percussion; Chris Gekker, trumpet; Stephen Gosling, piano, Joan Tower, conductor. **D5**

See: **B85, B190, B248, B449**

W29. Breakfast Rhythms I and II

Written 1974–1975, ©1983 Associated Music Publishers, Inc. AMP 7857-7
Duration: 15 minutes
Instrumentation: clarinet, flute (pic), violin, 'cello; piano, percussion: vibra-
    phone, marimba, 3 tom-toms (high, medium, low), woodblock (large)
Dedicated to Anand Devendra (Allen Blustine)
Commissioned by the National Endowment for the Arts
Composer's note:

> *This piece is influenced by Beethoven's use of textural and rhythmic
> contrast. In both movements, there is a sense of large- and small-scale
> balancing. Pitch patterns form the basis of the harmonic structure and
> melodic activity as they are isolated, completed, or combined with
> other patterns. Orderly yet angular ensemble writing regularly gives
> way to more lyrical passages for the clarinet, which lend an at-home
> and away-from-home feeling.*

Premiere:
- April 30, 1975. Da Capo Chamber Players. Town Hall, New York, NY

Selected Performances:
- February 22, 1974. Da Capo Chamber Players, American Society of
  University Composers, New York, NY
- May 31, 1981. New World Players. National Academy of Science,
  Washington, DC
- February 15, 1983. New Music Ensemble. Carnegie Recital Hall, New
  York, NY

Recordings:
- *American Contemporary.* 1976. CRI SD354 (LP). Da Capo Chamber
  Players. Allen Blustine, clarinet. **D6**
- *Joan Tower: Chamber and Solo Works.* 1994. CRI 582. Da Capo
  Chamber Players. Allen Blustine, clarinet. **D7**
- *Joan Tower Music for Clarinet.* 1995. Summit Records DCD 124. En-
  semble 21, Robert Spring, clarinet. **D8**

See: **B29, B293, B301, B450, B592**

W30. Brimset

©1965 American Composers' Alliance
Duration: 6 minutes
Instrumentation: 2 flutes, percussion
Selected Performances:
- July 3, 1973. 21st-Century Flute Quartet, Joan Tower, conductor. Loeb
  Student Center, New York University, NY

W31. Chamber Dance

Written 2005, ©2006 Associated Music Publishers, Inc.
Duration: 15 minutes

Commissioned by and dedicated to the Orpheus Chamber Orchestra
Instrumentation: 2(2nd doubles pic) 222/2200, timpani/percussion, strings
Premiere:
- May 6, 2006. Orpheus Chamber Orchestra. Carnegie Hall, New York,
  NY

Selected Performances:
- October 19–21, 2006. Nashville Symphony, Anu Talli, conductor.
  Schermerhorn Symphony Center, Nashville, TN

See: **B453**

W32. Copperwave
Written 2005; Not yet published
Duration: 10 minutes
Dedicated to the American Brass Quintet
Commissioned by the Juilliard School on the occasion of its 100th anniver-
sary with the generous support of Francis Goelet
Instrumentation: brass quintet
Premiere:
- May 4, 2006. American Brass Quintet: Raymond Mase and Kevin
  Cobb, trumpets; David Wakefield, horn; Michael Powell, trombone;
  John D. Rojak, bass trombone. Peter Jay Sharp Theatre, Juilliard
  School of Music, New York, NY
- July 29, 2006. American Brass Quintet. Aspen Music Festival, Aspen,
  CO.

See: **B366, B460**

W33. DNA
©2003 Associated Music Publishers, Inc. AMP 8195
Duration: 9 minutes
Dedicated to Frank Epstein, percussionist with the Boston Symphony Or-
chestra
Commissioned by Bradford and Dorothea Endicott for Frank Epstein and
the New England Conservatory Percussion Ensemble
Instrumentation: 5 percussion
Premiere:
- April 13, 2003. New England Conservatory Percussion Ensemble,
  Frank Epstein, conductor. Jordon Hall, New England Conservatory,
  Boston, MA

Selected Performances:
- October 3, 2003. Oberlin Percussion Group, Michael Rosen, conductor.
  Finney Chapel, Oberlin College, Oberlin, OH
- January 16, 2004. New England Conservatory Percussion Ensemble,
  Frank Epstein, conductor. Carnegie Hall Making Music Series, New
  York, NY
- October 2, 2004. Percussion Consort of the New World Symphony.
  Lincoln Theatre, Miami Beach, FL

- August 3, 2005. Aspen Percussion Ensemble, Jonathan Haas, conductor. Harris Concert Hall, Aspen Music Festival, Aspen, CO
- August 11, 2005. New England Conservatory Percussion Ensemble, Frank Epstein, conductor. Tanglewood, Lenox, MA

Composer's note:

DNA *is written for percussion quintet as a way of capitalizing on the notion of DNA and its role as the building block of all biological life. Deoxyribonucleic acid, as we know it chemically, is an elegant form, made up of double helixes and double strands in an endless spiraling ribbon. Using this feature as a starting point—the piece is built around pairs of instruments which are featured prominently throughout: high-hats, castanets, timbales, and snares appear in duos—and like the base pairs of DNA—conspire to make a whole work. The fifth percussionist is primarily a soloist, an outsider to the pairs—playing on temple blocks, tambourine, and congas until he joins them in passages of trios, quartets, and quintets.*

Recording:

- In Progress on Naxos label: New England Conservatory Percussion Ensemble, Frank Epstein, director. **D89**

See: **B11, B156, B283, B461**

W34. Elegy ("... Forgive These Wild and Wandering Cries ...")
©1993, revised 1994
Duration: 5 minutes
Commissioned by the Norfolk (CT) Chamber Music Festival, for its trombonist John Swallow
Instrumentation: trombone and string quartet
Premiere:

- August 6, 1993. Cleveland Quartet, John Swallow, trombone. Norfolk Chamber Music Festival, Norfolk, CT

Selected Performances:

- November 2, 1993. St. Ronan Quartet: Christine Frank, Mariana Lorens, violins; John Largess, viola; Erkki Lahesmaa, 'cello. John Swallow, trombone. Morse Recital Hall, Norfolk Chamber Music Festival, Norfolk, CT
- January 31, 2003. Degas Quartet: James Dickenson, Tamaki Higashi, violins; Simon Ertz, viola; Philip von Maltzahn, 'cello. Haim Avitsur, trombone. Auditorium of the Arts and Science Center, Hickory, NC
- November 24, 2005. Annalee Patipatanakoon, Carol Lynn Fujino, violins; Teng Li, viola; David Hetherington, 'cello. Alain Trudel, trombone. Women's Music Club of Toronto. Walter Hall, Edward Johnson Building, University of Toronto, Toronto, ON

See: **B9, B323, B348, B463**

W35. Fanfare for the Uncommon Woman, No. 1
Date: written 1986, ©1987. Associated Music Publishers, Inc.

Duration: 3 minutes
Dedicated to conductor Marin Alsop
Written under the Fanfare Project and commissioned by the Houston Symphony
Instrumentation: 4 horns in F, 3 trumpets in C, 3 trombones, tuba, timpani, 2 percussion: percussion #1: snare drum, medium bass drum, 3 cymbals, high gong, medium gong. percussion #2: large tam-tam, 2 cymbals, tom-toms, large bass drum, medium temple blocks, triangle
Performance material available as rental
Composer's note:
> Fanfare for the Uncommon Woman, No. 1 *was inspired by Copland's* Fanfare for the Common Man *and employs the same instrumentation. In addition, the original theme resembles the first theme in the Copland. It is dedicated to women who take risks and who are adventurous.*

Premiere:
- January 10, 1987. Houston Symphony, Hans Vonk, conductor. Jones Hall, Houston, TX

Selected Performances:
- July 15, 1994. Colorado Symphony, Marin Alsop, conductor. Red Rocks Amphitheatre, Denver, CO
- December 2, 1995. Louisiana Philharmonic, Marin Alsop, conductor. Orpheum Theatre, New Orleans, LA
- February 13, 1997. Buffalo Symphony Orchestra, Elizabeth Schulze, conductor. Kleinhas Music Hall, Buffalo, NY
- June 2, 1997. Toronto Symphony Orchestra, Marin Alsop, conductor. Roy Thomson Hall, Toronto, ON
- May 2, 1998. National Symphony Orchestra, Elizabeth Schulze, conductor. National Museum of Women in the Arts, Washington, DC
- June 30, 1999. Colorado Symphony Orchestra, Marin Alsop, conductor. Vail Valley Music Festival, Ford Amphitheatre, Vail, CO
- June 8, 2000. Buffalo Philharmonic Orchestra, Randy Fleischer, conductor. Kleinhans Music Hall, Buffalo, NY
- May 18, 2002. Alexandria Symphony Orchestra, Kim Allen Kluge, conductor. Schlesinger Concert Hall and Arts Center, Alexandria, VA
- July 22, 2002. Brass and Percussion Fellows of the Tanglewood Music Center, Bryan Nies, conductor. Lenox, MA
- August 3, 2002. Eastern Philharmonic Orchestra, JoAnn Faletta, conductor. Eastern Music Festival, Greensboro, NC
- February 8, 2003. Royal Scottish National Orchestra, Marin Alsop, conductor. Royal Concert Hall, Glasgow, Scotland
- January 9, 2004. Kitchener-Waterloo Symphony, Yannick Nezet-Seguin, conductor. Centre in the Square, Kitchener, ON
- March 24, 2004. Cincinnati College-Conservatory Orchestra, Xian Zhang, conductor. Corbett Auditorium, Cincinnati College Conservatory of Music, Cincinnati, OH

- September 18, 2004. Akron Symphony, Uriel Segal, conductor. EJ Thomas Hall, Akron, OH
- February 17, 2005. Baltimore Symphony Orchestra, Marin Alsop, conductor. Meyerhoff Hall, Baltimore, MD

Recordings:

- *The American Album.* 1991. RCA 60778. St. Louis Symphony Orchestra, Leonard Slatkin, conductor. **D16**
- *Red Seal Century—Soloists & Conductors.* 2001. RCA Victor Red Seal CD 60778, RCA Victor Red Seal CD 63861. 2 disks. St. Louis Symphony Orchestra, Leonard Slatkin, conductor. **D17**
- *Fanfares for the Uncommon Woman.* 1999. Koch Int'l Classics 7469. Colorado Symphony Orchestra, Marin Alsop, conductor. **D18**

See: **B15, B76, B90, B207, B255, B295, B300, B307, B320, B324, B354, B361, B392, B415, B422, B428, B464, B526, B527**

W36. Fanfare for the Uncommon Woman, No. 2
©1989, revised 1997. Associated Music Publishers, Inc.
Duration: 3 ½ minutes
Dedicated with affection to the former general manager of the St. Louis Symphony, Joan Briccetti
Commissioned by Carillon Importers on behalf of Absolut Vodka
Instrumentation: 4 horns, 3 trumpets in C, 3 trombones, tuba, timpani, 3 percussion: percussion #1: glockenspiel, 2 cymbals, snare drum, mounted castanets, low temple blocks, wood block. percussion #2: 2 cymbals, 2 timbales, tenor drum, low tom-toms, low tam-tam, tambourine, triangle. percussion #3: marimba, chimes, medium cymbal, 2 bass drums, wood block, bell tree.

Premiere:

- November 29, 1989. Orchestra of St. Luke's, Peter Connelly, conductor. Avery Fisher Hall, New York, NY

Selected Performances:

- November 16, 1999. New Music Festival Orchestra, Robert Aitken, conductor. Massey Hall, Toronto, ON

Recording:

- *Fanfares for the Uncommon Woman.* 1999. Koch Int'l Classics 7469. Colorado Symphony Orchestra, Marin Alsop, conductor. **D19**

See: **B387, B465**

W37. Fanfare for the Uncommon Woman, No. 3
©1991. Associated Music Publishers, Inc.
Duration: 6 minutes
Instrumentation: double brass quintet. Quintet I: 2 trumpets in C, horn in F, trombone, tuba. Quintet II: 2 trumpets in C, horn in F, trombone, tuba
Composer's note:

Fanfare for the Uncommon Woman, No. 3 *was commissioned by Carnegie Hall Corporation. It is dedicated to Frances Richard, director of concert music at ASCAP.*

Performance material available as rental from publisher

Premiere:

- May 5, 1991. Empire Brass Quintet and members of the New York Philharmonic, Zubin Mehta, conductor. Carnegie Hall, New York, NY [Broadcast on KERA-TV with co-anchors Beverly Sills and Peter Jennings]

Selected Performances:

- September 7, 1981. Members of the Minnesota Orchestra, Edo de Waart, conductor. Orchestra Hall, Minneapolis, MN
- July 22, 2002. Brass and Percussion Fellows of the Tanglewood Music Center, Bryan Nies, conductor. Tanglewood, Lenox, MA

Recordings:

- *Fanfares for the Uncommon Woman.* 1999. Koch Int'l Classics 7469. Colorado Symphony Orchestra, Marin Alsop, conductor. **D20**
- *Feminine Escapes.* 2002. Koch International Classics. Colorado Symphony Orchestra, Marin Alsop, conductor. **D21**

See: **B53, B92, B275, B466**

W38. Fanfare for the Uncommon Woman, No. 5

©1993 Associated Music Publishers, Inc. AMP 8122

Duration: 4 minutes

Dedicated to Joan Harris, whose donation built a new concert hall at the Aspen (CO) Music Festival

Instrumentation: trumpet quartet

Premiere:

- Aug 20, 1993. Empire Brass Quartet, Joan Tower, conductor. Joan and Irving Harris Concert Hall, Aspen Music Festival. Aspen, CO

Selected Performances:

- November 2, 1993. Allan Dean, Mario Bertoluzzi, Neil Mueller, Paula Swartz, trumpets; Joan Tower, conductor. Morse Recital Hall, Norfolk Chamber Festival, Norfolk, CT

Recordings:

- *Fanfares for the Uncommon Woman.* 1999. Koch International Classics 7469/Koch International Classics KIC 7630. Colorado Symphony Orchestra, Marin Alsop, conductor. **D23**
- *American Visions/American Brass Quintet.* 2003. Summit Records DCD 365. **D24**

See: **B91, B181, B333, B468**

W39. Fantasy . . . (Those Harbor Lights)

©1983 Associated Music Publishers, Inc. AMP 8005. First printing: April 1989

Duration: 14 minutes

Commissioned by and dedicated to Richard Stoltzman
Instrumentation: for clarinet and piano
Premiere:
- November 4, 1983. Richard Stoltzman, clarinet; Irma Vallecillo, piano. Bangor, ME
Selected Performances:
- June 9, 1998. Encounters Chamber Ensemble, Joaquin Valdepenas, clarinet; Stephen Clarke, piano. Glenn Gould Studio, Toronto, ON
- July 28, 1998. Michele Zukovsky, clarinet; Max Levinson, piano. Santa Fe Chamber Music Festival
Recordings:
- *Joan Tower: Music for Clarinet.* 1995. Summit Records DCD 124. Robert Spring, clarinet; Eckart Sellheim, piano. **D25**
- *20th Century Works for Clarinet.* 2004. Katson Productions. Keith Lemmons, clarinet; Maribeth Gunning, piano. **D26**
See: **B29, B109, B169, B298, B470, B539, B579**

W40. For Daniel
©2004 Associated Music Publishers, Inc.
Duration: 19 minutes
Written for the Kalichstein-Laredo-Robinson Trio in memory of Daniel MacArthur
Commissioned by the Arizona Friends of Chamber Music
Instrumentation: violin, 'cello, piano
Premiere:
- March 2, 2004. Kalichstein-Laredo-Robinson Trio. Tucson Winter Festival, Leo Rich Theater, Tucson Community Center, Tucson, AZ
- August 5, 2004. Members of the Muir String Quartet: Michael Reynolds, 'cello; Peter Zazofsky, violin; Joan Tower, piano. Deer Valley Music Festival, St. Mary's Catholic Church, Park City, UT
- November 22, 2004. Kalichstein-Laredo-Robinson Trio. Lincoln Performance Hall, Portland, OR
- May 28, 2005. Yehuda Hanani, 'cello; Joan Tower, piano; Yehonatan Berick, violin. Close Encounters with Music series, First United Church, Pittsfield, MA
- June 26, 2005. Kalichstein-Laredo-Robinson Trio. Chamber Music Albuquerque, Symphony Center, Albuquerque, NM
- August 18, 2005. Kalichstein-Laredo-Robinson Trio. Seiji Ozawa Hall, Tanglewood, Lenox, MA
- April 1, 2006. Members of the Orchestra of St. Luke's. Chelsea Museum of Art, New York, NY
- June 14, 2006. Erin Keefe, violin, Raman Ramakrishnan, 'cello; Joyce Yang, piano. OKMozart Festival, Bartlesville, OK
- January 27, 2007. Kalichstein-Laredo-Robinson Trio. Hamburg, Germany

See: **B13, B79, B120, B153, B233, B322, B338, B358, B375, B377, B416, B418, B431, B473**

W41. Incandescent
©2003 Associated Music Publishers, Inc.
Duration: 18 minutes
Written for and dedicated to the Emerson String Quartet "with affection and admiration"
Joint commission between the South Mountain Concerts and Bard College, Annandale-on-Hudson, NY
Instrumentation: string quartet
Composer's note:

> The word "incandescent" is not one that I would usually include in a title because it seems to be more poetic than what I am thinking about. My titles are usually more up front and visceral, and in this case I would have preferred to call it White Heat, but was outvoted by friends who found that title carried too many associations (titles are not easy for composers—especially for me). What I try to do in my music, and particularly in this piece, is create a heat from within, so that what unfolds is not only motivated by the architecture of the piece (which I consider the most important goal), but also that each idea or phrase contains a strong "radiance" of texture and feeling about it. In other words, the complete "action" of rhythm, texture, dynamic, harmony, and register has a strong enough profile that it creates an identity with a "temperature," one felt rather than observed. In Incandescent, my third string quartet, basically five actions or ideas unfold, develop, interact, and gradually change their "temperatures." They are a three-note collection that initially appears as an upper and lower neighbor to a central note at he very opening of the piece and later turns around on itself repeatedly in the first violin; a repetitive, dense, held-in-place, and narrowly registered dissonant chord; a consonant arpeggiation that creases a "melody" distributed throughout the instruments; a climbing motive that initially outlines an octatonic scale (whole steps alternating with half steps) and later shifts into both whole-tone and chromatic scales; and, finally, wide leaps that first appear in the first violin and are subsequently picked up by the viola. The extended 16th-note passages that occur throughout, finally arriving at a virtuosic, Vivaldi-like 'cello solo, include all these motives in different guises and temperatures.

Premiere:
• April 26, 2003. Emerson String Quartet. Richard B. Fisher Center, Bard College, Annandale-on-Hudson, NY
Selected Performances:
• January 28, 2004. Emerson String Quartet. University of Washington International Chamber Music Series, Meany Theater, University of Washington, Seattle, WA

- July 21, 2004. Emerson String Quartet. Ozawa Hall, Tanglewood, Lenox, MA
- October 7, 2004. Emerson String Quartet: Philip Setzer and Eugene Drucker, violins, Lawrence Dutton, viola; David Finckel, 'cello. Jane Mallett Theatre, Toronto
- November 21, 2004. Emerson String Quartet. Wigmore Hall, London, England
- January 11, 2005. Emerson String Quartet. Friends of Chamber Music, Vancouver Playhouse, Vancouver, BC
- May 12, 2005. Emerson String Quartet. Music Center, Strathmore Hall, Bethesda, MD
- July 28, 2006. Muir String Quartet. Deer Valley Music Festival, Park City, UT

See: **B39, B56, B94, B148, B161, B238, B269, B299, B339, B340, B345, B362, B374, B476, B542**

W42. In Memory
©2002 Associated Music Publishers, Inc.
Duration: c. 15 minutes
Dedication: in memory of Margaret Shafer
Commissioned by Tokyo String Quartet
Instrumentations
   (1) string quartet
   (2) string ensemble—arranged by the composer from string quartet (Available as rental from the publisher)
Composer's note:

The fifteen-minute, one-movement piece is about death and loss, and was written in memory of one of the composer's old friends, Margaret Shafer, who passed away the summer the piece was begun. About two months later, the September 11th event occurred and this increased the loss to include the many people who lost their lives in the WTC tragedy. This "amplified" feeling of so much pain in the world played a major role in increasing the intensity of the music. The writing contains high, celestial material, some of which descends very slowly. This is paired with more forceful and driving repetitive musical ideas that try to express the anger and pain that results from the loss of people in one's life.

Premiere: string quartet version
- February 23, 2002. Tokyo String Quartet. 92nd Street Y, New York, NY

Premiere: string ensemble version
- May 21, 2004. American Symphony Orchestra, Leon Botstein, conductor. Richard B. Fisher Center for the Performing Arts, Bard College, Annandale-on-Hudson, NY

Selected Performances: quartet version

- August 10, 2002. Colorado String Quartet: Julie Rosenfeld, Deborah Redding, violins; Marka Gustavsson, viola; Diane Chaplin, 'cello. Maverick Concert Hall, Woodstock, NY
- February 24, 2003. Tokyo String Quartet. Pittsburgh Chamber Music Society, Carnegie Music Hall, Pittsburgh, PA
- October 5, 2003. Cavani String Quartet. Aki Festival of New Music, Cleveland Museum of Art, Cleveland, OH
- January 16, 2004. Tokyo String Quartet. Making Music Series, Carnegie Hall, New York, NY
- May 8, 2006. Members of Chicago Symphony Orchestra. Symphony Center, Chicago, IL

Selected Performances: string ensemble version

- June 5, 2004. Orchestra of St. Luke's. Chelsea Museum of Art, New York, NY
- November 19, 2004. Kalistos Chamber Orchestra, Joan Tower, conductor. St. Paul Church, Brookline, MA
- May 28, 2005. Kalistos Chamber Orchestra, Chris Younghoon Kim, conductor. Merkin Hall, New York, NY

Recording:

- *Joan Tower: Instrumental Music.* 2005. Naxos 8559215. Tokyo String Quartet. **D32**

See: **B11, B98, B102, B103, B135, B141, B182, B282, B284, B400, B477, B541, B570**

W43. Island Prelude

Written 1989, ©1992 Associated Music Publishers, Inc. AMP 8042. First Printing: September 1992

Duration: 10 minutes

Dedication: "with love to Jeff Litfin"

Commissioned by the National Endowment for the Arts for Quintessence and the Dorian and Dakota quintets

Instrumentations

(1) oboe and wind quartet (flute, clarinet, horn, bassoon)

(2) oboe and string quintet (2 violins, viola, 'cello, bass)

Composer's note:

I tried for something with love and sensuousness, and thought of the setting as a tropical island somewhere in the Bahamas. The island is remote, lush, tropical, with stretches of white beach interspersed with thick green jungle. Above is a large, powerful, and brightly colored bird (the oboe) which soars and glides, spirals up, and plummets with folded wings as it dominates but lives in complete harmony with its island home. The wind quintet version is a heavier piece because of the weight of the different timbres under the oboe. The counterpoint, however, is more easily heard in this version.

Premiere: oboe/wind quartet

- April 9, 1989. Quintessence. Antonio Fernándes-Viñas, horn; Amy Ridings, flute; Nancy Clauter, oboe; Jill Marderness, bassoon; Ed Matthew, clarinet. Kerr Cultural Center of Arizona State University, Scottsdale, AZ

Premiere: oboe/string quintet

- August 23, 1989. Jennifer Sperry, oboe; Charles Sherba and Louis Finkel, violins; Consuelo Sherba, viola; Ian Ginsburg, 'cello; Roger Ruggeri, bass; Joan Tower, conductor. Grand Teton Festival, Teton Village, WY

Selected Performances:

- May 15, 1992. Chicago String Ensemble. Robert Morgan, oboe; Alan Heatherington, conductor. St. Paul's Church, Chicago, IL
- September 26, 1993. Dorian Woodwind Quintet. Elizabeth Mann, flute; Jerry Kirkbride, clarinet; Gerard Reuter, oboe; Jane Taylor, bassoon; Nancy Billmann, horn. Merkin Concert Hall, New York, NY
- October 30, 1993. Wingra Woodwind Quintet. Linda Kimball, horn; Stephanie Jutt, flute; Marc Fink, oboe/English horn; Linda Bartley, clarinet; Richard Lottridge, bassoon. Morphy Hall, University of Wisconsin–Madison, Madison, WI
- June 9, 1998. Encounters Chamber Ensemble. Lawrence Cherney, oboe. Glenn Gould Studio, Toronto, ON
- February 27, 1999. Members of Seattle Symphony. Randall Ellis, oboe. Illsley Ball Nordstrom Recital Hall, Seattle, WA
- April 27, 2003. New York Virtuosi Chamber Symphony. Richard Dallessio, oboe; Kenneth Klein, conductor. The New York Historical Society, New York, NY
- January 16, 2004. Tokyo String Quartet. Richard Woodhams, oboe. Carnegie Hall, New York, NY
- October 30, 2005. Wingra Woodwind Quintet. Linda Kimball, horn; Stephanie Jutt, flute; Marc Fink, oboe/English horn; Linda Bartley, clarinet; Marc Vallon, bassoon. University of Wisconsin–Madison, Madison, WI
- December 9, 2005. Wingra Woodwind Quintet. Conservatoire Nationale Superier, Paris, France

Recordings:

- *Meet the Composer Orchestra Residency Series: Joan Tower.* 1990. Electra/Nonesuch Records 79245. Peter Bowman, oboe; St. Louis Symphony Orchestra, Leonard Slatkin, conductor. **D33**
- *Joan Tower.* 2004. First Edition FECD25. Peter Bowman, oboe; St. Louis Symphony Orchestra, Leonard Slatkin, conductor. **D34**
- *Joan Tower: Instrumental Music.* 1995. Naxos. 8.559215. Tokyo String Quartet and Richard Woodhams, oboe. **D35**
- *Dorian Wind Quintet: American Premieres.* 1995. Summit DCD 117. Dorian Wind Quintet. **D36**

See: **B11, B28, B98, B103, B108, B130, B135, B182, B254, B298, B309, B397, B406, B440, B484, B548, B583, B588**

W44. Movements
Written 1967, ©1968 American Composers' Alliance
Duration: 10 minutes
Instrumentation: flute and piano
Premiere:
- April 17, 1968. Patricia Spencer, flute; Joan Tower, piano. Greenwich House Music School, New York, NY
Selected Performances:
- May 24, 1968. Patricia Spencer, flute; Joan Tower, piano. Greenwich House Music School, New York, NY
- February 22, 1970. Patricia Spencer, flute; Joan Tower, piano. The New York Historical Society, New York, NY
- February 28, 1970. Patricia Spencer, flute; Joan Tower, piano. Mahattan School of Music, New York, NY
Recording:
- *American Society of University Composers, vols. 1–4. Journal of Music Scores.* 1978. Advance Recording FGR-24S (LP). Patricia Spencer, flute; Joan Tower, piano. **D40**
See: **B488**

W45. Noon Dance
Written 1982, ©1987 Associated Music Publishers, Inc. AMP 7958–4
Duration: 17 minutes
Instrumentation: Fl (alto flute, piccolo), clarinet in A, violin, 'cello, piano, percussion
Commissioned by the Massachusetts State Arts Council
Composer's note:
> The word "noon" in the title refers to this piece as a sequel to an earlier piece, Breakfast Rhythms, written in 1974, which has the same instrumentation. Although there are some dance-type rhythms in the pieces, such as square dance and folk dance motifs, the real impetus for the word "dance" in the title comes from my idea of how close chamber music playing is to dancing: how players "move" with each other, sometimes following and sometimes leading, other times blending different kinds of energies in the pacing of sections; in toto, learning the "choreography" of the piece. Noon Dance is a piece that explores some of those "movements."

Premiere:
- February 28, 1983. Collage. Sanders Theatre, Cambridge, MA
Selected Performances:
- April 28, 1983. Da Capo Chamber Players. Carnegie Hall, New York, NY
- October 7, 1991. Currents New Music Group. Fred Cohen, conductor. North Court Recital Hall, University of Richmond, Richmond, VA.
- October 14, 1992. New York New Music Ensemble. Miller Theatre, Columbia University, New York, NY

- April 2, 1998. eighth blackbird. Corbett Theatre, University of Cincinnati, Cincinnati, OH
- February 21, 1999. Auros Group for New Music. Hyperprism Contemporary Music Series, Gasson Hall, Boston College, Boston, MA
- March 28, 2006. University of Texas New Music Ensemble, Dan Welcher, director and conductor. Bates Recital Hall, University of Texas, Austin, TX

Recordings:

- *Joan Tower: Platinum Spirals, Noon Dance, Wings, Amazon.* 1984. Composers' Recordings CRI SD517. Collage Ensemble. **D47**
- *Joan Tower: Chamber and Solo Works.* 1994. Composers' Recordings CRI SD582. Da Capo Chamber Players. **D48**

See: **B75, B139, B178, B276, B310, B360, B398, B407, B441, B492**

W46. Night Fields

©1994. Associated Music Publishers, Inc.
Duration: 15 minutes
Dedicated to the Muir String Quartet "with affection and admiration"
Commissioned by Hancher Auditorium at University of Iowa and the Snowbird Institute for Arts and Humanities. Funded in part by Chamber Music America with funds from the Pew Charitable Trust
Instrumentation: string quartet
Composer's note:

The title was conceived after the work was completed and provides an image or setting for some of the moods of the piece: a cold, windy night in a wheat field lit up by a bright, full moon, where waves of fast-moving colors ripple over the fields, occasionally settling on a patch of gold.

Premiere:

- March 1, 1994. Muir String Quartet. Hancher Auditorium, University of Iowa, Iowa City, IA

Selected Performances:

- November 1, 1995. Muir String Quartet. Convention Center, Philadelphia, PA
- December 11, 1995. Muir String Quartet. Pittsburgh Chamber Music Society, Carnegie Music Hall, Pittsburgh, PA
- May 20, 1996. Members of the St. Louis Symphony: Manuel Ramos, Jenny Lind Jones, violins; Morris Jacob, viola; Anne Fagerberg, 'cello. Powell Hall, St. Louis, MO
- July 16, 1998. Muir String Quartet. Deer Valley Chamber Music Festival. Snow Park Lodge, Deer Valley Resort, Deer Valley, UT
- September 6, 1998. Cassatt String Quartet: Muneko Otani, Jennifer Leshnower, violins; Tawnya Popoff, viola; Caroline Stinson, 'cello. Olin Auditorium, Bard College, Annandale-on-Hudson, NY
- September 10, 1998. Muir String Quartet. Merkin Concert Hall, New York, NY

- October 27, 1999. Da Vinci Quartet: Jerilyn Jorgenson, Wendolyn Olson, violins, Margaret Miller, viola; Katherine Knight, 'cello. Foote Hall, Lamont School of Music, University of Denver, Denver, CO
- March 19, 2001. Arianna Quartet: John McGrosso, Rebecca Rhee, violins; Sheila Browne, viola; Kurt Baldwin, 'cello. Sheldon Concert Hall, St. Louis, MO
- April 22, 2001. Maia Quartet. Columbus Museum of Art, Columbus, OH
- August 10, 2002. Cassatt String Quartet. Maverick Concert Hall, Woodstock, NY
- April 8, 2003. Lyra String Quartet. Gould Room Chamber Series, Cathedral of St. Philips, Atlanta, GA
- July 17, 2003. Del Sol Quartet. Deer Valley Music Festival, Park City, UT
- November 16, 2003. Enso Quartet: Maureen Nelson, Tereza Stanislav, violins; Robert Brophy, viola; Richard Belcher, 'cello. Frick Fine Arts Auditorium, Pittsburgh, PA
- September 2, 2004. Enso Quartet. Banff International String Quartet Competition. Banff, BC
- January 23, 2005. Parker String Quartet: Daniel Chong, Karen Kim, violins; Jessica Bodner, viola; Kee-Hyun Kim, 'cello. Philips Collection, Washington, DC

Recordings:

- *Degas Quartet.* 2003. Degas Quartet. **D43**
- *Black Topaz.* 1995. New World Records 80470–2. Muir String Quartet. **D44**
- *Boston Conservatory Chamber Players.* 1999. ST DAT .F73 N5. **D45**

See: **B8, B110, B111, B177, B186, B190, B230, B260, B284, B297, B349, B378, B380, B414, B490, B545, B557**

W47. Opa Eboni

©1967 American Composers' Alliance
Duration: 8 minutes
Instrumentation: Oboe and piano
Selected Performances:

- November 17, 1967. Judith Martin, oboe; Joan Tower, piano. Greenwich House Music School, New York, NY
- December 4, 1967. Judith Martin, oboe; Joan Tower, piano. New York Public Library, New York, NY

See: **B493**

W48. Percussion Quartet

©1963 American Composers' Alliance (revised 1969)
Duration: 7 minutes

Instrumentation: 4 percussionists: percussion #1: small bell, small cow bell, anvil pipe, large wood block. percussion #2: large triangle, 2 tom-toms (low and medium). percussion #3: medium cymbal, 2 timpani. percussion #4: large gong, medium bass drum

Premiere:

- January 24, 1964. Richard Wildermuth, Robert Lepre, Richard Fritz, John Williams, percussion. Manhattan School of Music Percussion Ensemble, Manhattan School of Music, New York, NY

Selected Performances:

- March 17, 1973. Ronald Glass, David Mancini, Steven Richards, John Sherry, percussion. American Society of University Composers. Eastman School of Music, Rochester, NY

See: **B495**

W49. Petroushskates

Written 1980, © 1983 Associated Music Publishers, Inc.

Duration: 5 minutes

Written for and premiered by Da Capo Chamber Players

Commissioned by Da Capo Chamber Players and the New York State Council on the Arts in celebration of the group's 10th anniversary

Instrumentations:

(1) flute, clarinet, violin, 'cello, piano

(2) Arrangement by Allen Otte with added percussion (2003)

Composer's note:

In an attempt to understand why figure skating, especially pair skating, was so beautiful and moving to me, I discovered a musical corollary I had been working on for a while—the idea of a seamless action— something I had started to explore in Amazon. *I also always loved* Petrouchka *and wanted to create an homage to Stravinsky and that piece in particular. As it turned out, the figure skating pairs became a whole company of skaters, thereby creating a sort of musical carnival on ice.*

Premiere:

- March 23, 1980. Da Capo Chamber Players, in celebration of Da Capo's 10th anniversary. Alice Tully Hall, New York, NY

Selected Performances:

- October 20, 1984. 20th-Century Consort: Sara Stern, flute; Loren Kitt, clarinet; Lambert Orkis, piano; Elisabeth Adkins, violin; David Hardy, 'cello; Christopher Kendall, conductor. Ring Auditorium, Hirshhorn Museum and Sculpture Garden, Washington, DC
- May 4, 1987. Columbia Players. National Democratic Club, Washington, DC
- October 7, 1991. Currents New Music Group, Fred Cohen, conductor. North Court Recital Hall, University of Richmond, Richmond, VA.
- July 1, 1995. Speculum Musicae. Music Mountain, Falls Village, CT

- April 2, 1998. eighth blackbird. Corbett Theatre, University of Cincinnati, Cincinnati, OH
- September 10, 1998. Da Capo Chamber Players. Merkin Concert Hall, New York, NY
- March 21, 1999. eighth blackbird. Gartner Auditorium, Cleveland Museum of Art, Cleveland, OH
- June 7, 2000. Orchestra of St. Luke's. Dia Center for the Arts, New York, NY
- February 11, 2002. Chicago Chamber Musicians, Composer Perspectives Series. Museum of Contemporary Art, Chicago, IL
- April 30, 2002. Eva Gruesser, violin; Andre Emelianoff, 'cello; Joan Tower, piano; Charles Niedich, clarinet; Carol Wincenc, flute. Kennedy Center Terrace Theatre, Washington, DC
- October 4, 2003. Da Camera of Houston: Sarah Rothenberg, piano; Tara O'Connor, flute; Michael Webster, clarinet; Jennifer Frautschi, violin; and Bion Tsang, 'cello. Cullen Theater, Wortham Center, Houston, TX
- October 5, 2003. Oberlin Contemporary Music Ensemble, Joan Tower, conductor. Aki Festival of New Music, Cleveland Museum of Art, Cleveland, OH
- July 29, 2004. Pittsburgh New Music Ensemble, choreographed/danced by Danielle Brewer, Jeremy Sment, Rudolfo Villela. Hazlett Theater, Pittsburgh, PA
- April 9, 2005. The Da Capo Chamber Players. Watson Hall, North Carolina School of the Arts, Winston-Salem, NC
- November 8, 2005. Da Capo Chamber Players and Yass Hakoshima Movement Theater. Symphony Center, New York, NY

Recordings:
- *The Da Capo Chamber Players Celebrate Their Tenth Anniversary.* 1981. Composers' Recordings CRI SD441. Da Capo Chamber Players. **D49**
- *The Composer–Performer: Forty Years of Discovery, 1954–1994.* 1994. Composers' Recordings CD670. Da Capo Chamber Players. **D50**
- *Joan Tower: Chamber and Solo Works.* 1994. Composers' Recordings CRI 582. Da Capo Chamber Players. **D51**
- *Thirteen Ways.* 2003. Cedille Records CD67. *eighth blackbird.* **D52**
- *New Music Recital.* Arkansas State University Department of Music. 2000. CD 1054. **D53**

See: **B14, B18, B69, B77, B86, B87, B140, B244, B286, B288, B290, B315, B332, B349, B356, B363, B367, B391, B412, B414, B496, B532**

W50. Prelude for Five Players
©1970 American Composers' Alliance
Duration: 6 minutes

Instrumentation: flute, oboe/violin, clarinet, bassoon/'cello, piano
Premiere:

- October 21, 1971. Da Capo Chamber Players. Carnegie Recital Hall, New York, NY

Selected Performances:

- December 2, 1971. Da Capo Chamber Players. Greenwich Music House, New York, NY
- March 6, 1972. University Contemporary Music Ensemble, M. William Karlins, conductor. Northwestern University, Evanston, IL
- March 13, 1972. Da Capo Chamber Players. New York University, New York, NY

Recording:

- *Three Movements for Quintet.* 1972. CRI 302 (LP). Da Capo Chamber Players. **D58**

See: **B499**

W51. Rain Waves

©1997 Associated Music Publishers, Inc. AMP 8154. First printing: January 2002.
Duration: 14 minutes
Commissioned by the Verdehr trio
Instrumentation: violin, clarinet, piano
Composer's note:

> Rain Waves *explores the motion of a wave form. Starting with a pointillistic rain-like pattern, the notes float upwards and downwards in increasing intensities. In the less staccato and more flowing sections, there is a sense of a wind pushing the notes into longer and wider arched patterns—perhaps like the undulating sheets of rain created in a light tropical rainfall.*
>
> *The work was commissioned by Michigan State University for the Verdehr Trio. It was written in 1997 and is dedicated to the Verdehr Trio in admiration for their unfailing support of the music of our time, and for their devoted efforts to give a composer's new work a "life" through their worldwide performance tours and recordings.*

Premiere:

- December 14, 1997. Verdehr Trio: Walter Verdehr, violin; Elsa Ludewig-Verdehr, clarinet; Silvia Roederer, piano. Frick Collection, New York, NY

Selected Performances:

- March 1, 1998. Verdehr Trio. Phillips Collection, Washington, DC
- January 16, 2001. Viviane Hagner, violin; Christopher Taylor, piano; David Shifrin, clarinet. Alice Tully Hall, New York, NY
- April 3, 2004. Quorum Chamber Arts Ensemble. School of Music, Michigan State University, East Lansing, MI
- June 5, 2004. Orchestra of St. Luke's. Chelsea Museum of Art, New York, NY

Recording:
- *The Making of a Medium, vol. 13: American Images 2.* 1993. Crystal Records 943. Verdehr Trio. Elsa Ludewig-Verdehr, clarinet; Silvia Roederer, piano; Walter Verdehr, violin. **D59**

See: **B45, B54, B102, B203, B344, B351, B400, B501**

W52. Toccanta
©1997 Associated Music Publishers, Inc.
Duration: 6 minutes
Instrumentation: oboe and harpsichord
Commissioned by Cynthia Green Libby
Premiere:
- June 27 1997. Cynthia Green Libby, oboe; Barbara Harbach, harpsichord. International Double Reed Society Conference. Steiger Concert Hall, Northwestern University, Evanston, IL

See: **B514**

W53. Trés Lent (Hommage à Messiaen)
©1994 Associated Music Publishers, Inc. AMP 8080. First printing: January 1995
Duration: 8 minutes
Dedicated to André Emelianoff
Instrumentation: 'cello and piano
Composer's note:

> Trés Lent *was written as an homage to Olivier Messiaen, particularly to his* Quartet for the End of Time, *which had a special influence on my work.*
>
> *When I was the pianist for the Da Capo Chamber Players, we frequently performed Messiaen's quartet over a seven-year period. During this time, I grew to love the many risks Messiaen took—particularly the use of very slow "time," both in tempo and in the flow of ideas and events.* Trés Lent *is my attempt to make "slow" music work. It is affectionately dedicated to my long-time friend and colleague, who never stops growing as a musician and 'cellist, André Emelianoff.*

Performer's (and dedicatee's) note:

> *In most of Joan's compositions, her "melodies" tend to be more intervallic arches, surrounded, even overwhelmed, by highly energized rhythmic and colorful material. In* Trés Lent *I sense a melody being born. Out of the opening D octaves grow embryonic intervals and a rhythmic motive: short-long-D (the only real Messiaen quote). The expansion and contraction of harmonic bands and pedal points, punctuated by embellishments and grace notes, create a profoundly expressive homage, entirely in Joan's own language.*

Premiere:
- May 8, 1994. André Emelianoff, 'cello; Joan Tower, piano. Merkin Concert Hall, New York, NY

Selected Performances:

- July 21, 1997. Sharon Robinson, 'cello; Reiko Uchida, piano. Tawes Theatre, University of Maryland, College Park, MD
- February 15, 1998. Judith Glyde, 'cello; Joan Tower, piano. Modern Music Festival University of Colorado–Boulder, Boulder, CO
- June 13, 1998. Paul Katz, 'cello; James Tocco, piano. Great Lakes Chamber Festival. Detroit, MI
- August 5, 2000. Andres Diaz, 'cello; Max Levinson, piano. Summerfest 2000. Sherwood Auditiorium, La Jolla, CA
- April 30, 2002. André Emelianoff, 'cello; Joan Tower, piano. Kennedy Center Terrace Theatre, Washington, DC
- August 10, 2002. Caroline Stinson, 'cello; Joan Tower, piano. Maverick Concert Hall, Woodstock, NY
- October 5, 2003. Darrett Adkins, 'cello; Teresa McCollough, piano. Aki Festival of New Music, Cleveland Museum of Art, Cleveland, OH
- June 13, 2006. Fred Sherry, 'cello; Joan Tower, piano. OKMozart Festival, Bartlesville, OK

Recordings:

- *Born in America 1938: Music for 'Cello.* 2002. Gasparo Records GSCD 351. Norman Fischer, 'cello; Jeanne Kierman, piano. **D74**
- *Black Topaz.* 1995. New World Records 80470–2. André Emelianoff, 'cello; Joan Tower, piano. **D75**

See: **B303, B414, B515**

W54. Snow Dreams

Written in 1983; ©1986 Associated Music Publishers, Inc.
Duration: 9 minutes
Dedicated to Carol Wincenc and Sharon Isbin
Commissioned by the Schubert Club
Instrumentation: flute and guitar. Flute part edited by Carol
    Wincenc; guitar fingerings by Sharon Isbin.
Composer's note:

> There are many different images of snow, its forms and its movements: light snow flakes, pockets of swirls of snow, rounded drifts, long white plains of blankets of snow, light and heavy snowfalls, and so forth. Many of these images can be found in the piece if, in fact, they need to be found at all. The listener will determine that choice.

Premiere:

- April 18, 1983. Sharon Isbin, guitar; Carol Wincenc, flute. Meeting of Schubert Club, St. Paul, MN

Selected Performances:

- March 13, 1984. Sharon Isbin, guitar; Carol Wincenc, flute. Kaufmann Concert Hall, New York, NY
- October 7, 1991. Currents New Music Group. North Court Recital Hall, University of Richmond, Richmond, VA

- October 21, 1993. Bonita Boyd, flute; Nicholas Goluses, guitar. Slee Hall, University of Buffalo, Buffalo, NY
- April 26, 1994. Laurel Ann Maurer, flute; Jerry Willard, guitar. Weill Recital Hall, Carnegie Hall, New York, NY

Recordings:

- *Black Topaz.* 1995. New World Records 80470–2. Carol Wincenc, flute; Sharon Isbin, guitar. **D70**
- *Chronicles of Discovery: American Music for Flute and Guitar.* 2000. Albany Records 379. Bonita Boyd, flute; Nicholas Goluses, guitar. **D71**
- *Terry Riley: Cantos Desiertos.* 2003. Naxos 8.559146. Alexandra Hawley, flute; Jeffrey McFadden, guitar. **D72**

See: **B97, B139, B256, B270, B278, B310, B355, B507, B525**

W55. Turning Points

©1995. Associated Music Publishers, Inc. First printing: February 1999
Duration: 16 minutes
Instrumentation: clarinet and string quartet
Composer's note:

> *An opening clarinet solo introduces the main thematic material for the whole of this one-movement piece. There are four distinct melodic ideas that form the basis of the piece. The first idea is a long held note which, after a crescendo, briefly touches the notes above and below and returns to itself. This idea is dramatic yet "held" in place. The second idea ascends slowly and quietly. The third is a consonant short arpeggiation that rises, rests, and falls. Although this has the effect of an interlude, it later becomes the basis for a larger section. (For those of you who like Bartók, you might recognize this from his* Contrasts. *I never have been able to shed this particular motive!) The fourth theme is another "held" motive, this time a wide interval (a tenth) that is slow and dolce. It appears at the end of the solo when the quartet quietly comes in, picking up the final notes of the clarinet solo. These four ideas are developed and transformed throughout the piece, taking on recognizable but different identities as they interact more and more with each other.*

Premiere:

- April 21, 1995. Chamber Music Society of Lincoln Center: David Shifrin, clarinet; Theodore Arm, Ani Kavafian, violins; Paul Neubauer, viola; Fred Sherry, 'cello. Alice Tully Hall, New York, NY

Selected Performances:

- September 6, 1998. Da Capo Chamber Players, Meighan Stoops, clarinet. Bard College, Annandale-on-Hudson, NY
- September 10, 1998. Chamber Music Society of Lincoln Center with David Shifrin, clarinet. Merkin Concert Hall, New York, NY
- February 21, 1999. Muir String Quartet and Mark Miller, clarinet. Hyperprism Contemporary Music Series, Gasson Hall, Boston College, Boston, MA

- May 27, 2003. Da Capo Chamber Players. Merkin Recital Hall, New York, NY

Recording:

- *Five American Clarinet Quintets.* 1998. Delos 3183. David Shifrin and members of the Chamber Music Society of Lincoln Center. **D76**

See: **B69, B232, B277, B326, B349, B516, B582**

Works for Solo Instruments

W56. Ascent
©1996 Associated Music Publishers, Inc.
Duration: 10 minutes
Dedicated to Cherry Rhodes
Commissioned by the American Guild of Organists
Instrumentation: organ solo
Composer's note:
> *When I was approached to write this piece, I decided to keep the length deliberately brief (about ten minutes) mainly because this was the first time I had ever written music for the organ. The title* Ascent *is quite direct in its description of the upward-moving scales in the piece, which form the central thematic action. I would like to thank Cherry Rhodes for her invaluable help in determining registrations.*

Premiere:

- July 8, 1996. Cherry Rhodes, organ. American Guild of Organists National Convention, St. Ignatius Loyola Church, New York, NY

Recording:

- *Viaticum: A Journey of the Mind, Body, and Soul.* 2000. Loft Recordings LRCD 1005/06/07. 3 disks. Robert F. Bates, organ. **D3**

See: **B382, B447**

W57. Big Steps (Homage to Debussy's *Pas Sur la Neige*)
Written in 2004. Not yet published
Duration: 3 minutes
Instrumentation: solo piano

W58. Circles
©1964 American Composers' Alliance
Duration: 7 minutes
Instrumentation: solo piano
See: **B455**

W59. Clocks
©1985 Associated Music Publishers, Inc. AMP 7999. First printing: January 1989
Duration: 9 minutes

Dedicated to Sharon Isbin; suggested fingerings by Sharon Isbin
Instrumentation: solo guitar
Premiere:
- August 3, 1985. Sharon Isbin, guitar. Ordway Music Theatre, St Paul, MN
- October 24, 1994. David Leisner, guitar. Jordan Hall, Boston, MA
Recordings:
- *Nightshade Rounds: Virtuoso.* 1994. Virgin Records 45024. Sharon Isbin, guitar. **D12**
- *Marimba Tracks.* 2000. Orchard 7785. Transcribed for marimba and performed by Janis Potter. **D13**
See: **B72, B149, B408, B457**

W60. Composition for Oboe
©1965 American Composers' Alliance
Duration: 4 minutes
Written for Judith Martin
Instrumentation: solo oboe
Selected Performances:
- February 19, 1971. Livio Caroli, oboe. American Music Festival. New York, NY
See: **B458**

W61. Fantasia
©1966 American Composers' Alliance
Duration: 10 minutes
Instrumentation: solo piano
See: **B469**

W62. Hexachords
©1972 American Composers' Alliance
Duration: 6 minutes
Written for Patricia Spencer
Instrumentation: solo flute
Composer's note:
> *The title refers to the basic harmony of the piece, which is based on a six-note, unordered chromatic collection of pitches. The use of different vibrato speeds as applied to individual notes (or groups of notes) combined with different rhythmic-dynamic articulations placed in different registers, creates a counterpoint of tunes that hopefully keeps the listener's attention moving through all the registers. The piece is divided into five sections which are most easily differentiated by a sense of either going somewhere or staying somewhere.*

Premiere:
- February 26, 1972. Patricia Spencer, flute. Vanderbilt Hall, New York University, New York, NY

Selected Performances:
- April 8, 1972. Patricia Spencer, flute. Carnegie Hall, New York, NY
- November 16, 1972. Patricia Spencer, flute. Princeton University, Princeton, NJ
- March 7, 1982. Sara Stern, flute. Ring Auditorium, Hirshhorn Museum and Sculpture Garden, Washington, DC

Recordings:
- *American Contemporary-ACA Recording Award.* 1976. CRI S354 (LP). Da Capo Chamber Players: Patricia Spencer, flute. **D29**
- *Joan Tower: Chamber and Solo Works.* 1994. Composers' Recordings CRI 582. Patricia Spencer, flute. **D30**
- *American Flute Works.* 1995. Albany Records 167. Laurel Ann Maurer, flute. **D31**

See: **B167, B474, B580**

W63. No Longer Very Clear: A Suite for Piano

©2005 Associated Music Publishers, Inc. First printing: June 2005
Instrumentation: solo piano
Duration: 17 minutes
Composer's note:

> The titles for these pieces were taken from lines of a poem by John Ashbery called "No Longer Very Clear." (However, as with Debussy's Preludes, *the music came first.) The four pieces may be played individually or in the printed order as a suite. If* Throbbing Still *is to be played separately, it is preferable that it be preceded by* Vast Antique Cubes.

Recording:
- *Joan Tower: Instrumental Music.* 2005. Naxos 8.559215. Melvin Chen, Ursula Oppens, piano. **D46**

See: **B103, B182, B258, B491**

I. Holding a Daisy

Written 1996, ©2005 Associated Music Publishers, Inc.
Duration: 4 minutes
Dedicated to and commissioned by Sarah Rothenberg
Instrumentation: solo piano
Composer's note:

> The image is of a Georgia O'Keefe flower painting, not as innocent as it appears.

Premiere:
- March 19, 1996. Sarah Rothenberg, piano. Miller Theatre, Columbia University, New York, NY

Selected Performances:
- July 28, 1998. Stephanie Brown, piano. Santa Fe Chamber Music Festival, Santa Fe, NM

- February 21, 1999. John McDonald, piano. Hyperprism Contemporary Music Series. Gasson Hall, Boston College, Boston, MA
- February 23, 2000. Bari Mort, piano. Olin Auditorium, Bard College, Annandale-on-Hudson, NY
- January 16, 2004. Ursula Oppens, piano. Making Music Series. Carnegie Hall, New York, NY
- October 11, 2005. Sarah Rothenberg, piano. Menil Collection, Houston, TX

See: **B11, B98, B135, B475, B539, B540**

II. Or Like a . . . an Engine
©1994, ©2005 Associated Music Publishers, Inc.
Duration: 3 minutes
For Ursula Oppens
For WNYC-FM's 50th Anniversary
Instrumentation: solo piano
Also published in *American Contemporary Masters: A Collection of Works for Piano*. New York: G. Schirmer, Inc., 1995.
Composer's note:
> *This is a motoric piece, somewhat like a virtuosic Chopin etude.*

Premiere:
- June 13, 1994. Ursula Oppens, piano. Alice Tully Hall, New York, NY

Selected Performances:
- July 28, 1998. Stephanie Brown, piano. Santa Fe Chamber Music Festival, Santa Fe, NM
- February 21 1999. John McDonald, piano. Hyperprism Contemporary Music Series. Gasson Hall, Boston College, Boston, MA
- August 10, 2002. Melvin Chen, piano. Maverick Concert Series, Woodstock, NY
- January 16, 2004. Ursula Oppens, piano. Making Music Series. Carnegie Hall, New York, NY
- October 11, 2005. Sarah Rothenberg, piano. Menil Collection, Houston, TX

See: **B11, B98, B135, B258, B352, B494, B539, B540**

III. Vast Antique Cubes
©2000, ©2005 Associated Music Publishers, Inc.
Duration: 3 minutes
Commissioned by Franklin and Marshall College for John Browning
Instrumentation: solo piano
Composer's note:

In Vast Antique Cubes, *I wanted to create a sense of a very large space that moved quite slowly from low to high and higher still. Within this reaching upwards are suggestions of Debussy and Chopin, two composers whom I play frequently as a pianist.*

Premiere:
- September 16, 2000. John Browning, piano. Barshinger Center for the Arts at Franklin and Marshall College, Lancaster, PA

Selected Performances:
- May 24, 2001. Emma Tahmizián, piano. Merkin Concert Hall, New York, NY
- February 22, 2002. Melvin Chen, piano. Olin Hall, Bard College, Annandale-on-Hudson, NY
- January 16, 2004. Melvin Chen, piano. Making Music Series. Carnegie Hall, New York, NY

See: **B11, B42, B98, B135, B145, B284, B325, B519**

IV. Throbbing Still

Written 2000, ©2005 Associated Music Publishers, Inc.
Duration: 7 minutes
Commissioned by Franklin and Marshall College for John Browning
Instrumentation: solo piano
Composer's note:

In the much more energetic and faster Throbbing Still, *the music of Stravinsky and the Latin Inca rhythms I grew up with in South America continue to play a powerful role—to "throb still" in my music.*

Premiere:
- September 16, 2000. John Browning, piano. Barshinger Center for the Arts at Franklin and Marshall College, Lancaster, PA

Selected Performances:
- May 24, 2001. Emma Tahmizián, piano. Merkin Concert Hall, New York, NY
- February 22, 2002. Melvin Chen, piano. Olin Hall, Bard College, Annandale-on-Hudson, NY
- January 16, 2004. Melvin Chen, piano. Making Music Series. Carnegie Hall, New York, NY

See: **B11, B42, B98, B135, B145, B284, B325, B513**

W64. Platinum Spirals

Written 1976, ©1981 Associated Music Publishers, Inc.
Duration: 7 minutes
Dedicated "to the memory of my father"
Commissioned by the National Endowment for the Arts
Instrumentation: violin solo

Composer's note:

> Platinum Spirals . . . *is dedicated to the memory of my father, who was a geologist and mining engineer. Platinum is a mineral whose internal properties reveal a very malleable and flexible set of characteristics. It is said that an ounce of platinum can be stretched into a mile. A lot of this piece is about the stretching of lines upward in "spirals." Other times there is a quiet kind of "rocking" pattern that "holds" the action in place.*

Premiere:

- April 21, 1976. Joel Lester, violin. Carnegie Recital Hall, New York, NY

Selected Performances:

- November 13, 1984. John Baldwin, violin. Oberlin College Conservatory of Music, Oberlin, OH
- February 12, 1999. ALEA III with Peter Zazofsky, violin. Tsai Performance Center, Boston University, Boston, MA

Recordings:

- *Joan Tower: Platinum Spirals, Noon Dance, Wings, Amazon.* 1984. CRI SD517. Joel Smirnoff, violin. **D56**
- *Joan Tower: Chamber and Solo Works.* 1994. Composers' Recordings CRI 582. Joel Smirnoff, violin. **D57**
  See: **B109, B360, B498**

W65. Red Garnet Waltz

Written 1977, © 1978
Dedicated "with love to Bob"
Published in *Waltzes by 25 Contemporary Composers.* New York: C.F. Peters, 1978.
Recordings:

- *The Waltz Project Revisited: New Waltzes for Piano.* 2004. Albany Records. Eric Moe, piano. **D61**
- *The Waltz Project.* 1981. Nonesuch D-79011. Alan Feinberg, piano. **D62**
  See: **B84, B291, B503**

W66. Six Variations

©1971 American Composers' Alliance
Duration: 10 minutes
Dedicated to Helen Harbison
Instrumentation: solo 'cello
Premiere:

- May 17, 1971. Helen Harbison, 'cello. Greenwich House Music School, New York, NY

Selected Performances:

- January 17, 1972. Fred Sherry, 'cello. Manhattan School of Music, New York, NY

See: **B506**

W67. Wild Purple
©1998 Associated Music Publishers, Inc. First printing: December 2001
Duration: 6 minutes
Dedicated to Paul Neubauer
Instrumentation: viola solo
Composer's note:

> *I've always thought of the viola sound as being the color purple. Its deep, resonant, and luscious timbre seems to embody all kinds of hues of purple. I never thought of the viola as being particularly wild. So I decided to try and see if I could create a piece that had wild energy in it and meet the challenge of creating a virtuosic piece for solo viola.*

Premiere:
- September 10, 1998. Paul Neubauer, viola. Merkin Concert Hall, New York, NY.

Selected Performances:
- November 23, 1998. Phyllis Kamrin, viola. War Memorial and Performing Arts Center, San Francisco, CA
- February 19, 1999. Paul Nebauer, viola. Fine Arts Concert Hall, University of Wyoming, Laramie, WY
- August 10, 2002. Marka Gustavsson, viola. Maverick Concert Hall, Woodstock, NY
- January 16, 2004. Paul Neubauer, viola. Making Music Series. Carnegie Hall, New York, NY

Recording:
- *Joan Tower: Instrumental Music.* 2005. Naxos 8559215. Paul Neubauer, viola. **D78**

See: **B11, B69, B78, B98, B103, B135, B182, B284, B327, B349, B521**

W68. Wings
Written 1981, ©1983 Associated Music Publishers, Inc.
Duration: 9 minutes
Dedicated to Laura Flax
Instrumentation: solo clarinet or bass clarinet
Composer's note:

> *The image behind the piece is one of a large bird—perhaps a falcon— at times flying very high, gliding along the thermal currents, barely moving. At other moments, the bird goes into elaborate flight patterns that loop around, diving downwards, gaining tremendous speeds.*

Premiere:
- December 14, 1981. Laura Flax, clarinet, Merkin Recital Hall, New York, NY

Selected Performances:
- April 28, 1983. Laura Flax, clarinet. Carnegie Recital Hall, New York, NY

- November 13, 1984. Lawrence McDonald, clarinet. Oberlin College Conservatory of Music, Oberlin, OH
- May 16, 1988. Laura Flax, clarinet. Performed with dancer Peter Sparling. Merkin Concert Hall, New York, NY
- December 3, 1994. Loren Kitt, clarinet. Ring Auditorium, Hirshhorn Museum, Washington, DC
- February 11, 1996. Paul Roe, clarinet. Hugh Lane Gallery, Dublin, Ireland
- February 15, 1998. Bil Jackson, clarinet. Modern Music Festival, University of Colorado–Boulder, CO
- October 8, 1998. Daniel Silver, clarinet. Festival of American Music. Corcoran Art Gallery, Washington, DC
- February 21, 1999. Mark Miller, clarinet. Hyperprism Contemporary Music Series. Gasson Hall, Boston College, Boston, MA
- April 30, 2002. Charles Neidich, clarinet. Kennedy Center Terrace Theatre, Washington, DC

Recordings:
- *Joan Tower: Platinum Spirals, Noon Dance, Wings, Amazon.* 1984. Composers' Recordings CRI SD517. Laura Flax, clarinet. **D79**
- *Joan Tower: Chamber and Solo Works.* 1994. Composers' Recordings CRI 582. Laura Flax, clarinet. **D80**
- *Joan Tower Music for Clarinet.* 1995. Summit Records DCD 124. Robert Spring, clarinet. **D81**

See: **B14, B29, B75, B77, B134, B219, B288, B301, B321, B355, B360, B384, B407, B409, B522, B572**

W69. Wings (arranged for saxophone)
©1991 Associated Music Publishers, Inc.
Duration: 9 minutes
Dedicated to John Sampen, Steve Stusek, and Arno Bornkamp "with thanks for their help and advice in transcribing this piece for saxophone"
Instrumentation: solo alto saxophone
Selected Performances:
- February 9, 1997. Jeffrey Collins, saxophone. Moore Auditorium, Webster University, Kansas City, MO

Recordings:
- *The Electric Saxophone.* 1997. Capstone 8636. John Sampen, electric saxophone. **D82**
- *America's Millenium Tribute to Adolphe Sax, Vol. 2.* 1999. Arizona State University Recordings 3068. Bill Perconti, saxophone. **D83**
- *Juggernaut.* 2002. Equilibrium Records 49. Jeremy Justeson, alto saxophone. **D84**
- *Visions in Metaphor.* 2001. Albany Records 442. John Sampen, saxophone. **D85**

- *Sequenza: The Boston Conservatory New Music Festival.* 2001. ST TBCCD. B447 S4 n.9b Disk 1, 2. Saxophone studio of Kenneth Radnofsky. **D86**
- *When Wind Comes to Sparse Bamboo.* 2003. Capstone Records CPS-8717. Demetrius Spaneas, tenor saxophone (solo saxophone with electronic effects). **D87**

See: **B262, B385, B523, B578**

W70. Valentine Trills for Flute
©1996 Associated Music Publishers, Inc.
Duration: 2 minutes
Dedicated to and edited by Carol Wincenc
Instrumentation: solo flute
Also published in *Valentines.* New York: Carl Fischer, 1999. Carol Wincenc, ed.
Performer's (and dedicatee's) note:

> Valentine Trills *is one of the most effective solo pieces I play. Audiences are awed by the continuous trilling, turning, spinning, and seemingly breathless quality in the piece—all which builds to a thrilling climax. Keep the pace "on the edge" right up to the last few trilling statements. The articulation needs to be brilliantly clear, and all the dynamic changes exaggerated from the surging fff to the hushed ppp at the end. If you can circular breathe, all the better.*

Premiere:

- February 14, 1996. Carol Wincenc, flute. Merkin Concert Hall, New York, NY

Selected Performances:

- April 6, 2000. Carol Wincenc, flute. Flute Society of St. Louis, Sheldon Concert Hall, St. Louis, MO
- March 29, 2005. Carol Wincenc, flute. Trinity Baptist Church, San Antonio, TX

See: **B32, B80, B517, B559, B560**

W71. Valentine Trills for Orchestra
Written 1996, ©1998 Associated Music Publishers, Inc.
Duration: 2 minutes
Instrumentation: Arranged by the composer for orchestra in honor of Leonard Slatkin's last performance with the St. Louis Symphony Orchestra
Available as rental from the publisher
Premiere:

- May 19, 1996. St. Louis Symphony, Leonard Slatkin, conductor. Powell Hall, St. Louis, MO

See: **B518**

Works in Progress

Dumbarton Quintet
Duration: 14 minutes
Commissioned by Dumbarton Oaks Research Library, Washington, DC
Instrumentation: piano and string quartet

Can I?
Duration: 7 minutes
Anticipated premiere: Spring 2008
Commissioned by Young People's Chorus of New York City: Transient
    Glory, Francesco Nunez, conductor
Instrumentation: children's choir

A Gift
Instrumentation: piano and wind quartet
Duration: 15 minutes
Commissioned by Chamber Music Northwest for performances in July
    2008
Anticipated performers: David Shifrin, clarinet; Tara O'Connor, flute; Mi-
    lan Turkovic, bassoon; William Purvis, horn; Anne Marie McDermott,
    piano

Untitled
Instrumentation: piano trio
Commissioned by a consortium including: La Jolla Chamber Music Festi-
    val, Seattle Chamber Music Festival, Virginia Arts Festival, Chamber
    Music Society of Lincoln Center
Anticipated premiere: August 2007
Anticipated performers: Cho-Liang, violin; André Michel Schub, piano;
    Gary Hoffman, 'cello

Early, Unpublished Works

Aspect I–V
From the 1960s
Instrumentation: violin, cello, clarinet

Composition
September 1965
Duration: 4 minutes
Instrumentation: solo oboe

Composition for Orchestra

1967, corrected 1972.
Instrumentation: 2 flutes (pic), 2 oboes, English Horn, 2 clarinets, 4 horns, 3
    trumpets, 2 trombones, (BTrb), tuba, 4 percussion: percussion #1: 3
    timpani, marimba, triangle. percussion #2: 3 tom-toms (high, medium,
    low), woodblock, pipe, high cymbal. percussion #3: low cymbal, large
    gong, bass drum. percussion #4: xylophone, vibraphone, piano, strings
Selected Performances:
- December 30, 1971. Buffalo Philharmonic Orchestra, John Landis,
    conductor. Readings of Works by New York State Composers, Buffalo,
    NY

Five Pieces
October 1969
Instrumentation: violin and piano

Motet
1963
Instrumentation: 2 sopranos, tenor, bass or violin, clarinet, viola, bassoon

Octet
1968
Duration: 8 minutes
Instrumentation: flute, clarinet, violin, viola, 'cello, bass, vibraphone or ma-
    rimba, piano

Piano Piece
January 1964
Duration: 3 minutes
Instrumentation: solo piano

Pillars
1961
Dedicated "to Messrs. Calabro and Novak"
Instrumentation: 2 pianos and percussion: xylophone, cymbal, snare, gong,
    glockenspiel, timpani, bass drum, triangle
Premiere:
- April 19, 1961. Lionel Nowak and Reinhoud van der Linde, pianos;
    Kay Reynolds, Louis Calabro, Henry Brant, and George Finckel, per-
    cussion. Bennington College, Bennington, VT

Prelude (arr. for woodwind quartet and piano)
1970
Instrumentation: flute, oboe, clarinet, bassoon, piano
Selected Performances:
- February 20, 1971. Joan Tower, piano; Patricia Spencer, flute; Steven
    Bernstein, oboe; Christopher Sereque, clarinet; David Miller, bassoon;

Joe Spivacke, conductor. American Music Festival, New York, NY
- March 12, 1971. Joan Tower, piano; Patricia Spencer, flute; Steven Bernstein, oboe; Christopher Sereque, clarinet; David Miller, bassoon; Joe Spivacke, conductor. Greenwich House Music School, New York, NY

Study I
March 1965
Duration: 5 minutes
Instrumentation: horn, violin, clarinet, 'cello

Quintet
From the 1960s
Instrumentation: 2 flutes, 2 clarinets, bass clarinet

Works Written for or Dedicated to Joan Tower

Piano and tape piece by Joan La Barbara
Performed: March 20, 1978. Joan Tower, piano. Christ and St. Stephen's Episcopal Church, New York, NY

Joan's by Charles Wuorinen
Instrumentation: piano, clarinet, flute, violin, 'cello
Written for the 10th anniversary of the Da Capo Chamber Players
Premiere: March 23, 1980. Alice Tully Hall, New York, NY

For Joan on her 50th by John Corigliano
Instrumentation: Quintet
Commissioned by the Da Capo Chamber Players for Joan's 50th birthday
Premiere: October 24, 1988. Merkin Concert Hall, New York, NY

Minuet from Short Suite by John Harbison
Instrumentation: Quartet
Commissioned by the Da Capo Chamber Players for Joan's 50th birthday
Premiere: October 24, 1988. Merkin Concert Hall, New York, NY

Fifty Bars for Joan by Bruce MacCombie
Instrumentation: Quintet
Commissioned by the Da Capo Chamber Players for Joan's 50th birthday
Premiere: October 24, 1988. Merkin Concert Hall, New York, NY

Tower Power by Joseph Schwantner
Instrumentation: Quintet

Commissioned by the Da Capo Chamber Players for Joan's 50th birthday
Premiere: October 24, 1988. Merkin Concert Hall, New York, NY

Para Jote Delate by Tania León
Instrumentation: Quintet
Commissioned by the Da Capo Chamber Players for Joan's 50th birthday
Premiere: October 24, 1988. Merkin Concert Hall, New York, NY

Spiraling Towers for Violin Alone by Elmar Oliveira
Instrumentation: violin
Commissioned by the Da Capo Chamber Players for Joan's 60th birthday
Premiere: September 10, 1998. Merkin Concert Hall, New York, NY

A Perrrrft Day by Rhoda Levine
Instrumentation: improvisational vocal group
Premiere: September 10, 1998. Merkin Concert Hall, New York, NY, for
Joan's 60th birthday. Performed by *Play It By Ear,* Rhoda Levine, director

Arcana XVI by Kyle Gann
Instrumentation: solo piano
1998

Piano Trio by Jennifer Higdon
I. Pale Yellow II. Fiery Red
Instrumentation: piano trio
Duration: 15 minutes
Premiere: July 15, 2003. Bravo!Vail Music Festival. Adam Neiman, piano,
Alisa Weilerstein, 'cello; Anne Akiko Meyers, violin

Divertimento in F: Fury (to Joan Tower) by Jack Stamp
1995. Citadel Records 88108. Keystone Wind Ensemble, Indiana University
of Pennsylvania. Jack Stamp, conductor.
See: **D9**

Trio by Steven Burke
Instrumentation: piano trio

Impala by Marcus Parris
Instrumentation: orchestra
Premiere: May 19, 2006. American Symphony Orchestra, Leon Botstein,
conductor. Bard College, Annandale-on-Hudson, NY

Music for Film and **Lost in the Long Grass** by Cameron Bossert
Instrumentation: orchestra

Premiere: May 19, 2006. American Symphony Orchestra, Leon Botstein, conductor. Bard College, Annandale-on-Hudson, NY

The Instant Gathers by Joan Panetti
Instrumentation: violin, 'cello, piano
Premiere: June 3, 2006. Mayucki Fukuhara, violin; Daire Fitzgerald, 'cello, and Joan Panetti, piano. Second Helpings, Chelsea Museum, New York, NY

Joan Tower and Aymara, La Paz, Bolivia, circa 1949.

The Tower family prepares to board an international flight in 1951. From left: Joan Tower, George Warren Tower III, George Tower IV, and Anna Peabody Robinson Tower. Joan's sister Ellen was enrolled in college at the time.

Joan Tower's high school graduation picture, circa 1958. *Photo courtesy of Walnut Hill School, Natick, Massachusetts.*

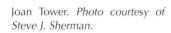

Joan Tower. *Photo courtesy of Steve J. Sherman.*

Joan Tower with her husband Jeff Litfin. *Photo courtesy of Douglas Baz, Barrytown, New York.*

Tower's workspace in Red Hook, New York. *Photo courtesy of Ellen K. Grolman.*

The Da Capo Chamber Players. Bottom row from left: Joel Lester and Joan Tower. Middle row from left: Patricia Spencer and Laura Flax. Top: André Emelianoff. *Photo courtesy of Jane Hamborsky.*

Joan Tower and former St. Louis Symphony conductor Leonard Slatkin after the 1987 premiere of *Silver Ladders*. *Photo courtesy of the St. Louis Symphony Orchestra.*

Joan Tower and former New York Philharmonic conductor Zubin Mehta peruse the score of Tower's *Sequoia* before the 1982 performance. *Photo courtesy of Kathleen M. Ron.*

Part IV: Discography

Discography

D1. **Amazon** in *Joan Tower: Platinum Spirals, Noon Dance, Wings, Amazon*
Composers' Recordings CRI SD517
Vinyl LP (1984)
Da Capo Chamber Players
Recorded at the American Academy and Institute of Arts and Letters,
New York, NY, December 12, 1984
See: **W23, W24**

D2. **Amazon** in *Joan Tower: Chamber and Solo Works*
Composers' Recordings CRI 582. ASIN: B000005TU9
Compact Disk (1994)
Da Capo Chamber Players
See: **W23, W24**

D3. **Ascent** in *Viaticum: A Journey of the Mind, Body, and Soul*
Loft Recordings LRCD 1005/06/07. ASIN: B00005231Y
3 Compact Disks (2000)
Robert F. Bates, organ
Recorded January 23–28, 2000, Stanford Memorial Church, Seattle, WA
Also on the CD: works by Arvo Pärt, Robert Bates, Jean Guillou, György
Ligeti, Jehan Alain, Jeanne Demessieux, and others
See: **W56**

D4. **Big Sky** in *Joan Tower: Instrumental Music*
Naxos 8559215. ASIN: B000A17GHY
Compact Disk (2005)
Chee-Yun, violin; André Emelianoff, 'cello; Joan Tower, piano
Recorded at the American Academy of Arts and Letters, New York, NY,
January 17–18, 2004
See: **W27**

D5. **Black Topaz** in *Black Topaz*
New World Records 80470-2. ASIN: B0000030IQ
Compact Disk (1995)
Laura Flax, clarinet; Patricia Spencer, flute; Jonathan Haas, Deborah
Moore, percussion; Stephen Gosling, piano; Michael Powell,
trombone; Chris Gekker, trumpet, Joan Tower, conductor
See: **W28**

D6.   Breakfast Rhythms I and II in *American Contemporary-ACA Recording Award*
Composers' Recordings CRI SD354
Vinyl LP (1976)
Da Capo Chamber Players
Also on the album: works by Elias Tanenbaum
See: **W29**

D7.   Breakfast Rhythms I and II in *Joan Tower: Chamber and Solo Works*
Composers' Recordings CRI 582. ASIN: B000005TU9
Compact Disk (1994)
Da Capo Chamber Players
See: **W29**

D8.   Breakfast Rhythms I and II in *Joan Tower Music for Clarinet*
Summit Records DCD 124. ASIN: B0000038IW
Compact Disk (1995)
Robert Spring, clarinet; Ensemble 21: J.B. Smith, Magdalena Martinic, Richard Bock, Marc Stocker, Arthur Weisberg, director
See: **W29**

D9.   Celebration Fanfare from Stepping Stones in *Divertimento/Wind Music of American Composers*
Citadel Records 88108. ASIN: B000003JVV
Compact Disk (1995)
Keystone Wind Ensemble, Jack Stamp, conductor
Also on CD: works by David Diamond, Fisher Tull, Robert Washburn, and a piece by Jack Stamp dedicated to Joan Tower: *Divertimento in F: Fury (to Joan Tower)*
See: **W1**

D10. Clarinet Concerto in *Joan Tower Music for Clarinet*
Summit Records DCD 124. ASIN: B0000038IW
Compact Disk (1995)
Robert Spring, clarinet; Eckart Sellheim, piano
See: **W5**

D11. Clarinet Concerto in *Joan Tower Concertos*
D'note Classics 1016. ASIN: B000003YNK
Compact Disk (1997)
David Shifrin, clarinet; Louisville Orchestra, Max Bragado-Darman, conductor
See: **W5**

D12. Clocks in *Nightshade Rounds: Virtuoso: Sharon Isbin*

Virgin Records 45024. ASIN: B000002SQ9
Compact Disk (1994)
Also on the CD: works by William Walton, George Gershwin, John
   Duarte, Benjamin Britten, and Bruce MacCombie
See: **W59**

D13. Clocks in *Marimba Tracks*
Orchard 7785. ASIN: B000056NY9
Compact Disk (2000)
Transcribed for marimba and performed by Janis Potter
Also on the CD: works by Maurice Ravel, Heitor Villa-Lobos, Eric
   Ewazen, J.S. Bach, Paul Bissell, and Francisco Tarrega
See: **W59**

D14. Concerto for Orchestra in *Fanfares for the Uncommon Woman*
Koch International Classics 7469/Koch International Classics KIC 7630.
   ASIN: B00000JIND
Compact Disk (1999)
Colorado Symphony Orchestra, Marin Alsop, conductor
Recorded at Boettcher Concert Hall, Denver, CO
See: **W6**

D15. Duets for Orchestra in *Fanfares for the Uncommon Woman*
Koch International Classics 7469/ Koch International Classics KIC 7630.
   ASIN: B00000JIND
Compact Disk (1999)
Colorado Symphony Orchestra, Marin Alsop, conductor
Recorded at Boettcher Concert Hall, Denver, CO
See: **W7**

D16. Fanfare for the Uncommon Woman, No. 1 in *The American Album*
RCA 60778. ASIN: B000003F4K
Compact Disk (1991)
St. Louis Symphony Orchestra, Leonard Slatkin, conductor
Also on the CD: works by Aaron Copland, Morton Gould, John Philip
   Sousa, William Schuman, Charles Ives, Morton Gould, Victor
   Herbert, Virgil Thomson, Ferde Grofé, Katherine Gladney Wells,
   Samuel A. Ward
See: **W35**

D17. Fanfare for the Uncommon Woman, No. 1 in *Red Seal Century—
Soloists & Conductors*
RCA Victor Red Seal 63861. ASIN: B00005OLDB
2 Compact Disks (2001)
St. Louis Symphony Orchestra, Leonard Slatkin, conductor

Also on the CD: works by Fritz Kreisler, Pyotr Il'yich Tchaikovsky,
     Johann Sebastian Bach, Evelyn Glennie, Aaron Copland, and others
See: **W35**

D18. Fanfare for the Uncommon Woman, No. 1 in *Fanfares for the
Uncommon Woman*
     Koch International Classics 7469/Koch International Classics KIC 7630.
          ASIN: B00000JIND
     Compact Disk (1999)
     Colorado Symphony Orchestra, Marin Alsop, conductor
     Recorded at Boettcher Concert Hall, Denver, CO
     See: **W35**

D19. Fanfare for the Uncommon Woman, No. 2 in *Fanfares for the
Uncommon Woman*
     Koch International Classics 7469/Koch International Classics KIC 7630.
          ASIN: B00000JIND
     Compact Disk 1999
     Colorado Symphony Orchestra, Marin Alsop, conductor
     Recorded at Boettcher Concert Hall, Denver, CO
     See: **W36**

D20. Fanfare for the Uncommon Woman, No. 3 in *Fanfares for the
Uncommon Woman*
     Koch International Classics 7469/Koch International Classics KIC 7630.
          ASIN: B00000JIND
     Compact Disk (1999)
     Colorado Symphony Orchestra, Marin Alsop, conductor
     Recorded at Boettcher Concert Hall, Denver, CO
     See: **W37**

D21. Fanfare for the Uncommon Woman, No. 3 in *Feminine Escapes*
     Koch International Classics. ASIN: B00006GO8B
     2 compact disks (2002)
     Colorado Symphony Orchestra, Marin Alsop, conductor
     Also on the CD: works by Stella Sung, Amy Beach, Rebecca Clarke,
          Barbara Strozzi, Libby Larsen, Hildegard of Bingen, Florence B.
          Price
     See: **W37**

D22. Fanfare for the Uncommon Woman, No. 4 in *Fanfares for the
Uncommon Woman*
     Koch International Classics 7469/ Koch International Classics KIC 7630.
          ASIN: B00000JIND
     Compact Disk (1999)

Colorado Symphony Orchestra, Marin Alsop, conductor
Recorded at Boettcher Concert hall, Denver, CO
See: **W8**

D23. Fanfare for the Uncommon Woman, No. 5 in *Fanfares for the Uncommon Woman*
Koch International Classics 7469/Koch International Classics KIC 7630.
  ASIN: B00000JIND
Compact Disk (1999)
Colorado Symphony Orchestra, Marin Alsop, conductor
Recorded at Boettcher Concert hall, Denver, CO
See: **W38**

D24. Fanfare for the Uncommon Woman, No. 5 in *American Visions/American Brass Quintet*
Summit Records DCD 365. ASIN: B0000AINLU
Compact Disk (2003)
American Brass Quintet
Also on the CD: works by William Schuman, Robert Beaser, Melinda
  Wagner, Samuel Adler, Thomas Andrew
See: **W38**

D25. Fantasy . . . (Those Harbor Lights) in *Joan Tower: Music for Clarinet*
Summit Records DCD 124. ASIN: B0000038IW
Compact Disk (1995)
Robert Spring, clarinet; Eckart Sellheim, piano
See: **W39**

D26. Fantasy . . . (Those Harbor Lights) in *20th Century Works for Clarinet*
Katson Productions
Compact Disk (2004)
Keith Lemmons, clarinet; Maribeth Gunning, piano
Also on the CD: works by Katherine Hoover, Ida Gotkovsky, William
  Woods
See: **W39**

D27. Fascinating Ribbons in *The Bandorama*
Compact Disk (2000)
Indiana University Concert Band, Symphonic Band, and
  Wind Ensemble, Timothy Mahr, conductor
Archived at Indiana University (Bloomington, IN), CD 1060
See: **W2**

D28. Flute Concerto in *Joan Tower Concertos*

D'note Classics 1016. ASIN B000003YNK
Compact Disk (1997)
Carol Wincenc, flute; Louisville Orchestra, Max Bragado-Darman,
    conductor
See: **W9**

D29. Hexachords in *American Contemporary-ACA Recording Award*
Composers' Recordings CRI SD354
Vinyl LP (1976)
Patricia Spencer, flute
Also on the album: works by Elias Tanenbaum
See: **W62**

D30. Hexachords in *Joan Tower: Chamber and Solo Works*
Composers' Recordings CRI 582. ASIN: B000005TU9
Compact Disk (1994)
Patricia Spencer, flute
See: **W62**

D31. Hexachords *in American Flute Works*
Albany Records 167. ASIN: B00000049OY
Compact Disk (1995)
Laurel Ann Maurer, flute
Also on the CD: works by Aaron Copland, Samuel Barber, Meyer
    Kupferman, Leo Kraft, Robert Muczynski
See: **W62**

D32. In Memory in *Joan Tower: Instrumental Music*
Naxos 8559215. ASIN B000A17GHY
Compact Disk (2005)
Tokyo String Quartet
Recorded at the American Academy of Arts and Letters, New York, NY,
    January 17–18, 2004
See: **W42**

D33. Island Prelude for Solo Oboe and String Orchestra in *Meet the
Composer Orchestra Residency Series: Joan Tower*
Electra/Nonesuch Records 79245. ASIN: B000005J0F
Compact Disk (1990)
Peter Bowman, oboe, St. Louis Symphony Orchestra, Leonard Slatkin,
    conductor
Recorded at Powell Symphony Hall, St. Louis, MO
Previously released on Elektra/Nonesuch 79118 (string orchestra version)
See: **W43**

D34. Island Prelude for Oboe and String Orchestra in *Joan Tower*
First Edition Recordings FECD0025. ASIN: B0001WJNCS
Compact Disk (2004)
Peter Bowman, oboe; St. Louis Symphony Orchestra, Leonard Slatkin, conductor
Originally recorded in 1984 and released on Elektra/Nonesuch 79245 in 1990
See: **W43**

D35. Island Prelude for Oboe and String Quartet in *Joan Tower: Instrumental Music*
Naxos 8.559215. ASIN B000A17GHY
Compact Disk (2005)
Richard Woodhams, oboe; Tokyo String Quartet
See: **W43**

D36. Island Prelude for Oboe and Wind Quartet in *Dorian Wind Quintet: American Premieres*
Summit DCD 117. ASIN: B00000ICPC
Compact Disk (1995)
Dorian Wind Quintet
Also on the CD: works by Bruce Adolphe, Lalo Schifrin, Conrad de Jong, Lee Hoiby
See: **W43**

D37. Island Rhythms in *First Edition Recordings Recordings: The Louisville Symphony*
First Edition Recordings LCD006
Compact Disk (1991)
Louisville Symphony, Lawrence Leighton Smith, conductor
Also on the CD: works by Otto Luening, Sofia Gubaidulina
See: **W10**

D38. Island Rhythms in *Joan Tower*
First Edition Recordings FECD0025. ASIN: B0001WJNCS
Compact Disk (2004)
Louisville Orchestra, Lawrence Leighton Smith, conductor
Originally recorded in 1990 and released as LCD-006 in 1991
See: **W10**

D39. Island Rhythms in *The Slatkin Years*
Archmedia/St. Louis Symphony Orchestra
Compact Disk (1995)
St. Louis Symphony, Leonard Slatkin, conductor

Also on the CD: works by Karol Husa, Joseph Schwantner John Adams,
    Felix Mendelssohn, Franz Joseph Haydn, W.A. Mozart, and others
Available through the St. Louis Symphony Orchestra
See: **W10**

D40. Movements for Flute and Piano in *American Society of University
Composers, vols. 1–4, Journal of Music Scores*
    Advance Recording FGR-24S
    Vinyl LP (1978)
    Patricia Spencer, flute; Joan Tower, piano
    Also on the album: works by Bruce Taub, Robert Stern, James Hartway
    Previously released on Elektra/Nonesuch 79118
    See: **W44**

D41. Music for 'Cello and Orchestra in *Joan Tower*
    First Edition Recordings FECD0025. ASIN: B0001WJNCS
    Compact Disk (2004)
    Lynn Harrell, 'cello; St. Louis Symphony Orchestra, Leonard Slatkin,
        conductor
    Originally recorded in 1984 and released on Elektra/Nonesuch 79245 in
        1990
    See: **W12**

D42. Music for 'Cello and Orchestra in *Meet the Composer Orchestra
Residency Series: Joan Tower*
    Electra/Nonesuch Records 79245. ASIN: B000005J0F
    Compact Disk (1990)
    Lynn Harrell, 'cello; St. Louis Symphony Orchestra, Leonard Slatkin,
        conductor
    Recorded at Powell Symphony Hall, St. Louis, MO
    See: **W12**

D43. Night Fields in *Degas Quartet: Beethoven/Tower*
    Compact Disk (2003)
    Available from the Degas Quartet: www.degasquartet.com
    Also on this disk: Beethoven: *String Quartet Op. 18 No. 6*
    See: **W46**

D44. Night Fields in *Black Topaz*
    New World Records 80470-2. ASIN: B0000030IQ
    Compact Disk (1995)
    Muir String Quartet
    See: **W46**

D45. Night Fields in *Boston Conservatory Chamber Players: All-American Presidents' Day Concert*
Recorded February 14, 1999, by WGBH, Boston, MA
Digital audio tape available at Boston Conservatory:
ST DAT .F73 N5 (1999)
Also on the CD: works by Arthur Foote, Aaron Copland, Amy Beach
See: **W46**

D46. No Longer Very Clear: Vast Antique Cubes,[1] Throbbing Still,[2] Holding a Daisy,[3] Or Like a . . . an Engine[4] in *Joan Tower: Instrumental Music*
Naxos 8.559215. ASIN: B000A17GHY
Compact Disk (2005)
[1] and [2]: Ursula Oppens; [3] and [4]: Melvin Chen, piano
Recorded at the American Academy of Arts and Letters, New York, NY, January 17–18, 2004
See: **W63**

D47. Noon Dance in *Joan Tower: Platinum Spirals, Noon Dance, Wings, Amazon*
Composers' Recordings CRI SD517
Vinyl LP (1984)
Collage Ensemble
See: **W45**

D48. Noon Dance in *Joan Tower: Chamber and Solo Works*
Composers' Recordings CRI 582. ASIN: B000005TU9
Compact Disk (1994)
Collage Ensemble
Recorded previously on CRI SD517
See: **W45**

D49. Petroushskates in *Da Capo Chamber Players Celebrate Their 10th Anniversary*
Composers' Recordings CRI SD441
Vinyl LP (1981)
Da Capo Chamber Players
Also on the album: works by Joseph C. Schwantner, Shulamit Ran, Charles Wuorinen, George Perle, and Philip Glass
See: **W49**

D50. Petroushskates in *The Composer-Performer: Forty Years of Discovery, 1954–1994*
Composers' Recordings CD670. ASIN: B000005TWL
Compact Disk (1994)

Da Capo Chamber Players
Recorded February 23–24, 1981, Church of the Holy Trinity, New York,
NY
Original recording released on SD441: *Da Capo Chamber Players
Celebrate Their 10th Anniversary.* Subsequently re-recorded by Da
Capo and released on CRI CD582.
Also on the CD: works by Henry Cowell, Harry Partch, Irving Fine, Otto
Luening, Virgil Thomson, William Albright, George Walker, Harvey
Sollberger, Ned Rorem, Guy Klucevsek, Michael Gordon, Victoria
Jordanova, Tan Dun, Alice Shields, and others
See: **W49**

D51. Petroushskates in *Joan Tower: Chamber and Solo Works*
Composers' Recordings CRI 582. ASIN: B000005TU9
Compact Disk (1994)
Da Capo Chamber Players
See: **W49**

D52. Petroushskates in *eighth blackbird: Thirteen Ways*
Cedille Records CD67. ASIN: B00008ZL55
Compact Disk (2003)
eighth blackbird
Also on the CD: works by George Perle, David Schober
See: **W49**

D53. Petroushskates in *New Music Recital,* Arkansas State University,
College of Fine Arts, Department of Music
CD 1054
Compact Disk (2000)
Recorded November 20, 2000
See: **W49**

D54. Piano Concerto No. 1 (Homage to Beethoven) in *Joan Tower
Concertos*
D'note Classics 1016. ASIN: B000003YNK
Compact Disk (1997)
Ursula Oppens, piano; Louisville Orchestra, Joseph Silverstein, conductor
See: **W13**

D55. Piano Concerto No. 1 (Homage to Beethoven) in *American Piano
Concertos*
Koch Schwann 313332. ASIN: B00000K2FO
Also sold under the title *Amerikanische Klavierkonzerte*
Compact Disk (1999)

Paul Barnes, piano; Bohuslav Martinu Philharmonic, Kirk Trevor, conductor
Also on the CD: works by Victoria Bond and David Ott
See: **W13**

D56. Platinum Spirals in *Joan Tower: Platinum Spirals, Noon Dance, Wings, Amazon.*
Composers' Recordings CRI SD517
Vinyl LP (1984)
Joel Smirnoff, violin
Recorded at First and Second Church, Boston, MA, June 6, 1984
See: **W64**

D57. Platinum Spirals in *Joan Tower: Chamber and Solo Works*
Composers' Recordings CRI 582. ASIN: B000005TU9
Compact Disk (1994)
Joel Smirnoff, violin
See: **W64**

D58. Prelude for Five Players in *Three Movements for Quintet*
Composers' Recordings CRI 302/Douglass Phonodisc DMds 5003
Vinyl LP (1972)
Rolf Schulte, violin; Allen Blustein, clarinet; Sophie Sollberger flute; Fred Sherry, 'cello; Robert Miller, piano; Charles Wuorinen, conductor
Also on the album: works by Raoul Pleskow, Edward Miller, Elie Yarden
See: **W50**

D59. Rain Waves in *The Making of a Medium, vol. 13: American Images 2*
Crystal Records 943. ASIN: B000065V7R
Compact Disk (1993)
Verdehr Trio
Also on the CD: works by Sebastian Currier, William David Brohn
See: **W51**

D60. Rapids in *The Centennial Commissions: Celebrating the 100th Anniversary of the University of Wisconsin–Madison School of Music*
2 Compact Disks (2000)
Archived at University of Wisconsin–Madison, Madison, WI
Ursula Oppens, piano; University of Wisconsin–Madison Symphony Orchestra, David E. Becker, conductor
See: **W17**

D61. Red Garnet Waltz in *The Waltz Project Revisited: New Waltzes for Piano*

Albany Records. ASIN: B0006A9FQE
Compact Disk (2004)
Eric Moe, piano
Also on the CD: works by Hayes Biggs, Wayne Peterson, Robert Helps,
    Akin Euba, Andrew Imbrie, Anthony Cornicello, Charles Wuorinen,
    Karl Hohn, Lee Hyla, Lou Harrison, Matthew Rosenblum, Milton
    Babbitt, Philip Glass, Ricky Ian Gordon, Roger Sessions, Roger
    Zahab, Ronale Caltabiano, and Zygmunt Krauze
See: **W65**

D62. **Red Garnet Waltz** in *The Waltz Project*
Nonesuch D-79011/Douglass Phonodisc DMds 10954
Vinyl LP (1981)
Alan Feinberg, piano
Also on the album: works by Philip Glass, Milton Babbit, Lou Harrison,
    Roger Sessions, Joseph Fennimore, Zygmunt Krauze, Alden
    Ashforth, Tom Constanten, Robert Helps, Ivan Tcherepnin, Alan
    Stout, Peter Gena, Richard Feliciano, John Cage, and Virgil
    Thomson
See: **W65**

D63. **Sequoia** in *Meet the Composer Orchestra Residency Series: Joan Tower*
Electra/Nonesuch Records 79245. ASIN: B000005J0F
Compact Disk (1990)
St. Louis Symphony Orchestra, Leonard Slatkin, conductor
Recorded at Powell Symphony Hall, St. Louis, MO
Previously released on Elektra/Nonesuch 79118
See: **W15**

D64. **Sequoia** in *The Infernal Machine*
Nonesuch 79118/Douglass Phonodisc DMds 9119
Vinyl LP (1986)
St. Louis Symphony Orchestra, Leonard Slatkin, conductor
Recorded November 25, 1984, Powell Symphony Hall, St. Louis, MO
Also on the album: works by Donald Erb and Christopher Rouse
See: **W15**

D65. **Sequoia** in *New York Philharmonic: An American Celebration Sampler,
vol. 2*
New York Philharmonic 1955. ASIN: B0001PEB18
10 Compact Disks (1999)
Sequoia originally recorded in 1982
New York Philharmonic, Zubin Mehta, conductor
Also on the CD: works by Samuel Barber, Leonard Bernstein, John
    Bolcom, Aaron Copland, George Crumb, David Diamond, Duke

Ellington, Lukas Foss, Ned Rorem, Gunther Schuller, Ellen Taaffe Zwilich, and others
See: **W15**

D66. Sequoia in *Joan Tower*
First Edition Recordings FECD0025. ASIN: B0001WJNCS
Compact Disk (2004)
St. Louis Symphony Orchestra, Leonard Slatkin, conductor
Originally recorded in 1984 and released on Elektra/Nonesuch 79245 in 1990
See: **W15**

D67. Silver Ladders in *Meet the Composer Orchestra Residency Series: Joan Tower*
Electra/Nonesuch Records 79245. ASIN: B000005J0F
Compact Disk (1990)
St. Louis Symphony Orchestra, Leonard Slatkin, conductor
Recorded at Powell Symphony Hall, St. Louis, MO
See: **W16**

D68. Silver Ladders in *First Edition Music: World Premiere Collection*
Naxos FECD 32. ASIN: B0007DA4GA
Compact Disk (2005)
Re-release of the 1990 recording of *Silver Ladders* on *Meet the Composer Orchestra Residency Series: Joan Tower*
Electra/Nonesuch Records 79245. ASIN: B000005J0F
St. Louis Symphony Orchestra, Peter Bowman, oboe, Leonard Slatkin, conductor
Also on the CD: works by Alan Hovhaness, Andrzej Panufnik, Christopher Rouse, George Crumb, Heitor Villa-Lobos, Henry Cowell, John Corigliano, John Harbison, Karel Husa, Lou Harrison, Luigi Dallapiccola, Ned Rorem, Roy Harris, and Walter Piston
See: **W16**

D69. Silver Ladders in *Joan Tower*
First Edition Recordings LCD 006
Compact Disk (2004)
St. Louis Symphony Orchestra, Leonard Slatkin, conductor
See: **W16**

D70. Snow Dreams in *Black Topaz*
New World Records 80470. ASIN: B0000030IQ
Compact Disk (1995)
Carol Wincenc, flute; Sharon Isbin, guitar
See: **W54**

D71. **Snow Dreams** in *Chronicles of Discovery: American Music for Flute and Guitar*
Albany Records 379. ASIN: B00004SQZZ
Compact Disk (2000)
Bonita Boyd, flute; Nicholas Goluses, guitar
Also on the CD: works by Augusta Read Thomas, Katherine Hoover, and Roberto Sierra
See: **W54**

D72. **Snow Dreams** in *Terry Riley: Cantos Desiertos*
Naxos 8.559146. ASIN: B00009NHBP
Compact Disk (2003)
Alexandra Hawley, flute; Jeffrey McFadden, guitar
Also on the CD: works by Terry Riley, Robert Beaser, Lowell Liebermann
See: **W54**

D73. **Stepping Stones** in *Black Topaz*
New World Records 80470. ASIN: B0000030IQ
Compact Disk (1995)
Double Edge: Edmund Niemann and Nurit Tiles, piano
See: **W3, W4**

D74. **Trés Lent (Hommage à Messiaen)** in *Born in America 1938: Music for 'Cello*
Gasparo Records GSCD 351
Compact Disk (2002)
Norman Fischer, 'cello; Jeanne Kierman, piano
See: **W53**

D75. **Trés Lent (Hommage à Messiaen)** in *Black Topaz*
New World Records 80470. ASIN: B0000030IQ
Compact Disk (1995)
André Emelianoff, 'cello; Joan Tower, piano
See: **W53**

D76. **Turning Points** in *Five American Clarinet Quintets*
Delos 3183. ASIN: B00000G4LI
Compact Disk (1998)
David Shifrin, clarinet; Theodore Arm and Ani Kavafian, violins; Paul Neubauer, viola; Fred Sherry, 'cello
Also on the CD: works by John Corigliano, Ellen Taaffe Zwilich, Bright Sheng, Bruce Adolphe
See: **W55**

D77. Violin Concerto in *Joan Tower Concertos*
D'note Classics 1016. ASIN: B000003YNK
Compact Disk (1997)
Elmar Oliveira, violin; Louisville Orchestra, Joseph Silverstein, conductor
See: **W21**

D78. Wild Purple in *Joan Tower: Instrumental Music*
Naxos 8559215. ASIN: B000A17GHY
Compact Disk (2005)
Paul Neubauer, viola
Recorded at the American Academy of Arts and Letters, New York, NY, January 17–18, 2004
See: **W67**

D79. Wings in *Joan Tower: Platinum Spirals, Noon Dance, Wings, Amazon*
Composers' Recordings CRI SD517
Vinyl LP (1984)
Laura Flax, clarinet
Recorded at the American Academy and Institute of Arts and Letters, New York, NY, December 12, 1984
See: **W68**

D80. Wings in *Joan Tower: Chamber and Solo Works*
Composers' Recordings CRI 582. ASIN: B000005TU9
Compact Disk (1994)
Laura Flax, clarinet
See: **W68**

D81. Wings in *Joan Tower Music for Clarinet*
Summit Records DCD 124. ASIN: B0000038IW
Compact Disk (1995)
Robert Spring, clarinet
See: **W68**

D82. Wings in *The Electric Saxophone*
Capstone 8636. ASIN: B000001YVA
Compact Disk (1997)
John Sampen, electric saxophone
Also on the CD: works by John Cage, Marilyn Shrude, Vladimir Ussachevsky, James Mobberley, Mary Stanley Bunce, Pablo Furman
See: **W69**

D83. Wings in *America's Millenium Tribute to Adolphe Sax, Vol. 2*
Arizona State University Recordings 3068. ASIN: B00000IM5X

Compact Disk (1999)
Bill Perconti, saxophone
Also on this CD: works by Robert Muczynski, Alfred Descenclos, Jay
    Vosk, Andrew Earle Simpson, Gregory W. Yasinitsky, Allan Blank,
    Wolfgang Amadeus Mozart
See: **W69**

D84. **Wings** in *Juggernaut*
Equilibrium Records 49. ASIN: B00006JJ2E
Compact Disk (2002)
Jeremy Justeson, alto saxophone
Also on the CD: David Maslanka, Rob Smith, and David Heuser
See: **W69**

D85. **Wings** in *Visions in Metaphor*
Albany Records 442. ASIN: B00005NF2U
Compact Disk (2001)
John Sampen, saxophone
Also on the CD: works by John Adams, Karel Husa, Pauline Oliveros,
    William Albright, Samuel Adler, Marilyn Shrude, Bernard Rands
See: **W69**

D86. **Wings** in *Sequenza: The Boston Conservatory New Music Festival*
ST TBCCD .B447 S4 n.9b Disk 1, 2
2 Compact Disks (2001)
Saxophone studio of Kenneth Radnofsky, Boston Conservatory
Archived at Boston Conservatory Library
Also on the CD: works by Luciano Berio, Marilyn Shrude, Charles
    Wuorinen, William Albright, Jeremy Beck, and others
See: **W69**

D87. **Wings** in *When Wind Comes to Sparse Bamboo*
Capstone Records CPS-8717. ASIN: B0000AQS87
Compact Disk (2003)
Demetrius Spaneas, tenor saxophone
Also on the CD: works by Johann Sebastian Bach, Benjamin Britten,
    Vincent Persichetti, Claude Debussy, Donald Martino, Sean Heim
See: **W69**

In Progress

D88. **Made in America, Tambor, Concerto for Orchestra**
Naxos 8.559328
Compact Disk (2007)

Nashville Symphony, Leonard Slatkin, conductor
See: **W6, W11, W19**

D89. DNA
New England Conservatory Percussion Ensemble, Frank Epstein, director
Not yet released
See: **W33**

Joan Tower Performs Works by Other Composers

D90. Riding the Wind in *New York Retrospective: Works by Harvey Sollberger*
CRI SD352. ASIN: B000005TYL
Compact Disk (1997)
Joan Tower with the Da Capo Chamber Players

D91. Voices from Elysium by Miriam Gideon in *Voices from Elysium*
New World Records 80543. ASIN: B00000AGK9
Compact Disk (1998)
Joan Tower with the Da Capo Chamber Players
Also on the CD: works by Louise Talma, Aaron Copland, Henry Cowell, Ruth Crawford-Seeger

D92. Diadem by Louise Talma in *Voices from Elysium*
New World Records 80543. ASIN: B00000AGK9
Compact Disk (1998)
Joan Tower with the Da Capo Chamber Players
Also on the CD: works by Miriam Gideon, Aaron Copland, Henry Cowell, Ruth Crawford-Seeger

D93. Vocalise by Henry Cowell in *Voices from Elysium*
New World Records 80543. ASIN: B00000AGK9
Compact Disk (1998)
Joan Tower with the Da Capo Chamber Players
Also on the CD: works by Miriam Gideon, Louise Talma, Aaron Copland, Ruth Crawford-Seeger

D94. When Summer Sang by Ursula Mamlok in *Chamber Works of Ursula Mamlok*
Composers' Recordings CRI 891
Compact Disk (2002)
Joan Tower with the Da Capo Chamber Players
Originally released by CRI as analog disk in 1966 (SD518)

Part V: Peer Reflections

Peer Reflections

Leonard Slatkin, Music Director of the National Symphony Orchestra in Washington D.C., Principal Guest Conductor of the Los Angeles Philharmonic, and former conductor of the St. Louis Symphony: During my years as Music Director in St. Louis I helped establish a Composers-in-Residence program. Joan was the second of a very distinguished group of creators. But Joan was also the most insecure. She never took the time to pat herself on the back for a composition well written. All of us would say, "Joan, this is a great piece!" But Joan refused to believe it. Every so often I would offer a friendly and experienced word of advice, usually pertaining to a bowing or an instrumental touch. Joan would berate herself for not having thought of it. I would tell her that this was only a suggestion, and that she shouldn't take my word as gospel. Thank heavens she didn't. Maybe more important was Joan's choice of wardrobe. When she arrived in St. Louis I don't believe "fashion" was the word you associated with her. One day my wife got a hold of Joan and they went shopping. I think this was a turning point in Joan's life. All of a sudden she had a newfound confidence and wrote her music with increasing skill. I understand she has turned a great deal of her attention to conducting. Fair enough—I do a little composing on the side. But like everything else with Joan, I'm certain that she undertakes this with a seriousness of purpose unlike anyone I know. Maybe someday she will conduct one of my pieces and then we will have come full circle. No—Joan has to take me shopping first.

Emerson Quartet (by David Finckel, 'cellist): I first heard of Joan Tower in the early 1980s. At that time, famous women composers were few and far between, and her success caught my attention, perhaps for the wrong reason. However, it was not long before I began to hear glowing reports about her music, especially from my colleagues in the chamber music world. By the mid-1990s I had heard much of her work and began to hope that we (my quartet, the Emerson, or my duo with Wu Han) would find the opportunity to commission works from her. My good fortunes brought me both: a marvelous String Quartet, *Incandescent,* which was premiered at Bard College and which has toured with us in the U.S., Europe, and the UK; and the piano trio *Big Sky,* which was commissioned by La Jolla Summerfest during the years that Wu Han and I artistic-directed the festival, 1980–2000.

It was in La Jolla that Joan and I first really worked together; she was composer-in-residence and I was the 'cellist for the trio's premiere. Being an intensely no-nonsense personality, anxious to get past formalities to the more important things in life, she set the stage for our collaboration by describing her work with my late uncle George Finckel, who was the 'cello teacher at Bennington College, where Joan went to school. George was a large personality and a magnetic teacher, whose enthusiasm, curiosity, and courage knew no bounds. Joan, who was studying piano, was conscripted by George to read through the Beethoven 'cello and piano sonatas on a daily basis, which apparently had a profound effect on her, as she still speaks of this experience with great relish and nostalgia.

After a short time working with Joan on her trio, we learned that her casual, unpretentious demeanor masks her astounding musical brilliance and exacting expectations—of herself, her music, and her performances. Never critical in a restrictive way, she is nonetheless demanding of her interpreters and extracts the best of them. She is a reasonable composer who is always ready to listen to suggestions, and she torments herself more than anyone else to ensure the quality of her pieces. At virtually every performance of her quartet that she has heard, she has tinkered with details, always searching for something that pleases her more. She is one of a diminishing number of composers who seem to really know what they have written, and what they have not, and this further increases the desire of her performers to do her scores justice.

Perhaps one of the most striking qualities of Joan's music is its vitality. Even in quiet passages there is a sense of her own joy of living, that something is always happening or about to happen. Frequently her music is imbued with wildness that borders on abandon, tossing technical anxieties to the wind and "going for it" with athletic exhilaration. I don't think she would be unhappy hearing anyone say that her music is fun to play, and I'm sure she'd rather her performers take some corners a bit too fast than be cautious for safety's sake. In this way, Joan's music lives in the moment and is completely human. It celebrates the present—performers and listeners in a room together experiencing something living and vital. Maybe it is this innate quality that allows her to speak so directly to audiences of all persuasions, and which keeps them at attention, hanging on every next note. Her voice is a precious presence in our time, when musicians and listeners are searching hungrily for meaning in new music. Truly interesting ideas, realized with compositional skill and informed by simple human passions, have brought Joan the prominence she deserves and the listeners who eagerly await her next compositions. I look forward to hearing, and hopefully performing, many of them.

Frances Richard, former associate director of Meet the Composer and current director of Concert Music for ASCAP: I first knew Joan Tower as the inspired force behind the Da Capo Chamber Players. I knew she was a good composer, and was impressed that she collaborated with great musicians to publicly perform works in which she believed. She was not about promoting herself and her music above all else. She was an excellent pianist, chamber musician, and a supportive colleague for her fellow composers. In other words, she was already an impressive musical citizen in the days when so many composers sat home by the telephone, hoping someone would call and want to play their music. And then, when it was played, they skulked in the recesses of concert halls; way in the back orchestra, under the balcony, hoping no one would see them.

She was right up there on the stage, with a presence and a cause! We became friends and I remember a few moments of that long friendship as outstanding, funny, revealing, and poignant. When the New York Philharmonic asked her to write them an orchestral piece (her first), we spoke about what she would write. I said, "You are the first woman composer commissioned by these old boys. There are enough of the flute and harp pieces. Announce your piece with a big bang. You are a woman. Show them you can make noise!" And she sure did. Then we talked about those four subscription performances for *Sequoia*, and she wanted to buy a different gown for each night to acknowledge the audience's applause. We discussed the fact that after all, the men wear the same tuxedo every night, and there was no reason to break the bank with four different gowns!

Then there was the time she called me and said she wanted to be rich and famous like Aaron Copland, and would write a *Fanfare for the Common Woman*. I told her that women were not common—that word had been used pejoratively about women for far too long. So she wrote the *Fanfare for the Uncommon Woman*, and I am very proud that she dedicated the third one to me. She invited me to attend the premiere. It was at the newly refurbished Carnegie Hall and was a televised special concert. There were flowers all across the front of the stage, and we had just sat down in our aisle seats when she was told that she had to stay behind the scenes, in the wings, during the performance so that she could come out and bow at the end. I told the Carnegie Hall functionary that she was the composer, and that she was attending the premiere of her new work and that she had to hear it in the hall, not in the wings. So they moved the flowers to make the little staircase in front of the stage accessible for her at the end of the piece. She did hear it in the hall, and then when the audience applauded walked up onto the stage to receive the applause she deserved. Joan Tower is funny, very human, very loyal, and incredibly modest. She is now a formidable American icon and has earned all the recognition and applause she gets. There may be other composers out there, but no one has the ability to laugh that Joan has.

Paul Barnes, pianist: I first met Joan Tower in March of 1995 when I organized a women's music festival with the Indianapolis Chamber Orchestra. I fell in love with her first *Piano Concerto* (1985) and eventually ended up recording it the following year for Koch International. I remember having a most fascinating conversation with Joan during the rehearsals for the concerto performance about her problematic relationship with Beethoven. She's a pianist and therefore had several of the sonatas in her hands. She was initially concerned that she would have to consciously shut out this obvious influence, thinking that her own voice would be confused with Beethoven's. After much struggling with this aesthetic issue, Joan finally said to Beethoven, "All right, just come on in but sit over there and be quiet!" Thus Joan no longer tried to repress her obvious love for Beethoven's piano music, but embraced it as part of herself. The 1985 *Piano Concerto* is a wonderful musical monument to her love of Beethoven.

Since that initial encounter with Joan, I have performed her solo compositions for piano (an unfortunately small number of works!) in several interesting and exotic locations. In 1999 I had the opportunity to perform in Jerusalem both *Holding a Daisy* and *Or like a . . . an Engine*, both based on the poem "No Longer Very Clear" by John Ashbery. But a most bizarre encounter occurred during this trip. After the recital, I was walking home to my hotel in the evening and looked across the street to find a most interesting poetry reading taking place. It was a bilingual event dedicated to both English and Hebrew poetry. I decided to walk in and look around. In the lobby of the auditorium where the readings were taking place, I saw several tables with books of poetry on them. To my great surprise, I found several works by John Ashbery, Joan Tower's colleague at Bard College on whose poem she had based her piano compositions I had just performed.

Filled with a certain guilt that I had actually not read the complete poem upon which these wonderful piano works were based, I was lucky to find the book that contained "No Longer Very Clear." I was elated as I read the beautiful poem. And then I realized that there were an unusually large number of John Ashbery books on the table. I look up from reading my poem and there in front of me is the poet himself! He actually knew who I was because Joan had mentioned the recording of the piano concerto I had done. So he signed my book and now at each performance of *Holding a Daisy* and *Or like a . . . an Engine*. I proudly read the poem from my personally autographed copy!

Since that bizarre encounter in Jerusalem, I've performed Joan's solo piano works in several cities including Moscow, St. Petersburg, Minsk, and also the Music Teacher's National Association Convention in Minneapolis. And I've also encouraged my piano students at the University of Nebraska–Lincoln School of Music to program her works. In fact, Joan was just in Lincoln a few weeks ago for the premiere of her *Viola Concerto* with the Omaha Symphony. I had two of my students play *Or like a . . . an Engine* for her. She loved it!

In fact, working with Joan back in 1995 began my own journey of working with living composers. The musical exhilaration that can result has really changed my professional life. Much of my performing life is now consumed with world premieres, most recently Philip Glass's *Piano Concerto No. 2 (After Lewis and Clark)* which I premiered last year with the Omaha Symphony. I really can trace this all back to Joan and the energy she exudes for new music. And to see this energy transfer to my students, to the next generation of pianists, was one of the most musically satisfying events of my life.

JoAnn Falletta, conductor: I had the happy opportunity of first meeting Joan Tower in the late 1980s when we were performing her *Amazon* with the Women's Philharmonic. I realized then that Joan was an absolutely extraordinary woman—a great composer, a superb musician, and a warm and wonderful person. Over the years I have had the chance to collaborate with her on many of her works and have found each a thrilling musical experience. The power of Joan's music is matched by the power of her personality—she is passionate, humorous, caring, and fiercely intelligent. I am sure that Joan did not have herself in mind when she wrote the extraordinary *Fanfare for the Uncommon Woman*, yet that is exactly what she is—a unique and uncommonly gifted artist and person. I am proud to call her my friend.

Kalichstein-Laredo-Robinson Trio (by Joseph Kalichstein, pianist): Joan e-mailed me recently to express her reaction to a taped Tanglewood performance she had just heard of her first piano trio, *For Daniel*, played by me and my trio partners, Jaime Laredo and Sharon Robinson. After sharing her very emotional response, she added that she got a special kick out of noticing that I had missed the same notes she always does when performing the Trio! That is Joan to a T: exuberant and enthusiastic, but honest; dead serious about music yet playfully funny; critical but always friendly. And with a great pair of ears! She belongs to that rare echelon of composers who, while very adamant and exact and knowl-edgeable about what they want, want more than anything else to get back from their works something extra that had not been anticipated, planned, or even imagined while being written.

Her caring is contagious, so when you work with her on her pieces you are forced to care; you get caught in her intensity, and then the involvement be-comes your own. I remember so clearly one of our first rehearsals, where she, when asked to help guide us, actually conducted us. We were floored by her musicianship and natural talent! It is such a thrill to help her music come to life and to see her reaction to it: it certainly makes all the work you put in worth it!!

Elmar Oliveira, violinist: I first met Joan Tower many years ago when I was appearing as the soloist with the St. Louis Symphony under the direction of Leo-nard Slatkin. Joan was then the composer-in-residence with the orchestra. When I heard her music I was immediately impressed by her great compositional skills and the directness of the emotional impact of her music. We immediately be-came great friends. Several years later Joan surprised me by presenting me with a violin concerto she had written especially for me. She had gotten a commis-sion from an organization in Utah and I gave the premiere of the *Violin Con-certo* with the Utah Symphony under the direction of Joseph Silverstein. I later recorded the concerto with the Louisville Orchestra with Joseph Silverstein con-ducting. Just before the premiere in Utah my life was sadly affected by the death of my older brother John who was also a violinist. John was eleven years older than me and was my first teacher and very dear to me. It was a great loss to bear. Joan also knew my brother John, as she had met him at one of my performances. What was amazing was that Joan had incorporated into her *Violin Concerto* a section where I played a duet with the concertmaster signifying my relationship to my brother. It was more or less a memorial to him.

David Shifrin, clarinetist: Joan Tower has made one of the most significant contributions to the repertory of the clarinet in a generation. I have been privi-leged to perform most of her clarinet pieces and to record her quintet and con-certo. She has contributed masterfully to every important genre for the instru-ment. From solo, to duo with piano, to quintet with strings to her brilliant concerto, she honors past traditions while bringing new depths, horizons, and challenges to every clarinetist and audience member. Her wonderful sense of expression, color, and kinetic energy combined with a wonderful understanding of form and proportion makes her a truly great composer. Her empathy for her fellow performers is evident in her instrumental writing, even when she presents us with enormous challenges. I am sure that her years as pianist in a chamber group with clarinet (Da Capo Chamber Players) have a lot to do with the sensitivity and brilliance she brings to her compositions for clarinet. I look forward to hearing and playing her music for many years to come and I am sure that this tradition will continue with future generations.

Tania León, composer: Tres Memorables Anecdotas de Juana de la Torre (Three Memorable Anecdotes about Joan Tower): First Anecdote: We met at the first panel I ever sat on for the New York State Council for the Arts. I was terrified; my English wasn't very good yet. Then I heard this woman across the table ranting at the top of her lungs, defending a particular application that she felt strongly about. I didn't understand all her words, but I understood the tone of her voice, her body language, and the sincerity and zealousness with which she defended this application. It so happened that this application was one of the first for Meet the Composer. Later on I found out she was the composer Joan Tower. I so admired her passion in standing up for what she believed in that we became friends from that point on.

Second Anecdote: Joan and Jeff would have parties at their loft, located in SoHo at Wooster and Prince Streets. I remember well the interminable six flights of stairs that we'd have to ascend to join in the festivities. Joan would gather her close friends, musicians, and artists and the evenings always culminated in spontaneous improvised performances. I would bring a dish of *frijoles negros* (black beans); others brought their favorite dishes. Following the performance, we would all end up dancing—Joan would be the first to hit the floor, like a pro. That's how I discovered one more of the many facets of her personality that she allowed us to see on these occasions. Every time I pass that corner I look up and relish the wonderful memories of those celebratory gatherings.

Third Anecdote: *Silver Ladders'* Premiere: I was part of the team of friends that Joan would call when she needed to think of a title for her latest composition. She was quite passionate about *Silver Ladders'* title, which reflected the climbing succession of pitches with which the work opens. I had the privilege of witnessing the creation of *Silver Ladders*, as she played me excerpts of the piece in her studio, overlooking a beautiful landscape in upstate New York. On the day of the premiere, there I was sitting next to Joan in a box at Carnegie Hall. What happened next defied my comprehension. The piece began, and as soon as the first note was heard, Joan closed her eyes and went into some sort of trance, as if each note was playing through her soul. She didn't emerge from this trance until the work was finished and that is when I understood how much her sounds mean to her. Until then she had never revealed to me the inner complexities of her musical spirit. To this day, I have that inspiring image of Joan in my mind.

Paul Neubauer, violist: I first met Joan when the Chamber Music Society of Lincoln Center premiered her *Clarinet Quintet*. As Joan likes to say, "I wasn't happy with the ending of the Quintet and Fred Sherry and Paul jumped right in offering ideas, much to the chagrin of their colleagues!" Well, after that she decided that she would like to write a piece for me on the occasion of her 60th birthday. That was my, and all, violists' great fortune, because she turned out *Wild Purple* for solo viola, which is an extremely dramatic and wild piece. Since the premiere, the work has become a staple of the solo viola literature. It was then my turn to ask Joan to write a piece—and what a piece it turned out to be! Keeping the "purple" idea going, she wrote a hauntingly beautiful and dramatic viola concerto called *Purple Rhapsody* which was premiered at the opening of a new concert hall in Omaha in 2005. This was a co-commission of seven orchestras with a grant from the Koussevitzky Foundation. What's next for Joan and the viola is anyone's guess.

Emerson Quartet (by Eugene Drucker, violinist): We in the Emerson Quartet very much enjoyed working with Joan Tower on *Incandescent,* which I believe is her fourth string quartet. It is a very effective piece, with lots of variety, alternating between lyrical, almost impressionist passages and sections dominated by pounding, propulsive rhythms. There are brilliant cadenzas for violin, viola, and 'cello. The quartet has a great ending, and has always elicited a strong response from audiences. In rehearsals, Joan was quite concerned about tempo relationships, balance between the instruments so that the dominant lines in a given measure or phrase could come out, and overall dynamic pacing. I remember that when she first heard us run through it in a rehearsal, she sat there with intense concentration, her eyes tightly shut. It struck me that she wasn't following a score, that the music and her desires for how it should be realized were securely in her head. As I'm sure you've heard from other respondents, Joan has a very lively personality and a great sense of humor. When she attended our performances of her work—the premiere at Bard College, then in Aspen, and finally in London (there may be others that I don't remember at the moment, but we certainly played it many times without Joan in attendance)—it always lent further excitement to the atmosphere, for us and for the audience.

Patricia Spencer, flutist and member of Da Capo Chamber Players: To talk about all the fabulous interactions I've had with Joan Tower—even just about the first 15 years of Da Capo, plus my own prior and continuing experiences—would already be an entire book. The paragraphs below are monumentally inadequate. I've tried to organize them into some early memories, rehearsals (an ongoing pleasure), the origins of the Da Capo Chamber Players, and commissioned works by Joan.

Early reminiscences: The flutist Sophie Sollberger (at that time married to Harvey Sollberger) first introduced me to Joan in the late 1960s. Joan gave one an immediate impression of the intensity, the depth of her musical commitment. This was confirmed in rehearsals—with the intensity always balanced by humor and warmth. The first piece she and I played together was Kazuo Fukushima's

Three Pieces from Chu-U, performing it for the Greenwich House Concert Series of Contemporary Music, which Joan had started. This was followed by
Chou Wen-Chung's *Cursive,* then the premiere and recording of Joan's *Movements for Flute and Piano,* then Stefan Wolpe's *Piece in Two Parts for Flute
and Piano* (which Joan is still complaining about), and others: Haydn, Roussel
(another piece she didn't like). These collaborations were expanded to chamber
music concerts at the New York Historical Society, Donnell Library, and similar
venues, merging eventually with the formation of Da Capo Chamber Players.

Those early years of working with Joan were deeply influential for me.
Partly from her came the idea that it might be okay to be a chamber musician,
rather than seeking an orchestral career. Also, as a young and very inexperi-
enced player, the idea that a performer could "reject" a piece that had actually
been published was totally foreign to me. (How things change.) The idea of
rhythmic subdivisions (for negotiating 5 against 3, and so on), as well as the
dynamic extremes called for in the performance of new music—all this was new
to me. Rehearsal procedures took a long time to work out—partly due to my
inexperience, partly because performing contemporary chamber music was itself
a young field, and partly again because so much of the training at that time was
geared toward orchestral skills. Learning how to rehearse efficiently and produc-
tively in a chamber setting was new territory. Joan helped me, in this regard,
more than I would dare to admit!

Rehearsals with Joan: From the beginnings of Da Capo to the present, rehearsals with Joan were and still are creative; keeping the piece alive, finding
images that help the "sculpting" of the sound. For Joan, it almost seems as if
musical sound is a live animal bouncing around the walls of the room (or the
concert hall). There was always a warmth in her piano sound. Not only did she
have great images (one section of a Cowell piece would be "like a snake
charmer, exotic"), but she was always trying to find a way to communicate the
architecture of a piece, whether through color, or awareness of deep, long-range
registral shapes, or dynamic extremes. All of these and more continue to be very
much a part of her rehearsing technique. Da Capo is tremendously fortunate to
have continuing opportunities to work with her, at Bard College and at the new
Bard College Conservatory of Music, where we are the Ensemble-in-Residence
with the Composition Department. This means that twice a year, we spend several days on campus rehearsing and performing pieces by student composers—
often with Joan present or conducting the works of her students. It's a stimulat-
ing program!

A recent and very exciting rehearsal experience for me was working with
Joan on her *Flute Concerto.* (She and I performed it together in the version with
piano, and I subsequently played it with orchestra for the National Flute Association Convention in August 2004, conducted by Ransom Wilson.) In the expressive sections, she asks for the flute to be almost literally a "voice"—not with
words, but with its emotional impact and its energy. This is something that is
really important to me, as well, and is a constant challenge.

Origins of the Da Capo Chamber Players: As mentioned above, Joan had
started a concert series of contemporary music at the Greenwich House in New

York City. Gradually, as she and I were also plotting concerts at other venues (the New York Historical Society and such), the idea evolved of having a specific group. The instrumentation was chosen with regard to the musicians who were interested in and committed to new music. We had an oboist, Judy Martin (for whom oboe pieces were written by Charles Wuorinen, Harvey Sollberger, Charles Whittenberg, Ursula Mamlok, and of course, Joan); we had a soprano for a while, then a clarinet (Allen Blustine), 'cello (Helen Harbison), and violin (Joel Lester). The repertoire was at first mightily influenced by the pieces we heard on the Group for Contemporary Music concerts; they were the most prestigious, best show in town, at that time, for new music. However, after some time all of us, and Joan especially, became interested in tapping into a wider, more diverse repertoire. At first, Joan did all of the organizational stuff—incorporation, booking the halls, getting Carnegie Hall sponsorship (in the late '70s), setting up the commissions for our Naumburg Chamber Music Award (Milton Babbit's *Arie da capo* and Harvey Sollberger's *Riding the Wind I*). Although we all participated in the choices of composers and other decisions, none of the rest of us realized how much work there was to do. (And though I know I helped, or tried to, in retrospect I would call myself pretty inept in comparison to Joan!)

Joan frequently comments that being a member of a group, being able to work from the "inside" on the sounds and shaping of a piece (especially her own, of course, but works by other composers as well), was extremely important for her composing. One hears this in the emotional connection of her music with that of Messiaen. From our perspective, having a composer as a member of the group added a really exciting dimension, and to this day I know that I understand music differently because of so many years of having Joan in the group. "Differently" means better, of course, in my perception! But I also remember a review early on, when Da Capo had performed in Baltimore, that commented that "the flutist and pianist were the weakest members of the group . . . bringing out inner voices that should have remained submerged."

Commissioned pieces by Joan: There is always a sense of history about receiving a new piece written for you or your ensemble. With Joan, this is particularly strong, since the pieces have often become classics: *Amazon*, first written for Da Capo in 1978, not only became a classic, but also morphed into an orchestra piece; *Petroushskates*, written for our 10th anniversary in 1980, has received hundreds of performances, and been programmed by virtually every group of our instrumentation. Right from the start *Amazon* felt like a landmark work in Joan's development as a composer, with its orchestral textures drawn from just five instruments. The first rehearsal for *Petroushskates* was a good example of why composers should never be allowed to come to the early rehearsals of their pieces. It was unavoidable, of course, since Joan was the pianist. But, since the balances were all totally off, and nothing was together, and the difficult parts were still at a very slow and/or sketchy stage of mastery (one should say "non-mastery"), Joan was hysterical because it was the first time she was hearing her piece and it sounded absolutely terrible. We somehow got through that, and at the next rehearsal her famous sense of humor took over: as we walked in, in response to Joel's question about how it was going, she announced that she "already taken it off the program." (Only one person almost believed her.)

Joan's *Hexachords* for solo flute is particularly memorable because it was the first piece written for me. I still remember the excitement I felt when she told me she had started "my piece"! The meetings we had on it were explorations of the dynamic nature of the flute; she was particularly fascinated with the sustaining quality. Her use of different vibratos was influenced by Charles Wuorinen's *Flute Variations II* (which was in turn influenced by shakuhaci sounds and techniques), and by the playing of Harvey Sollberger, who incorporated a wide range of vibrato variation into his interpretations. Joan now feels uncomfortable with her compositional style from that period; I guess she thinks it is academic. However, I think she's wrong. *Hexachords* always speaks to listeners in a very personal way, expanding the dimensions of musical space, then exploding with an exuberant, tumultuous drive.

A couple of little anecdotes: One evening in the late 1970s, after an International Society of Contemporary Music board meeting, a group of us (who are now well-established composers or performers, but were then quite young) went to a restaurant for drinks and camaraderie. It was a memorable evening because it advanced from the usual fund-raising soul-searching to a game of "strip-spin-the-bottle"—most probably Joan's idea. The rules are obvious: as the bottle pointed to you, you took something off. Jewelry, belts, shoes, and continuing (no one was arrested.)

In the first year after the creation of the New York State Council on the Arts, Da Capo happened to be giving a performance and interview for WQXR. Joan's approach to this interview was like something from Alice in Wonderland. In response to whatever bland question the interviewer had asked her, she immediately started talking about the importance of NYSCA, even though it was a complete non sequitur. Smart!

Muir String Quartet (by Michael P. Reynolds, 'cellist): Our interaction with Joan Tower began about 1990. We'd received a commission through the Snowbird Institute and the Hancher Center to have Joan write her first string quartet (*Night Fields*) for the Muir Quartet. That event began a very enjoyable friendship and collaboration with her that continues to this day. The working sessions with Joan for the premiere performance were great—lots of arguing, experimentation, laughter, and the usual birthing pains for a new work. Joan was great about articulating what her real intentions were, which resulted in many rewritings and new interpretations. We then had the pleasure of coming back to the piece many times, often in her presence, and it was fun to see the piece evolve as a real collaboration. On top of that, Joan's become a terrific colleague in the mentoring of young composers and string quartets that we tutor through the Deer Valley Festival's Emerging Quartets and Composers program. This program, which started at the Snowbird Institute in 1990, moved to Deer Valley in the late 1990s, and in 2004 became the educational component of the Deer Valley Festival, presented by the Utah Symphony/Opera. Each year, Joan chooses two young composers to interact with two young quartets the Muir has selected. The quartets and composers have a few weeks together to interact and prepare premieres of new works that the young composers create. She also co-mentors the young quartets in the standard literature—in addition to being a great composer, she's a very dynamic and popular quartet coach. Each year, we also perform one of Joan's quartets or other literature that she's written for strings—including piano trios with her at the piano. This all leaves out the most enjoyable part—Joan and her husband, Jeff, have become dear friends of us all. We think that Joan's having spent many years in the trenches as a performer has helped us to bond and understand each of our quirks and predilections.

John Duffy, composer, conductor, founder of Meet the Composer: I met Joan in 1974, the year I founded Meet the Composer. Joan, Steve Reich, Leroy Jenkins, Billy Taylor, Charles Dodge, and a small band of other composers helped spearhead the organization. Several years later, when Meet the Composer initiated its landmark orchestra residencies program, I attended a performance in a small church at 69th and Columbus Street. It was a revelation. Da Capo Chamber Players, with Joan on piano, performed Joan's latest chamber work. It was stunning! From that moment, I knew Joan was a natural to be a resident with a major orchestra. Leonard Slatkin, soon after, asked her to join the St. Louis Symphony, and the rest is musical history. Given her outgoing nature, her sharp musical gifts and easy collaborations with fellow musicians, Joan was a memorable representative of our composer community in St. Louis. She created many works there, programmed fellow composers, and spoke passionately on the role of living composers in the everyday lives of Americans. Each day of the week Joan was on the trail like "Joanny Appleseed," spreading the good news about living American composers and their music. She was such a passionate, visible pioneer that local policemen stopped traffic as she made her way to concerts. I've spent a lot of time with Joan, over Chinese meals, after Meet the Composer annual composer meetings, in St. Louis asking a clarinetist how best to write a part "that sounds," in rural Utah where she got the crowd laughing, and always there's Joan's authentic self, Joan's beautifully expressive music, Joan's deep humanism that people love.

Frank Epstein, percussionist, director of the New England Conservatory Percussion Ensemble: I can't remember when I first met Joan Tower. However, I do remember commissioning Joan to write a piece for Collage New Music Ensemble, which I founded back in the early '70s. The piece in question, *Noon Dance*, was recorded in 1983 after its premiere in Boston and became part of an all-Tower recording. Since then, I have kept in contact with Joan, who is a person who becomes an immediate friend and remains a friend. She is fun, down-to-earth, wise, and understanding, and, as she often would say: "I'm a performer and I understand the problems."

Joan as a performer is practical and this comes out in her music. The most recent piece I commissioned is a piece for percussion ensemble. She jumped in with both feet. But before writing a note she made sure she knew the medium and asked many questions. She asked about instruments, sticks, mallet choice, and different types of sounds. I know she asked other people as well. Consequently the piece entitled *DNA* for 5 percussion is a dream. It works! In fact I have performed the piece at least 5 times since its premiere, including a performance at Carnegie Hall as part of a concert dedicated to Joan, and have recorded it for a future album of works commissioned for the New England Conservatory Percussion Ensemble. I have met Joan on many other occasions; I have attended numerous performances of her music at the Tanglewood Music Center and performed in several of her pieces as a member of the Boston Symphony Orchestra percussion section. Her energy and passion comes out in her music. Joan is a person with a message and the message is: here I am, a woman, a performer, a perfectionist, and I write music. I write for you, the performer; I hope the listener will enjoy what I write as well, but I write for you.

Jennifer Higdon, composer: Joan Tower is the one composer whose path I have crossed the most throughout my compositional life. That statement says more than one might initially think, because though I was crossing Joan's path, she was affecting mine in so many different ways. From the very first time in 1989 that I heard her music in a rehearsal with the Curtis Institute Orchestra, which was preparing for the Friedheim Competition, to our talks at various receptions at concerts and festivals (the "how do I become a composer?" and "how do I get a career?" questions), to teaching as her sabbatical replacement at Bard College (thereby necessitating many wonderful meals where I would get teaching advice and keep her up to date on her students), to watching Leonard Slatkin conduct her *Concerto for Orchestra* with the New York Philharmonic (successfully balancing a program with Stravinsky's *Rite of Spring*), to being a good musical citizen of the world (Joan gives of herself completely). I learned that gender is not any kind of barrier to creating bold music; that being able to conduct your music is a very, very good thing; that teaching must be done in a way that is measured to fit each and every individual student; that being a good performer is significant to being a good composer; that despite the fact that something is scary to write (we both struggled over string quartets at the same time), you must persevere because good things can come of that effort; that a sense of humor through it all is important; that grace in all that you do is everything. And the best part is that she continues to inspire me!

Robert Spring, clarinetist: I was approached by Summit Records in—I think maybe 1990. They wanted me to do a CD of all one composer. I submitted a list of people who had written for the clarinet and they picked Joan Tower. I had to audition with her for permission to record her music. Luck had it that she was coming to Tempe (AZ) for a visiting composer series workshop, and I played *Wings* for her. She really seemed to like the performance, and at the end said she would allow me to record her music. She was taking a huge step, as I had never done anything like this before, and was really an unknown performer in every way.

Well, she sent me the music for the recording. The big pieces were the *Fantasy . . . (Those Harbor Lights)* and the *Clarinet Concerto*. I remember that it was a Saturday when I received a package in the mail from her. I called her to tell her that I received the music, and that I had a few questions. One was that there was no place to breathe in the first two pages of the *Concerto*. Her line was, "Well, you do circular breathe, don't you!?" I said that of course I did, but wanted to make certain that this was what she wanted. I hung up the phone and when my wife asked what was wrong, I said, "I have to learn to circular breathe!"

She would not let us record for 9 months so we would have plenty of time to really prepare the music. I remember the recording session well. She was extremely exact in what she wanted. In retrospect, I'm really glad she was, as this recording has been a bench mark in her music for clarinet. I performed the *Concerto* twice with her in attendance. In both cases, I can honestly say that I'd never been this nervous. She is an amazing force in both her creativity and her personal presence. Another story about the recording session: After I spent all that time learning to circular breathe, we got to the recording and it was too noisy for her, so we did it all by splicing the sections together! And the opening of *Wings* was always too loud for her, so I turned my back to the microphone—and she loved the volume!!!

Laura Flax, clarinetist/former member, Da Capo Chamber Players: Joan Tower, what an apt name. Tower of Strength. Tower of Power. Ivory Tower. Towering Inferno. Joan Tower does in fact tower above most of us regular folks. When I first met Joan in 1976, she had recently founded the Da Capo Chamber Players with several of her colleagues. It was a wonderful collection of talent that came together to bring new compositions to audiences in a different way, a chance to hear a new piece twice on one concert. Terrific idea. Joan had so many terrific ideas. In those days she was splitting her time between performing as a pianist and composing. She had a boundless energy that enabled her to be a present and inspiring teacher, an open chamber music colleague always willing to share and take musical risks, and a supportive, generous friend.

Joan once had an idea for a class that Da Capo presented at Bard College. She posed the question, "What makes a performance exciting: the performer or the piece?" We had lots of provocative discussion on the topic. When I think about it now, more than 25 years later, I realize that having Joan perform anything was exciting. And when her incredibly high performance energy was directed to her own music, it was brilliant. That's what I thought of Joan then, and now as well: strong, powerful, innovative, inspired, inspiring, open, supportive, generous, funny, exciting, high energy, and brilliant. Happy 70th!

eighth blackbird (by Nick Photinos 'cellist, and Lisa Kaplan, pianist). Lisa: The summer of 1997 was the first that eighth blackbird spent together. We had put together audition tapes and sent them to various summer music festivals. Amazingly, we got into them all (not bad considering we knew how to play a total of four pieces). One of those was *Noon Dance* by Joan Tower. We knew that Joan was one of the composers-in-residence at the Norfolk Festival in Connecticut and we were thrilled at the possibility of playing her piece for her. Nick: Since it was our first summer at Norfolk, we were there as students (i.e., we paid to go). At that point we had hung out with Joan a little bit, but didn't really know the depth of her coolness, when we asked her to listen to us play through *Noon Dance*. So we were a bit nervous (we didn't know what she was going to think). Lisa: I'll never forget that day in July. All six of us were crammed into the shed annex with its noisy air conditioner, friendly mice, and out-of-tune upright piano. Joan sat about two feet away from us as she closed her eyes and listened to us play. Nick: When we were done, she was silent for some time. She first said, "Wow," and then made a comment that I remember well, but not precisely. She said that I had actually made the 'cello solo sound good (she had never been very pleased about how she had composed it and thought that it just would never really work). Suffice it to say this made me very happy. Lisa: She had tears in her eyes, and told us the reason she hadn't immediately agreed to listen to us play *Noon Dance* was that she had never really been comfortable with the work. But she said our performance that day had changed her mind about the piece. Nick: Since then, how could we not have gotten along with her famously? And how could we not include a work of hers on our first commercial release?

Our experience with *Petroushskates* is like an old friend—it manages to pop up nearly every season, since a lot of people ask for it, and is relatively easy to bring back up. It seems a very "bright" piece to me—very sparkling, with all the energy of *Petrouchka* (the opening, anyway) yet very much Joan Tower. We also had a great time playing *Big Sky* with her. We were asked to appear on a festival that featured her music, and she was coming as well, and Lisa (our pianist) was rather sick and didn't know if she could make it. We ended up playing *Big Sky*, which was a revelation on many levels. Not only is she an excellent collaborator and musician, but it really opened our eyes about what is possible with the piece. Often in music, and especially new music, you try very hard to do what's on the page, but Joan was relatively free with her own music, and made it sing in different ways than we had. Besides that, I would say that I, and everyone I know, is always struck by Joan's down-to-earth nature—while she is brilliant, she is pretty much the antithesis of stuffy, and her laugh is contagious.

Ursula Oppens, pianist: I first met Joan in the mid-'60s, when she was a brilliant Ph.D. student at Columbia University and I, newly finished with college, had become entranced by all the living composers around me. No, the definition of composer did not have to include the word "dead"! Joan was also a terrific pianist, and so she wrote over the years some fantastic piano music, including two concerti and a number of solo pieces. One day, when her 60th birthday was looming, Joan said to me: "I've written all these pieces for you over the years; now it is your turn to write something for me." What a horror! I had never composed anything in my life. But Joan was (and is) a dear friend. In the end, writing this piece was some of the greatest fun I've had. After I decided on a structure that would have 60 parts (one for each year), I was able to write a 5-minute piece. But usually it is the other way around. Joan's music is fun to play (though hard) and it is wonderful to play a piece that you know the audience will love. Just recently I was in Glens Falls, NY, where a month earlier the orchestra had played the premiere of *Made in America*. The whole town was still giddy with excitement. The orchestra had been challenged to play its very best, the townspeople were moved, excited, and thrilled by hearing the work, and everyone knew that history had been made there. And of course, they all loved Joan.

Greg Sandow, composer, critic, and consultant: Joan and I have known each other a long time. When she introduced a piece of mine at a recent concert, she said we'd known each other for 20 years. But I realized with a shock that it's more like 30. I wouldn't have realized that if I hadn't thought back to the time we met, and then done some subtraction. That's because when Joan became a presence in my life, she somehow became timeless. She's about as unforgettable as any person could be—always strong, always truthful, always honest, always open, always herself. There was a long period in which, as our lives took us in different directions, we didn't see each other. Then we reconnected at a party, and it was as if we'd been in touch just the day before. That's also the way Joan is—always present in the moment.

I have so many memories of her. I've sat with her while her music was being played, on one occasion when she wasn't sure she liked what she heard (she was worried about her piece, not the performance), and on another when the playing was just stunning, but the conductor got angry with the orchestra and stalked offstage, shocking Joan, I think, more than anyone. Her vulnerability lies right on the surface, but that doesn't make her any less forceful or determined when she's got something that she wants to do, or wants other people to do. She's one of the fiercest advocates for composers that I've ever met. She won't let the subject alone when she's part of a discussion or a conference where composers need an advocate. She also thinks all musicians should compose—and that they can compose, which is just as important, since so many people have the idea that composing is a special talent, limited to just a few blessed souls. Though Joan clearly has that talent (is overflowing with it), she doesn't want to exclude anyone. I love that about her.

Her music knocks me out. I've heard it during all the time I've known her, but got to know it best when she flattered me by asking me to write liner notes for her recent Naxos CD. (I would have happily written them without being paid.) Joan insisted I put my ideas about the music in the notes, and resisted (until I persuaded her) giving me her own. Which is something else about her: as far as I can see, she doesn't think she owns the music that she writes. She wants it to belong to the entire musical community. But the best thing about writing these notes was that I got to know her music intimately (or at least the pieces I was writing about). The more I heard these pieces, the stronger, more personal, inevitable, and powerful they became. I admired so many things about the way she writes, not least the way her music naturally takes shape according to the nature of each instrument she's writing for. I don't think that's a gift many composers have (I certainly don't have it), or maybe, at best, we might have it only for one or two instruments. Joan has it, as far as I can see, for every instrument. That's one way in which studying her scores can be an education. You breathe the flavor—and the playing technique—of all the instruments.

Maybe my happiest Joan experience was having a piece played on the "Second Helpings" series she runs for St. Luke's Orchestra. Here I found that her care for composers goes far beyond advocacy. She works warmly and eagerly to create a supportive environment. She takes the composers featured on each concert out to dinner. She sits in on rehearsals. I can't stress the value of her presence—she's had more experience bringing new works to life than probably all the other composers and the musicians on the program added together. She won't speak up unless she has to, but when she does, it's usually to help solve a problem that might, for the moment, have seemed really difficult. She'll offer her thoughts with warmth, good humor, common sense, and of course vast knowledge. My piece and I benefited from that. And most of all, she was an inspiring presence. She helped the concert develop a very special feeling, which both made everyone involved happy that they were involved, and made the performances even better (more committed, more caring, more engaged) than they would have been without her. I'm happy to honor Joan. Everywhere she goes, she makes the world better.

Carol Wincenc, flutist: To The Mighty Joan Tower, Friend, Colleague, and Masterful Musician: I wish you endless, continued joy and productivity in your already rich life. You have so been a source of inspiration to me, with not only all the magical compositions that you have written for me that have impacted my soul and performing career, but with all the sharing of personal events and happenings with me, from all our performances together, and in such thrilling places. Shall we ever forget the Kennedy Center, recording the *Flute Concerto* in Louisville, performing the Concerto in Banff when one of the piano strings erupted and flew across the room, your 60th birthday, when you had such unshakable faith that you asked me to write an original composition for the occasion, to your wedding celebration and all the other wonderful events in the past.

I am in complete admiration of your stamina, your vision as an artist, your impeccable performances and willingness to take complete risks on stage and in life; your love that manifests itself in exceptional team work, sensitivity to all the artists that you engage, your inimitable sense of humor, and your compassion as a total being: woman, partner, playmate, mentor, and teacher to name a few. I know that we shall continue to connect and take inventories of our lives together, and I thank you for all that you have given to me.

Zubin Mehta, conductor: I remember with great pleasure my many associations with Joan Tower, especially when we collaborated with the New York Philharmonic and the United Nations in 1982, performing *Sequoia*. I would like to wish Joan a very happy [70th] birthday with many more years for her creative activities.

Timothy Russell, conductor: I have had the great privilege of collaborating with Joan Tower on numerous occasions over the last decade. Ten years ago she visited Arizona State University as part of a residency sponsored by the University's Public Events concert series. The ASU Symphony Orchestra performed Joan's *Piano Concerto*, with Ursula Oppens as soloist, and her *Clarinet Concerto*, with ASU Professor Robert Spring. This was my first interaction with Joan and her music. I have been a fan and proponent ever since. I'm sure that Joan has many fans, but I would be happy to run for President of her Fan Club, should such an official organization be founded!

Subsequently, she has visited Columbus, OH, three times as the ProMusica Chamber Orchestra, of which I am the co-founder and music director of 27 seasons, has offered multiple performances of a number of Joan's works. In 1998, we offered a 60th birthday party for Joan, one of our favorite visiting composers. This is what *The Columbus Dispatch* wrote on April 6, 1998, following the concert:

> Music Director Timothy Russell was superb conducting the wide-ranging repertoire that combined the Irmelin Prelude of Delius with Mozart's *Piano Concerto in B flat major*, K. 456 on the first half and two by Joan Tower on the second: *Duets* and *Piano Concerto (Homage to Beethoven)*. As fine as the proceedings were to this point, ProMusica soared to a new plateau as it delivered in stunning fashion the two amazing works by Tower. It was Tower's blockbuster *Duets* that capped the evening's artistic achievements for orchestra and conductor. . . . It opened the ears, stimulated the mind, and aroused the emotions.

I have conducted Joan Tower's music at the Interlochen Center for the Arts, with the World Youth Symphony, as well as with the Charlotte Symphony. I also helped to produce a CD recording of four of Joan's concertos (for flute, clarinet, violin, and piano) with the Louisville Symphony for d'Note Records. Wherever I go to conduct her music, the musicians of the orchestra (young and old) love rehearsing and performing these spectacular compositions and audiences truly enjoy their encounters with this remarkable artist. Joan and I have not only shared in the music-making process, but also in many opportunities to talk with audiences—about the role of classical music (historically and in our world today), "new music," and Joan's music specifically. Joan Tower is a wonderful teacher and colleague. These happy occasions always serve to renew me and energize me. Samuel Johnson once wrote that "great art is that which pleases many and pleases long." I truly believe that Joan Tower's music fits this definition.

When the history of music is written, Joan Tower will hold a very important place in that story. Joan simply knows how to make an orchestra "sound." Her music is filled with emotional intensity and rhythmic energy and like all great artists, Joan has something important to say. A unique and profound voice, she is also superb in crafting her compositions. She is a "colorist," a marvelous orchestrator. She communicates with passion and power. Great music is about making connections—composer to performer and performers to audiences. Joan connects! Just a few months ago, ProMusica and I were honored to participate in a performance which resulted from a consortium that commissioned Joan's remarkable new viola concerto. The atmosphere was electric. On February 13, 2006, *The Columbus Dispatch* wrote:

> Ferocious. Aggressive. Not something you want to encounter in a dark alley. An attack dog? No, new music by Joan Tower, whose piece for chamber orchestra and solo viola (of all things) keeps you nervously on the edge of your seat like film noir or a good suspense thriller. Tower's *Purple Rhapsody* premiered last night with concert violist Paul Neubauer and the ProMusica Chamber Orchestra of Columbus conducted by Timothy Russell. It is an astonishing work—if you can live through it. It assaults your senses and the emotions over and over, climbing scales in loud, jabbing, dissonant chords, ratcheting up intensity by layering agitated sounds on top of one another. Neubauer led the charge throughout, projecting powerful emissions from the lower registers, sawing on repeated pitches until the music came close to explosion, which is finally what it did at the end. His was an amazing performance by any standard.

Joan Tower is a great gift, a very special person. She is a joy to know and a pleasure to work with. Many of my fondest musical memories are of conducting music by Joan Tower. I look forward to many more such experiences in the years ahead.

Joan Panetti, pianist, composer, director of the Norfolk Chamber Music Festival: Joan is a vivacious, kaleidoscopic, endearing dynamo . . . all of this plus an honest, trustworthy, loyal person, and of course a distinctive and masterful musician. Our working relationship began around fifteen years ago when we listened separately to over 100 tapes of young composers hoping to be admitted to the Contemporary Music Program of the Norfolk Chamber Music Festival. As we compared notes, I was immediately impressed that she had obviously listened all the way through each piece and that she zeroed in on the positive aspects of each one. Connections, imagination, and having an individual voice were important to her; the style didn't matter. At Norfolk, she instantly made everyone—performers composers, staff, visitors, audiences, my children—feel comfortable. She's a great listener. She speaks straightforwardly and vividly. She cares. And she loves long glittery earrings! She consistently asked provocative questions, helped young composers put finishing touches on their pieces, and then coached these pieces. She coaxed innumerable interpretations out of each work and at the same time paid close attention to the opinions of the composers and performers. The process and sense of community were always more important than the final result. Whenever Joan came to Norfolk she asked for a block of time to compose, but I don't know how she ever wrote a note! She devoted herself fully to our program (and our wines or beers around the big kitchen table). Joan made everything such fun! Our workshop traditionally ended with skits, complete with "costumes," in which we poked fun at each other. Invariably she would guffaw where she wasn't supposed to in her own skits! These are truly precious memories. But the real point here is that amidst all the laughter, there was immense respect, gratitude, and affection for everyone's beloved "J.T."

Appendix A: Alphabetical Listing of Published Compositions

Appendix A: Alphabetical Listing of Published Compositions

Music for 'Cello and Orchestra	**W12**
Night Fields	**W46**
No Longer Very Clear	**W63**
Noon Dance	**W45**
Opa Eboni	**W47**
Or Like a . . . an Engine	**W63**
Percussion Quartet	**W48**
Petroushskates	**W49**
Piano Concerto No. 1 (Homage to Beethoven)	**W13**
Platinum Spirals	**W64**
Prelude for Five Players	**W50**
Purple Rhapsody	**W14**
Rain Waves	**W51**
Rapids (Piano Concerto No. 2)	**W17**
Red Garnet Waltz	**W65**
Sequoia	**W15**
Silver Ladders	**W16**
Six Variations	**W66**
Snow Dreams	**W54**
Stepping Stones	**W3**
Stepping Stones: A Ballet for Two Pianos	**W4**
Strike Zones	**W18**
Tambor	**W19**
The Last Dance	**W20**
Throbbing Still	**W63**
Toccanta	**W52**
Trés Lent (Hommage à Messiaen)	**W53**
Turning Points	**W55**
Valentine Trills	**W70, W71**
Vast Antique Cubes	**W63**
Violin Concerto	**W21**
Wild Purple	**W67**
Wings	**W68, W69**
Yet Another Set of Variations (Paganini Trills)	**W22**

Bibliography

Bibliography

B1.   "1987–1988 Premieres and Season Highlights." *Symphony Magazine* 38, no. 5 (October–November 1987): 31. Announces the premiere of *Clarinet Concerto* by the American Symphony Orchestra, Jorge Meister conducting; Charles Neidich, soloist. See: **D10, D11, W5**

B2.   "1979–1980 Premieres and Season Highlights." *Symphony News* 30, no. 6 (December 4, 1979): 49. Announces the premiere of *Amazon II* by the Hudson Valley Philharmonic, Imre Pallo conducting. See: **D1, D2, W24**

B3.   "1981–1982 "Premieres and Season Highlights." *Symphony Magazine* 32, no. 3 (June–July 1981): 154. Announces the premiere of *Sequoia* by the American Composers Orchestra, Dennis Russell Davies conducting. See: **D63, D64, D65, D66, W15**

B4.   "1986–1987 Premieres and Season Highlights." *Symphony Magazine* 37, no. 5 (October–November 1987): 17. Announces the premiere of *Silver Ladders* by the St. Louis Symphony Orchestra, Leonard Slatkin conducting. See: **D67, D68, D69, W16**

B5.   "1995–1996 Premieres and Season Highlights." *Symphony* 46, no. 5 (December 1996): 70. Announces premiere of *Piano Concerto No. 2*, Ursula Oppens, piano, with the University of Wisconsin Symphony Orchestra, David Becker conducting. See: **D60, W17**

B6.   "American Academy of Arts and Letters Music Winners." *American Music Teacher* 52, no. 1 (August–September 2002): 12. Tower sits on American Academy of Arts and Letters committee, which selected the winners of the 2003 music awards.

B7.   "An Autumn Filled with New Music." *Plain Dealer* (Cleveland, OH), September 26, 2003, 46. Announces an all-Tower recital, part of the Aki Festival of New Music.

B8.   "Between the Steelers and a String Quartet." *Pittsburgh Post-Gazette* (PA), November 16, 2003, E3. Reports a performance of *Night Fields* by the Enso Quartet. See: **D43, D44, D45, W46**

B9.   "Classical Calendar: Women's Musical Club of Toronto." *Toronto Life*, November 1, 2005. *Elegy* is performed, along with works by Berio, Beethoven, Ravel, and Alan Hovhaness. See: **W34**

B10.   "Classical Music and Dance Guide: St. Luke's Chamber Ensemble." *New York Times*, June 4, 2004, E1. The ensemble presents a program entitled "Tower Power," a tribute to the group's composer-in-residence.

B11.   "Classical Music and Dance Guide: Joan Tower." *New York Times*, January 16, 2004, E1. Carnegie Hall's Making Music Series features eight of Tower's works: *Vast Antique Cubes/Throbbing Still, DNA, Wild Purple,*

In Memory, Island Prelude, Holding a Daisy and *Like a . . . an Engine.* See:
D32, D33, D34, D35, D36, D46, D76, D89, W33, W42, W43, W63, W67

B12. "Cleveland Group to Play." *Columbus Dispatch* (OH), February 24, 1993, H8. Cleveland Chamber Symphony performs the first *Piano Concerto.*
See: **D54, D55, W13**

B13. "Concert to Honor Notable Women." *The Berkshire Eagle*, May 27, 2005, D2. Announcement and description of the Close Encounters with Music Series, which includes Tower's *For Daniel,* performed by Yehuda Hanani, Joan Tower, and Yehonatan Berick. See: **W40**

B14. "Concerts and Operas Listings: District of Columbia." *Music Magazine*, April 1, 2002, 2. Kennedy Center programs for the spring 2002 season include *Wings, Petroushskates, Flute Concerto.* See: **D28, D49, D50, D51, D52, D53, D79, D80, D81, D82, D83, D84, D85, D86, D87, W9, W49, W68, W69**

B15. "Critics' Choice." *The Denver Post*, June 23, 2002, F3. Music Director Marin Alsop and the Colorado Symphony kick off the 15th anniversary season of the Vail Valley Music Festival with a program that includes *Fanfare for the Uncommon Woman, No. 1.* See: **D16, D17, D18, W35**

B16. "Ford *Made in America.*" www.fordmadeinamerica.org (Accessed November 10, 2005). Comprehensive site devoted to the national premieres of *Made in America,* with video and audio clips, photos, interviews, calendar of premieres, and more. See: **D88, W11**

B17. "Glens Falls Symphony Orchestra Premieres Joan Tower's *Made in America.*" *The Times Union* (Albany, NY), September 18, 2005, S4. See: **D88, W11**

B18. "Great American Ensemble Works." Schirmer, Inc/Associated Music Publishers, Inc. 2005. www.schirmer.com/repertoire/great_us_ensemble_works.html (Accessed January 2, 2006). *Petroushskates* is nominated by Chamber Music America as one of 101 most significant compositions in the repertoire for small ensembles. See: **D49, D50, D51, D52, D53, W49**

B19. "High Notes." *Musical Opinion* 113 (July 1990): 222. Report of Tower's having been awarded the 1990 Grawemeyer for *Silver Ladders.* Notes that the Grawemeyer is the largest award of its kind in music. See: **D67, D68, D69, W16**

B20. "IDRS Awards Six Grants-in-Aid for Double Reed Projects." *The Double Reed* 18, no. 1 (1995): 7–10. Oboist Cynthia Green Libby was awarded funds from the executive committee of the International Double Reed Society to commission a recital piece for oboe and harpsichord from Joan Tower.

B21. "Joan Tower." Schirmer, Inc./Associated Music Publishers, Inc. www.schirmer.com/composers/tower_bio.html (Accessed September 28, 2005). Brief biography of composer.

B22. "Joan Tower Summerfest." June 1997 Schirmer News. www.schirmer.com/news/jun97/news.html#tower (Accessed December 20, 2005). Outlines Tower's four summer residencies for 1997.

B23.   "Joan Tower: Four *Concertos*." [CD review] December 1997–January 1998. Schirmer News. www.schirmer.com/composers/tow-bio.html (Accessed January 26, 2005). Quotes Robert Croan's *Pittsburgh Post-Gazette's* review: "A splendid new recording. . . . With the toughness of the *Violin Concerto* and the lyricism and humor of the *Flute Concerto*, all four works are beautifully and idiomatically written for the solo instruments and orchestrated with an ear for color and contrast." See: **D10, D11, D28, D54, D55, D77, W5, W9, W13, W21**

B24.   "La Jolla Music Society's 2005–06 Season." *The San Diego Union-Tribune*, April 24, 2004, F5. Notes the planned performance of *Made in America*. See: **D88, W11**

B25.   "*Joan Tower*." Hutchinson Encyclopedia. CD Rom. Oxford, England: Helicon, 2003.

B26.   "Local Premieres Highlight Symphony Season Opener." *St. Louis Globe-Democrat*, September 14, 1984, D1. Tower addresses a St. Louis Symphony audience before *Sequoia*'s local premiere. See: **D63, D64, D65, D66, W15**

B27.   "May 1998 Schirmer News." G. Schirmer, Inc./Associated Music Publishers, Inc. www.schirmer.com/news/may98/tower.html (Accessed November 15, 2005). Announces premiere of *Tambor*. See: **D88, W19**

B28.   "New Music Review: Joan Tower's *Island Prelude*." *Instrumentalist* 43, no. 11 (June 1989): 55. Announcement of *Island Prelude's* premiere by Leonard Slatkin, conductor; oboist Peter Bowman; and members of the Saint Louis Symphony. See: **D33, D34, D35, D36, W43**

B29.   "News Section: Reviews." *Tempo* 188 (September 1993): 45–6. Lengthy, thorough review of the Summit Record CD which features *Fantasy . . . (Those Harbor Lights), Breakfast Rhythms I and II, Wings, Clarinet Concerto*. "Her music inhabits a realm which, although not unvisited by others, is nonetheless capable, at her instigation, of yielding up new secrets and revelations." See: **D6, D7, D8, D10, D11, D25, D26, D79, D80, D81, D82, D83, D84, D85, D86, D87, W5, W29, W39, W68, W69**

B30.   "News Section: Composers." *Tempo* 192 (April 1995): 63. Announces the premieres of Tower's *Duets for Orchestra* by the Los Angeles Chamber Orchestra, Christof Perick, conductor. See: **D15, W7**

B31.   "News Section: Composers." *Tempo* 193 (July 1995): 62–63. Reports the Alice Tully Hall premiere of *Clarinet Quintet* with David Shifrin, clarinet, and the Chamber Music Society of Lincoln Center.

B32.   "News Section: Composers." *Tempo* 196 (April 1996): 71–72. Reports the premiere of *Valentine Trills* in New York by Carol Wincenc, flute, as well as the premiere of *Stepping Stones* (version for synthesized piano and tape) in Columbus, OH. See: **W70**

B33.   "News Section: Composers." *Tempo* 214 (October 2000): 61–63. Reports the premiere of *Big Sky* in La Jolla, CA, on August 6, 2000. See: **D4, W27**

B34. "Omaha Symphony 2005–06 Season." *Omaha World-Herald,* March 6, 2005, Sunrise Edition, 3. Outlines 2005–06 concert season which includes the world premiere of *Purple Rhapsody* with violist Paul Neubauer. See: **W14**

B35. "Pine Bluff Symphony to Offer Bit of Spirit, Bit of Adventure." *Arkansas Democrat Gazette,* September 4, 2005, Style section, E4. Reports the regional premiere of *Made in America* by the Pine Bluffs Symphony. See: **D88, W11**

B36. "Pine Bluff Concert to Give New Work Regional Premiere." *Arkansas Democrat Gazette* (Little Rock), October 14, 2005, E3. Announces the regional premiere of *Made in America,* performed by the Pine Bluff Symphony. See: **D88, W11**

B37. "Premieres." *Chamber Music Magazine* 3, no. 1 (1986): 48. Announces the world premiere of *Piano Concerto* by the Hudson Valley Philharmonic Chamber Orchestra, Jacquelyn Helin, pianist. See: **D54, D55, W13**

B38. "Profile: Bay-Atlantic Symphony of New Jersey." Broadcast on National Public Radio, Weekend Edition, October 9, 2004. Scott Simon, Jeff Lunden, hosts. Profiles the Bay-Atlantic Symphony; details their commissioning works with a consortium of regional orchestras.

B39. "The Emerson String Quartet Play Their Compatriot Joan Tower." *Time Out London,* November 17, 2004, 146. The Emerson Quartet performs *Incandescent* at Blackheath Halls, London. See: **W41**

B40. "Tower Triumphant." *Symphony Magazine* 41, no. 3 (1980): 22. Tower receives the Grawemeyer Award for Music Composition.

B41. "Tower [*Clarinet*] *Concerto* Performed as Part of Women's History Month." *Clarinotes* 23, no. 2 (1996): 10. Linda Bartley and the Madison (Wisconsin) Symphony Orchestra give Tower's *Clarinet Concerto* its second performance. Elizabeth Schulze conducts. Tower comments that to her recollection it was the first time one of her compositions had been performed by both a woman soloist and a woman conductor. See: **D10, D11, W5**

B42. "Upbeats." *Piano and Keyboard* 208 (January–February 2001): 12. Announces the premiere of *Vast Antique Cubes/Throbbing Still* at Franklin and Marshall College. Tower explains the origin of the work's title. See: **D46, W63**

B43. "Woman Ends Drought at NY Phil." *The Boston Globe,* September 24, 1982. Reuters. *Sequoia* is performed by the New York Philharmonic. See: **D63, D64, D65, D66, W15**

B44. "Women Composers." Television Broadcast, CBS Sunday Morning with Charles Kurault. November 1, 1992. Eugenia Zuckerman, host.

B45. "Winter Rain." Schirmer News. Newsletter. 1997. www.schirmer.com/news/dec97_jan98/tower.html (Accessed January 26, 2005). Schirmer Associate Music Publishers announce the premiere of *Rain Waves* by the Verdehr Trio. See: **D59, W51**

B46. Adler, Andrew. "CD Review: Tower CD Rededicates Orchestra Mission." *The Louisville Courier-Journal*, May 11, 1997, Arts and Leisure, I-1. This reviewer praises the composer, the compositions, the orchestra, the soloist, and the production. "The d'Note CD is an exemplary introduction to a vital American composer, and a rededication of the mission of an intrinsically American orchestra."

B47. ———. "CD Review: Tower Concerto CD." *The Louisville Courier-Journal*, May 10, 1996, D8. "Much of the concerto is written in a lush, approachable manner, opening with shimmering upper strings under which the pianist enters in soft treble."

B48. Alcott, Dan. 2006. "Explore the Bryan Symphony Orchestra: Notes from the Music Director for the February Concert—An Interview with Joan Tower." www.bryansymphony.org.current42/BSOconductorFeb.asp (Accessed February 17, 2006). A transcript of a telephone interview Tower had with the conductor of the orchestra prior to a performance of *Made in America*. See: **D88, W11**

B49. Alvarado, Maria. "Students Attend Kansas City Symphony Concert." *Kansas City Kansas Community College Notes* 4 (December 1993): 1. Describes the *Violin Concerto* as the highlight of the concert, which also included works by Chausson, Bach, and Debussy. See: **D77, W21**

B50. Anthony, Michael. "Tower of Power: Composer Happily Endures the Popularity of her Uncommon *Fanfare*." *Star Tribune* (Minneapolis, MN), February 24, 2002, F2. Tower talks about the enduring popularity of the first *Fanfare*, as well as the past and current challenges that women composers encounter. See: **D16, D17, D18, W35**

B51. ———. "Tower in Residence." *Star Tribune* (Minneapolis, MN), November 18, 2001. Among other musical announcements: Tower in residence at the University of Minnesota School of Music.

B52. Ardoin, John. "DSO's Patchwork Doesn't Fully Work." *The Dallas Morning News*, April 10, 1989, C6. A mixed review of a Dallas Symphony Orchestra concert. On the program: *Silver Ladders* and works by Mozart and Rimsky-Korsakov and Ives. "Total professional in [Tower's] understanding of a modern symphony . . . filled with an imaginative use of instrumental color." See: **D67, D68, D69, W16**

B53. ———. "Fitting Tribute to Carnegie Hall." *The Dallas Morning News*, May 12, 1991, C2. A performance of *Fanfare for the Uncommon Woman, No. 3* is part of the 100th anniversary celebration for Carnegie Hall. See: **D20, D21, W37**

B54. Banno, Joe. "Verdehr Trio." *The Washington Post,* March 3, 1998, B8. The trio's concert at the Philips Collection features some of their most successful commissions for violin, clarinet and piano. *Rain Waves* "abound(s) in pictorial detail. [Tower] bookends an ambiguous rainy-day conversation between the clarinet and violin with whirls of splashing, drizzling, dripping and cascading notes." See: **D59, W51**

B55.   Bargreen, Melinda. "Weekend Programs Stroke the Strings." *The Seattle Times*, February 1, 2002, H28. Arianna String Quartet performs *Nightfields*.

B56.   ———. "Emerson at Its Best in Meany Concert." *The Times*, January 30, 2004, C2. A lukewarm review of *Incandescent*, which the reviewer found "was more tepid than white-hot, with tone clusters that expanded and contracted, but failed to develop much excitement." See: **W41**

B57.   Barkin, Elaine. "New Music Performance: An Interview with Joan Tower." *The Bennington Review* (1980): 34–40. One of the earliest extended interviews; covers a wide variety of subjects including the formation of the Da Capo Chamber Players, audience development, good and bad publicity, and programming.

B58.   Battisti, Frank. "Joan Tower: How She Came to Write *Fascinating Ribbons*." *The Instrumentalist* 59, no. 9 (April 2005): 32–34. See: **D27**

B59.   Bernstein, Tamara. www.cyorchestra.org/repertoire/?p=6 (Accessed November 18, 2005). Review and analysis of *Fanfare for the Uncommon Woman, No. 5*.

B60.   ———. Liner notes to *Fanfares for the Uncommon Woman*. Koch International Classics 7469, 1999. See: **D16, D17, D18, W10, W35, W36**

B61.   Bickelhaupt, Susan. "From Jefferson to Williams: Music for an All-American Fourth." *The Boston Globe*, July 2, 1993, 55. Announces Boston's WCRB-FM's all-American broadcast which includes the first *Fanfare for the Uncommon Woman*. See: **D16, D17, D18, W35**

B62.   Blocker, Susan. "Anniversary Carries Special Benefit: Renowned Musicians to Compose Music Marking School's 100 Years." *Wisconsin State Journal*, September 3, 1995, A4. See: **D60, W17**

B63.   ———. "MSO to Feature *Clarinet Concerto*." *Wisconsin State Journal*, March 23, 1995, Rhythm, 7. A preview of the Madison Symphony Orchestra's performance of *Clarinet Concerto* with soloist Linda Bartley. Tower comments in this article that she finds the clarinet "one of the most extraordinarily flexible of all instruments, capable of producing an incredibly wide range of dynamics and expression." See: **D10, D11, W5**

B64.   ———. "She Composes—Composer Adds Life to Symphonies." *Wisconsin State Journal*, March 24, 1995, C1. Tower discusses with Blocker her start in the composing world and expresses excitement at hearing a performance of her *Clarinet Concerto* by the Madison Symphony Orchestra; Charles Neidich, clarinet, Elizabeth Schulze, conductor. Humorously: "I'm really looking forward to hearing this delinquent child of mine." See: **D10, D11, W5**

B65.   ———."Hand in Hand—Pianist Seeks out Composers." *Wisconsin State Journal*, March 1, 1996, Daybreak, D1. An interview with Ursula Oppens, who prepares to premiere *Rapids* with the University of Wisconsin–Madison School of Music Orchestra. The work was commissioned by the school to mark its centennial. See: **D60, W17**

B66.   Blomster, Wes. "Omaha: Paul Neubauer and the Holland Performing Arts Center." *American Record Guide* 69, no. 1 (February 2005): 17. Comments on both the premiere of *Purple Rhapsody* and the new hall in which it was performed. ". . . a powerful and pleasantly percussive score that pushes tonality to the edge." See: **W14**

B67.   Blumenthal, Fred. "St. Louis Symphony Orchestra Opens 1984–1985 Season with Joan Tower's *Sequoia*." *St. Louis Globe-Democrat*, September 18, 1984, C4. A feature article about *Sequoia*, the centerpiece of the season's opening concert. See: **D63, D64, D65, D66, W15**

B68.   Borak, Jeffrey. "Pianist, Composer Are a Premiere Team." *Poughkeepsie Journal*, January 31, 1986. An interview with Jacquelyn Helin as she prepares to premiere the *Piano Concerto (Homage to Beethoven)*. See: **D54, D55, W13**

B69.   Bowers, Faubion. "Joan Tower Celebration." *American Record Guide* 62 (March–April 1999): 50–51. Upbeat review of the Merkin Hall celebration concert in honor of Tower's 60th birthday. Peformed: *Petroushskates, Trés Lent, And . . . They're Off!, Wild Purple,* and *Turning Points.* ". . . making a flute, clarinet, violin, 'cello and piano sound like a full orchestra while Tower filched from the Stravinsky ballet and established her skill in orchestration. *Trés Lent* . . . was also an homage, this time to Messiaen, a stunning study in sonorities . . . . *Turning Points* . . . had excellent craftsman-like moments built on four slender ideas. [Tower's work] is not Romantic, not too dissonant, neither cerebral nor personal, never taxing, always accessible, strength and roughness intersticed with sweet lyricism." See: **D49, D50, D51, D52, D53, D74, D75, D76, D78, W26, W49, W53, W55, W67**

B70.   Bradley, Jeff. "Tower, CSO Combine for CD." *Denver Post*, October 3, 1999, I8. Positive review of the newly released *Concerto* CD. "(This CD is) a superb introduction to her sometimes atonal, often difficult but always rewarding music." See: **D28, D75, W5, W9, W13, W21**

B71.   ———. "National Events Honor Composer Joan Tower's 60th." *Denver Post*, February 7, 1998, E5. Details the concert in honor of Tower's birthday as part of the Modern Music Festival in Boulder, Colorado. "Tower often begins with simple gestures but builds spectacular rhythmic and sonic textures."

B72.   ———. "CD Review: Recordings." *Denver Post*, August 26, 1994, 37. Reviews Sharon Isbin's Nightshade Rounds CD, which includes *Clocks*. See: **D12, D13, W59**

B73.   Briscoe, James R. *Contemporary Anthology of Music by Women.* Bloomington: Indiana University Press, 1997.

B74.   Brixley, Elizabeth. "Bartley Is Stunning in *Clarinet Concerto*." *Wisconsin State Journal*, March 27, 1995. Glowing review of a "stunning performance" of the *Clarinet Concerto* by the Madison Symphony Orchestra, Elizabeth Schulze, conductor, and Linda Bartley, clarinet. "The solo part demands athletic technique—use of the extreme high register, for example—and artful rolling between the technical and lyrical lines." See: **D10, D11, W5**

B75. Broun, Ronald. "Thoroughly Modern Milieu." *The Washington Post,* October 10, 1998, Style, C8. The Contemporary Music Forum presents its initial concert at the Corcoran in Washington, D.C. The program includes *Noon Dance* and *Wings.* See: **D47, D48, D79, D80, D81, D82, D83, D84, D85, D86, D87, W45, W68, W69**

B76. ————. "NSO's Strong Show of Works by Women." *The Washington Post,* June 4, 2001, C5. Brief review of a concert which included *Fanfare, No. 1* and works by Zwilich, Beach, and Larsen. "[*Fanfare for the Uncommon Woman* was] . . . brief but effective." See: **D16, D17, D18, W35**

B77. ————. "Ned Rorem and Joan Tower." *The Washington Post,* May 2, 2002, C8. Review of the concert "Two American Composers Play Their Own Works" at the Kennedy Center. Concert included *Petroushskates* ("irresistibly giddy and brilliantly made"), the *Flute Concerto, Wings, Big Sky,* and *Trés Lent.* See: **D4, D28, D49, D50, D51, D52, D53, D79, D80, D81, D82, D83, D84, D85, D86, D87, W9, W27, W49, W53, W68, W69**

B78. ————. "Neubauer's Bloch Party." *The Washington Post,* May 8, 1999, C3. Short review (" . . . mysterious and evocative, well worth repeated listening") of *Wild Purple,* performed by Paul Nebauer in the Sackler Gallery, Washington, D.C. See: **D78, W67**

B79. Brown, Geoff. "Emerson String Quartet." *The Times (London),* November 25, 2004, 22. Rave review of Emerson String Quartet's rendition of *For Daniel* at Wigmore Hall in London. "Why hadn't we heard Joan Tower's music before? Audiences of a conservative bent don't usually uncork the wild applause for recent pieces, but the 66 year-old American composer's dance of constantly transforming, radiant light, deserved every single clap. Over 18 minutes, melodic motifs, chordal crunches, and high diving leaps of the fingerboard sparked and fused in a flow of exhilarating invention." See: **W40**

B80. Brozan, Nadine. "Chronicle." *New York Times,* February 6, 1996, B4, column 6. Carol Wincenc includes *Valentine Trills* on a Valentine's Day concert in Merkin Concert Hall. See: **W70**

B81. Breuer, Robert. "Werke von Steve Reich und Joan Tower in New York erstaufgeführt." *Neue Zeitschrift fur Musik* 1 (January 1983): 33. Announces a performance of *Sequoia* in New York. See: **D63, D64, D65, D66, W15**

B82. Budzak, Gary. "Quartet Boasts Columbus Connection." *Columbus Dispatch* (OH), April 19, 2001, 16. Announces an upcoming concert by the Maia Quartet.

B83. Buell, Richard. "Noting Joan Tower's Niche at 60th Birthday Celebration." *The Boston Globe,* February 16, 1999, C5. Review of the Auros Group for New Music, the Muir String Quartet, John McDonald, and others at Boston College.

B84. Burge, David. "Music Reviews: Waltzes by 25 Contemporary Composers." *MLA Notes* 2 (December 1979): 476–79. The reviewer praises this collection, which includes the "imaginative fantasy" of *Red Garnet Waltz.* See: **D61, D62, W65**

B85.   Burwasser, Peter. "CD Review: Joan Tower: *Black Topaz.*" *Fanfare Magazine* 18, no. 6 (July–August 1995). "Tower is among a handful of American composers to have successfully mastered the art of eclecticism. The music on this disc serves as a superb showcase of Tower's success at both inspiring musicians with beautifully written material and giving a broad range of listeners an opportunity to connect to a vibrant stream of new music." See: **D5, W28**

B86.   Bustard, Clarke. "Composer Sings Praises of eighth blackbird." *Richmond Times-Dispatch*, February 15, 2004, H2. Brief interview before a performance of *Petroushskates* at University of Richmond. See: **D49, D50, D51, D52, D53, W49**

B87.   ———. "Fresh Approach to Music: eighth blackbird Revels in the Challenge of Contemporary Classical Works." *Richmond Times-Dispatch*, February 19, 2004. An interview with eight blackbird before a University of Richmond performance of *Big Sky* and *Petroushskates.* See: **D4, D49, D50, D51, D52, D53, W27, W49**

B88.   ———. "Tower Tired of Explaining Her Music." *Richmond Times-Dispatch*, October 6, 1991. Tower discusses the prejudice against new music.

B89.   Byrne, Frank. "An Interview with Leonard Slatkin." *College Band Directors National Association Report* (Spring 1998): 13. Slatkin singles out Tower as one of three outstanding American composers.

B90.   Camet, Therese J. "The Magic of Music Begins." *Manila Bulletin*, September 5, 2005. Details the Philippines Philharmonic Orchestra's 2005–2006 season, which includes *Fanfare for the Uncommon Woman, No. 1.* See: **D16, D17, D18, W35**

B91.   Campbell, Larry. "Review: American Brass Quintet—American Visions." *International Trombone Association Journal* 32, no. 3 (July 2004): 53–54. Reviewer describes *Fanfare for the Uncommon Woman, No. 5* as a "virtuosic work for all of the trumpets . . . exciting to hear." See: **D23, D24, W38**

B92.   Campbell, Mary. "Carnegie to Mark 100th." *Washington Post*, January 12, 1989, C13. A series of nine concerts mark Carnegie Hall's 100th anniversary. Tower wrote *Fanfare, No. 3* specifically for the May 1991 premiere by members of the New York Philharmonic and Empire Brass. See: **D20, D21, W37**

B93.   Cantrell, Scott. "Tower Rising in Music World." *Times-Union* (Albany, NY), November 9, 1984, C1. Well-written article focusing on Tower's musical education, her connection with the performers of her music, and her relationship with her completed compositions.

B94.   ———. "Emerson Quartet Polishes Exhilarating Works." *Dallas Morning News,* March 30, 2004. A glowing review of *Incandescent*: "Proved engaging both intellectually and viscerally. . . . The basically atonal language finds room for some appealing bittersweet harmonies." See: **W41**

B95. ————. "Edge Lost in Future." *Dallas Morning News*, June 22, 2002. Mixed review of *Tambor*: "Textures are lively, interplays interesting, but the basic motivic material is banal." See: **D88, W19**

B96. ————. "Future Classics." *American Record Guide* 65, no. 5 (Sept–October 2002): 41, 44. "*Tambor* opened the concert with a chatter and clatter of percussion, beneath which the music has something of Aaron Copland's plainspoken manner. A striding motif answered by timpani echoes a memorable gesture from Holst's *Planets*." See: **D88, W19**

B97. Carr, Victor, Jr. "Classics Today. Terry Riley: *Cantos Desiertos*." www.classicstoday.com/search.asp.?ReviewNum=7148 (Accessed January 7, 2005). A review of the CD which Tower's *Snow Dreams* shares with composers Riley, Beaser, Liebermann, and Schickele. "Joan Tower's quasi-impressionistic *Snow Dreams* initially conjures up idyllic, pastoral images before the composer's spiky harmonic style slightly sharpens the music's edges." See: **D70, D71, D72, W54**

B98. ————. "Classics Today: Joan Tower: Instrumental Music." www.classicstoday.com/review.asp?ReviewNum=9266 (Accessed January 10, 2006). Review of the Naxos instrumental CD with *In Memory, Big Sky, Wild Purple, Holding a Daisy, Or Like a . . . An Engine, Vast Antique Cubes, Throbbing Still*, and *Island Prelude*. "Joan Tower's chamber music has much the same emotional intensity and gestural ferocity as her orchestral works. Her primarily angular harmonic language, with its predominantly dissonant cast, evokes a sense of agitation bordering on rage." See: **D4, D32, D33, D34, D35, D36, D46, D78, W27, W42, W43, W63, W67**

B99. Charles, Gerard. "Stepping Stones." *Balletnotes* of BalletMet, www.balletmet.org/ Notes/ Stones.html (Accessed January 10, 2005). Article dealing with the inception of *Stepping Stones* (choreography by Kathryn Posin), which the Milwaukee Ballet premiered in April 1993. "As a composer, I've always thought of myself as a closet choreographer. Texture, space, speed, direction, all the words that apply to dance also apply to music." See: **D73, W3**

B100. Chism, Olin. "Concertos Get to Heart of Dramatics." *Dallas Morning News*, February 8, 1998. Review of the *Concertos* CD. "[The concertos] are bold and melodic and glory in stretching the capabilities of each solo instrument . . . showpieces." See: **D10, D11, D28, D54, D55, D77, W5, W9, W13, W21**

B101. Clark, Robert. "Critic's Pick." *The Calgary Herald* (Alberta), September 2, 2004, F6. Article about the Banff International String Quartet Competition where Tower is one of the featured composers.

B102. ————. "Music Chronicle I." *Hudson Review* 57, no. 3 (2004): 479. Lengthy article about Tower and an all-Tower concert in New York City, performed by the St. Luke's Chamber Ensemble. The program included *Rain Waves, Big Sky, In Memory*. See: **D4, D32, D59, W27, W42, W51**

B103. Clements, Andrew. "Classical CD Releases." *The Guardian* (London), August 5, 2005, Final Edition, 19. Review of new Tower CD. Includes *In Memory; Big Sky; Wild Purple; No Longer Very Clear; Island Prelude*.

"[Tower] has forged a distinctive style from a variety of contemporary models including serialism and Messiaen. . . . [Her] music is all very carefully crafted but never seems to lose its rhythmic vitality in the process. The most impressive piece here, the string quartet, *In Memory,* composed after 9/11, is a perfectly paced, steadily evolving single movement, while the piano trio, *Big Sky,* and the freewheeling quintet for oboe and strings, *Island Prelude,* from 1989, show how, as a professional pianist herself, Tower understands the minutiae of chamber-music playing. *No Longer Very Clear,* the four piano pieces, vividly played on the disc by Ursula Oppens, take their individual titles from lines by John Ashbery; they are intense, study-like, and shaped with absolute precision." See: **D4, D32, D33, D34, D35, D36, D46, D78, W27, W42, W43, W63, W67**

B104.   Clements, Carol. "HPR Interview: Joan Tower." *High Performance Review* (Winter 1991–1992): 60–64. Extensive article dealing with Tower's compositional process and philosophy of composing.

B105.   Commanday, Robert. "Conductor Shows His Outgoing Side: Herbig's American Program with Symphony." *The San Francisco Chronicle,* March 20, 1992, D5. This reviewer could find nothing positive to write about *Sequoia,* which shared a San Francisco Symphony program with the Barber *Cello Concerto,* and Dvorak's *New World Symphony.* See: **D63, D64, D65, D66, W15**

B106.   Conrad, Willa. "From New World to Telemann, an Evening of Wonderful Pairings." *The Charlotte Observer,* March 1, 1997. The Charlotte Symphony performs the *Flute Concerto,* Dvorak's *New World Symphony,* and Telemann. "Intricately balanced inner lines, bright orchestral effects." See: **D28, W9**

B107.   Cowan, Rob. "Rob Cowan on the Week's CD Releases." *The Independent* (London), October 22, 1999, 18. The focus of the review is the release of the 10-disk set *American Celebration* by the New York Philharmonic. Included in the set is *Sequoia.* See: **D63, D64, D65, D66, W15**

B108.   Creditor, Bruce. "Quintessence." *The Clarinet* 17, no. 4 (July–August 1990): 6–7. Reviewer summarizes/reprints a portion of clarinetist Ed Matthew's *Chamber Music America* article about the commission and premiere of *Island Prelude.* See: **D33, D34, D35, D36, W43**

B109.   Croan, Robert. "*Fantasy* Brings Tower to Town." *Pittsburgh Post-Gazette,* March 28, 1994, D2. Tower to lecture on *Fantasy* and *Platinum Spirals* before their performance in Frick Auditorium at the University of Pittsburgh. See: **D25, D26, D56, D57, W39, W64**

B110.   ———. "Juilliard Group to Open PCMS Season." *The Pittsburgh Post-Gazette,* February 13, 1995, C2. The Pittsburgh Chamber Music Society slates the Muir Quartet to perform *Night Fields.* See: **D43, D44, D45, W46**

B111.   ———. "Muir String Quartet's Performance Towering." *Pittsburgh Post-Gazette,* December 12, 1995, C9. Review of Muir Quartet's performance of *Night Fields.* "[*Night Fields*'] single-movement structure frames an emotional elegiac outpouring with outer sections of intense vigor and harmonic strength. It . . . contains a gamut of human expression couched in a harmonically colorful aural garb." See: **D43, D44, D45, W46**

B112. ———."Highlighting American Composers." *Pittsburgh Post-Gazette,* April 14, 1998, G4. Pittsburgh Symphony commissions and programs the premiere of *Tambor.* Tower shares this program with Ellen Taaffe Zwilich. See: **D88, W19**

B113. ———. "Symphony Excels with New Music and Old." *Pittsburgh Post-Gazette,* May 8, 1998, B2. Mariss Jansons and the Pittsburgh Symphony premiere *Tambor.* "Its knockout moments alternate with lyrical melodic fragments. . . . Tower's rhythmic vocabulary is varied and inventive." See: **D88, W19**

B114. ———. "Tower of Sound: Composer Emphasized the Rhythm and Timbre for New PSO Piece." *Pittsburgh Post-Gazette,* May 8, 1998, 23. Tower speaks with the reporter about the composing process in advance of the Pittsburgh Symphony's premiere of *Tambor.* See: **D88, W19**

B115. ———. "Pittsburgh Symphony: Tower's *Tambor." American Record Guide* 61 (July–August 1998): 53. A review of *Tambor,* followed by Tower's explanation of her affinity for percussion. Croan writes: "Essentially a terse concerto for the percussion section, Tower's score has color and variety. It starts with a showcase of percussion techniques and sound possibilities, then shows the remaining instruments of the orchestra striving for comparable sounds, each within its own physical capabilities. Tower revels in cross-rhythms and off-the-beat accents, as well as rhythmic patterns repeated for several measures that, fleetingly, sound minimalistic." See: **D88, W19**

B116. Culot, Hubert. "CD Review: Joan Tower Instrumental Works." www.musicweb.uk.net/classrev/2005/Oct05/Tower8559215.htm (Accessed February 18, 2006). Enthusiastic review of this release. "Tower's music is clearly of its time, closer to Bartók and Stravinsky than to Copland, and it is always colorful, well-crafted and immensely accessible."

B117. Cunningham, Carl. "Music: Contemporary Trends." *The Houston Post,* March 13, 1983, B2. Review of a Houston Symphony performance of *Amazon* ". . . pleasant, peaceful. . . ." See: **D1, D2, W23, W24**

B118. Dalton, Jody. "New Music News." *Ear Magazine* 15 (June 1990): 13. Tower receives the Grawemeyer Award for *Silver Ladders.* See: **D67, D68, D69, W16**

B119. Dalton, Joseph. "Small Orchestra Gains Notice." *The Times Union* (Albany, NY*),* July 4, 2004, I5. Discusses Tower's involvement with *Made in America,* a consortium of small orchestras which commissions works from high-profile American composers. Tower, at the time of the article's publication, was working on a 15-minute composition for the Glens Falls (NY) Symphony Orchestra. See: **D88, W11**

B120. ———. "Real Women." *The Times Union* (Albany, NY), May 26, 2005, P12. Reviewer interviews cellist Yehuda Hanani about the Close Encounters with Music Series, which she directs. The program will include Tower at the piano for a performance of her trio *For Daniel.* See: **W40**

B121. ———. "A Sound Way to Keep America the Beautiful." *The Times Union* (Albany), September 25, 2005. Arts-Events, I3. Announces the world premiere of *Made in America*, performed by the Glens Falls Symphony, under the baton of Charles Peltz. He describes the new work as "an uncanny balance of the clear expansion of melody with a fragmented, disguised creative use of the tune." See: **D88, W11**

B122. ———. "*Made in America* Debuts with Polish." *The Times Union* (Albany, NY), October 3, 2005, C4. The Glens Falls Symphony debuts *Made in America*. "Tower has a well-established style—propulsive rhythmic landscapes with vibrant orchestration. *Made in America* hewed closely to that model but with an added element. Fragments of the melody of *America the Beautiful* are subtly woven throughout the piece. The familiar tune gave a thread of beauty, possibly hope, to Tower's tense and edgy sounds. Something always seemed to be impending, but the only true climax came in the end in a giant roll of the bass drum. The score's feeling of industry and striving made it very American." See: **D88, W11**

B123. ———. "Glens Falls Orchestra Reaches Out." *The Times Union* (Albany, NY), September 25, 2005, I1. The orchestra wants to tighten community ties to classical music, and one way of doing that is to feature specially commissioned works like *Made in America*. See: **D88, W11**

B124. Darrow, Emily. "Conductors' Institute at Bard College Announces Its Summer 2005 Program." *Bard College Press Release.* www.bard.edu/news/releases/pr/fstory.php?id=829 (Accessed February 10, 2006). An extensive article detailing the program's conductors and composers-in-residence. In-depth coverage of Tower's career; includes a quote from the *New Yorker*, hailing her as "one of the most successful woman composers of all time."

B125. Davidson, Justin. "Something Extra for the Ordinary." *Newsday*, February 25, 2000. Review of the premiere of *The Last Dance* by the Orchestra of St. Luke's. ". . . alternates intense percussion frenzy with slow, tense strings." See: **W20**

B126. Davis, Peter G. "Music: Minorities, Minimalism, and Melodrama." *New York,* October 11, 1982. A lengthy article reviewing the New York Philharmonic's performance of *Sequoia*. "What gives *Sequoia* its expressive individuality . . . is the strong poetic impulse that motivates the notes as they translate a visual image into sound. . . . A busy, energetic score that cleverly proportions and balances the elements. . . . The effort necessary to appreciate such craftsmanship pays off handsomely." See: **D63, D64, D65, D66, W15**

B127. ———. "Switch." *New York Magazine* 27, no. 4 (1994): 79. Features the composer and *Concerto for Orchestra*, her life in Bolivia, South America's influence on her creative work, and CDs of Tower's music. Tower speaks to a New York Philharmonic audience prior to her *Concerto for Orchestra's* performance. Article also includes review of *Concerto:* "contrasting spacious, long-held chords with passages of rapidly whirling notes that fairly explode with action and energy, all carefully controlled and proportioned to communicate a satisfying sense of coherency . . . interesting musical challenges for every player." See: **D14, D88, W6**

B128. Dees, Pamela. *Piano Music by Women Composers: Women Born After 1900*, vol. 2. Westport: Praeger Publishers, 2004.

B129. Delacoma, Wynne. "Fine Finale for Grant Park Orchestra." *Chicago Sun-Times*, August 24, 1992, 36. A review of a Grant Park Symphony Orchestra concert which began with Copland's and Tower's *Fanfares*. "[Tower's *Fanfare*] was a prickly, energetic companion to Copland's classic." See: **D16, D17, D18, W35**

B130. ———. "String Ensemble Ends Season on a Positive Note." *Chicago Sun-Times*, May 18, 1992, 32. Glowing review of the local premiere of *Island Prelude*, which shared the program with works by Barber, Bach, Elgar, and Shostakovich. "Tower set pure, burnished oboe melodies, beautifully shaped . . . against murmuring strings." See: **D33, D34, D35, D36, W43**

B131. ———. "Slatkin Leads CSO in Energetic Tower Concerto." *Chicago Sun-Times*, April 9, 1993, 27. Positive review of a Chicago Symphony Orchestra performance of *Concerto for Orchestra*. ". . . a study in high energy rather than expansiveness. . . . [The work contained] . . . a hint of minimalism but . . . [Tower's] repetition was not obsessive." See: **D14, D88, W6**

B132. ———. "Classical's Pre-Easter Basket Full of Concerts." *Chicago Sun-Times*, March 18, 2005, Weekend Edition, 10. The Fulcrum Point Ensemble programs *Amazon I* on a March 2005 recital. See: **D1, D2, W23**

B133. DeLapp, Jennifer. "Essential Cowell: Selected Writings on Music." *Notes* 59, no. 3 (2003): 630–32. When the re-release of Cowell's book encountered problems with a publisher, Tower and Pauline Oliveros rallied to bring the book's publication to fruition.

B134. Dennis, Ron. "Music Review: *Wings*." Unpublished review in composer's collection. ". . . a broad, serious essay in contemporary idiom for the mature clarinetist . . . characterized by sophisticated exploitation of the clarinet's sonic potential in realizing the musical idea." See: **D79, D80, D81, D82, D83, D84, D85, D86, D87, W68, W69**

B135. Denton, David. "David's Review Corner: Tower: *In Memory, Big Sky, Wild Purple, Holding a Daisy, Or Like a . . . an Engine, Antique Cubes, Throbbing Still, Island Prelude*." Positive review of Tower's music. "[Her orchestral works] continue where Bartók left off, with just a whiff of Copland and a hint of Bernstein's colourful orchestration. This is the first time I have come across Tower's chamber music, and the experience proves rewarding." www.naxos.com/sharefile/rview/David_reviewcorner_AUG.asp (Accessed April 20, 2006). See: **D4, D32, D33, D34, D35, D36, D46, D78, W27, W42, W43, W63, W67**

B136. Dervan, Michael. "Sound and Vision: Reviews." *The Irish Times*, March 19, 1999, 13. The briefest of reviews of *Silver Ladders*, as well as a mention of the Grawemeyer Award. See: **D67, D68, D69, W16**

B137. Dettmer, Roger. "CD Classical Review: New York Philharmonic—An American Celebration, Volume 2." www.classical_cdreview.com/nyp2.htm (Accessed April 20, 2005). Reviews the 5-disk set which includes *Sequoia*:

"It is a serious piece in an astringent but accessible idiom." See: **D63, D64, D65, D66, W15**

B138. Dowling, Susan, producer. *Soundings: The Music of Joan Tower.* WGBH-New Television Workshop documentary, 1982.

B139. Drone, Jeanette. "American Composer Update." *Pan Pipes of Sigma Alpha Iota* 75, no. 2 (1983): 43. Details the premieres of several [at that point] untitled works: one by Collage (*Noon Dance*) at Harvard University and one by Carol Wincenc and Sharon Isbin (*Snow Dreams*) in St. Paul, Minnesota. See: **D47, D48, D70, D71, D72, W45, W54**

B140. Druckenbrod, Andrew. "Short Takes: Pittsburgh New Music Ensemble Impressive." *Pittsburgh Post-Gazette*, July 22, 2003. The ensemble presents choreographed versions of originally all-instrumental works, including *Petroushskates.* See: **D49, D50, D51, D52, D53, W49**

B141. ———. "Music Review: String Quartet Undone by Lack of Cohesion." *Pittsburgh Post-Gazette*, February 26, 2003. Having replaced their second violinist recently, the Tokyo String Quartet encountered some ensemble problems in this recital that included *In Memory.* "Opening with a descending, lamenting figure and later overwhelmed with naked anger. . . . Strident writing emphasizes the anxiety of not knowing ultimately at whom to gnash one's teeth when death comes unexpectedly." See: **D32, W42**

B142. ———. "Concert Review: Tortelier Tested in Galway Concert." *Pittsburgh Post-Gazette,* June 11, 2004. During a three-day festival, Yan Pascal Tortelier conducts a Pittsburgh Symphony Orchestra performance which featured *Tambor* and works by Richard Strauss, Claude Debussy, and David Amram. "[*Tambor*] is a work of percussive splendor. . . ." See: **D88, W19**

B143. ———. "Reviews: The Best New Recordings from North America– The Waltz Project Revisited." *Gramophone* 82 (February 2005): A14

B144. Dubins, Jerry. "CD Review: Joan Tower: Instrumental Music." *Fanfare Magazine* 29, no. 3 (January–February 2006): 239–40. "This latest Naxos release in their 'American Classics' series is a superb introduction to a woman who deserves, in my opinion, to be one of America's laureate composers."

B145. Dubroff, Marcy. "Franklin & Marshall College Presents Five New York Premieres." Franklin and Marshall Archived Release: server1.fandm.edu/departments/CollegeRelations/PressReleases/2000–01/P 167.html (Accessed February 21, 2006). This Merkin Hall concert included *Vast Antique Cubes/Throbbing Still.* See: **D46, W63**

B146. Duffie, Bruce. "Joan Tower: The Composer in Conversation with Bruce Duffie." *New Music Connoisseur Magazine* 9, no. 1 (Spring 2001): 23. An excellent interview covering the state of contemporary music, women composers, and concert programming.

B147. ———. "Joan Tower: The Composer in Conversation with Bruce Duffie." my.voyager.net/~duffie/tower.html (Accessed January 8, 2005). Revised, online version of Duffie article listed in **B146**.

B148. Duke, David Gordon. "Eclectic But Intelligent Program: Emerson Quartet a Reliable Favourite for Friends of Chamber Music." *The Vancouver Sun*, January 14, 2005, Arts and Life, H10. "*Incandescent* is a taut and logical work, spectacularly conceived for the Emerson, and brought to life by appropriately incandescent and rhythmically vibrant playing." See: **W41**

B149. Dyer, Richard. "A Musical Personality Finds His Voice in Guitar." *The Boston Globe*, October 25, 1994, 68. David Leisner performs *Clocks*: "Vigorous in idea, strong in profile." This performance included a very minor revision of the composition: a single note, with which Tower had always been unhappy, was changed, even though it added considerably to the level of difficulty for the guitarist. See: **D12, D13, W59**

B150. ———. "Joan Tower's Bold Music Hits Boston." *The Boston Globe*, May 3, 1987, 101. *Silver Ladders* enjoys its Boston premiere with the St. Louis Symphony under Leonard Slatkin. See: **D67, D68, D69, W16**

B151. ———. "Boston Symphony Century to Be Captured in a Box." *The Boston Globe*, November 5, 1999, D15. Notes the trend of major orchestras to record and issue retrospective sets. Mentions the New York Philharmonic's boxed set which included *Sequoia*. See: **D63, D64, D65, D66, W15**

B152. ———. "Stirring Tower Fanfares Launch Festive Evening." *The Boston Globe*, July 24, 2002, F6. Reviews a Tanglewood concert which began with the first three *Fanfares*. See: **D16, D17, D18, W35, W36, W37**

B153. ———. "Trio Shows Command of Light and Dark." *The Boston Globe*, August 20, 2005, C2. Very favorable review of *For Daniel*. "The rhythms of the piece are governed by the efforts of breathing. . . . The anguish is unremitting, but so is the vitality and the rush of raw emotions . . . a ravishing splash of water that recalls Liszt or Ravel." Kalichstein-Laredo-Robinson Trio performed. See: **W40**

B154. ———. "*Made in America* is a Major Group Effort." *The Boston Globe*, November 18, 2005, Entertainment, C8. Outlines the co-commissioning process and highlights the four Massachusetts performances of *Made in America*. See: **D88, W11**

B155. ———. "A Subdued Celebration of Composers." *Boston Globe*, August 11, 1994, 29. Details the Composers' Conference performances at Wellesley College. "*Amazon* is not the feminist piece one might expect from the composer of *Fanfare for the Uncommon Woman*. Instead, it is a lyrical evocation of the mighty river. The rippling rills and the crosscurrents of rhythm place this in the delightful company of the very best water music by Liszt, Debussy and Ravel." See: **D1, D2, W23, W24**

B156. ———. "Tanglewood Fest Focused on Pleasure." *The Boston Globe*, August 14, 2005, Third Edition, N5. Tanglewood premiere of the "invigorating *DNA*." See: **D89, W33**

B157. Ehrensaft, Philip. "CD Reviews: Joan Tower: Instrumental Music." www.chronogram.com/issue/2006/01/arts/music/cd.php (Accessed February 6, 2006). "Her engaging music shifts from languid tonal sensuality to loud dissonance to shades of atonality in function of immediate emotional goals and musical context."

B158.   Eichler, Jeremy. "A Somber Salute to American History." *Newsday*, January 26, 2000. Mixed review of the National Symphony Orchestra's performance of *Tambor* in Carnegie Hall. "Tightly charged rhythmic statements held the music together, but unfortunately, the rhythms themselves were not particularly interesting or complex. . . . Earnest but flawed. . . opened . . . in rambunctious, almost raucous style." See: **D88, W19**

B159.   ———. "Youth Is Served Classically." *New York Times,* August 10, 2005, Final Edition, 5, column 2. Details Tower's involvement with the Young Composers' Development Program of the Orchestra of St. Luke's.

B160.   Erdmann, Thomas. "An Interview with Joan Tower." *Journal of the Conductors' Guild* 25, no. 1 (2004): 1–9. Lengthy interview that covers Tower's early years, her composition process, and the current state of contemporary music.

B161.   Erikson, Matthew. "Emerson at Tanglewood." *Hartford Courant* (CT), July 15, 2004, 30. Announces a forthcoming performance which includes Shostakovich, Britten, and Tower's *Incandescent.* See: **W41**

B162.   Fairman, Richard. "The Philharmonia; Royal Festival Hall." *Financial Times*, May 30, 1991, 21. Review of *Sequoia*, conducted by Leonard Slatkin in London. See: **D63, D64, D65, D66, W15**

B163.   Farmer, Ann. "Joint Effort." *Classical Music*, November 20, 2004, 54. Article treats the *Made in America* consortium. See: **D88, W11**

B164.   Felton-Coletti, Mario. Critiques de DC. *La Scena Musicale* 11, no. 2. www.scena.org/LSMCritics.asp?Volume=11&No=2&Type=0&lan=2 (Accessed February 8, 2006). Glowing review of 2005's instrumental CD. "La musique . . . d'une extraordinaire sophistication . . . une grande sensibilité artistique."

B165.   Feder, Susan. Liner notes to *Meet the Composer Orchestra Residency Series: Joan Tower*, Electra/Nonesuch Records 79245, 1990. See: **D33, D34, D35, D36, D41, D42, D63, D64, D65, D66, D67, D68, D69, W12, W15, W16, W43**

B166.   ———. Liner notes to *Meet the Composer Orchestra Residency Series: Joan Tower*, Electra/Nonesuch Records FECD0025, 2004. See: **D33, D34, D35, D36, D37, D38, D39, D41, D42, D63, D64, D65, D66, D67, D68, D69, W10, W12, W15, W16, W43**

B167.   Fennelly, Brian. "Reviews: Joan Tower: *Hexachords*." *Notes* 34, no. 1 (September 1977): 204–6. The review focuses on the publication *Solo Flute Series,* which includes *Hexachords*, a work which "addresses itself to an instrumental polyphony in traditional terms." See: **D29, D30, D31, W62**

B168.   Fischbach, Bob, and Ashley Hassebroek. "Classical and Jazz Arts Preview." *Omaha World-Herald,* September 11, 2005, Sunrise Edition, AT4. New York Philharmonic violist Paul Neubauer performs the world premiere of *Purple Rhapsody*, co-commissioned by the Omaha Symphony. See: **W14**

B169.   Fisher, George, and Judy Lochhead. "Analyzing from the Body." *Theory and Practice: Newsletter-Journal of the Music Theory Society of New York State* 27 (2002): 37–67. Using portions of Tower's *Fantasy . . . (Those*

Harbor Lights) and Brahms' *Sonata for Clarinet* in E-flat, Op. 120, the authors explore the idea of "the central role of bodily activity in the projection, apprehension and constitution of musical meaning." See: **D25, D26, W39**

B170. Fleming, John. "Kinder, Gentler Composers They're Not." *St. Petersburg Times* (FL), August 11, 1998, D1. Tower, Zwilich, and Musgrave on being identified as women composers rather than composers, as well as the impact the feminist movement has had on their composition.

B171. Fleming, Michael. "Two Reasons the St. Louis Symphony is Nudging to Top." *St. Petersburg Times,* May 25, 1986, E2. A review of the Slatkin/ St. Louis recording of *Sequoia*: "Shows a . . . mastery of the orchestra and an instinctive understanding of form." See: **D63, D64, D65, D66, W15**

B172. Fleming, Shirley. "New York Philharmonic: Tower *Concerto for Orchestra.*" *American Record Guide* 57, no. 2 (March 1, 1994): 47. "Tower shows a very adept skill in handling large orchestral forces and also in creating, in quieter moments, some attractive and translucent episodes." See: **D14, D88, W6**

B173. Fletcher, John. "Analysis of *Fascinating Ribbons.*" *The Instrumentalist* 59, no. 9 (April 2005): 34–40. See: **D27**

B174. Fox, Larry. "Waterford, Fair Waterford." *Washington Post,* October 5, 2001, T3. Percussionist Evelyn Glennie and the National Symphony Orchestra premiere *Strike Zones* at the Kennedy Center in Washington, DC See: **W18**

B175. Fox, Margalit. "A Living Composer." *Newsday,* January 2, 1994, 16. Lengthy interview with the composer before the premiere of *Concerto for Orchestra.* See: **D14, D88, W6**

B176. Freymann-Weyr, Jeffrey. Radio Broadcast. "Unique Performances of the Chamber Music Group eighth blackbird." All Things Considered, National Public Radio, March 10, 2004. Interview with Tower and the members of eighth blackbird.

B177. Gann, Kyle. 2001. "American Composer: Joan Tower." *Chamber Music* 18, no. 6 (December 2001): 28–29. Details Tower's composing origins, her compositional aesthetic and development, and her passion for chamber music. "It is an earthy, tactile body of music, steeped in body movement and performance practice. Its most unvarying characteristic is that it never stays still, but dedicates itself to the art of continual transition. In the works of the 90s and 80s, that restlessness results in a tension that feels somewhat nervous and disembodied; in the recent works such as *Night Fields* and *Big Sky,* the tension is still present but now underlain by a profound calm. It's an amazing—and appropriately gradual—transformation in a composer's development, as though the music has slowly shed its fear without losing its lust for life." See: **D4, D43, D44, D45, W27, W46**

B178. ———. "Contoured Sheets." *Village Voice,* March 3, 1987, 70. Review of a concert on which Tower's *Noon Dance* shared the stage with works by Krzystof Penderecki and George Perle. "[*Noon Dance* exhibited] "ingratiating excitement. . . . Amid scurrying alternations of notes and chords, several strong motives led the ear and unified the melodic contour . . . richly patterned fabric." See: **D47, D48, W45**

B179. ———. "Uptown Dropout." *Village Voice*, September 22, 1998, 132. The article profiles Tower and the upcoming series of concerts across North America which celebrate her 60th birthday. Tower discusses her alienation from serial music and the increased satisfaction she gets by composing more intuitively.

B180. Gay, Yvonne. "Oberlin Ensembles Celebrate Composer Joan Tower's Music in Finney Chapel and at Aki Festival of New Music in Cleveland." Oberlin Online: Backstage Pass. www.oberlin.edu/con/bkstage/20 0310/JoanTower.htm (Accessed January 9, 2005). A lengthy article detailing Tower's accomplishments and announcing her Oberlin residency and a pair of concerts featuring her music, performed by the Oberlin Contemporary Music Ensemble and Percussion Group.

B181. Giffin, Glenn. "A New Sound at Aspen." *American Record Guide* 57, no. 1 (January–February 1994): 30. For the opening of Aspen's Harris Concert Hall, Tower's *Fanfare for the Uncommon Woman, No. 5* is premiered: "Serious enough for the occasion, sassy enough for its title." See: **D23, D24, W38**

B182. Gimbel, Alan. "Review: Tower: *In Memory; Big Sky; Wild Purple; No Longer Very Clear; Island Prelude.*" *American Record Guide* 69, no. 1 (January–February 2006): 210. A lukewarm reception for this Naxos CD: "[Tower] has always favored expanded diatonic languages like octatonicism (like middle Stravinsky and the French composers of the century) over the more heated chromatic styles of many of her urban colleagues. Her music is vaguely tonal and thus generally approachable, though it is usually constructed for use in small doses." See: **D4, D32, D33, D34, D35, D36, D46, D78, W27, W42, W43, W63, W67**

B183. Ginell, Richard S. "Los Angeles Chamber Orchestra: Tower *Duets.*" *American Record Guide* 58, no. 3 (1995): 53. Enthusiastic review of a Los Angeles Chamber Orchestra performance which included the premiere of *Duets*. "*Duets* is a particularly pleasing sampling of her stylistically amorphous ways. . . . The language is tonal, lyrical, and a bit vague; like a few of Tower works, we notice more sheer craft and cunning orchestration at work than arresting musical ideas."

B184. Godfrey, John. "From the Height of a Sequoia." *Christian Science Monitor*, May 1, 1992, 16. Glowing review of a Toronto Symphony performance of *Sequoia*. "Power and grandeur cohere in *Sequoia.*" See: **D63, D64, D65, D65, W15**

B185. Goldman, Mary Kunz. "Review: BPO Soars with Brahms' First." *The Buffalo News*, March 5, 2006. Review of *Purple Rhapsody*: "It's rhapsodic in a spiritual, rather than melodic, sense. Unpredictable, stream-of-consciousness interludes give way to plateaus of calm. . . . The music also showed the wealth of textures, from caressing, mournful lines to a clear, whistling tone in the stratosphere of the viola's range." See: **W14**

B186. Goldsmith, Harris. "Muir String Quartet." *American Record Guide* 58 no. 3 (1995): 51. Focuses on the premiere of *Night Fields* by the Muir String Quartet at New York City's Weill Hall. "Dynamic, forward-directed, replete with reference to the chattering repeated notes of the first movement of Bartok's *Fifth Quartet*, to the slashing chords of the *Fourth*, to the dynamic muscularity and stringent compression of the *Third*. Still, Tower's essay was an effective musical statement in its own right. The work lent itself well to the Muir's tight, aggressive, militant style and showed the group to its best advantage." See: **D43, D44, D45, W46**

B187. Goodfellow, William S. "Joan Tower: Music Must Unfold." *The American Record Guide* 55, no. 4 (1992): 20. A brief article that focuses on Tower's presence at the rehearsals leading up to the premiere of her *Violin Concerto* with Joseph Silverstein, Elmar Oliveira, and the Utah Symphony. See: **D77, W21**

B188. ———. "Utah Symphony/Silverstein: Tower *Violin Concerto* (premiere)." *The American Record Guide* 55, no. 4 (1992): 73. The *Violin Concerto* "strikes me as prime Tower, typically bold and colorful yet with a pronounced lyrical streak and an unexpectedly strong formal design . . . . The orchestral writing . . . runs the gamut, from the forcefulness of the brass, at times jazzily inflected, to the almost Impressionistic central section, with its shimmering percussion and strings." See: **D77, W21**

B189. ———. "Record Review: Previn, Slatkin Bring Us More New Voices on Nonesuch." *Deseret News* (Salt Lake City), October 26, 1986. Review of *Sequoia* as recorded by Leonard Slatkin and the St. Louis Symphony: "Brilliant, often dazzling. . . ." See: **D63, D64, D65, D66, W15**

B190. ———. "Introspective *Night Fields* dominates new Tower CD." *Deseret News* (Salt Lake City), April 14, 1996. Review of the *Black Topaz* CD, in which the writer focuses mainly on *Night Fields*: "Its shifting moods and tensions and dark, tautly introspective writing hold up well, combining a Shostakovichian terseness and acridity with her own energy and creative vitality—even in the music's quieter pages." See: **D5, D43, D44, D45, W28, W46**

B191. Goodman, Peter. "Joan Tower, Scaling the Heights." *New York Newsday,* April 30, 1987, Entertainment Section. Brief article covering Tower's passion for contemporary music and approach to composition.

B192. Goodman, Virginia. "Program Gives Big-time Debut to Small Orchestra." Broadcast, National Public Radio, Morning Edition, October 19, 2005. An interview with Joan Tower describes the *Made in America* commissioning consortium. See: **D88, W11**

B193. Goulart, Karen. "Concert Sunday at Norwell Library." *The Patriot Ledger* (Quincy, MA), January 19, 2004, 15. The Calyx Trio performs *Big Sky* at the James Library. See: **D4, W27**

B194. Gould, Neil. "Hudson Valley Philharmonic: Tower Premiere." *High Fidelity/Musical America* 30 (March 1980): 24. At the urging of conductor Imre Pallo, Tower fully orchestrated her *Amazon II,* originally for quintet. Pallo and the Hudson Valley Philharmonic then premiered the work at the

Kingston Center for the Performing Arts. "The aspect of Tower's composition that most impresses is her ability to create a structurally cogent and moving work out of motivic materials that are concise and arresting to the ear. . . . If there is a weakness in this work at all, it involves the transformation of triplets originally conceived for the piano into string figures. At the tempo demanded by this score, these figures do not work and the result is a blurring of the orchestral sound that is at variance with the translucent clarity of the rest of the score." See: **D1, D2, W24**

B195. ———. "A Moving Premiere, Warm Debut Launch the Philharmonic's Season." *Poughkeepsie Journal,* November 12, 1979. The Hudson Valley Philharmonic premieres *Amazon.* See: **D1, D2, W23, W24**

B196. Gowen, Bradford. "The Latest CDs." *Piano and Keyboard: the Bimonthly Piano Quarterly* 192 (May–June 1998): 60–61. A glowing review of the *Concertos* CD. "As a recording, it is a document of what is possible in the CD era, and a vivid tribute to the reputation of an impressive composer. These concertos . . . show Tower to be a composer of music that is spontaneous, colorful, poetic, theatrical, commanding, and accessible. She creates moments of intimacy, of rapt quietness, of pushed-from-behind urgency, and of soaring sweep, tied together with prismatic orchestration, and infused with an anything-can-happen atmosphere." See: **D10, D11, D28, D54, D55, D77, W5, W9, W13, W21**

B197. Gray, Channing. "*Made in America* Composer Embraced by 50 States." *The Providence Journal* (RI), November 17, 2005, Live this Weekend, L14. *Made in America* is performed by the Rhode Island Philharmonic. See: **D88, W11**

B198. ———. "Philharmonic at Veterans Saturday Night: *Made in America* Makes It to R.I." *The Providence Journal* (RI), November 21, 2005, A2. "Masterful." See: **D88, W11**

B199. Green, Judith. "Catch These." *The Atlanta Journal-Constitution*, March 26, 1999. Announces a week-long residency by Tower at the University of Georgia in Athens.

B200. ———. "Uncommon Composer Holds Court at UGA." *The Atlanta Journal-Constitution,* March 24, 1999, E2. Previews Tower's activities as composer in residence at University of Georgia and outlines her thoughts regarding women composers. "The statistics are not good for us females. We have to balance things out a little bit around here."

B201. Greenberg, Mike. "Concert Works Sassy, Serious by Turns." *San Antonio Express-News*, January 24, 2002, F2. Review of the SOLI Chamber Ensemble's performance of *Amazon*: "[*Amazon*] opens darkly, with spare but nervous textures. The center is an extended passage of driving rhythms, with melodic material, delivered sometimes in unison, that suggests the indigenous cultures of the rain forest. The closing is serene. . . . Tower's music . . . draws from a deep well of pathos and urgency." See: **D1, D2, W23, W24**

B202. Griffiths, Paul. "Women's Music: Who Can Tell?" *New York Times,* July 7, 1998, E1, column 4. "The lesson may be that sex is much less important than national origin in influencing a composer's music."

B203. ———. "It's a Wonderful Town for Underexposed Composers." *New York Times,* January 20, 2001, B15. Rather poorly written review of an Alice Tully Hall concert, part of A Great Day in New York Festival, which included *Rain Waves.* See: **D59, W51**

B204. ———. "From Delicate Whispers to a Furious Clamor." *New York Times,* October 15, 2001, Arts, E3. Musings about a pair of National Symphony concerts.

B205. Groeling, Charles R. *"Joan Tower: Celebration Fanfare." The Instrumentalist* 51, no. 9 (April 1997): 44A. Descriptive review of *Celebration Fanfare.* See: **D9, W1**

B206. ———. *"Joan Tower: Clarinet Concerto." The Instrumentalist* 47, no. 3 (October 1992): 103. A descriptive review of *Clarinet Concerto.* See: **D10, D11, W5**

B207. Gruber, Dan. "A Rare Combination." *Buffalo News,* June 13, 2000, N4. Review of a Buffalo Philharmonic Orchestra which included *Fanfare, No. 1.* See: **D16, D17, D18, W35**

B208. Hamilton, David. "Review: New York Philharmonic: An American Celebration." *Association for Recorded Sound Journal* 32, no. 2 (Fall 2001): 293–96. "Joan Tower's *Sequoia,* though a first effort at orchestral writing, is impressive in its fluent and flexible rhythmic flow." See: **D63, D64, D65, D66, W15**

B209. Harding, Catherine. "Milwaukee Ballet's Twenty-Fifth Season." *Dance Magazine* 68, no. 9 (September 1994): 24–25. The Ballet mounts *Stepping Stones* as part of its 1994–1995 season. The work was a 1992 commission for choreographer Kathryn Posin and Tower. See: **D73, W3**

B210. Harman, Nan. Liner notes to *First Edition Recordings: Tower, Luening, Gubaidulina.* First Edition Recordings, FECD 006, 1991. See: **D37, D38, D39, W10**

B211. Harris, J. David. "Compact Disc Reviews: Joan Tower: Music for Clarinet." *The Clarinet* 20, no. 4 (July–August 1993): 41. "One is thoroughly engrossed and challenged by the wit and expressiveness of composer Joan Tower."

B212. Hassebroek, Ashley. "Symphony to Debut Tower Viola Concerto." *Omaha World Herald,* February 22, 2001, 31. Announces the Omaha Symphony's part in co-commissioning *Purple Rhapsody.* See: **W14**

B213. ———. "Symphony's Coming Season Has Extra Glitter: 2005–06 Highlights." *Omaha World Herald,* February 17, 2005, Sunrise Edition, E1. Details the symphony's 2005–2006 season, which includes the premiere of *Purple Rhapsody.* See: **W14**

B214. ———. "Hall a First Step for Symphony." *Omaha World Herald,* March 6, 2005, Arts and Leisure, 1. Announcement of a new concert hall for the orchestra; the season includes *Purple Rhapsody.* See: **W14**

B215. ———. "Opening Events Conclude with New Sounds: A Youth Orchestra Sunday Will Premiere *Made in America* at the Holland Center." *Omaha World-Herald*, October 27, 2005, Go section, 3. The Omaha Youth Orchestra prepares to perform *Made in America*. Conductor Aviva Segall speaks about the commissioning consortium. See: **D88, W11**

B216. ———. "Singing, Virtuosic Concerto to Premiere Dawn of a New Era." *Omaha World-Herald*, October 30, 2005, Arts and Travel, 1. Details the consortium commissioning of *Purple Rhapsody* before its premiere by Paul Neubauer and the Omaha Symphony. See: **W14**

B217. ———. "Symphony's Holland Hall Debut." *Omaha World-Herald*, November 5, 2005, Sunrise Edition, Living Section, 1. Omaha Symphony's inaugural concert in the Holland Center features the world premiere of *Purple Rhapsody*. "Tower's writing gave the audience a chance to hear the rich sounds of the instrument through gorgeous melody, but also the kind of fancy string techniques commonly reserved for violin or 'cello concertos." See: **W14**

B218. Helps, Robert, and Robert Moran. *Waltzes by 25 Contemporary Composers*. New York: C.F. Peters Corporation, 1978.

B219. Henahan, Donald. "Métier of Modern Dance." *New York Times*, May 18, 1988, C17. Dancer/choreographer Peter Sparling performs to compositions including *Wings;* Laura Flax performs the work on clarinet. See: **D79, D80, D81, D82, D83, D84, D85, D86, D87, W68, W69**

B220. Henken, John. "Written in a Key All Her Own." *Los Angeles Times,* October 1, 2000, 58. A lengthy interview that highlights Tower's residency at University of Southern California, during which she conducted some of her works.

B221. Henry, Derrick. "Centuries After Their Contributions Began, Female Composers Are Getting Recognition." *The Atlanta Journal-Constitution*, April 4, 1991, E1. Tower is mentioned in an article chronicling the challenges women composers have faced over the past few centuries.

B222. Heresniak, M.F. "HVO Chamber Concert Was Accomplished." *Poughkeepsie Journal,* February 4, 1986, A14. Review of the premiere of the *Piano Concerto (Homage to Beethoven),* performed by the Hudson Valley Philharmonic. This reviewer found little to like in the composition: "There is some truly magnificent orchestral writing . . . far outstripping the writing for the solo instrument. The work's problems crop up in the compositional glue that holds it together as well as in the solo piano part." See: **D54, D55, W13**

B223. Hershenson, Roberta. "Footlights." *New York Times*, July 4, 2004, 14WC (Westchester County), 4. The resident chamber ensemble of Copland House presents "Sounds of Westchester," a program of works by composers who at one time lived in Westchester, NY. An unspecified Tower work was performed.

B224. Hertelendy, Paul. "Awards Pour in for Composer Joan Tower." *San Jose Mercury News,* April 30, 1998, E8. Article dealing with the premiere of the choreographed version of *Silver Ladders.* See: **D67, D68, D69, W16**

B225. ———. "San Francisco Ballet Goes Back to the Future With *Silver Ladders.*" May 2, 1998, E10. Rave reviews for the San Francisco Ballet's rendition of *Silver Ladders.* See: **D67, D68, D69, W16**

B226. Hoag, Charles. "In Quest of *Silver Ladders* in the Americas." *Contemporary Music Forum* 3 (1992): 9–16. A lengthy article dealing with the various ways that contemporary American composers use octatonicism in their compositions. See: **D67, D68, D69, W16**

B227. Holland, Bernard. "20th Century American, and Nothing But." *New York Times,* January 31, 1990, C16, column 4. Details the premiere of the *Flute Concerto* by Carol Wincenc and the American Composers Orchestra under Hugh Wolff. "Low registers set against finely separated ensemble colors give the flute a strong and intelligible identity. . . . Elsewhere, its racing, skittering passages explore and expand on the instrument's natural trilling character. . . . An honest sentiment and energy here. . . ." See: **D28, W9**

B228. ———. "Music: Tower *Concerto, Homage to Beethoven.*" *New York Times,* February 3, 1986, C21. *Piano Concerto (Homage to Beethoven)* is premiered in New York in a pair of concerts. "Listening to this concerto's Beethovian allusions, its little bursts of minimalist repetition, its whole-tone methodology, its warmly chiming percussion effects—all smoothly glued one to the next—was a little like walking into a shiny new split-level house that has been crammed with antiques." See: **D54, D55, W13**

B229. ———. "Concert: Chamber Symphony Opens Season at Y." *New York Times,* October 2, 1984. "*Music for 'Cello and Orchestra* [had an] angular sense of drama, bright primary colors and edge-of-the-chair intensity . . . busy, tense, and very effective." See: **D41, D42, W12**

B230. ———. "Anger in Chromatics." *New York Times,* December 12, 1994. C18. *Night Fields* shares a program with Schubert and Dvorak. "[*Night Fields* is] propelled by unrelenting emotional pressure." See: **D43, D44, D45, W46**

B231. ———. "Classical Music in Review: New York Philharmonic." *New York Times,* January 8, 1994, A18. Review of a performance of *Concerto for Orchestra* presented by the New York Philharmonic and Leonard Slatkin. "The *Concerto* is more about restless energy than grace." See: **D14, D88, W6**

B232. ———. "An Ensemble Indeed, but Not Graven in Stone." *New York Times,* April 24, 1995, C13. *Turning Points* is among the featured works at this Alice Tully Hall performance. "[*Turning Points*] was notable in part for what it did not do: namely, ride bandwagons or exploit stylistic fashions. [It is] chamber-music argument that is clear, literate, and heartfelt." See: **D76, W55**

B233. Houdek, Richard. "Ladies' Night in Pittsfield." *The Berkshire Eagle,* May 31, 2005, Arts and Entertainment section. Details the Close Encounters with Music concert series which featured Tower at the keyboard, along with Yehuda Hanani and Yehonatan Berick, performing *For Daniel.* See: **W40**

B234. Horsley, Paul. "Music: The Prime of Joan Tower." *Kansas City Star,* November 10, 2005. On the evening before the Kansas City Symphony performs *Purple Rhapsody,* Tower grants a lengthy interview. See: **W14**

B235. Howard, Sharon Prado. "Joan Tower," *Grove Music Online,* ed. L. Macy. www.grovemusic.com (Accessed January 7, 2005).

B236. Howard, Rebecca. "Musician Working to Help Children." *Deseret Morning News* (Salt Lake City), July 24, 2005, E6. Overview of Mike Reynolds' (of Muir Quartet) work with the Emerging Quartets and Composers Program, in which Tower participates.

B237. Hubley, Doug. "Symphony Displays Strengths in Uneven Opening Concert." *Portland Press Herald,* A9. Review of a Portland Symphony performance which included *Sequoia,* which was "the high point of the evening." See: **D63, D64, D65, D66, W15**

B238. Huebner, Michael. "Emerson Show Mostly Excellent." *Birmingham News* (AL), October 3, 2004. "Lush dissonance met head-on with Debussy-esque harmonies in Tower's *Incandescent.* . . . It is essential Tower—kinetic rhythmic exchanges, dizzying whirls and swirls of notes, single pitches that flower to expansive phrases. It was custom-fit for this ensemble, which has an uncanny knack for drawing listeners into its momentum-building processes." See: **W41**

B239. Hughes, Andrew. "Unmasking the Music's Spirit." *South Bend Tribune* (IN), April 15, 2005, Home Section, D3. Mentions the Emerson Quartet's wide range in performing works from Beethoven to Tower.

B240. Humphries, Stephen. "Glennie Creates Fresh Vibes; Aims to Revitalize Classical Music Around the World with Energetic Percussion." *Christian Science Monitor,* October 12, 2001, 20. A discussion with Evelyn Glennie, who premieres *Strike Zones* with Leonard Slatkin and the National Symphony Orchestra at Carnegie Hall. Other premieres on the program included works by Chen Yi, George Tsontakis, and Stewart Wallace. See: **W18**

B241. Humphrey, Mary Lou. "An Uncommon Woman." Carnegie Hall edition of *Stagebill* Magazine (January 1990). New York: Levitt Communications, 1990, 8–11.

B242. ———. *Joan Tower.* Biographical Pamphlet. New York: G. Schirmer, 1988, rev. 1991.

B243. Humphrey, Mary Lou, and David Wright. *Joan Tower-Composer Essay.* New York: Associated Music Publishers. www.schirmer.com/DefaultId=2419&State_2872=2&composerId_2872=1605 (Accessed January 31, 2006).

B244. Hurwitz, David. "Classics Today: *eighth blackbird: Thirteen Ways.*" www.classicstoday.com/review.asp?ReviewNum=6383 (Accessed January 10, 2006). A review of eighth blackbird's performance of *Petroushskates.* "a delightful little homage to both Stravinsky and figure skating,

Petroushskates makes an effervescent curtain-raiser that brilliantly shows off the group's timbral range." See: **D49, D50, D51, D52, D53, W49**

B245.   Hutton, Mary Ellyn. "New, Chamber, Spiritual Music Take Center Stage." *Cincinnati Post,* June 9, 2005. Lists the 2005 concert line-up of the annual Norse Festival, which includes *Trés Lent,* performed by Nicola Ruzevic, 'cello, and Shiau-uen Ding, piano. See: **D74, D75, W53**

B246.   Huxhold, John. "Slatkin Picks His Favorites; New Box Set Showcases the Maestro's Best Work." *St. Louis Post-Dispatch,* September 10, 1995, D3. *Island Rhythms* gets its first recording in a 5 CD set by Slatkin and the St. Louis Symphony Orchestra See: **D37, D38, D39 W10**

B247.   ———. "Classical Music Review Chamber Group at Ease in Contemporary Tricks." *St. Louis Post-Dispatch,* March 30, 1988, F8. Before leaving her St. Louis Symphony residency to return to teaching at Bard College, Tower arranges her final "On Stage" concert with Chamber Music St. Louis.

B248.   Hyslop, Sandra. Program notes for *Black Topaz* CD. New World Records 80470. See: **D5, W28**

B249.   Jacobson, Joel. "People, Players Composer's Reward." *The Chronicle-Herald,* May 28, 1997, A6. Tower is composer-in-residence at the Scotia Festival Music, Nova Scotia.

B250.   Jepson, Barbara. "Composer Overcomes Obstacles; Joan Tower Successful Despite Many Musicians' Antipathy to New Works." *St. Louis Post-Dispatch,* January 2, 1994, D9. An interview in which Tower restates her advocacy of contemporary music. Includes an announcement of the premiere of *Concerto for Orchestra.* See: **D14, D88, W6**

B251.   ———. "For an Uncommon Woman, Fanfare Comes Full Circle." *New York Times,* January 2, 1994, Section 2, 29. Tower, who has "helped break down the barriers to women in classical music," is profiled.

B252.   ———. "Music that Lives Beyond its Premiere." *New York Times,* February 3, 2006, E23. The vision and success of the Ford *Made in America* commissioning consortium is outlined; a performance by the Greenwich Village Orchestra in New York is announced. See: **D88, W11**

B253.   ———. "Music Quenching the Desert's Classical Thirst." *Wall Street Journal,* August 12, 1998, 13. The Santa Fe Chamber Music Festival, under Marc Neikrug, shows a strong commitment to contemporary music. The 1998 summer season includes 16 works by eight living composers, among which are Tower, Carter, Ligeti, and Neikrug himself.

B254.   Johnson, Brett. "Record Review: Tower: *Silver Ladders; Island Prelude; Music for 'Cello and Orchestra and Sequoia* by the Saint Louis Symphony Orchestra, Leonard Slatkin, conductor." *Tempo* 186 (September 1993): 45–46. "Her music inhabits a realms which . . . is capable . . . of yielding up new secrets and revelations." See: **D33, D34, D35, D36, D41, D42, D63, D64, D65, D66, D67, D68, D69, W12, W15, W16, W43**

B255.   Johnson, Colleen. "Concert's Passion Warms Cold Winter Night." *The Record* (Kitchener-Waterloo, Ontario), January 10, 2004, Saturday Final Edition, Arts, C3. The Kitchener-Waterloo Symphony performed *Fanfare* *for the Uncommon Woman, No. 1.* "Huge blocks of sound in strident fan-fares caught the audience's attention. This short work in clever ways was reminiscent of Gregorian chant, while being thoroughly modernistic." See: **D16, D17, D18, W35**

B256. Johnson, Jessica. "CD Review: *Snow Dreams, Cantos Desiertos, and Others.*" *American Record Guide* 66, no. 6 (November/December 2003): 222. Announcement/review of a recently released Naxos CD which includes *Snow Dreams* along with compositions by Lowell Liebermann, Terry Riley, and Robert Beaser. See: **D70, D71, D72, W54**

B257. Johnson, Lawrence. "Recordings: Mr. Slatkin Goes to Washington, But First . . ." *New York Times,* January 21, 1996, 2. Review of St. Louis Symphony performance of *Island Rhythms.* "Bravura ensemble display mustered for Tower's complex *Rhythms.*" See: **D37, D38, D39, W10**

B258. Keller, James. "Don't Touch that Dial." *Piano and Keyboard* 171 (November–December 1994): 35. To preserve one of the last city-supported classical music stations in New York City, poet John Ashbery contributed "No Longer Very Clear," a poem that served as inspiration for new compositions by twelve composers, including Tower. Of *Or like a . . . an Engine:* "an industrially propulsive toccata that traces the spatial, easily visualized 'choreography of tones' that is a Tower trademark." See: **D46, W63**

B259. Kennicott, Philip. "Grand Finale: Maestro Slatkin's Farewell is Light-hearted, Sincere." *St. Louis Post-Dispatch,* May 20, 1996, A1. A review of conductor Slatkin's last performance with the St. Louis Symphony Orchestra. On the program was *Yet Another Set of Variations* team-composed by Tower, Joseph Schwantner, William Bolcom, Clau de Baker, Donald Erb, and Leonard Slatkin. See: **W22**

B260. ———. "Little Discovery, but Worthy Music in Series Finale." *St. Louis Post-Dispatch,* May 23, 1996, G4. Positive review of *Night Fields,* which the reviewer calls "Shostakovich's *16th Quartet,*" performed by members of the St. Louis Symphony. "A knockoff this convincing is worth high marks." See: **D43, D44, D45, W46**

B261. ———. "Joan Tower Unwraps Her Concerto." *New York Newsday,* January 8, 1994, 23. Enthusiastic review of a Slatkin/St. Louis Symphony performance of *Concerto for Orchestra* in Lincoln Center. "The *Concerto for Orchestra* has an easy, unpretentious dramatic momentum." See: **D14, D88, W6**

B262. ———. "Synchronia Spotlights Two New Music Stars." *St. Louis Post-Dispatch,* February 13, 1997, G5. Review of a Webster University concert that included *Wings.* "A saxophone solo that begins from silence and rises to a frenzy of trills throughout the instrument's range brought forth the most fluid and naturally flowing performance of the evening." See: **D79, D80, D81, D82, D83, D84, D85, D86, D87, W68, W69**

B263. ———. "The NSO, Pounding Home Its Support of Percussion." *The Washington Post,* October 5, 2001, C1. In-depth review of Washington, DC's percussion-fest, "More Drums Along the Potomac," which gave *Strike*

Zones its premiere. "Tower focuses the action on the instruments them-selves, using them sequentially rather than simultaneously; she explores the sonic possibilities of each one, from the lightest touch to the heaviest bat-tery; she mostly eschews the easy hypnosis of repetitive rhythmic struc-tures. The vibraphone is used meditatively, with its pulsing vibrato set against a hazy orchestral background. There is also a not-so-latent strain of brutality and aggression that propels the work forward. . . ." See: **W18**

B264. ———. "St. Louis and Slatkin Say Goodbye." *The Dallas Morning News,* May 20, 1996, A17. An article about the farewell concert, which in-cluded *Yet Another Set of Variations (on a Theme by Paganini)* in Slatkin's honor. See: **W22**

B265. Kenyon, Nicholas. "Musical Events." *The New Yorker,* June 1, 1981, 128–32. Lengthy review of an American Composers' Orchestra perform-ance of *Sequoia,* along with works by William Schuman, Keith Jarrett, and Ralph Shapey. "[*Sequoia* is] an ambitious, energetic, and exhausting por-trait. . . ." See: **D63, D64, D65, D66, W15**

B266. Kerner, Leighton. "Non-Ivory Tower." *The Village Voice,* February 1, 1994, 80. *Concerto for Orchestra,* performed by the New York Philhar-monic and Leonard Slatkin, receives high praise. "Well-positioned contrasts between hushed, sustained unisons and peppery bursts of cadenza, between grand chordal pillars and supercharged ostinati. . . ." See: **D14, D88, W6**

B267. Keuffel, Ken. "Familiar Melodies Recast; Chamber Group to Perform Saturday." *Winston-Salem Journal,* April 3, 2005, F1. The Da Capo Cham-ber Players to perform *Petroushskates* in Winston-Salem, NC. See: **D49, D50, D51, D52, D53, W49**

B268. Kimball, Robert. "Well-Rounded Concert by Philharmonic." *New York Post,* September 25, 1982. A review of the New York Philharmonic per-formance of *Sequoia.* The reviewer comments on the "distinctly Latin fla-vor" of the work. See: **D63, D64, D65, D66, W15**

B269. Kiraly, Phillipa. "Emerson Soars in a Challenging Program." *Seattle Post-Intelligencer,* January 30, 2004, D2. Very positive review of Emerson Quartet's rendition of *Incandescent.* "Full of rich color, like stained glass in sound at one moment and with rhythmic playfulness the next, often urgent, always vital, it is dissonant but never dry. Tower has larded it with solos that are almost mini-cadenzas for violin, viola and 'cello. . . ." See: **W41**

B270. Kirzinger, Robert. "Review: *Cantos Desiertos.*" *Fanfare* 27, no. 5 (May–June 2004): 257–58. Review of a recording containing flute and gui-tar duos, among which is Tower's *Snow Dreams.* See: **D70, D71, D72, W54**

B271. Kisselgoff, Anna. "A Moment to Unveil the New." *New York Times,* October 24, 1998, B14. A lukewarm review of the San Francisco Ballet's (Helgi Tomasson, artistic director) choreography of *Silver Ladders.* "*Silver Ladders* is a[n] . . . uneasy blend whose content is not entirely supported by its means of expression. The style is Neo-Classical and too refined for the onstage ritual that Mr. Tomasson has conjured up from the music." See: **D67, D68, D69, W16**

B272. Koplewitz, Laura. "Joan Tower: Building Bridges for New Music." *Symphony Magazine* 34, no. 3 (June–July 1983): 36–40. An article about Tower's style. "[Her] work is bold, uniquely orchestrated, neither tending toward great dissonances nor wistful lyricism, and it manages high intensity without overwhelming the ear," as well as her origins as a performer, and the connection between composer and performer.

B273. Kosman, Joshua. "Herbst Constrains Women's Philharmonic Opening." *The San Francisco Chronicle*, October 7, 1991, E2.

B274. ———. "Women's Philharmonic Tunes Up Orchestra." *San Francisco Chronicle*, January 27, 1997, D2. A critical review of the orchestra's performance in general and of *Island Rhythms* in particular. See: **D37, D38, D39, W10**

B275. Kozinn, Allan. "Super Sunday at Carnegie Hall." *New York Times*, May 3, 1991, C20, column 1. The opening concert of the new hall includes *Fanfare for the Uncommon Woman, No. 3,* written specifically for the occasion. See: **D20, D21, W37**

B276. ———. "Music Notes." *New York Times*, October 13, 1992, C12, column 3. The New York Consortium for New Music includes *Noon Dance* in its first Sonic Boom Festival. See: **D47, D48, W45**

B277. ———. "Chamber Music Society to Present Premieres." *New York Times,* March 31, 1994, C15. The Chamber Music Society of Lincoln Center slates a trio of premieres: Tower's *Turning Points* and works by Ned Rorem and Wynton Marsalis. See: **D76, W55**

B278. ———. "Classical Music in Review: Laurel Ann Maurer." *New York Times*, April 30, 1994, 16, column 3. *Snow Dreams* is on a program of American contemporary music. See: **D70, D71, D72, W54**

B279. ———. "A Celebration of America, With the Future in Question." *New York Times,* February 7, 2006, Arts Section, 1. Barbara Yahr conducts the Greenwich Village Orchestra in a performance of *Made in America.* See: **D88, W11**

B280. ———. "A New Stage and Lineup for Concerts at Carnegie." *New York Times*, January 12, 1999, E1. Tower invited to participate in American Composers' Orchestra 20th Century Snapshots commission. The concert series will celebrate the new Carnegie Hall; the work will receive its premiere during the 2000–2001 season.

B281. ———. "Chinese-Born Composer Wins $225,000 Ives Prize." *New York Times*, December 21, 2000, E.11. Tower sits on the nominating committee for the Charles Ives Living Award. The 2000 recipient was Chen Yi.

B282. ———. "From Brahms' Passion to Contemporary Melancholy." *New York Times*, March 2, 2002, B19. Among this season's offerings from New York's 92nd Street Y are four recitals by the Tokyo String Quartet, each featuring chamber music by Brahms, along with a newly commissioned work. The third concert included *In Memory,* Tower's second string quartet. "Ms. Tower's new quartet is a passionate work. . . . The language here is accessible and unambiguous, with modulations of melancholy, grief and anger that were all conveyed powerfully in the Tokyo players' vigorous reading." See: **D32, W42**

B283. ———. "Composers in a 5-day Berkshires Jamboree." *New York Times*, August 10, 2005, E-1. Notes the performance of *DNA* during a Festival of Contemporary Composers at Tanglewood. See: **D89, W33**

B284. ———. "Classical Music and Dance Guide." *New York Times*, August 9, 2002, E1. Maverick Festival announces a concert featuring Tower's music. The Cassatt and Colorado String Quartets and pianists Melvin Chen and Tower perform a program of Tower's music, including *Trés Lent, Vast Antique Cubes/Throbbing Still, Wild Purple, Night Fields,* and *In Memory.* See: **D32, D43, D44, D45, D46, D78, W42, W46, W53, W63, W67**

B285. ———. "A New Hand in a Music Barn." *New York Times*, July 11, 2003, E1. Announcement regarding a new director and the season lineup of the 88th Maverick Festival, which mounted an all-Tower program.

B286. ———. "Classical Music Guide." *New York Times*, July 2, 1999, E16. Announces the performance at the Caramoor festival of *Petroushskates* by eighth blackbird. The concert also includes works by Bowers, Lerdahls, and Albert. See: **D49, D50, D51, D52, D53, W49**

B287. ———. "Classical Music and Dance Guide." *New York Times,* September 4, 1998, E14. Announcement of Bard College program, with American Symphony Chamber Orchestra, Leon Botstein, director, in honor of Tower's 60th birthday. Tower conducts *Duets* and *Flute Concerto,* with Carol Wincenc, soloist. See: **D15, D28, W7, W9**

B288. ———. "Works of Crumb and Tower, with Stylized Mime as Well." *New York Times*, November 10, 2005, E5. The Da Capo Chamber Players collaborate with Yass Hakoshima Movement Theater in performances of *Petroushskates* and *Wings.* See: **D49, D50, D51, D52, D53, D79, D80, D81, D82, D83, D84, D85, D86, D87, W49, W68, W69**

B289. LeComte, Richard. "Reno Chamber Orchestra." *American Record Guide* 69, no. 1 (January/February 2006): 14. *Made in America* is premiered in Reno: "Thunderous, seismic rumblings arose from the percussion section, and off the orchestra went with a breathy, slightly hesitant performance. The stridency and immediacy of the music surprised me, and at the end the audience needed a second to catch its breath before launching into applause. The effect did not enthrall totally, but I was kept at the edge of my seat." See: **D88, W11**

B290. Lehman, Mark L. "CD Review: 13 Ways, *Petroushskates* and other Works." *American Record Guide* 66, no. 5 (November–December 2003): 212. Lehman reviews this CD by eighth blackbird, which includes *Petroushskates* and works by George Perle, Thomas Albert, and David Schober. "*Petroushskates* is a 6-minute overture-like cascade of bright, shimmering riffs on the proto-minimalist activity and carnival gaiety of Stravinsky's ballet." See: **D49, D50, D51, D52, D53, W49**

B291. ———. "Waltz Project Revisited." *American Record Guide* 68, no. 2 (May–June 2005): 208. Positive review of a newly released CD which includes *Red Garnet Waltz.* See: **D61, D62, W65**

B292. Lehr, John. "Review: Fanfares and Celebrations." *The Toronto Star*, November 17, 1999. Massey Hall New Music Festival includes *Fanfares 1* and *2* on a concert program in Toronto. See: **D16, D17, D18, W35, W36**

B293. Levin, Gregory. "Current Chronicle: American Society of University Composers." *Musical Quarterly* LX, no. 4 (October 1974): 625–32. Review of a concert presented during an annual meeting of the American Society of University Composers. Tower's *Breakfast Rhythms (I)* shared the program with works by Harvery Sollberger, Jean Eichelberger Ivey, and others. "*Breakfast Rhythms* is a stylish and elegant work, marked by great sectional clarity and nuance." See: **D6, D7, D8, W29**

B294. Libby, Cynthia Green. "Discovery: Compact Discs in Review." *Women of Note Quarterly* 1, no. 1 (May 1993): 7–8. Positive review of the *Joan Tower: Chamber and Solo Works* CD.

B295. Lindeman, Tim. "Season Ends with Brilliant Concert." *The News and Record* (Piedmont Triad, North Carolina), August 5, 2002. Glowing review of an Eastern Philharmonic Orchestra performance of *Fanfare for the Uncommon Woman, No. 1.* "Nothing timid about this composition. It begins with a bang, and the energy is unrelenting." **D16, D17, D18, W35**

B296. Littler, William. "American's Music Argues its Own Case." *The Toronto Star*, March 27, 1992, C12.

B297. ———. "Muir's Virtuosity the Means to a Stylish End." *The Toronto Star*, November 5, 1995, B3. Review of a Muir Quartet concert which included *Night Fields.* "Tower built her musical arguments cogently through three connected movements, the outer pair dramatically assertive, the slower middle movement surprisingly melodic by contemporary standards." See: **D43, D44, D45, W46**

B298. ———. "Engaging Musical Encounters." *The Toronto Star*, June 10, 1998, E3. Reviews a performance by the Encounters Chamber Ensemble: *Fantasy, Island Prelude,* and *Stepping Stones for Two Pianos.* "Tower's ability to fashion and energize complicated textures animated all three of her contributions to the program." See: **D25, D26, D33, D34, D35, D36, D73, W4, W39, W43**

B299. ———. "Emerson Quartet Sparkles as America's Finest." *The Toronto Star*, October 8, 2004, D14. Less a review than a report of the Emerson's performance of *Incandescent.* "It is her third quartet, a one-movement opus she reportedly felt tempted to title *White Heat*, because of the way the music appears to well up from within a potent core." See: **W41**

B300. ———. "A Fanfare for Today's Woman Composer." *Toronto Star*, June 3, 1997, E1. Brief overview of a Toronto Symphony concert conducted by Marin Alsop. The program included *Fanfare for the Uncommon Woman, No. 1.* See: **D16, D17, D18, W35**

B301. Lochhead, Judy. "Joan Tower's *Wings* and *Breakfast Rhythms I and II*: Some Thoughts on Form and Repetition." *Perspectives of New Music* 30 (Winter 1992): 132–56. See: **D6, D7, D8, D79, D80, D81, D82, D83, D84, D85, D86, D87, W29, W68, W69**

B302. Loft, Kurt. "Composer's Special Work Suggests Island Milieu." *Tampa Tribune-Times,* June 30, 1985. The Florida Orchestra premieres *Island Rhythms:* " . . . a wide range of broken instrumental colors. . . ." See: **D37, D38, D39, W10**

B303. Longaker, Mark. "Performing Arts: Sharon Robinson." *Washington Post,* July 23, 1997, C6. Robinson performs *Trés Lent (Homage to Messiaen).* See: **D74, D75, W53**

B304. Lowe, Jim. "VSO Opens Season With Joan Tower, Peter Serkin." *The Times Argus,* October 14, 2005, D1–2. The Vermont Symphony prepares to premiere *Made in America.* Sce: **D88, W11**

B305. Lynch, Kevin. "U of Wisconsin Festival Orchestra: Tower *Rapids* Premiere." *American Record Guide* 59, no. 3 (May–June 1996): 53. Review of the March 2, 1996, premiere of *Rapids* for piano and orchestra as performed by Ursula Oppens, piano, and the University of Wisconsin–Madison School of Music Orchestra, David Becker, conductor. "Though originally advertised as a concerto, it amounted to a 13-minute one-movement work of a kind of hyper-impressionism. It opened with a cascading whirl of lines in which piano and orchestra echo each other; a primal Stravinskian excitement grew as the piece swept on to punchy interplay between solo and orchestra, and it peaked with exultant cries from the brass." See: **D60, W17**

B306. Maddox, David. "The Poetics of Sound: Composer Joan Tower Challenges the Hegemony of Drama in Music." Nashville Scene. www.nashvillescene.com/Stories/Arts/2005/01/27/The_Poetics_of_Sound/index.shtml (Accessed April 27, 2006).

B307. Mahne, Theodore P. "Casual Concert Sounds Fancy." *Times-Picayune* (New Orleans, LA), December 2, 1995, A25. *Fanfare for the Uncommon Woman, No. 1* shares a Louisiana Philharmonic program with Aaron Copland's *Fanfare for the Common Man.* "Copland's Olympian burst of glory is full of majesty; Tower's shares that sense of stateliness but livens it up with a jazzier beat." See: **D16, D17, D18, W35**

B308. ———. "Composer Urges Audiences Not to Fear New Music." *Times-Picayune,* Feb 21, 1999, E12. In advance of the local premiere of *Rapids,* Tower speaks about audiences' discomfort with contemporary music. See: **D60, W17**

B309. Matthew, Ed. "Artists on Repertoire II." *Chamber Music* 7, no. 1 (Spring 1990): 15. Written by the clarinetist of Quintessence, for whom *Island Prelude* was written. About working with the group, Tower said: "[It's] like having a painting in front of you and actually being able to work on it. I got to put in a little red there, a little pink, a little white." See: **D33, D34, D35, D36, W43**

B310. McBride, Jerry. "Review: Joan Tower *Noon Dance, Snow Dreams.*" *Notes* 46, no. 3 (March 1990): 818–19. In-depth article about *Noon Dance* and *Snow Dreams. Noon Dance has* "many shifting meters and unison sections . . . requiring vituoso skills from all the players. . . . Tonal centers are defined by repeated and sustained single pitches and ostinatos. Chordal structures are then built by branching out from these tonal centers." *Snow*

Dreams "also shows a masterful knowledge of instrumental timbral possibilities." See: **D47, D48, D70, D71, D72, W45, W54**

B311.   McCardell, Charles. "National Symphony: Percussion and Premieres." *American Record Guide* 65, no. 1 (January–February 2002): 45. Covers the "More Drums along the Potomac" Festival, co-directed by Evelyn Glennie and Leonard Slatkin. *Strike Zones* had its second playing during the festival. "[*Strike Zones* is] thoughtfully organized and not disjointed. . . . Interesting touches include a cadenza on hi-hat cymbal and drumkit . . . and two percussionists armed with castanets, sleigh bells, and a portable glockenspiel who add another dimension from their vantage points elsewhere in the hall." See: **W18**

B312.   ——. "Debuts and Reappearances: Washington Kennedy Center Friedheim Awards." *Musical America* 109, no. 2 (March 1989): 47. *Silver Ladders* places fourth in the Kennedy Center Friedheim Awards. See: **D67, D68, D69, W16**

B313.   Maclean, Don. "20th Century Consort." *Washington Post*, December 9, 1992, C9. 20th Century Consort's impressive performance of *Amazon* is the subject of this very positive review. "Tower's magnificent *Amazon* is . . . an intriguing impressionistic piece that seeks to evoke the power of a river. Alternating between hazy, quiet dissonances and thunderous rushing climaxes, this work is a worthy addition to the chamber music repertoire." See: **D1, D2, W23, W24**

B314.   McClary, Susan. *Feminine Endings: Music, Gender, and Sexuality*, reprint edition. Minneapolis: University of Minnesota Press, 2002.

B315.   McConnico, Patricia. "Around the State." *Texas Monthly,* October 2003: 35. Da Camera of Houston announces an upcoming concert program which includes *Petroushskates*. See: **D49, D50, D51, D52, D53, W49**

B316.   McCutchan, Ann. *The Muse that Sings: Composers Speak about the Creative Process*. New York: Oxford University Press, 1999.

B317.   McLellan, Joseph. "From Europe and America, Collections from Women of Note." *Washington Post*, January 10, 1993, G10. Reviewer picks *Meet the Composer* CD as his favorite Tower recording.

B318.   ——. "On Center Stage: The Neoromantics." *Washington Post*, October 29, 1988, C2. The four 1988 Kennedy Center/Friedheim Awards finalists are profiled, along with their entries. Tower submitted *Silver Ladders.* See: **D67, D68, D69, W16**

B319.   ——. "20th Century Consort's Inspired Performance." *Washington Post*, June 26, 1997, E7. This performance in the Washington National Cathedral included the two-piano arrangement of *Stepping Stones*. "Dramatic and rhetorical. . . ." See: **D73, W4**

B320.   ——. "Alexandria Symphony Orchestra and *Percussion Blast!*" *Washington Post*, May 20, 2002, C5. Review of a performance of *Fanfare for the Uncommon Woman, No. 1* by the Alexandria Symphony Orchestra, Kim Allen Kluge, conductor. The reviewer notes that Tower's *Fanfare* has the same instrumentation as Copland's *Fanfare* but that in its "more frenzied way, Tower's take is equally impressive." See: **D16, D17, D18, W35**

B321. ———."Theatre Chamber Players." *Washington Post*, May 16, 2003, C8. Review of Theatre Chamber Players' performance of, among other works, *Wings*. Tower's "vividly descriptive" work was performed by Edward Walters. See: **D79, D80, D81, D82, D83, D84, D85, D86, D87, W68, W69**

B322. McQuillen, James. "Creativity, Poignance Tie Pieces That KLR Trio Delicately Renders." *The Oregonian*, November 24, 2004, E3. Review of a Kalichstein-Laredo-Robinson Trio concert which included *For Daniel* and works by Brahms and Mendelssohn. "*For Daniel* provided an emotional anchor for the evening. . . . The spare textures, terse phrases and anguished anger recalled Shostakovich, and the references to breathing—the crescendos and descrescendos in the strings; repeated ascending scales in the piano—made the music both physically palpable and painful to hear, however fine the performance." See: **W40**

B323. Metcalf, Steve. "Audience Key in Success of Cleveland Quartet." *Hartford Courant,* August 8, 1993, B2. The Cleveland Quartet premieres *Elegy*. See: **W34**

B324. Meyer, Marianne. "Alexandria Symphony Orchestra's Percussion Blast!" *Washington Post*, May 16, 2002, T12. Performance of *Fanfare for the Uncommon Woman, No. 1* by the Alexandria Symphony Orchestra. See: **D16, D17, D18, W35**

B325. Midgette, Anne. "A Multitude of Voices, All From Pianos." *New York Times*, December 17, 2002, E6. The Rock Hotel Pianofest: 2 months, 20 pianists, 32 premieres, including *Vast Antique Cubes/Throbbing Still*. See: **D46, W63**

B326. ———. "Music Review: Play it Again, On Purpose or By Accident." *New York Times*, May 29, 2003, E3, column 5. The Da Capo Chamber Players perform at Merkin Hall in New York City. *Turning Points* "simply spoke music, fluently and melodically to say something new." See: **D76, W55**

B327. Mistak, Alvin. "New Music Reviews: *Wild Purple* for Solo Viola." *The Instrumentalist* 56, no. 10 (May 2002): 72. A descriptive review of *Wild Purple*. See: **D78, W67**

B328. Monson, Karen. "Ovation Record Review: Erb, Rouse, and Tower." *Ovation*, June 1987. A review of the Slatkin/St. Louis recording of *Sequoia:* "This album can be highly recommended for its *Sequoia*." See: **D63, D64, D65, D66, W15**

B329. Montgomery, Virginia. "*Sequoia* a Success Story." *Cincinnati Enquirer,* May 2, 1986. Article dealing with a Cincinnati Symphony Orchestra performance of *Sequoia*; includes a summary of her best-known works and her history with the Da Capo Chamber Players. See: **D63, D64, D65, D66, W15**

B330. Montgomery, Kitty. "HVP Chamber Plays Ginastera." *Sunday Freeman*, February 9, 1986, 40. Review of the premiere of *Piano Concerto*

(Homage to Beethoven); "[The work] . . . may owe its conscious inspiration to a lifetime of musical influence by that great man . . . but there is a raw, emotive quality to the composition that reflects another source. . . . Call it *Rites of Beethoven.*" See: **D54, D55, W13**

B331. Moore, David W. "Review: Born in America in 1938." *American Record Guide* 65, no. 3 (May–June 2002): 184–85. "Joan Tower's piece (*Trés Lent)* in memory of Messiaen recalls that composer's otherworldly spaciousness." See: **D74, D75, W53**

B332. Morrison, Mairi N. "Reference Points." *Washington Post*, May 3, 1987, G3. Tower speaks with this reporter regarding her generally referential music and the upcoming performance of *Petroushskates* by the Columbia Players. "Every piece I write contains some reference to another composer." See: **D49, D50, D51, D52, D53, W49**

B333. Moss, Bruce. "*Fanfare for the Uncommon Woman No. 5.*" *The Instrumentalist* 52, no. 10 (May 1998): 76. A descriptive review of *Fanfare, No. 5.* "Abounds with energy." See: **D23, D24, W38**

B334. Munger, Philip. "From Player to Composer to Conductor." *Anchorage Daily News*, November 3, 2000, 15–16. This article treats Tower's interest in conducting and highlights her appearance as conductor of the Anchorage Symphony Orchestra.

B335. Nachman, Myrna S., and Lisa Robinson. "Joan Tower." *The Norton/Grove Dictionary of Women Composers,* Julie Anne Sadie and Rhian Samuel, eds. New York: W.W. Norton and Co., 1995.

B336. Neal, Jack. "Reno Chamber Orchestra to Perform." www.nevada-events.net/cgi-bin/cal_manager2/review433.shtml (Accessed April 24, 2006). A review of a Reno Chamber Orchestra performance of *Made in America.* "A prism of texture and tonal clusters that radiate an abstract energized spirit. . . ." See: **D88, W11**

B337. Neuls-Bates, Carol. *Women in Music: an Anthology of Source Readings from the Middle Ages to the Present.* Rev. ed. Boston: Northeastern University Press, 1996.

B338. Newton, Catherine Reese. "Composer Tower, Symphony Show Tunes Up at Deer Valley." *Salt Lake Tribune*, August 3, 2004, D4. Tower performs *For Daniel* with the Muir Quartet at the Deer Valley Music Festival. See: **W40**

B339. ———. "Emerson Quartet Above Reproach." *Salt Lake Tribune*, October 22, 2004, B3. Emerson performs *Incandescent.* "Beginning with bow strokes reminiscent of a match being struck, the 18-minute piece burned and glowed more with rhythm and color than with melody." See: **W41**

B340. ———. "Emerson Quartet to Show Utah Why They Are Grammy Winners." *Salt Lake Tribune*, October 17, 2004, D6. Interview with Emerson String Quartet members about the upcoming concert which will include *Incandescent.* See: **W41**

B341. Nichols, Janet. *Women Music Makers: An Introduction to Women Composers.* New York: Walker and Company, 1992.

B342. Nichols, William. "CD Review: Audio Notes: Joan Tower Concertos." *Clarinet Journal* 24, no. 2 (February–March 1997): 20, 22. "Strongly recommended. Tower has a keen sense of instrumental capabilities and the performing process. Her years of performance experience provide an invaluable tool in creating music which is accessible and yet sophisticated and finely wrought." See: **D10, D11, D28, D54, D55, D77, W5, W9, W13, W21**

B343. Nilsson, B.A. "Symphony's Featured Work a Cellist-Composer Effort." *The Knickerbocker News,* November 9, 1984, 9. Tower and André Emelianoff discuss their collaboration on *Music for 'Cello and Orchestra.* See: **D41, D42, W12**

B344. North, James. "CD Review : Joan Tower: American Images 2/ Verdehr Trio." *Fanfare* 26, no. 1 (September–October 2002): 250. "Joan Tower's single-movement *Rain Waves* also demonstrates that there are perfectly fine musical structures beyond sonata form." See: **D59, W51**

B345. Ochoa, Gracie. "Sneak Preview." *Houston Chronicle,* January 29, 2004, 18. The Emerson Quartet performs *Incandescent* on a Rice University program. See: **W41**

B346. O'Brien, Valerie. "Musician of the Month: Joan Tower: Her *Sequoia* Gains Establishment Status, But She Won't Rest On Her Laurels." *High Fidelity/Musical America edition* 32, no. 9 (September 1982): 6–8. Detailed review deals with *Sequoia* ("gutsy, lushly orchestrated work with some outrageous percussion passages"), her thoughts on the state of contemporary music ("The composer today is not present—there is no person to identify with. To me, that is the main reason why new music has suffered so much"), and the evolution of Tower's compositional style. See: **D63, D64, D65, D66, W15**

B347. O'Dette, Ralph. "ProMusica Offers Engaging Blend of New, Old." *Columbus Dispatch,* April 1, 1996, B6. Rave review for the *Clarinet Concerto* and its performance by ProMusica Chamber Ensemble and soloist Robert Spring. "With this challenging 19-minute work, Tower has made a substantial contribution to the contemporary orchestral literature as well as to the relatively small clarinet concerto repertoire." See: **D10, D11, W5**

B348. Oestreich, James R. "Classic Improvisation (As in Quick Thinking)." *New York Times,* August 10, 1993, C13, column 5. The premiere of *Elegy* by the Cleveland Quartet and trombonist John Swallow. "In it, an agitated, disjunct trombone line enlivens the slow-moving strings to a febrile excitement imbued with an element of ecstasy before the whole ensemble slumps back towards stasis. . . . Touching and effective." See: **W34**

B349. ———. "Composer's Birthday Tribute." *New York Times,* September 15, 1998, E5, column 3. Reviews a concert in celebration of Tower's 60th birthday at Merkin Concert Hall in New York City. Performances by the Da Capo Chamber Players of *Turning Points, Petroushskates, Night Fields,* and the premiere of *Wild Purple. "Night Fields* . . . failed to make its effect . . . unlike *Petroushskates,* which revels in its derivativeness. *Night Fields* draws distractingly on Shostakovich, right down to that composer's signature motto, to no apparent purpose." See: **D43, D44, D45, D49, D50, D51, D52, D53, D76, D78, W46, W49, W55, W67**

B350. ———. "Call Her a Musician, Pure and Simple." *New York Times*, September 30, 2001, 28. Article focuses on Evelyn Glennie's career and her premiere of *Strike Zones* with the National Symphony Orchestra, Leonard Slatkin, conductor. See: **W18**

B351. ———. "Snapshot of a City's Composers." *New York Times*, January 12, 2001, E1:1. Fred Sherry directs "A Great Day in New York," a festival featuring composers who are connected to the city. Tower's *Rain Waves* was performed. See: **D59, W51**

B352. Oppens, Ursula. "*Or Like a . . . an Engine.*" *Piano and Keyboard* 171 (November–December 1994): 36–41. *Or Like a . . . an Engine* appears in full in this issue of *Piano and Keyboard*, with introduction and performance suggestions by Oppens, for whom Tower wrote the piece. See: **D46, W63**

B353. Oteri, Frank J. "Joan Tower: *Made in America*." www.newmusicbox. org/article.nmbx?id=4369, September 15, 2005 (Accessed April 24, 2006). Video interview with Tower, on her responsibility to the audience, the chamber music world versus the orchestral world, the titles of her works, and *Made in America*. See: **D88, W11**

B354. Page, Tim. "Hilary Hahn and Prokofiev, A Classic Match." *Washington Post*, February 19, 2005, C1. The Baltimore Symphony Orchestra begins a concert with a performance of Copland's *Fanfare for the Common Man* followed by *Fanfare for the Uncommon Woman, No. 1*. "I'm glad Tower has a hit—her *Fanfare* has been played by more than 500 ensembles. . . . Still, this deeply gifted composer has not only written better works, she has written nothing else but better works." See: **D16, D17, D18, W35**

B355. Pappenheim, Mark. "Women Call the Tune." *The Independent* (London), November 29, 1990, 35. Profiles Tower before the opening of a festival which features performances of *Wings* and *Snow Dreams*. See: **D70, D71, D72, D79, D80, D81, D82, D83, D84, D85, D86, D87, W54, W68, W69**

B356. Pineiro, John de Clef. "Da Capo." *21st Century Music* 8, no. 10 (October 2001): 13–14. Reviews a concert in celebration of Da Capo Chamber Players' 30th anniversary. The program included *Big Sky* and *Petroushskates*, with the composer at the piano in the first work. About *Big Sky*: "As a contemporary piano trio, it just does not get any better than this." See: **D4, D49, D50, D51, D52, D53, W27, W49**

B357. Pfeifer, Ellen. "Classical Music." *Boston Herald*, February 12, 1999, S5. Tower decries the paucity of performances of music by women composers in current orchestral programs, chamber music series, and radio programs. "Women composers still need a lot of help. . . . Look at your Boston Symphony programs, the programs of your biggest chamber music series. Look at the programs for the month. Look even at the contemporary groups. See how few women are represented. It's not a great scene. It's better than it was, but still pretty dismal."

B358.   Pincus, Andrew. "An Evening of Contrasts." *Berkshire Eagle,* August 20, 2005, Arts Section. Review of the well-received Tanglewood performance of *For Daniel* by the Kalichstein-Laredo-Robinson Trio. "[The work] seems overly bleak, Tower too close to her material. Or it may be that, with its lengthy fortissimo passages and strident chords, the piece needs orchestral dress. Skillful as the writing is, [it] wound up being like the person who tells you how miserable she is. She becomes so insistent about it that she leaves no room for the sympathy you might want to give." See: **W40**

B359.   ———. "Symphony's Cycle of Concertos by Women Opens With Class." *Berkshire Eagle,* October 29, 1990, Arts Section. Article about a Berkshire Symphony performance that featured *Music for 'Cello and Orchestra,* part of a season-long survey of concertos by living American women composers. See: **D41, D42, W12**

B360.   Pollack, Howard. "Review: Joan Tower: *Platinum Spirals, Noon Dance, Amazon, Wings.*" *American Music* 5, no. 4 (1987): 469–71. A generally positive review of the chamber and solo works CD, the solo works being praised more highly than the ensemble compositions. See: **D1, D2, D47, D48, D56, D57, D79, D80, D81, D82, D83, D84, D85, D86, D87, W23, W24, W45, W64, W68, W69**

B361.   Porter, Cecilia. "Portraits of Composure: Women in Music." *Washington Post,* May 2, 1998, C9. This concert, conducted by the National Symphony Orchestra's Elizabeth Schulze, salutes the 10th anniversary of the National Museum of Women in the Arts and included Tower's *Fanfare for the Uncommon Woman, No. 1.* "The NSO's reading of Tower's *Fanfare* highlighted its evocative timbres, antiphonal flashes of brilliant brass and percussion, and rhythmic complexity." See: **D16, D17, D18, W35**

B362.   ———. "Classical Music." *Washington Post,* May 14, 2005, C4. Review of the Emerson String Quartet's performance of *Incandescent.* "As the work unfolded, the Emerson gradually collected melodic strands, rhythms and textures, building them up to a white heat that exploded with blinding luminescence at the end." See: **W41**

B363.   Pineiro, John De Clef. "Review: Da Capo Chamber Players. " *21st Century Music* 8, no. 10 (October 2001): 13–14. Review of a concert in Merkin Hall in honor of the Da Capo Chamber Players' 30th anniversary. The program included *Big Sky* (with Tower at the keyboard) and *Petroushskates.* See: **D4, D49, D50, D51, D52, D53, W27, W49**

B364.   Potter, Jon. "Serkin joins VSO at Latchis." *Brattleboro Reformer* (Vermont), October 20, 2005, Entertainment section. Announces the Vermont premiere of *Made in America.* See: **D88, W11**

B365.   Prado, Sharon. "New Wine into Old Bottles: Traditional Media and Contemporary Women Composers." *Contemporary Music Review* 16 (1997): 45–57. Prado's abstract: "Traditional genres continue to attract contemporary women composers. . . . Though these women . . . choose conventional forms and performing forces, their music is fresh and their expression uncontained by formulaic approaches. Focusing upon specific pieces by Ellen Taaffe Zwilich, Tower, and Katherine Hoover, this article explores both what is old and new about their music, highlighting those ties to the past which are infused with new performer-friendly and accessible ideas. Included is a survey of women whose primary contributions fall within traditional boundaries—a categorization no longer readily defined."

B366. Pratt, David. 2006. "What's in a Name?" *The Juilliard Journal Online* 21, no. 8 (May 2006). www.juilliard.edu/update/journal/ j_articles887.html (Accessed May 3, 2006). Tower discusses the challenges of writing *Copperwave* for the American Brass Quintet. See: **W32**

B367. Quint, Andrew. "The Want List." *Fanfare* 27, no. 2 (November– December 2003): 90–91. Reviews the eighth blackbird's performance of *Petroushskates*: "Delightful." See: **D49, D50, D51, D52, D53, W49**

B368. Rafferty, Ann. 1983. "A Symphony Under Control." *Maine Times,* October 28, 1983. The Portland Symphony performs *Sequoia.* "A ruthlessly percussive opening blasted away time barriers, leaving a sort of misty, primeval glowering in its wake. This piece had moments of mystery and bombast, but demanded a complete sensory awareness throughout." See: **D63, D64, D65, D66, W15**

B369. Rath, Jay. "UW Symphony Soars in Student Concerto." *Wisconsin State Journal* (Madison, WI), March 11, 2003, D2. Review of a student performance of *Piano Concerto (Homage to Beethoven)* with the University of Wisconsin Orchestra. "Less a pastiche than a modern requiem. . . ." See: **D54, D55, W13**

B370. Raymond, David. 1997. Liner notes to *Joan Tower Concertos,* d'Note Classics, DND 1016. See: **D10, D11, D28, D54, D55, D77, W5, W9, W13, W21**

B371. Redmond, Michael. "Towering Uncommon Composer." *Plain Dealer* (Cleveland, OH), June 3, 1994, 30. A lengthy interview with Tower, focusing on the small number of living composers, especially women, present on programs of major symphonies.

B372. Reed, Jerome. "Piano Music by Women Composers: Women Born After 1900, vol. 2." *American Music Teacher* 55, no. 1 (August–September 2005): 96. Review of newly issued reference book by Pamela Dees.

B373. Reese, Catherine. "Composer Calls *Concerto* Fantasy for Orchestra." *Salt Lake Tribune,* April 19, 1992, E3. The *Violin Concerto* is premiered by Elmar Oliveira. See: **D77, W21**

B374. Reichel, Edward. "Emerson Delivers Ideal Performance." *Deseret Morning News* (Salt Lake City), October 23, 2004. Glowing review of *Incandescent* as performed by the Emerson String Quartet, for whom it was written. "The one movement work is intense, creating unremitting suspense through repeated phrases that are altered, sustained tones and intervals, and constant nervous motion. Tower seeemingly manages the impossible by creating riveting music out of nothing. She employs traditional means to create highly original music that is inventive to a high degree, making her one of the most fascinating composers working today." See: **W41**

B375. ————. "Muir Has Substance, Depth, Meaning." *Deseret Morning News* (Salt Lake City), August 7, 2004. The Emerson String Quartet, closely associated with Tower for decades, performed *For Daniel* at the Deer Valley Music festival. "Tower is without question this country's pre-eminent composer. What distinguishes her from many of her contemporary and younger colleagues is that her music has substance, depth and meaning." See: **W40**

B376. ————. "Early On, Tower Preferred the Piano to Composing." *Deseret News* (Salt Lake City), July 12, 1998, E4. Tower is composer-in-residence at the Deer Valley Chamber Music Festival in Utah.

B377. ————. "Quartet to Play Local Premiere of *For Daniel* Trio." *Deseret Morning News* (Salt Lake City), August 1, 2004. Previews a performance by Tower with (part of) the Muir String Quartet. Includes comments by Tower regarding the dedication of the work and her own occasional performances of her works ("I play slow pieces, things that are not too demanding"). See: **W40**

B378. ————. "Muir Showcases Tower's Intense *Night Fields.*" *Deseret Morning News* (Salt Lake City), August 6, 2005, E6. Review of Muir's performance of *Night Fields*: "One of the finest chamber works to have been written in the past decade . . . full of potency and dynamic vitality." See: **D43, D44, D45, W46**

B379. ————. "Symphony Gives Fabulous Performance." *Deseret Morning News* (Salt Lake City), August 9, 2005, C5. Review of Utah Symphony's performance of *Tambor:* "A vigorous piece propelled by a restless energy that turns the work into a perpetuum mobile." Edwin Outwater conducts. See: **D88, W19**

B380. Reinthaler, Joan. "The Parker Quartet: A Splash of Color at the Phillips." *Washington Post*, January 25, 2005, Final Edition, Style, C8. The Parker Quartet begins their performance with *Night Fields*: "The fine-tuning of Tower's play on timbres . . . were projected with energy and the exhilaration of a risk well taken." See: **D43, D44, D45, W46**

B381. Retzel, Frank. "Joan Tower, *Silver Ladders.*" *Music Library Association Notes* 48, no. 2 (December 1991): 686–88. Schwanter's *Toward Light* and Tower's *Silver Ladders* "superbly demonstrate the creators' handling of the orchestral forces at their disposal. Each piece achieves a highly original character free from gimmicks that might detract from the music itself. There is a classicism of approach in the use of prescribed ensembles, usual instrumental techniques and tunings and traditional notation; invention is focused instead on absolute music. . . . There is so much to laud in this piece that it's hard to know where to begin." There is brief discussion regarding the works' structure. See: **D67, D68, D69, W16**

B382. Rhodes, Cherry, ed. *Ascent.* New York: Associated Music Publishers, Inc., 1999. See: **D3, W56**

B383. Rice, Patricia. "The Composer Lends a Hand to the Baton." *St. Louis Post-Dispatch,* September 14, 1984, D3. Tower and Leonard Slatkin discuss aspects of *Sequoia* as the St. Louis Symphony prepares the work for its season's opening concert. See: **D63, D64, D65, D66, W15**

B384. Rischin, Rebecca. "Masterclass: *Wings* by Joan Tower." *The Clarinet* 26 (1999): 4–11. The author speaks with Tower regarding her affinity for the clarinet ("There's something about the instrument and the people playing it that's been just fascinating to me. . . . It can pull an idea from very soft to very loud and from very low to very high, and you can sense the power of that pull in a clarinet better than you can with other instruments."), how she titles her compositions, similarities between Messiaen's *Abime des Oiseaux* and her own *Wings*, and performance considerations regarding the latter. See: **D79, D80, D81, D82, D83, D84, D85, D86, D87, W68, W69**

B385. Ritter, Stephen E. "*Saxophone Sonata/Juggernaut/Wings/Deep Blue Spiral.* American Record Guide 67, no. 3 (1 May 2004): 137. Negative review of newly released CD that includes a transcription for saxophone of *Wings*. "It is supposed to be descriptive of the flight of falcons, and it is given wings by the use of techniques like large melodic leaps, trills, and tremelos. But at ten minutes there has to be more to the piece to keep it going, and this one falters mid-flight, lacking any sort of internal consistency for the listener to follow, aside from the programmatic aspects." See: **D79, D80, D81, D82, D83, D84, D85, D86, D87, W69**

B386. Rix, Christian. "Arianna Quartet Presents Another Fine Program." *St. Louis Post-Dispatch,* March 21, 2001, E2. Reviews a performance of Mozart, Schumann, and Tower's *Night Fields*, a " dark but interesting piece." See: **D43, D44, D45, W46**

B387. Rockwell, John. "Program of Premieres to Benefit Pro Musicians." *The New York Times,* December 3, 1989, Section 1, Part 2, 90. Reviews an Avery Fisher Hall concert of new works commissioned by Absolut Vodka, including *Fanfare for the Uncommon Woman, No. 2*. See: **D19, W36**

B388. ———. "New-Music Symposium Raises Some Hackles." *New York Times,* January 27, 1981, C7. The conference on contemporary music at the 92nd Street Y turns controversial, as some composers, including Tower, voice their opposition to the Y's timid and infrequent programming of contemporary music.

B389. Rosen, Lawrence. *American Contemporary Masters: A Collection of Works for Piano.* New York: G. Schirmer, Inc., 1995.

B390. Rosenberg, Donald. "Concert Was Referential and Well Received." *Plain Dealer* (Cleveland, OH), March 3, 1993, E6. Review of the *Piano Concerto (Homage to Beethoven).* "While Tower's writing for the soloist often is motoric and aggressive in the extreme, it also is filtered through an impressionistic sensibility. . . . The score . . . bursts with rhythmic vitality and . . . juxtapositions of struggle and repose." See: **D54, D55, W13**

B391. ———. "Group Takes Flight with Fresh Performances." *Plain Dealer* (Cleveland, OH), March 23, 1999, E4. eighth blackbird performs *Petroushskates* at the Cleveland Museum of Art's Gartner Auditorium: ". . . A five-minute brainstorm." See: **D49, D50, D51, D52, D53, W49**

B392. ———. "Composer Tower is an Uncommon Woman." *Plain Dealer* (Cleveland, OH), March 23, 2001, E1. Brief interview with Tower and an announcement of the Contemporary Youth Ensemble's upcoming performance of an all-Tower program: *Fanfare for the Uncommon Woman, No. 1, Tambor,* and the *Flute Concerto.* See: **D16, D17, D18, D28, D88, W9, W19, W35**

B393. ———. "Wonderful Weaving of Soloist, Conductor." *Plain Dealer* (Cleveland, OH), September 20, 2004, D5. Reviews the Akron Symphony Orchestra's performance of *Fanfare* and other works. "[*Fanfare*] goes about its business in a series of handsome flourishes, especially from the timpani." See: **D16, D17, D18, W35**

B394. ———. "Musicians Capture the Many Composers Inside Tower." *Plain Dealer* (Cleveland, OH), October 7, 2003, E8. Reviews an all-Tower program. "The six pieces suggested that Tower has continued to explore without regard to specific trends or sensibilities. Her music can be astringent and brooding or colorful and lyrical or all of the above, depending on the needs of the moment."

B395. Rosenbaum, Lee. "No-Go CoCo (Concert Companion) Gadget." *Wall Street Journal,* July 8, 2004, D10. The New York Philharmonic, Kansas City Symphony, and the Philadelphia Orchestras, among others, test-drive an electronic handheld device which is intended to assist audience members in understanding the music they hear at concerts. The device was used during a Pittsburgh Symphony performance of Tower's *Tambor* recently. Although she has mixed feelings about using words to "try and educate" audiences, she conceded that "in an age of multi-tasking, some people will have a great time with this thing."

B396. Rosenblum, Phyllis. "Joan Tower *Concerto for Orchestra*." *Santa Cruz County Sentinel,* August 3, 1996. Reviews the August premiere of Tower's *Concerto for Orchestra* performed by Cabrillo Festival Orchestra, Marin Alsop, conductor. "Uneven, infectious rhythms decorated a forward driving motion, broken occasionally by shimmering islands of calm." See: **D14, D88, W6**

B397. Ross, Alex. "Classical Music in Review: Dorian Wind Quartet." *New York Times,* September 28, 1993, C14, column 5. Merkin Concert Hall was the venue for this performance of *Island Prelude.* "Hovering sonorities, slowly unfolding lines, patient construction of motifs . . . chattering Stravinskyite episodes and florid cadenzas for the soloist . . . thoroughly distinctive shape overall." See: **D33, D34, D35, D36, W43**

B398. Rothbart, Peter. "Da Capo Presents Innovate Program at IC." *Ithaca Journal,* April 11, 1983, 5. The Da Capo Chamber Players perform Tower's *Noon Dance,* along with works by Schwantner, Janacek, and Debussy. "Considerable compositional skills. . . ." See: **D47, D48, W45**

B399. Ruhe, Pierre. "Ex-Atlantan a Hot Ticket in Classical Music World." *The Atlanta Journal-Constitution,* May 5, 2002. Article focuses on composer Jennifer Higdon; includes Tower quotes about being a woman composer. "There are stronger women composers, and more of them now than before, but women are still not part of the big discussion. We're not considered the major players—we're still put into a niche called Women Composers."

B400. Samiljan, Tom. "Notes on Art." *New York Magazine* 37, no. 20 (June 7, 2004): 87. Chelsea Art Museum's "Second Helpings" presents the Orchestra of St. Luke's performing *Rain Waves, Big Sky,* and *In Memory.* See: **D4, D32, D59, W27, W42, W51**

B401. Sandow, Greg. Liner notes to *American Classics: Joan Tower: Instrumental Music.* Naxos, 8.559215, 2004. See: **D4, D32, D33, D34, D35, D36, D46, D78, W27, W42, W67**

B402. Scher, Valerie. "Fest's Composer Makes a Contemporary Splash." *San Diego Tribune,* August 8, 2000, E3. Tower's *And . . . They're Off!* and *Big Sky* share a program at SummerFest La Jolla. "*Big Sky* brimmed with powerful dynamic contrasts and pointillistic effects. . . . [The] galloping, Bartokian intensity of *And . . . They're Off!*" See: **D4, W26, W27, W43, W63**

B403. Schetzel, Florence. "Premiere Performance." *Poughkeepsie Journal,* January 6, 1994, D1. The New York Philharmonic gives the New York City debut of *Concerto for Orchestra.* See: **D14, D88, W6**

B404. Schirmer, Inc. *Composer Handbook:* New York: G. Schirmer, 1994. Biographies, selective worklists, and discographies of approximately two dozen composers.

B405. Schwartz, Elliott, and Daniel Godfrey. *Music Since 1945.* New York: Schirmer Books, 1993.

B406. Schwarz, K. Robert. "Recent Releases: Joan Tower: *Silver Ladders, Island Prelude, Music for 'Cello and Orchestra, Sequoia.*" *New York Times,* November 4, 1990, H34. "All [the compositions on the CD] possess a propulsive, Stravinskyan rhythmic force, but temper that impulse with a luminous sense of color . . . beautifully orchestrated and immensely appealing without ever being simplistic." See: **D33, D34, D35, D36, D41, D42, D63, D64, D65, D66, D67, D68, D69, W12, W15, W16, W43**

B407. ———. "Copland's Third: Language of Hope." *New York Times,* April 19, 1987. A brief review of the newly released all-Tower recording of *Platinum Spiral, Amazon, Noon Dance,* and *Wings.* "Clearly focused, possessing distinct climaxes and bold contrasts of mood. An almost Stravinskyan rhythmic sense lends a propellant unifying thrust. . . ." See: **D1, D2, D47, D48, D79, D80, D81, D82, D83, D84, D85, D86, D87, W23, W24, W45, W68, W69**

B408. Schwenk, Noel. "Analyzing Contemporary Music from a Performer's Perspective." *Soundboard: Guitar Foundation of America* 26, no. 2 (Fall 1999): 21–23. Using examples from *Clocks,* Schwenk examines the difficulty of using traditional theoretical language to label elements in contemporary music. See: **D12, D13, W59**

B409. Sealy, Douglas. "Reviews." *Irish Times,* February 13, 1996, 12. This Dublin concert featured *Amazon* and *Wings.* See: **D1, D2, D78, D79, D80, D81, D82, D83, D84, D85, D86, W23, W24, W68, W69**

B410.   Sheridan, Molly. "Start Small, Think Big: A Grass-Roots Commissioning Consortium Thrives Among America's Smaller-Budget Orchestras." *Symphony* 57, no. 2 (Spring 2006): 30–35. A close-up of the *Made in America* commissioning consortium and Tower's role in this ground-breaking project. See: **D88, W11**

B411.   Sherman, Robert. "Looking Back to 1855 for July 4 Celebration." *New York Times,* July 2, 1995, Section 13WC. Announces upcoming performance of *Celebration Fanfare* by the American Russian Youth Orchestra.

B412.   ———. "New Orleans Sounds in Storrs." *New York Times,* June 25, 1995, Section 13CN, 16. Details the season's programs at the Norfolk and Music Mountain festivals, including a performance of *Petroushskates* by Speculum Musicae. See: **D49, D50, D51, D52, D53, W49**

B413.   ———. "Music: New Orchestra Focuses on 20th Century Works." *New York Times,* September 8, 1991, A23. The New Orchestra of Westchester presents *Sequoia,* as well as works by Prokofiev and Beethoven. See: **D63, D64, D65, D66, W15**

B414.   Shen, Ted. "Tower Leads Instrumental Journey, Orchestrates a Lesson on Rhythm." *Chicago Tribune,* February 1, 2002. Superlatives characterize this review of a Chicago Chamber Musicians' concert, which included *Big Sky, Trés Lent, Night Fields, Petroushskates,* and works by Beethoven and Messiaen. "[Tower has] rendered the label 'woman composer' superfluous. [She] understands and can convey the urgency and visceral immediacy of chamber music . . . [earning] a place among innovators of her generation." See: **D4, D43, D44, D45, D49, D50, D51, D52, D53, D73, D74, D75, W27, W46, W49, W53**

B415.   Shulgold, Marc. "Red Rocks Hosts CSO and Winds." *Rocky Mountain News,* July 16, 1994, A70. Marin Alsop begins this outdoor performance with the *Fanfare for the Uncommon Woman, No. 1* and Copland's *Fanfare for the Common Man.* See: **D16, D17, D18, W35**

B416.   ———. "Dream-Come-True Venue Awakens with Trio's Rousing Performance." *Rocky Mountain News,* May 5, 2005, Final Edition, Spotlight, 50A. Reviews a performance of *For Daniel* by the Kalichstein-Laredo-Robinson Trio. "The thundering music those two giants [Beethoven and Brahms] created might appear at first glance to serve as the program's roof-rattling contributions. In fact, they pale next to the centerpiece, Joan Tower's single-movement tribute to her recently departed young nephew, who had suffered from long-term lung disease." See: **W40**

B417.   ———. "CSO is All-American Now." *Rocky Mountain News,* November 23, 1996. Reviews a set of Colorado Symphony Orchestra concerts featuring *Concerto for Orchestra* and *Fanfares.* "A single-movement spectacular . . . blistering climaxes." See: **D14, D16, D17, D18, D88, W6, W35, W36**

B418.   ———. "Time Apart Has Helped Trio Mesh Nearly 30 Years." *Rocky Mountain News,* May 4, 2005, Final Edition, Spotlight, 10D. Reviewer interviews members of the Kalichstein-Laredo-Robinson Trio, scheduled to play *For Daniel* in Denver, CO. See: **W40**

B419. ———. "Colorado Symphony Soars for Audience, CNN Cameras." *Rocky Mountain News*, January 17, 1997. Review of Colorado Symphony Orchestra's performance of *Duets* ("Dramatic sweep . . . lyrical repose").

B420. ———. "Ancient, Modern Themes Tug at 20th Century Composers." *Rocky Mountain News*, April 20, 1997, D14. Reviewer praises the new *Concertos* CD. "One of America's leading woman composers unblushingly uses the traditional form of the concerto to express her forward-leaning ideas. These four [concertos] explore the virtuoso possibilities of the violin, flute, piano and clarinet. This is fresh, new music that is gimmick-free." See: **D10, D11, D28, D54, D55, D77, W5, W9, W13, W21**

B421. ———. "Present's Perfect as Composer Nears 60." *Rocky Mountain News*, February 15, 1998, D4. Reviewer talks with Tower about her 60th birthday, her success in the composing world, and the upcoming concert in Boulder which will feature four of her works.

B422. ———. "Symphony Starts Vail with a Bang." *Rocky Mountain News*, July 1, 1999. Announces that *Fanfare, No. 1* will share a Colorado Symphony Orchestra program with Copland, Weber, and Beethoven. See: **D16, D17, D18, W35**

B423. ———. "Festival Shatters Stereotypes." *Rocky Mountain News*, February 16, 1998, A53. Review of a program dominated by Tower compositions during the Modern Music Festival at the University of Colorado. "[Tower's work] ranged from the shamelessly accessible to the intellectually challenging, but it never bored."

B424. ———. "Moving (Ahead) with the Music on Upcoming CD, Composer, CSO Will Sound a Contemporary Theme." *Rocky Mountain News*, February 17, 1997, D6. Chronicles the recording of a new CD by Marin Alsop and the Colorado Symphony Orchestra in Boettcher Hall in Denver. Includes *Concerto for Orchestra, Duets,* and the *Fanfares.* See: **D14, D15, D16, D17, D18, D19, D20, D21, D22, D23, D24, D88, W6, W7, W8, W35, W36, W37, W38**

B425. ———. "Musically Speaking, Accessible CSO Conducts Harmonious Exchanges with Concertgoers." *Rocky Mountain News*, January 28, 1997. Marin Alsop and Joan Tower speak with concert attendees after a performance of *Duets.* See: **D15, W7**

B426. ———. "Oundjian's Loss Is Symphony's Gain." *Rocky Mountain News*, April 6, 2002, A26. Oundjian conducts the Colorado Symphony Orchestra in Tower's *Sequoia.* See: **D63, D64, D65, D66, W15**

B427. Smith, Mary. "*Sequoia* Composer Likes to be Visible." *Omaha World-Herald,* October 4, 1984, 13. An interview preceding the Omaha Symphony's performance of *Sequoia.* See: **D63, D64, D65, D66, W15**

B428. Smith, Tim. "A Night of Sharp Contrasts at BSO under Alsop's Baton: *Fanfares,* then Music with Subtler Sounds." *Baltimore Sun,* February 19, 2005, D1. A positive review of a BSO performance under Alsop. The program included *Fanfare, No. 1.* See: **D16, D17, D18, W35**

B429.　Slettom, Jeanlyn Bezoler. "Success Amazes Composer." *St. Paul Dispatch,* October 25, 1984, B13. Tower discusses the success of *Sequoia.* See: **D63, D64, D65, D66, W15**

B430.　Stein, Jerry. "Ballet Pieces Explore Celebrating Women."*Cincinnati Post,* March 11, 2000. The Cincinnati Ballet programs *Stepping Stones.* See: **D73, W3**

B431.　Steinberg, David. "Trio Ends Music Festival with Famous Composers." *Albuquerque Journal,* June 19, 2005, Final Edition, F1. *For Daniel* performed by the Kalichstein-Laredo-Robinson during the Chamber Music Albuquerque 2005 season. See: **W40**

B432.　Stiller, Andrew. "Tower: *Chamber and Solo Works* and Tower: *Orchestral Works.*" *Musical America* 111, no. 2 (1991): 90–91. A less than positive review of two Tower CDs. Most of the review is along these lines: "I don't think there are more than a dozen notes on these two discs where the scoring does not fit the guidelines of Walter Piston's textbook *Orchestration* . . . formulaic . . . uncontrasting."

B433.　Story, John. "CD Review: Tower: *Concerto for Orchestra, Duets for Orchestra, Fanfares for the Uncommon Woman nos. 1–5.*" *Fanfare* 24, no. 5 (May–June 2000): 251. A mixed review: "She has an interesting but entirely accessible harmonic pallette, a pleasant and sometimes memorable melodic sense, and a lot of rhythmic punch" and "The five *Fanfares* . . . all make theatrical use of not really climaxing." See: **D16, D17, D18, D19, D20, D21, D22, D23, D24, D88, W6, W7, W8, W35, W36, W37, W38,**

B434.　Strini, Tom. "A Voracious Appetite for Dance." *Dance Magazine* 73, no. 4 (1999): 72–74. Profiles dancer Kathryn Posin, who choreographed *Stepping Stones.* See: **D73, W3**

B435.　————. "Waukesha Symphony Bringing Its Music to Many Places During 2005–06 Season." *Milwaukee Journal Sentinel,* March 27, 2005, Final Edition, E3. Orchestra plans local premiere of Tower's *Made in America.* See: **D88, W11**

B436.　————. "Arts Preview: Music Calendar." *Milwaukee Journal Sentinel,* August 21, 2005. E5. Details the Waukesha Symphony Orchestra's 2005 season, which includes *Made in America* See: **D88, W11**

B437.　————. "Classical Music and Dance Briefing." *Milwaukee Journal Sentinel,* July 12, 2005, Final Edition, E5. Details the Ford *Made in America* Project, launched by The American Symphony Orchestra League and Meet the Composer. Tower was the first composer selected for the program. See: **D88, W11**

B438.　Stryker, Mark. "To Thine Own Talent Be True." *Detroit Free Press,* May 31, 1998, E1. Tower discusses her compositional aesthetic and process.

B439.　————. "Chamber Composer Shows off Her Precise Pace." *Detroit Free Press,* June 16, 1998. An evening of Tower's works presented at the Great Lakes Chamber Festival.

B440.　Sullivan, Jack. "Guide to Records." *American Record Guide* 67, no. 5 (September 1, 2004): 212. A somewhat lukewarm review of the First Edi-

Bibliography

tion orchestral release which contains *Silver Ladders, Island Prelude, Island Rhythms, Music for 'Cello and Orchestra,* and *Sequoia.* "Her best moments are meditative—the *Island Prelude* for oboe and string orchestra, the middle section of *Silver Ladders*—but too often loud effects substitute for power, repetitive poundings for rhythmic excitement." See: **D33, D34, D35, D36, D37, D38, D39, D41, D42, D63, D64, D65, D66, D67, D68, D69, W10, W12, W15, W16, W43**

B441. Tate, Nick. "Collage Offers Sometimes Tasty Buffet of New Music." *Cambridge Chronicle,* March 10, 1983. Review of *Noon Dance,* as performed by the Boston-based Collage Ensemble. See: **D47, D48, W45**

B442. Tommasini, Anthony. "Tower Faces the Musical Inquisition." *Boston Globe,* August 5, 1991. Reviews the 47th Annual Composers' Conference, at which Tower fielded questions from the audience.

B443. ———. *Amazon I.* New York: Associated Music Publishers, Inc., 1978. See: **D1, W23**

B444. ———. *Amazon II.* New York: Associated Music Publishers, Inc., 1979. See: **D1, D2, W24**

B445. ———. *And . . . They're Off!* New York: Associated Music Publishers, Inc., 1997. See: **W26**

B446. ———. "Approaching Senior Status as a Woman and a Composer." Audio cassette recording of Patten Foundation Lecture at Indiana University, October 27, 1998, Indiana University Library, Bloomington, IN

B447. ———. *Ascent.* New York: Associated Music Publishers, Inc., 1996. See: **D3, W56**

B448. ———. *Big Sky.* New York: Associated Music Publishers, Inc., 2000. See: **D4, W27**

B449. ———. *Black Topaz.* New York: Associated Music Publishers, Inc., 1976. See: **D5, W28**

B450. ———. *Breakfast Rhythms I and II.* New York: Associated Music Publishers, Inc.,1983. See: **D6, D7, D8, W29**

B451. ———. *Brimset.* New York: American Composers Alliance, 1965. See: **W30**

B452. ———. *Celebration Fanfare (from Stepping Stones).* New York: Associated Music Publishers, Inc., 1993. See: **D9, W1**

B453. ———. *Chamber Dance.* New York: Associated Music Publishers, Inc., 2006. See: **W31**

B454. ———. "Choreographing Sound." Audio cassette recording of Patten Foundation Lecture at Indiana University, October 26, 1998, Indiana University Library, Bloomington, IN

B455. ———. *Circles.* New York: American Composers Alliance, 1964. See: **W58**

B456. ———. *Clarinet Concerto.* New York: Associated Music Publishers, Inc., 1990. See: **D10, D11, W5**

B457. ———. *Clocks.* New York: Associated Music Publishers, Inc., 1985. See: **D12, D13, W59**

B458. ———. *Composition for Oboe.* New York: American Composers Alliance, 1965. See: **W60**

B459. ———. *Concerto for Orchestra.* New York: Associated Music Publishers, Inc., 1991. See: **D14, D88, W6**

B460. ———. *Copperwave.* New York: Associated Music Publishers, Inc., 2005. See: **W32**

B461. ———. *DNA.* New York: Associated Music Publishers, Inc., 2003. See: **D89, W33**

B462. ———. *Duets for Chamber Orchestra.* New York: Associated Music Publishers, Inc., 1995. See: **D15, W7**

B463. ———. *Elegy.* New York: Associated Music Publishers, Inc., 1993. See: **W34**

B464. ———. *Fanfare for the Uncommon Woman, No. 1.* New York: Associated Music Publishers, Inc.,1987. See: **D16, D17, D18, W35**

B465. ———. *Fanfare for the Uncommon Woman, No. 2.* New York: Associated Music Publishers, Inc.,1989. See: **D19, W36**

B466. ———. *Fanfare for the Uncommon Woman, No. 3.* New York: Associated Music Publishers, Inc.,1991. See: **D20, D21, W37**

B467. ———. *Fanfare For the Uncommon Woman, No. 4.* New York: Associated Music Publishers, Inc.,1992. See: **D22, W8**

B468. ———. *Fanfare for the Uncommon Woman, No. 5.* New York: Associated Music Publishers, Inc., 1993. See: **D23, D24, W38**

B469. ———. *Fantasia.* New York: American Composers Alliance, 1966. See: **W61**

B470. ———. *Fantasy . . . (Those Harbor Lights) .* New York: Associated Music Publishers, Inc., 1983. See: **D25, D26, W39**

B471. ———. *Fascinating Ribbons.* New York: Associated Music Publishers, Inc., 2002. See: **D27, W2**

B472. ———. *Flute Concerto.* New York: Associated Music Publishers, Inc., 1990. See: **D28, W9**

B473. ———. *For Daniel.* New York: Associated Music Publishers, Inc., 2004. See: **W40**

B474. ———. *Hexachords.* New York: American Composers Alliance, 1972. See: **D29, D30, D31, W62**

B475. ———. *Holding a Daisy.* New York: Associated Music Publishers, Inc., 2005. See: **D46, W63**

B476. ———. *Incandescent.* New York: Associated Music Publishers, Inc., 2003. See: **W41**

B477. ———. *In Memory.* New York: Associated Music Publishers, Inc., 2002. See: **D32, W42**

B478. ———. Interview by Frances Harmeyer. Transcripts of taped interviews conducted for Oral History American Music Project, Yale University School of Music, New Haven, CT, January 9, 1976. Tower speaks about her first composition, her early years in New York, the women's movement, and her approach to composition.

B479. ———. Interview by Jan Fournier. Transcripts of taped interviews conducted for Oral History American Music Project, Yale University School of Music, New Haven, CT, July 28, 1983. Subjects covered in this lengthy interview include Tower's years in South America, the relationship between composer and performer, and her vulnerability at premieres.

B480. ———. Interview by Julie Niemeyer. Transcripts of taped interviews conducted for Oral History American Music Project, Yale University School of Music, New Haven, CT, April 30, 1993. Tower waxes poetic about the clarinet, how she finds titles for her pieces, *Wings,* and her interest in percussion.

B481. ———. Interview by Jenny Raymond. Transcripts of taped interviews conducted for Oral History American Music Project, Yale University School of Music, New Haven, CT, January 4, 1998. Tower discusses her residency with the St. Louis Symphony; her first orchestral work, *Sequoia*; musical influences; and her fondness for one-movement works.

B482. ———. Interview by Kathryn Mishell. Radio Broadcast. March 28, 2006. The writing of *Sequoia,* how Joan Tower came to write for orchestra, what makes a good piece of music, writing for string quartet, the compositional process, and thoughts on the state of women composers and on contemporary music today. www.intothelightradio.org/special.html (Accessed June 5, 2006). See: **D63, D64, D65, D66, W15**

B483. ———. Interview by Lauren Rico. "Instrumental Women: Comparing Notes." Host: Minnesota Public Radio broadcast, February 1, 2001. music.minnesota.publicradio.org/features/0302_instrumental_women/ (Accessed February 17, 2006). Rico interviews composers including Tower, Libby Larsen, and Ellen Taaffe Zwilich about various aspects of their lives as composers, including their philosophy of composing and status of women composers.

B484. ———. *Island Prelude.* New York: Associated Music Publishers, Inc., 1992. See: **D33, D34, D35, D36, W43**

B485. ———. *Island Rhythms.* New York: Associated Music Publishers, Inc., See: **D37, D38, D39, W10**

B486. ———. Liner notes to *Joan Tower: Chamber Works,* Composers' Recordings, CRI 582, 1994. See: **D1, D6, D7, D8, D29, D30, D31, D47, D48, D49, D50, D51, D52, D53, D56, D78, D79, D80, D81, W23, W29, W49, W62,W64, W68**

B487. ———. *Made in America.* New York: Associated Music Publishers, Inc., 2005. See: **D88, W11**

B488. ———. *Movements.* New York: American Composers Alliance, 1968. See: **D40, W44**

B489. ———. *Music for 'Cello and Orchestra.* New York: Associated Music Publishers, Inc., 1984. See: **D41, D42, W12**

B490. ———. *Night Fields.* New York: Associated Music Publishers, Inc., 1994. See: **D43, D44, D45, W46**

B491. ———. *No Longer Very Clear*. New York: Associated Music Publishers, Inc., 2005. See: **D46, W63**

B492. ———. *Noon Dance*. New York: Associated Music Publishers, Inc., 1987. See: **D47, D48, W45**

B493. ———. *Opa Eboni*. New York: American Composers Alliance, 1967. See: **W47**

B494. ———. *Or Like a . . . an Engine*. New York: Associated Music Publishers, Inc., 1994, 2005. See: **D46, W63**

B495. ———. *Percussion Quartet*. New York: Inc., American Composers Alliance, 1963 (revised 1969). See: **W48**

B496. ———. *Petroushskates*. New York: Associated Music Publishers, Inc., 1983. See: **D49, D50, D51, D52, D53, W49**

B497. ———. *Piano Concerto No. 1 (Homage to Beethoven)*. New York: Associated Music Publishers, Inc., 1985. See: **D54, D55, W13**

B498. ———. *Platinum Spirals*. New York: Associated Music Publishers, Inc.,1981. See: **D56, D57, W64**

B499. ———. *Prelude for Five Players*. New York: American Composers Alliance, 1970. See: **D58, W50**

B500. ———. *Purple Rhapsody*. New York: Associated Music Publishers, Inc., 2005. See: **W14**

B501. ———. *Rain Waves*. New York: Associated Music Publishers, Inc., 1997. See: **D59, W51**

B502. ———. *Rapids (Piano Concerto No. 2)*. New York: Associated Music Publishers, Inc., 1996. See: **D60, W17**

B503. ———. *Red Garnet Waltz*. New York: Associated Music Publishers, Inc., 1978. See: **D61, D62, W65**

B504. ———. *Sequoia*. New York: Associated Music Publishers, Inc., 1981. See: **D63, D64, D65, D66, W15**

B505. ———. *Silver Ladders*. New York: Associated Music Publishers, Inc., 1987 . See: **D67, D68, D69, W16**

B506. ———. *Six Variations*. New York: American Composers Alliance, 1971. See: **W66**

B507. ———. *Snow Dreams*. New York: Associated Music Publishers, Inc., 1986. See: **D70, D71, D72, W54**

B508. ———. *Stepping Stones*. New York: Associated Music Publishers, Inc., 1993. See: **W3**

B509. ———. *Stepping Stones: A Ballet for Two Pianos*. New York: Associated Music Publishers, Inc., 1995. See: **D73, W4**

B510. ———. *Strike Zones*. New York: Associated Music Publishers, Inc., 2001. See: **W18**

B511. ———. *Tambor*. New York: Associated Music Publishers, Inc., 1998. See: **D88, W19**

B512. ———. *The Last Dance*. New York: Associated Music Publishers, Inc., 2000. See: **W20**

B513. ———. *Throbbing Still*. New York: Associated Music Publishers, Inc., 2005. See: **D46, W63**

B514. ———. *Toccanta.* New York: Associated Music Publishers, Inc., 1997. See: **W52**

B515. ———. *Trés Lent (Hommage à Messiaen).* New York: Associated Music Publishers, Inc., 1994. See: **W53**

B516. ———. *Turning Points.* New York: Associated Music Publishers, Inc., 1995. See: **D76, W55**

B517. ———. *Valentine Trills.* New York: Associated Music Publishers, Inc., 1996. See: **W70**

B518. ———. *Valentine Trills.* (arr. for orchestra). New York: Associated Music Publishers, Inc., 1998. See: **W71**

B519. ———. *Vast Antique Cubes.* New York: Associated Music Publishers, Inc., 2005. See: **D46, W63**

B520. ———. *Violin Concerto.* New York: Associated Music Publishers, 1992. See: **D77, W21**

B521. ———. *Wild Purple.* New York: Associated Music Publishers, Inc., 1998. See: **D78, W67**

B522. ———. *Wings* for clarinet. New York: Associated Music Publishers, Inc., 1983. See: **D79, D80, D81, W68**

B523. ———. *Wings* for saxophone. New York: Associated Music Publishers, Inc., 1991. See: **D82, D83, D84, D85, D86, D87, W69**

B524. ———. *Yet Another Set of Variations (on a Theme by Paganini): Paganini Trills.* New York: Associated Music Publishers, Inc., 1996. See: **W22**

B525. Trotter, Herman. "First-Class Guitar." *Buffalo News,* October 22, 1993, 25. *Snow Dreams* was this reviewer's favorite on a program of 20th-century music guitar and flute music. "[*Snow Dreams*] represented the recital's peak of interest. . . . Wonderfully chatty interplay for the two instruments." See: **D70, D71, D72, W54**

B526. ———. "In Chautauqua, Dueling *Fanfares.*" *Buffalo News* (New York), August 14, 1997, F8. The Chautauqua Symphony Orchestra performs *Fanfare for the Uncommon Woman, No. 1,* under Marin Alsop. "Tower made no attempt to replicate the stark, dramatic gestures of Copland. Her *Fanfare* moves in more agile brass figurations at the opening and throughout tends to provide a more homogeneous type of musical speech." See: **D16, D17, D18, W35**

B527. ———."Theme Music: Composers, Performers, and Film Honor Women." *Bufflao News* (NY), February 14, 1997, G23. The Buffalo Symphony Orchestra programs ten works, each accompanied by film clips, live dramatization and commentary. *Fanfare for the Uncommon Woman, No. 1* was included. See: **D16, D17, D18, W35**

B528. Ullman, Micheal. "1997 CD Review: Joan Tower *Concertos.*" *Schwann Opus.* www.dnote.com/jtreview.htm. (Accessed January 3, 2005). Review of the four-concerto CD with the Louisville Orchestra, Joseph Silverstein and Max Bragado-Darman, conductor. "These four concertos are full of straightforward zest, but the effects are always within the magisterial control of the composer. They are played by four accomplished soloists who are at home with the virtuoso demands of the works, and who beautifully convey the welcoming spirit of Tower's writing." See: **D10, D11, D28, D54, D55, D77, W5, W9, W13, W21**

B529. Ulrich, Allan. "A Dazzling Performance of *Sequoia.*" *San Francisco Examiner,* November 25, 1982, F1. *Sequoia* receives its West Coast premiere with the San Francisco Symphony under Dennis Russell Davies. "Coruscating sonorities, masterful sense of building to a climax . . . inventive talent." See: **D63, D64, D65, D66, W15**

B530. Valdes, Lesley. "New Recordings: Joan Tower *Concertos.*" *Philadelphia Inquirer,* January 11, 1998, 10, column 5. "Tower's music builds from traditions as logical and cellular as Beethoven's, as primal and motor-driven as Stravinsky's. . . . Ideas come from a sophisticate but not a pedant." See: **D10, D11, D28, D54, D55, D77, W5, W9, W13, W21**

B531. ———. "Women Composers Can Be in Harmony Without Making Music Together." *Baltimore Sun,* May 30, 1981, A7. A fairly extensive interview. Topics include honors received, unique challenges for women composers and musical influences on Tower's composition."

B532. Vernier, David. "Classics Today: Thirteen Ways." www.classicstoday.com/search.asp?ReviewNum=6383 (Accessed January 7, 2005). Review of eighth blackbird's performance of *Petroushskates* and works by Perle, Schober, and Albert. "Joan Tower's delightful little homage to both Stravinsky and figure skating, *Petroushskates* makes an effervescent curtain-raiser that brilliantly shows off the group's timbral range." See: **D49, D50, D51, D52, D53, W49**

B533. ———. "Classics Today. *Fanfares for the Uncommon Woman.*" www.classicstoday.com/review.asp?ReviewNum=517 (Accessed January 7, 2005). Review of CD *Fanfares for the Uncommon Woman*: "Producers of this disc, and the liner note commentator in particular, just can't seem to get past the need to also drive home the fact that she's a woman with an agenda. Tower's voice, like that of her main musical idol Beethoven, is strong and free and unafraid; it communicates using assured thematic strokes and well-chosen combinations of instruments." See: **D16, D17, D18 W35, W36**

B534. Vogel, Howard. "Joan Tower: *Rapids (Piano Concerto No. 2).*" *Woodstock Times* (NY), March 4, 1996. Reviews premiere of *Rapids,* Ursula Oppens, piano, American Symphony Orchestra, Joan Tower, conductor. "Cascading sound, rippling up the piano and down the strings, flew off into the other sections with musical material that grabbed this listener's ear and didn't let go. The piece was driven as much by linear movement as by the powerful rhythmic figures." See: **D60, W17**

B535. ———. "Stunning Tower, a Rare Bartok, and a Reformed Mendelssohn." *Woodstock Times* (NY), May 11, 1995, 2. Review of *Duets,* as performed by the American Symphony Chamber Orchestra: "We are regaled with musical results that beguile, inspire and challenge." See: **D15, W7**

B536. Von Rhein, John. "Ms. Tower's Opus: How 65 Orchestras United for an American Brand." *Chicago Tribune,* February 3, 2006. Details the commissioning consortium behind *Made in America.* See: **D88, W11**

B537. Waleson, Heidi. "Classical: Keeping Score." *Billboard,* October 7, 1995, 35. Subtitled "Hail and Farewell" this article mentions the 5-CD, 21-work compilation "The Slatkin Years," by departing conductor Leonard Slatkin and the St. Louis Symphony. The set includes Tower's *Island Rhythms.* See: **D37, D38, D39, W10**

B538. ———. "Women Composers Find Things Easier—Sort Of." *New York Times,* January 28, 1990, 27, column 3. Lengthy article about women composers. Highlights the premiere of the *Flute Concerto* in Carnegie Hall. See: **D28, W9**

B539. Ward, Charles. "Santa Fe More than an Operatic Paradise." *Houston Chronicle,* July 30, 1998, 1. Reviews a performance of *Fantasy . . . (Those Harbor Lights), Holding a Daisy,* and *Or Like a . . . an Engine.* "Tower's *Fantasy* had convincing shape and variety." See: **D25, D26, D46, W39, W63**

B540. — —. "Tough Music and Poetry Form Expressive Work." *Houston Chronicle,* October 14, 2005, 12. Da Camera of Houston offers compositions directly related to John Ashbery's poetry. "A sense of insistent simplicity prevailed, despite contrasting lush chords in *Holding a Daisy* and the frenetic energy of *Or Like a . . . an Engine.*" See: **D46, W63**

B541. ———. "*In Memory* Plays out as a Perfect Tribute." *Houston Chronicle,* April 11, 2002, 10. Tokyo Quartet performs *In Memory.* "A skilled use of pacing. . . ." See: **D32, W42**

B542. ———. "Quartet Stretches with New Works." *Houston Chronicle,* January 31, 2004, 9. Review of Emerson's performance of *Incandescent* at Rice University. "Typically, the single-movement piece began with a single note that expanded into clusters of notes. However, the clusters never veered from comfortably reinforcing consonance into the wilder noise more typical of the device. Throughout, the music glowed just as often as it erupted in tense virtuosic solos." See: **W41**

B543. ———. "Trends Concert Mixes Intriguing Performances of Women's Works with Audience Discussions." *Houston Chronicle,* March 14, 1983, Section 4, 3. *Amazon* shares a stage with works by Joan La Barbara and Libby Larsen. See: **D1, D2, W23, W24**

B544. Watts, James D. "Voila, the Viola." *The World Scene Writer.* June 11, 2006. www.tulsaworld.com/MusicStory.asp?ID=060611_mu_H3_Voila2 3037 (Accessed June 21, 2006). Tower grants an interview while in residence at the OKMozart Festival. *Purple Rhapsody* scheduled to be performed at the festival.

B545. Webster, Daniel. "Muir Quartet's New Violinist." *Philadelphia Inquirer,* November 4, 1995, D10. Muir introduces their new second violinist, Wei-Pin Kuo, in a recital which includes *Night Fields.* "The composer con-

centrated her musical ideas into an explosive, dark-hued piece." See: **D43,
D44, D45, W46**

B546. Wechsler, Bert. "Reviews, Concerts." *The Music Journal* 39, no. 4
(August–September 1981): 36. The American Composers' Orchestra performs *Sequoia,* as well works by Shapey, Hovhaness, and Schuman. "Ex-
cept where it got too loud, this could accompany an audio-visual presenta-
tion of how the tree grows and the nature life around said tree." See: **D63,
D64, D65, D66, W15**

B547. Wierzbicki, James. "Interview with Joan Tower." *St. Louis Post-
Dispatch,* January 4, 1987. A lengthy interview with the composer about the
composing process, being a composer-in-residence, and new music.

B548. ———. 1989. "New Joan Tower Piece Pretty But Lacks Impact." *St.
Louis Post-Dispatch,* May 6, 1989, D5. Lukewarm review of *Island Prelude,* performed by the St. Louis Symphony and Leonard Slatkin. "Had it
[*Island Prelude*] followed through on the sumptuous lyric ideas with which
it begins, it might well have been a meditation comparable in potency to the
Adagio for Strings of Samuel Barber that Tower says is one of its models.
But Tower abruptly changes the subject halfway through. . . . Instead of let-
ting the dreamy oboe theme evolve naturally into something more urgent,
she allows it to deteriorate into digressions that seem little connected to
what preceded them." See: **D33, D34, D35, D36, W43**

B549. ———. "Composer Gets Prize; Worked Here in 80s." *St. Louis Post-
Dispatch,* April 25, 1990, A6. Tower receives Grawemeyer Award.

B550. ———. "Composer Joan Tower Scores Big with Prestigious Award."
St. Louis Post-Dispatch, May 6, 1990, D4. Article dealing with Tower's re-
ceipt of the Grawemeyer Award.

B551. ____. "Every Instant of Music Has Past, Present and Future." *St. Louis
Post-Dispatch,* January 4, 1987, D4. In-depth article in which Tower details
her organic approach to composition.

B552. ———. "St. Louis Symphony: Tower's *Silver Ladders*" *Musical America* 107, no. 2 (May 1987): 50. Covers *Silver Ladders'* premiere by Leonard
Slatkin and the St. Louis Symphony Orchestra. "Fine-detailed craftsmanship and large scale structural elegance that characterize   most of the music
she has produced in the last ten years. It also features a quality of dynamism
perhaps not so regularly associated with her output. . . . Viscerally exciting
from start to finish." See: **D67, D68, D69, W16**

B553. ———. "CD Review: Tower: *Island Rhythms.*" *Musical America* 112,
no. 1 (January–February 1992): 45. Review of the new Louisville Orchestra's CD that *Island Rhythms* shares with Luening's *Kentucky Concerto* and
Gubaidulina's *Pro et Contra.* "Jaunty little curtain-raiser . . . solidity of the
string playing and the expressive flair of the wind solos suggest a new standard." See: **D37, D38, D39, W10**

B554. ———. "Deliberate Simplicity in Concerto." *St. Louis Post-Dispatch,*
February 29, 1992, D4. Positive review of the *Flute Concerto,* played by the
St. Louis Symphony with Carol Wincenc, flutist, and Joseph Silverstein,
conductor. "[There is] plenty of contrast in Tower's *Flute Concerto,* but it

involves textures and densities, not a dialectic of themes and counterthemes. The concerto makes just a single statement, and it does so very convincingly." See: **D28, W9**

B555. ———. "Symphony Season Enjoys Grand Finale." *St. Louis Post-Dispatch,* May 21, 1989. Review of *Music for 'Cello and Orchestra,* as performed by Lynn Harrell and the St. Louis Symphony. "A fine piece that demonstrates very well not just the craftsmanship but also the aesthetic upon which Tower has made her reputation . . . logic and art go hand in hand." See: **D41, D42, W12**

B556. Wigler, Stephen. "Women of Notes: Orchestra Will Keep Playing Music by Female Composers at Least Until Other Orchestras Do." *Baltimore Sun,* January 17, 1992, E1. The Women Composers' Orchestra under Antonio Joy Wilson performs *Para Jote Delate,* a musical birthday tribute to Tower by Tania Leon.

B557. Williams, David. "Quartet Spans Music Landscape." *Charleston Gazette* (WV), October 4, 2004, A7. The Cavani String Quartet performs *Night Fields* which "spun out darker melodies in a musical landscape teeming with dramatic contrasts and contrapuntal undercurrents. *Night Fields* suggests Shostakovich with its almost-parody of the rising-falling-falling motif . . . that was Dmitri Shostakovich's own musical signature." See: **D43, D44, D45, W46**

B558. Wincenc, Carol. "Performing Tower's *[Flute] Concerto.*" *Flute Talk* 19 (November 1999): 8–15. Wincenc shares performance suggestions, several pages of her own marked score, and Tower's thoughts about composing this work ("I was intimidated because you're always faced with the problem of the flute being overpowered by the orchestra") in this detailed review. See: **D28, W9**

B559. ____, ed. *Valentines.* New York, NY: Carl Fischer, 1999. A collection of works for solo flute, flute and piano, and voice and piano. Tower's *Valentine Trills,* written for Wincenc, is included in this collection. See: **W70**

B560. Windeler, Diane. "Flutist Ends Series on Expressive Note." *San Antonio Express-News,* March 31, 2005, State and Metro Edition, F3. Carol Wincenc performs the final concert in the Tuesday Musical Club Artist Series; includes *Valentine Trills.* See: **W70**

B561. Wise, Brian. *Composer Essay: Joan Tower.* New York: Associated Music Publishers, Inc., 2005.

B562. Wiser, John D. 1986. "HV Chamber Orchestra Performs." *Poughkeepsie Journal,* February 6, 1986. Review of Hudson Valley Chamber Orchestra's premiere of *Piano Concerto (Homage to Beethoven).* "Music of solid craftsmanship and allusive wit, never trivial, or merely facetious." See: **D54, D55, W13**

B563. Young, Jerry. "Composing Is Architecture for Tower." *Austin American Statesman,* September 28, 1996. Tower discusses her composing process before a performance of *Silver Ladders.* See: **D67, D68, D69, W16**

B564. Zakariasen, Bill. "Mehta Helps Tower Tower." *Daily News,* September 25, 1982. The New York Philharmonic programs *Sequoia.* "A work of healthy, purposeful sounds which connect to an audience with strength and directness." See: **D63, D64, D65, D66, W15**

B565. Zuck, Barbara. "Much Ado about Music: Joan Tower to Continue Lancaster Festival Tradition." *Columbus Dispatch* (OH), July 19, 1992, H1. Tower is composer-in-residence at the Lancaster Festival.

B566. ———. "ProMusica Event Spotlights American Pianist, Composer." *Columbus Dispatch* (OH), April 2, 1998, 28. ProMusica slates a concert in honor of Tower's 60th birthday. Program includes *Rapids (Piano Concerto No. 2)* and *Duets for Orchestra.* See: **D15, D60, W7, W17**

B567. ———. "ProMusica Chamber Orchestra." *Columbus Dispatch* (OH), April 10, 2005, D8. Outlines ProMusica Chamber Orchestra of Columbus' 2005–06 season, which includes Tower's *Purple Rhapsody.* See: **W14**

B568. ———. "Chamber Music: Purple Offers Golden Gift to Violists." *Columbus Dispatch* (OH), February 8, 2006, G1. ProMusica Chamber Orchestra presents the regional premiere of *Purple Rhapsody* with Tower in attendance. See: **W14**

B569. ———. "Review: Viola Taken on Wild Ride in Debut of Astonishing *Purple Rhapsody.*" *Columbus Dispatch* (OH), February 13, 2006, B4. "An astonishing work . . . assaults the senses and emotions over and over . . . ratcheting up intensity by layering agitated sounds on top of one another." See: **W14**

B570. Zuckerman, Alicia. "Tower's Power." *New York Magazine* 35, no. 6 25 (February 2002): 90. A brief "fluff piece" to accompany an announcement about the Tokyo Quartet's performance of *In Memory.* See: **D32, W42**

Dissertations and Theses

B571. Ball, James S. *A Conductor's Guide to Selected Contemporary American Orchestral Compositions.* Dissertation, University of Missouri–Kansas City, 1992.

B572. Bonds, Nancy E. Leckie. *An Analysis of Joan Tower's* Wings *for Solo Clarinet.* Dissertation, City University of New York, 2000. See: **D79, D80, D81, D82, D83, D84, D85, D86, D87, W68, W69**

B573. Bryden, Kristi. *Musical Conclusions: Exploring Closural Processes in Five Late Twentieth-Century Chamber Works.* Dissertation, University of Wisconsin–Madison. 2001.

B574. Chung, Mia. *The Contemporary Piano Concerto: A Blend of Old and New Treatments as Seen in Works by Peter Lieberson, Joan Tower, and Ellen Zwilich.* Dissertation, D.M.A. Performance, The Juilliard School, New York, New York, 1991. See: **D54, D55, D60, W13, W17**

B575. Crawford, Heather. 2002. *Joan Tower's* Violin Concerto*: An Organic Approach to Composition.* Dissertation, University of Texas–Austin. See: **D77, W21**

B576. Denman, James Louis. *Modes of Octatonic Discourse: Traditions, Terms and Techniques 1880–1999.* Dissertation, Ph.D., Music Theory, University of Washington. In progress.

B577. Fletcher, John. *Joan Tower's* Fascinating Ribbons *for Band: Genesis and Analysis.* Dissertation, D.M.A., University of Oklahoma. 2002. See: **D27**

B578. Ford, Shannon Marie. Wings*: A Performance Analysis of Joan Tower's Work for Solo Alto Saxophone.* M.M. Thesis, Bowling Green State University, 1995. See: **D82, D83, D84, D85, D86, D87, W68, W69**

B579. Janssen, Robert. *Intuition and Analysis: A Performer's Perspective on Joan Tower's* Fantasy *for Clarinet and Piano.* Dissertation, City University of New York, 2000. See: **D25, D26, W39**

B580. Jones, Margo S. *Joan Tower's* Hexachords *for Solo Flute: An Analysis and Comparison of Its Flute writing to Tower's* Flute Concerto*.* Dissertation, University of North Texas, 1993. See: **D28, D29, D30, D31, W9, W62**

B581. Lerner, Ellen Dale. *The Music of Selected Contemporary American Women Composers: A Stylistic Analysis.* Master's Thesis, University of Massachusetts, Amherst, 1976.

B582. Oddo, Rochelle Lynn. *Joan Tower's Compositional Profile, Use of the Clarinet, and Collaboration in* Turning Points *for Clarinet and String Quartet.* Dissertation, D.M.A., Rice University, 2004. See: **D76, W55**

B583. Reichardt, Sarah Jane. *An Analysis of Joan Tower's* Island Prelude*.* Master's Thesis, University of Texas at Austin, 1998. See: **D33, D34, D35, D36, W43**

B584. Robinson, Susan Louise Bailey. *Three Contemporary Orchestral Compositions by American Women: A Guide to Rehearsal and Performance for the University Orchestra Conductor.* Dissertation, Texas Tech University, 1991. See: **D63, D64, D65, D66, W15**

B585. Rylands, Ann. *The Violin Concertos of Ellen Taafe Zwilich (1997) and Joan Tower (1992): Evolution of an American Style.* Dissertation, University of South Carolina, 2002. See: **D77, W21**

B586. Schloss, Myrna. 1993. *Out of the Twentieth Century: Three Composers, Three Musics, One Femininity.* Dissertation, Weslyan University, 1993.

B587. Shih, Ching-ju. *Compositional Techniques in Joan Tower's* Silver Ladders*.* Dissertation, D.M.A., Composition, City University of New York. In progress. See: **D67, D68, D69, W16**

B588. Shouha, Laura. *The Musical Language of Joan Tower: An Energy Line Analysis of* Island Prelude *for Oboe and Wind Quartet.* Dissertation, University of North Texas, December 2001. See: **D33, D34, D35, D36, W43**

B589. Singleton, Glen R. *Contrast and Unity in* Silver Ladders *by Joan Tower.* Thesis, M.M., Baylor University, 1993. See: **D67, D68, W16**

B590.   Stoecker, Philip. *An Analysis of Joan Tower's* Sequoia. Thesis, Master of Arts in Music Theory, University of Ottawa, Ontario, Canada. 1997. See: **D63, D64, D65, D66, W15**

B591.   Taylor, Robert. *Joan Tower:* Fascinating Ribbons. Northwestern University Graduate Wind Conducting Seminar, 2002. See: **D27, W2**

B592.   Tower, Joan. *On* Breakfast Rhythms I *and* II. Dissertation, D.M.A., Columbia University, 1978. See: **D6, D7, D8, W29**

Index

Index

AT&T Foundation, 16
Academy of Arts and Sciences, 17
Adams, Abigail, 3
Adams, John, 3
Aida, 5
Alea III, 18
Alfred I. DuPont Award, 16
Alsop, Marin, 17
Amazon, 13, 30, 32, 33, 34, 35, 40, 71–72
American Academy of Arts and Letters, 16, 42
American Brass Quintet, 17
American Composers' Alliance, 42
American Composers' Orchestra, 13, 17
American Guild of Organists, 17
American Music Center, 18, 42
American Society of University Composers, 16
American Symphony, 20, 42
American Symphony Orchestra League, 18, 61, 43, 201
American Women Composers, 42, 44
Anchorage Symphony, 20
And . . . They're Off!, 18, 20, 34, 73
Arcana XVI, 107
Arianna String Quartet, 17
Ascent, 34, 95
Aspect I–V, 104–5
Ashbery, John, 20, 33, 35
Asher Edelman Professorship, 12
Aspen Music Festival, 21
Auros Group, 18
Autocaril, 5
Aymara, 5

Babbitt, Milton, 7, 8, 9, 21n21
Ball, James S., 210
Baltimore Symphony Orchestra, 20
Barber, Samuel, 122
Bard College, 12, 13, 14, 20, 22, 43, 44
Bargreen, Melinda, 162
Barkin, Elaine, 162
Barlow Foundation, 16
Barnes, Paul, 120, 133–34
Beeson, Jack, 8

Beethoven, Ludwig von, 15, 16, 30, 37, 38, 41
Bellows, Henry Whitney, 4
Bennington College, 6, 7, 13, 36, 38
Berlin Philharmonic, 17
Berlioz, Hector, 38
Bernstein, Tamara, 33, 47nn52–53, 49n123
Big Sky, 20, 73–74
Big Steps, 95
Black Topaz, 28, 33, 34, 40, 49n98, 74–75
Bloch Music Festival, 21
Blustine, Allen, 9, 10, 12. *See also* Devendra, Anand
Bolero, 7, 15
Bonds, Nancy Leckie, 22n28, 22nn40–41, 22n47, 31, 37, 46n3, 210
Boretz, Benjamin, 8, 45, 50n137
Bossert, Cameron, 108
Bowman, Peter, 67, 85
Bragado-Darman, Max, 56, 59
Brant, Henry, 6, 7
Breakfast Rhythms I and *II* , 8, 10, 11, 27, 29, 32, 34, 36, 37, 46n24–26, 46nn68–69, 75
Brimset, 36, 75
Browning, John, 17, 99
Bryden, Kristi, 210
Burke, Steven, 107

Calabro, Louis, 7, 105, 106
Can I?, 35, 104
Carnegie Hall, 17, 18, 19
Cassatt String Quartet, 17, 18
Cavani String Quartet, 17
Celebration Fanfare (from *Stepping Stones*), 18, 53
Chamber Dance, 20, 33, 75–76
Chamber Music America, 42
Chamber Music Northwest, 21
Chamber Music Society of Lincoln Center, 18
Chance, Nancy, 44
Chee-Yun, 17
Chen, Melvin, 19

215

Fletcher, John, 30, 34, 47n58, 48n87, 172, 211
Flute Concerto, 16, 20, 34, 45, 46n18, 59–60
For Daniel, 20, 34, 81–82
For Joan on Her 50th, 106
Ford Motor Company Fund, 18
Ford, Shannon Marie, 211
Forlano, Daniel, 35
Fournier, Jan, 21n3, 21n6, 21n8, 21n11, 47n49, 48n65, 48n95, 49n102
Frank, Gabriela, 45

Gann, Kyle, 10, 21n16, 21n26, 107
Gideon, Miriam, 44 127
A Gift, 20, 72, 104
Gilbert, Alan, 17
Glass, Philip, 38
Glennie, Evelyn, 17
Glens Fall Symphony, 18
Grawemeyer Award, 16, 17
Greenwich Music House, 8, 9, 44
Group for Contemporary Music, 8
Guggenheim Foundation, 10

Harbison, Helen, 9, 11
Harbison, John, 11
Harmeyer, Frances, 47n27, 48n70, 48n84, 48n88
Harrell, Lynn, 17
Hayes, Gerry, 3, 21n1
Heinz Foundation, 43
Hexachords, 8, 11, 12, 29, 46n18, 96–97
Higdon, Jennifer, 45, 107, 142
Hingham, England, 3
Hingham, Massachusetts, 3
Holding a Daisy, 18, 33, 97–98
Houston Symphony, 17
Howard, Sharon Prado, 22n27
Hudson Valley Philharmonic, 20
Humphrey, Mary Lou, 22n29, 46n9, 47n36, 47n55, 48n79, 49n98
Hyslop, Sandra, 180

Ibrook, Margaret, 3
Impala, 107–8
In Memory, 20, 33, 34, 83–84
Incandescent, 20, 34, 82–83
Indiana University of Pennsylvania, 35

The Instant Gathers, 108
International Society for Contemporary Music, 42
International Women's Forum, 53
Isbin, Sharon, 93, 94, 96
Island Prelude, 20, 29, 33, 34, 35, 37, 40 46n19, 84–86
Island Rhythms, 33, 60
Janssen, Robert, 211
Janssons, Mariss, 17
Jerome Foundation, 16
Joan's, 106
Jones, Margo S., 29, 46n18, 211
Juilliard School of Music, 17

Kafavian, Ani, 17
Kalichstein Joseph, 17
Kalichstein-Laredo-Robinson Trio, 17, 135
Kalistos Chamber Orchestra, 20
Kaplan, Lisa, 143–44
Kennedy Center Friedheim Award, 16
Keystone Winds, 35
King, Medora Award, 19
Koussevitsky Foundation, 16

La Barbara, Joan, 106
La Jolla Chamber Music Festival, 17, 21
La Paz, Bolivia, 4
Larchmont, NY, 4
Laredo, Jaime, 17
Larsen, Libby, 42
The Last Dance, 18, 20, 34, 69–70
León, Tania, 107, 136
Lester, Joel, 9, 10
Levine, Rhoda, 107
Lima, Peru, 6, 42
Lin, Cho-Liang, 17
Lincoln, Abraham, 4
Lincoln, Malachi, 3
Lincoln, Samuel, 3
Lincoln, Sarah, 3
Litfin, Jeff, 20, 84
Litton, Andrew, 17
Lochhead, Judy, 185
London Symphony Orchestra, 17
Los Angeles Philharmonic, 17
Lost in the Long Grass, 107–8
Louisville Symphony Orchestra, 17

11, 27–29, 32, 36; synesthesia in works
    by, 33–34; titles of works by, 32–34;
    unpublished works by, 104–6; use of
    clarinet in compositions of, 11, 12;
    works written for or dedicated to, 106–
    8
Tower, John, 3
Tower, Malachi, 3
Tower Power, 106–7
Trés Lent, 16, 18, 37, 92–93
Trio, 108
Turning Points, 11, 18, 34, 37, 94–95

University of Wisconsin–Madison School
    of Music, 17
Untitled, 104
Ussachevsky, Vladimir, 8

Valentine Trills, 18, 103
Vanderbilt University, 21
Varese, Edgar, 37
Vast Antique Cubes, 20, 33, 98–99
Verdehr Trio, 17
Vermeer String Quartet, 17
Violin Concerto, 18, 34, 70
Vocalise, 127

Voice of the Whale, 28
Voices from Elysium, 127
von Rhein, John, 19
von Stroheim, Denise, 5

Walnut Hill School, 6
Walpole, Massachusetts, 4
Walter W. Naumburg Award, 10
WGBH–TV, 16
Wheelock Teachers' College, 4, 6
When Summer Sang, 127
Wild Purple, 18, 101
Wincenc, Carol, 17, 45, 49n135, 146
Wings, 11, 12, 16, 18, 22n28, 22n36,
    22nn40–41, 22n47, 32, 33, 37, 40,
    46n3, 47n32, 101–3
Wise, Brian, 47n45, 48n64
Woodhams, Richard, 17, 19
Wright, David, 47n55
Wu-Han, 17
Wuorinen, Charles, 7, 8, 106

Yamaha, 39
Yarden, Eli, 12
*Yet Another Set of Variations, (Paganini
    Trills)*, 18, 70–71

About the Author

Ellen K. Grolman is professor of music at Frostburg State University, Frostburg, Maryland, and has served there as both Department Chair and Associate Chair of the Division of Performing Arts. Prior to relocating to Maryland, she held a faculty appointment at the Eilat Conservatory of Music in Israel.

She is active in musicological research, specifically in the field of women's participation in music; as a 'cellist, her solo and chamber music programming reflects a strong commitment to the music of both historical and contemporary women composers. She has authored the bio-bibliography of American composer Emma Lou Diemer and *A Catalogue of Published Works for String Orchestra and Piano Trio by 20th-Century American Women Composers*, and has edited a two-volume set of six string trios by 18th-Century composer Maddalena Lombardini-Sirmen. Dr. Grolman is a contributor to the *New Grove Dictionary of Music and Musicians* and *Women and Music in America Since 1900: An Encyclopedia*. She is reviews editor for the *Journal of the International Alliance for Women in Music*, and has written articles and reviews for the *Journal of the American String Teachers' Association*.